Y0-AGL-473

St. Martin's Paperbacks Titles
by Jeanne Williams

PRAIRIE BOUQUET
NO ROOF BUT HEAVEN

No Roof But Heaven

JEANNE WILLIAMS

ST. MARTIN'S PAPERBACKS

NO ROOF BUT HEAVEN

Copyright © 1990 by Jeanne Williams.

Cover photography by Marc Tauss; stepback photography by B & G Studio; antique desk courtesy of Gardeners II, Westwood, NJ.

All rights reserved. No part of this book may be used or reproduced in any manner whatsoever without written permission except in the case of brief quotations embodied in critical articles or reviews. For information address St. Martin's Press, 175 Fifth Avenue, New York, N.Y. 10010.

Library of Congress Catalog Card Number 89-24098

ISBN: 0-312-92639-1

Printed in the United States of America

St. Martin's Press hardcover edition published 1990
St. Martin's Paperbacks edition/October 1991

10 9 8 7 6 5 4 3 2 1

For Pi Irwin, Gerry Hernbrode, and Bill Broyles, who as teachers and educators make tremendous differences in the lives of many children, for my daughter, Kristin, who is discovering the challenges and rewards of working with youngsters, and for Michael Williams, a teacher who loves and inspires his students. He is also a writer—and my son.

❧ *Author's Note* ❧

My father grew up south of Dodge City. His memories of those years exist in letters and tapes we exchanged when far away, and somewhat tardily I got interested in the prairies of my birth. I saw the groves, mulberry trees, and Turkey Red wheat of the Mennonites long before I knew anything about these people or why they came to this country.

Living with my grandparents on their farm gave me a chance to attend a one-room school not too different from Susanna's though it wasn't a soddie. I studied by a kerosene lamp and carried water from a spring, so I have experience of living without electricity or plumbing, which has been useful in re-creating frontier times. My grandmother told me about her school days and life on various homesteads, and my brother, Lewis Kreie, told me about wheat harvest after Turkey Red became the dominant grain.

When I couldn't find out when the Pledge of Allegiance came into use, my son, Michael, himself a very fine teacher, tracked down the fact that the pledge was first published in "Youth's Companion" in 1892, so it could not have been a part of the Mason-Dixon school's opening exercises. Jackie Brotchner sent me the very useful *Cook-*

ery of the Prairie Homesteader by Louise K. Nickey (The Touchstone Press, Beaverton, Oregon, 1976), which also gives a wonderful feel of seasons and customs. My good friend Gaydell Collier sent me invaluable material on teachers' contracts, institutes, and other details as well as several interesting books on rural teachers. Ruth M. Johnson's sprightly *A Flea in My Tea* (Quick Printing Company, Sheridan, Wyoming, 1983) is full of delightful incidents and lore.

Ringing the Children In by Thad Sitton and Milam C. Rowold (Texas A&M University Press, College Station, Texas, 1987) is a fascinating account of early rural schools and makes a good case for their value as compared to huge consolidated schools. Stanley Vestal's *Short Grass Country* (Greenwood Press, Westport, Connecticut, 1970) evokes the region and its history. *The Sod House Frontier* by Everett Dick (Johnson Publishing Company, Lincoln, Nebraska, 1954) is the best single volume on settling the prairies. David Dary's *The Buffalo Book* (Discus, Avon, New York, 1975) tells of the world just ending when my book begins. Among the many books I read for historical background, the most useful were *Conquest of Southwest Kansas* by Leola Howard Blanchard (Wichita Eagle Press, Wichita, Kansas, 1931); Noble L. Prentis's classic *History of Kansas* (E. P. Green, Winfield, Kansas, 1899); *The Coming of the Russian Mennonites* by C. Henry Smith (Mennonite Book Concern, Berne, Indiana, 1927); the three-volume *Standard History of Kansas and Kansans* by William E. Connelley (Lewis Publishing Company, Chicago, 1919); Foster Harris's intriguing and irreplaceable *Look of the Old West* (Viking Press, New York, 1955); and John Ise's warmly human account of a homesteading family, *Sod and Stubble* (University of Nebraska Press, Lincoln, Nebraska, 1967).

The seasons and creatures of the plains are graphically portrayed in *Natural Kansas* by Joseph T. Collins (University Press of Kansas, Lawrence, Kansas, 1985) and *The*

Prairie World by David F. Costello (Crowell, New York, 1975). For details on women's clothing, I relied mostly on *Calico Chronicle* by Betty J. Mills (Texas Tech Press, Lubbock, Texas, 1985).

Lastly, thanks to my sister, Naomi, for retracing with me the prairie world where we were born.

Cave Creek Canyon
The Chiricahua Mountains
August 24, 1989

"A teacher affects eternity; he can never tell where his influence stops."
          —Henry Adams, *The Education of Henry Adams*

❀ *One* ❀

Buckboard was a fitting name for this—this vehicle! Susanna gripped the splintery board seat, nailed securely, she hoped, to either side of the wagon, which truly did buck, and cast a desperate glance at her trunk. Would Grandmother Alden's teapot and two remaining eggshell-thin cups survive this last part of the journey from Ohio? Susanna had carefully swaddled them in her garments and lilac-scented bedding, and the trunk was jammed among tools, sacks, and boxes so that it didn't slide around, but the dried mud of the rutted tracks kept everything in the wagon jouncing and vibrating, including Susanna.

The man who gripped the reins in one expert hand didn't jounce, and Susanna couldn't imagine him vibrating, though the thought made her want to chuckle for the first time since leaving Ohio. The whiskery station agent in Dodge City had called the spare, dark-haired young man "Doc," but Susanna would never have dared address him so. In spite of the hot day, he wore a coat. His mouth curved down in a way that made grooves in his taut, sun-browned skin. No beard disguised the spare cheekbones, square chin, or hard angle of jaw where carelessly

1

trimmed sideburns struggled to curl, black like the hair that fell across his right temple. His eyes, etched at the corners, had a disturbing luminescence like gray clouds lit by wintry sun.

He'd frowned as the agent explained her plight. "This here's the new Mason-Dixon schoolmarm, Doc. Henry Morton was supposed to meet her but he ain't back yet from Topeka."

The scrawny little man waved a hand at the broad street of flimsy false-fronted buildings, most of which were saloons and dance halls being left or entered by painted women, raffish men, and what had to be cowboys—leathery young men with bright neckerchiefs, big hats, and jingling spurs fastened to high-heeled boots. Sprung from a soddie erected only three years ago beside a lone cottonwood tree marking the ford of the Arkansas River, Buffalo City had changed its name as the rails approached. Susanna had heard on her journey this September of 1875 that three years' incredible slaughter of buffalo had almost exterminated the immense herds but hunters must still be finding some, as witnessed by piles of stinking, board-stiff hides black with flies and by a mountain of whitening bones heaped near the depot.

"No place for a decent woman," the agent went on. "When it was a hide hunters' town, it was hides, bones, dust, and hell. Since the stockyards and loading chutes were built last winter, now it's cows, cowboys, dust, and hell. Same gamblers and floozies that got the hunters' money are fleecin' cowboys. Won't be much out of your way, Doc, to set Miss Alden down at Ase McCanless's ranch."

"But I have to pass an examination from Mr. Morton," Susanna objected. "As county superintendent of schools, he has to give me my teaching certificate. I can't go out to the school as if I were already hired."

The man introduced as Matt Rawdon gave an impatient shrug. "Oh, Henry'll give you the certificate. Your big problem will be the school board. All right, Clem, I guess I'll have to haul her out there. Give me a hand with the trunk."

Haul! As if she were a sack of potatoes! Even though she was twenty-seven and painfully aware that she had been becoming one of Pleasant Grove's numerous old maids, Susanna wasn't used to being treated as a nuisance by men of whatever vintage, much less by those under middle age. Beautiful she wasn't, but she had swift, rippling laughter and rather heavy eyebrows winged above eyes that varied from gold to brown with sometimes a hint of green, depending on light and mood. Curly brown hair sparked with red glints in the sun, though it was now demurely rolled into a French knot hidden by her brown bonnet.

Brown, she had thought, would make her look responsible and didn't too much flout the custom that she should still be in mourning since her father had died only six months ago. Black seemed to her to be asking for sympathy and she had resolved not to wear it in this new life except for occasions when the lack would be callous. Though severely cut, the brown dress brought out the smooth creaminess of her skin and molded the slender, still youthful blooming of her figure.

Stung by Rawdon's ungracious manner, Susanna turned her back to him and gazed around to see if there might be a hackney or even a cart at the disposal of new arrivals, but she saw only a cloud of dust rising from a cattle herd being driven into the pens, and a pair of cowboys galloping down the street, whooping and yelling to announce their arrival.

A few buildings claimed to be hotels but she had her doubts. No, most definitely, she didn't want to spend the night here. "I'll pay for my transportation, sir," she said in her coolest tone as the agent helped the tall man stow the trunk among the sacks, tools, boards, and boxes in the wagon which offered not a hint of shelter from the noonday sun. "I'm sorry to put you to trouble and—"

"Save your money for your ticket home, miss."

Bewildered by his hostility, Susanna put her satchel under the seat and set her foot on the narrow iron step attached to the wagon bed, but she didn't scramble up soon enough to please Rawdon, for he gave an annoyed sigh. With an extraordinarily strong arm, he hoisted her almost bodily onto the bare plank seat, and as he did so she glimpsed his other hand, ridged with scars and hanging as if he had little use of it.

What a misfortune for a doctor! Susanna's face must have shown her dismayed sympathy. Rawdon let go of her as if burned and strode to the other side of the wagon. Leaping up easily, he settled his long legs and gave her a harsh, challenging grin as if prepared to enjoy her discomfort. "Well, Miss Alden, let's see how you like a buckboard. Don't ask me to drive slower. After I drop you off, I have to get to my claim in time to milk the cows."

An indelicate reference but Susanna ignored it. "I haven't asked you to drive slow, sir, and I won't." Folding her hands in her lap, she sat primly, determined not to complain if she died for it. She didn't complain but she very quickly unfolded her hands and held to the seat as the deeper bounces threatened to tumble her off her perch. She braced her feet, held tight, and scanned the plains in vain search for a tree, hill, or habitation.

Reaching to infinity, a cloudless, dazzling sky bowed at last to the prairie rim, and between, far as the eye could search, coppery grass with fringed leaftops bent before the wind and then swept back, darker, like a velvet pile rubbed the wrong way. Another kind of yellowing grass had crescent seed heads, some taller clumps flaunted golden plumes, and subtle hues of black, gray, silver, crimson, and white threaded stands of dun and reddish brown. Asters dipped purple heads and other flowers—yellow, orange, and white—spangled the tapestry.

So there was beauty here if you looked closely, something besides the lonely sweep of plains and sky that could be home only to winged creatures like the hawk lazily skimming circles till it suddenly plunged. Susanna's heart contracted and she felt the terror of whatever small, furry creature was now gripped in those talons.

"Hawks and eagles have wonderful vision but they miss more often than not," Rawdon said, raising his voice to be heard above the rattling and clanking.

He wore a battered gray hat. Could he have been in the Confederate army?

Susanna tensed. The man she had loved since putting on long skirts, the man she would have married, had died in the war; and her father had returned so crippled and pain-ridden that it took more and more whiskey to ease him.

Susanna still felt terrible guilt for the relief that flashed through her grief that morning in March when she took him his breakfast and found that his sleep had deepened into death. At the same time, she'd felt suddenly useless, deprived of her reason for existing. For ten years, except for the four hours daily that she taught literature and composition at her aunt's school for young ladies, Susanna had taken care of her father, read to him, written his letters. His death freed her, but with that came a sort of dread, a painful sensation of moving from an airless chamber into a blast of fierce winds that filled constricted lungs with stinging life.

Now she had a choice of what to do, a choice of what was left to a woman of a generation bereft of so many of its best young men like her Richard, who lay with many others at Gettysburg. She had to accept that there might never be another man for her, not simply because Richard, fair, reckless, and laughing, had been so dearly loved, but because in her small Ohio town there wasn't a man she could even consider. Aunt Mollie, of course, had invited her to move in with her and Uncle Frank and teach full-time, but to Susanna that had seemed like losing any chance to really live, accomplish something besides fulfilling her duty to her father.

Her reflections were suddenly shattered by a distant booming from the west. It sounded like a battle.

Indians? Comanche, Kiowa, Cheyenne, Arapaho—the names flashed through Susanna's head like flaming arrows. She knew that the South Plains Indians were supposed to live on reservations in Indian Territory situated between Kansas and Texas, but only the summer before, as Aunt Mollie had several times pointed out, there had been raids in western Kansas that took the lives of twenty-seven whites. Just that summer the last free Comanches, led by Quanah Parker, had come in to live at the Fort Sill agency down in Indian Territory, and that wasn't terribly far away.

"Buffalo hunters," Rawdon said with a jerk of his head. "Not many shaggies left around here but I reckon some strayed in sight. When I first came here three years ago, the big kill was just starting. Argentine pampas cattle had been slaughtered till there weren't enough to supply American and European tanneries so tanners figured out a way to make good leather from buffalo hides. When word spread that there was a big market, thousands of hunters swarmed over the prairies. An expert shot could kill seventy-five to a hundred in a day, though a few have brought down more than that in less than an hour." As Susanna gasped, he added, "The average hunter probably shoots about fifty a day. They peeled off the hides, leaving the meat to rot, all the way from Montana to Texas. Frank Mayer, one old hunter, told me he guesses over three million buffalo were killed on the southern plains and that didn't count well over a million killed in those three years by Indians. The railroad figures on shipped hides are a lot lower, but any way you count it, the herds are gone, and the ones left on the northern plains can't last long."

"Don't the Indians need them?"

"Sure. For food, shelter, clothing, everything. Killing off the herds forced the horse Indians onto the reservations a lot faster and more effectively than any number of soldiers could have. And what, Miss Alden, will you teach your pupils about that?"

Maturing during the war and then preoccupied with tending her father, Susanna had never thought much about Indians and when she did her feelings were a confused tangle of sympathy for their loss of a wild free roving life and shrinking horror at reports of scalped and tortured settlers and babies tossed on lances.

Goaded by Rawdon, she spoke curtly. "I'll try to teach the truth—when I find out what it is."

He hooted. "Which truth? Whose truth? That white Christians are obeying a moral imperative to civilize heathens? That since horse Indians don't farm the earth and settle on it, it's empty and should be put to use?"

"Isn't that what you're doing?"

"I'm using the land but without pious excuses. A simple matter of might makes right, as the North taught the South."

"Right? You call slavery right?"

He brushed away the question with a flick of his hand. "I never owned a man or woman and I never thought it just. But if you're to teach history, ma'am, do get your facts straight. The war was fought over whether states have the right to secede. I still maintain they have the right but they don't have the power. That's all that counts. And that's all that counts with Indian claims though you can take some comfort in remembering that battles and raids are a warrior's path to glory and stronger tribes have always pushed weaker ones off favored territory."

"If you think I'm going to teach children such cynical views—"

"No need. They'll find out soon enough. Just as you'll learn why your prospective school is called Mason-Dixon."

Curiosity about the school overcame her resentment. "Obviously it can't be the line between Pennsylvania and

7

Maryland surveyed by Charles Mason and Jeremiah Dixon in 1767 and later extended to be the boundary between slave states and free."

"Obviously."

Odious man! But she did want to learn all she could about the situation so she ignored his caustic reply. "Kansas entered the Union as a free-soil state in 1861—"

"With the help of a passel of New England abolitionists."

This man took a lot of ignoring. "So I suppose," Susanna concluded, after a slow count to twenty-five, "that the name means the district has some former Unionists and some former Confederates."

"For that brilliant deduction, Miss Alden, you get a big red A plus with a gold star."

If this was a sample of how Southern gentlemen behaved, she doubted that she could keep her equanimity and be an effective teacher. Since the school was in Kansas, Bleeding Kansas, which had been a stronghold of abolitionists years before the war, she had never dreamed she'd be living among former Confederates. It was time, she knew, for both sides to stop harboring angry grief, but she had lost her sweetheart and spent her youth and young womanhood nursing a father destroyed by the war. Another war raged in Susanna. She almost demanded that Rawdon drive her back to Dodge where she could state her objections to the superintendent and get another school or seek a position elsewhere, but Rawdon would rejoice in her defeat. For some inexplicable reason, she hated to give him that satisfaction.

Whirling on him, not forgetting to hold tight to the seat, she demanded, "Why are you so—so rude? Because I'm from Ohio? Because I'm a woman? Or did your teacher switch you as much as you probably deserved?"

He cast her a startled look before he laughed. That relaxed the stern set of his features and made him seem younger and less formidable, though from the lines at his eyes and mouth she judged him to be in his early thirties.

"You'd love to thrash me, wouldn't you?" he taunted. "Very well. I beg your pardon. But I didn't wish for your company, and since you bring it up, I don't much care for Yankees, women, or teachers. Nothing personal, I assure you."

"Nothing personal!" With great effort, Susanna resisted the urge to strike him across that jeering face. "Let me remind you, sir, that the North suffered, too, not that it'll do much good since you admit to being a bigoted, jaundiced misogynist." Swallowing hard, she fixed her eyes on that distant meeting of earth and sky. "I—I won't trouble you with further conversation."

"Can you spell that?"

"Spell what?"

"What you called me."

"Of course I can. Can you?"

He gave her an infuriating grin. "It seems that we're having us a further conversation."

"Oh!" Smothering the flood of hot words that rushed to her lips, Susanna vowed not to let him lure her into another outburst. It gave him the upper hand and, besides, he might be low enough to tell the school board that she had an inflammable temper.

The wheels struck an especially bad rut. Her teeth jarred together and from the cacophony emitted from the jumbled load behind her, she thought she detected the distressed squeak of her trunk's leather bindings against the wagon bed.

Looking back, she was reassured to see it was still there. Strange that everything she had in the world was in that trunk and the tapestry satchel snugged by her feet, which had done service as a handbag and held her necessities on the train.

It still hurt to remember winnowing her possessions down to what she could pack in the trunk, a gift from Uncle Frank and Aunt Mollie. They were almost like parents; she'd lived with them during the four years that her father had worked in field hospitals before an explosion blew off one leg and injured his spine. His hair had been more black than gray when he'd volunteered; it was pure white when he limped off the train that brought him home. He had withered like a seared branch. The blue eyes that had sparkled with interest in people and all creation were dulled with drugs and pain. No matter how she shamed herself, Susanna felt as if her father, her real father, had died in the blast and only a husk remained.

Charles Alden had once lived with zest and loving kindness though he had never remarried after childbed fever stole his adored wife, Serena, whom Susanna only knew from a daguerreotype. When he died this past spring, nearly everyone in the little town attended the funeral and told a dazed Susanna how Charles had sat up all night, wrapping a feverish child in wet sheets till the fever ebbed, delivered babies who had seemed too big or wrongly placed to ever be born alive; how he had comforted the dying, set many a broken bone, and sewed up gashes through which a life could have bled away.

Some of these people slipped coins or President Lincoln's green paper money into her pocket, murmuring that they still owed the doctor money after all these years and would pay her when they could, but the lamentable truth was that Charles had been a physician, not a businessman. He never sent bills, assuring his disapproving sister, Aunt Mollie, that his patients would pay him when they could. The pretty little white house among the lilacs where he'd brought his Serena as a bride and where he and Susanna had lived till he went to war, upon his death brought enough with its simple furnishings to pay for his burial and clear up outstanding debts, with enough left to buy Susanna's passage west. Her pay had provided their necessities but his constant need for drink had used up his small savings a year before he died, and the largest bill she had to pay was to the saloon owner who'd supplied him with whiskey. The fifty dollars she had left after buying her ticket was prudently lodged in a pocket Aunt Mollie had sewn to the underside of her bodice.

Over the puzzled and somewhat indignant objections of her aunt and uncle, she had insisted on leaving Pleasant Grove. "In a few years, you could take over as headmistress of the school," plump, rosy Aunt Mollie said tearfully. "Or you could marry that nice lawyer Bartholomew Harris."

"I can't. Mr. Harris managed to stay safely at home while Richard was killed and my father was wounded. And don't bother naming the other men I can marry, darling. They're twice my age or just want a housekeeper and stepmother for their children." She added with a fierceness that surprised her, "I may be an old maid, but I don't want a secondhand husband!"

At Uncle Frank's warning glance, Aunt Mollie wiped her eyes and gripped Susanna's hands. "If things don't go well, dear, come right back to us. You're like our own baby and you'll always have a home here."

Embracing her aunt though she'd winced at the word "baby," Susanna wept, too, but held to her purpose. "I love you both, but I want to go somewhere new, someplace different, where my teaching can really be important. Professor Morris at the normal school has had letters from the county superintendents of a dozen schools in Kansas and Nebraska. Teaching out there's not just another job, it—it's *pioneering.*"

"So you closed your eyes and picked this letter from Ford County!" Aunt Mollie wailed. "Why, that country's full of wild Indians and wilder cowboys, buffalo hunters, wolves, and rattlesnakes!"

And, it would seem, bigoted, jaundiced misogynists who were also dismayingly attractive. Thinking of her aunt and uncle brought a wave of homesickness and Susanna's eyes blurred till she couldn't distinguish between sky and prairie.

"Save your tears till you meet the school trustees,"

Rawdon advised. "Then you'll really have something to cry about."

"I'm not crying! Whatever the trustees are like, they can't be as horrid as you!"

"And bigoted, jaundiced, and misogynic?" he supplied.

"I hope you don't have children in my school and I feel mightily sorry for your wife, if you've got one."

His face closed. "I don't and the chance of my ever having children in your school is slim as a whisker."

He looked so forbidding that she didn't dare ask him why he was so sure he'd have no offspring. As if they had reached some kind of stalemate, they were both silent. Up ahead Susanna saw the first sign of human existence since leaving town, a ragged field of corn, the husks stripped down to let the ears dry on the browning stalks, just as was done in Ohio. This familiar sight raised her spirits till she saw a house of mud bricks, roofed with sod growing grass and weeds so that at a distance, the squat oblong dwelling would be indistinguishable from the prairie.

With all her heart, Susanna hoped no woman lived there and was glad when Rawdon said, "Pete Townsend hauls freight while he's proving up on his claim——has to live on it five years, build a house, and do some planting before he gets title."

"Are you homesteading?"

"Good gracious, teacher," he said in a sarcastic tone. "Don't you know that rebels can't? But Yanks are allowed to count the time they fought in the war against the five years it takes to prove up. I bought out a couple of settlers who were tired of drought, hail, blizzards, tornados, and grasshoppers." He cast her a sardonic grin. "Didn't cost much and that was before last year when the grasshoppers gnawed every green thing right into the ground."

"If western Kansas is so dreadful, why did you settle here?"

"I can't be much of a doctor with only one useful hand and I didn't choose to set up practice in Dallas, as my sister urged, to treat the megrims and vapors of her society friends. I owe Amanda a lot. We were orphaned when I was ten and she was only sixteen, left with nothing since our mother had died years earlier and our father had long ago given up the practice of law for the tilting of the bottle. Amanda kept me in school while she worked for little more than our board and room, cooking, housekeeping, whatever she could find. It was her dream that I'd be a doctor like our grandfather. A doctor she worked for took an interest in me, and arranged for me to work my way through medical school." Rawdon's smile was wry. "I was more inclined to go mustanging, but Amanda prodded me into it. During those two years of medical school, I became fascinated with surgery. Amanda, bless her heart, had meanwhile nursed a well-to-do widower through a serious illness. He was much older, but there was true affection between them. He died during the war. I know Amanda hoped that Melanie, my fiancée, and I would share her big house. But——" He shrugged. "Forgive me for boring you, Miss Alden. Suffice it to say that I left Texas in search of cheap land with good grass. I farm a little but mostly I'm raising horses."

Susanna frowned. She knew she should mind her own business yet it seemed such a waste that this man not use his talent and training. "Why can't you be a doctor? I'd think there'd be lots you could do with one hand."

"Not surgery."

Her father had taken a special pride in surgery so she understood something of Rawdon's frustration, but he was alive while her men weren't so she didn't bother to speak gently. "Delivering babies may not be as gratifying as carving away with a scalpel, Dr. Rawdon, but it's important. So is easing a dying person or setting broken bones and stitching up wounds. In a region like this, where you're surely needed, it seems almost wicked not to practice your profession."

"Make the best of things?" His eyes bored into her. "Is that what you're doing, Miss Alden?"

She could do nothing about the blood that rushed to her face but she didn't speak till she had control of her voice. "I'm doing just that, sir, and I'm not ashamed of it."

This time the silence lasted till they passed a mud house with a partially destroyed roof. The door was gone and a hide flapped at one small window. A few stalks of corn, unhusked, rose from a grown-over patch that had almost returned to sod. Rawdon veered out of the ruts and snapped off the ears. "No use their going to waste. Mrs. Osborn went sort of daft from the wind, their baby died, and they went back to Iowa two years ago."

Susanna repressed a shudder. Had she been foolish to come here? Even without the undefined menace of the school board, this vast plain made her feel as if—as if— She groped to define it. Aunt Mollie used to say that if you could understand what troubled you, you were halfway to dealing with it. Susanna felt as if—the roof and walls of a comfortable house had suddenly blown off and she was left with no roof but heaven, no floor but the grass, no neighbor but the wind.

She shivered, but there was something spacious and wonderfully free about this prairie, something that whispered there was all the room in the world to grow, to be what you couldn't be inside the walls. Susanna's head ached from the pins that had held her hair in place for three days. How good it would feel to pull off the sedate bonnet and let the wind blow her hair!

After one brief moment of shock at the audacity of unpinning her hair in front of a strange man, she tugged the ribbon and, as Rawdon shot her an amazed look, she loosed her hair. Hadn't she come out to lead a new kind of life and along with the hardships of the frontier taste its freedom? Defiantly heedless of this man who didn't approve of her anyway, she threw back her head and laughed into the western breeze, reveling in the way it soothed the chafed places on her scalp and touched the roots of her hair with cooling invisible fingers.

To her surprise, Rawdon's chuckle was almost sympathetic. "Bet that does feel good. Like a horse that's lathered up enjoys a good roll in the dust. Till you did that, I figured you for the perfect schoolmarm."

"Who never lets down her hair?"

His eyes touched her, only for a moment, but their curious light seemed to pierce her, see deep inside, and there was something more, a flash of danger, heady, intoxicating, a feeling she had never had before. She had been only seventeen when Richard kissed her shyly and asked her to wait for him. How many times since then had she wished that she'd been a little bolder, that each of them could have had more than a swift kiss to remember. Startled at the way Rawdon's glance sent her pulse racing, she looked away.

"You bet she doesn't let down her hair, Miss Alden." His tone was almost contemptuous. "She's careful of her clothes, her money, and her reputation."

Thinking of the money pocket sewn into her dress, Susanna nearly winced. "No more than they get paid, teachers have to be careful of the first two," she said defensively. "And any woman has to guard her reputation."

"Then you'd better twist that pretty hair back into a knot because the dust and smoke up ahead looks like a branding crew and Ase McCanless may be there. He's chairman of the board of trustees. Smile at him sweetly, Miss Alden, because if you don't get along with him, you won't last long."

"He's a rancher?"

"You could say that. His cattle range clear down to Texas where he started broke after the war. He wouldn't like homesteaders plowing up what he thinks is his grass anyway, but when they're Yankees, and most are, it really sticks in his craw."

As they approached the pall of dust, Susanna could hear

shouts and the angry, frightened bawling of cattle. Some distance from the track, mounted men kept watch over grazing cattle while others roped calves and hauled them to a fire where long irons glowed red. When a calf was wrestled down by two more men, a third applied one of the irons, made swifts cuts with a knife, and in a few minutes, the calf stumbled up and made for its mother who licked it tenderly and comforted it with her udder.

These cows looked very different from the sleek Jerseys and Holsteins and Guernseys of Ohio. Most of these had vicious long and curling horns, were rangy and lean, and came in a dusty rainbow of bovine colors—gray, dun, brindled, red, cream, and brown. The man with the iron called one of the herders, gave him the iron, and, appropriating his horse, rode over to the buckboard.

Sweeping off a wide-brimmed hat so soiled it was impossible to discern its original color, the big stranger gave a curt nod to Rawdon before he frankly stared at Susanna. "You the new schoolmarm, lady?" Lean and tough and dark as the leather of his saddle, he had piercing blue eyes and sandy brown hair. About Rawdon's age, she guessed, though it was hard to tell. "No offense," he continued in a lazy drawl, "but you don't look old enough to be traveling around by yourself."

Susanna couldn't keep from chuckling. "That's flattering, sir, but I'm twenty-seven and I've been teaching for years."

Eyeing her with increased caution, he sighed. "Seems Henry said you're from Ohio."

"Yes."

He sighed again. "Well, accordin' to Henry, you had the best qualifications of the teachers who applied—not that many did. Western Kansas isn't real popular. Too bad we couldn't get a Southern lady but I reckon their menfolk won't let 'em go gadding around the country."

"My fiancé was killed in the war," Susanna said icily. "And my father recently died after years of pain from his injuries. I'm willing to answer any reasonable questions about my competency, but when the county superintendent invited me to come, he knew I was what you doubtless call a Yankee."

"Now don't go flyin' off the handle, ma'am. Two of the board want you because you *are* from the North like them. But the main thing is, our kids need teachin' and if you can do that, more power to you." He set his hat firmly back on his head. "I'm Asa McCanless, ma'am, and I reckon you're Miss Susanna Alden. I got to get back to work, but Rawdon, just take her on to the house, and much obliged. Stay for supper and overnight if you want."

"Thanks, Ase, but I'll get on to my place. Cash Hardy's back is paining him. I promised I'd get him some medicine in Dodge and stop by tonight."

McCanless chuckled. "For a doctor who says he don't doctor, Doc, you sure pay a lot of calls. If you ask me, what Cash needs most is a good kick in the pants."

"Oh, he's got some injured vertebrae," said Rawdon. He spoke to the team and they were moving on when suddenly McCanless shot past them, making for a rider on the horizon, a rider whose horse skimmed the plains, tail and mane swept by the wind.

"One of your pupils," Rawdon said. "Ase's daughter. Regular little hellion and made a lot worse by the way he treats her." As the team started, he gave Susanna a grim smile. "You're going to have an—interesting time, Miss Alden. It's not just Yanks and Rebels still fighting the war, but some of the families have their little problems."

"Would you enjoy seeing me give up?"

"What's it to me? I told you, I've no youngsters and probably never will." He hesitated a second. "I'm—sorry about your father and fiancé."

That had taken an effort. Moved to honesty, she said, "I'm sorry about your hand."

His face went red, then pale. After a moment, he spoke in a tight, hard tone. "My hand, Miss Alden, is absolutely none of your concern. The revulsion it causes, especially

17

to ladies, is perfectly natural. I prefer honest shrinking to pity."

Stung, Susanna could think of no good answer. They drove along, the silence between them heavy and bitter with memories, till what must be McCanless's home came into view.

A wide-porched white frame house dominated a sprawl of sod buildings and corrals. None of the trees planted around the dwelling as yet rose higher than the windows of the gabled second story. This added to the impression that the big house had been conjured up in a place where it didn't belong.

"Here you are at Ace High." Rawdon got down, hitched the team to a post, and impatiently helped her alight. "Why will women wear corsets?" he grumbled. "At least you seem to have the sense not to lace yourself so tight you can't breathe."

"Sir!" His remark was so indecorous that she could think of no retort but a withering glance that only made him throw back his head and laugh.

"Sorry, ma'am. Consider it a physician's observation."

"*If* you go back into practice and *if* I seek your advice, then Dr. Rawdon, you may make such comments."

"I already did." Ignoring her displeasure, he greeted an old man who limped out of a shed and came to help with the trunk. The door of the house flew open and a plump, elderly lady hurried out, catching Susanna's hands.

"Come in, dear," she greeted, her smile spreading to warm shrewd hazel eyes as she took Susanna in with one swift toe-to-top glance. "Fagged, you must be, and wanting a bath, and to stretch out. Your room's ready. Johnny'll fill a tub for you. I'll bring you some nice soup and you won't need to come down to supper if you'd rather just go to bed. I'm Betty Flynn, Mr. McCanless's housekeeper."

She bore Susanna into a carpeted hall and motioned up the stairs. "First door on your right, dear. If you need anything, just call."

Overwhelmed by such a welcome after encountering Dodge City and two Southern men who hadn't exactly lived up to the tradition of chivalry attached to that region, Susanna started up the stairs. Rawdon met her on the landing.

"Thank you for your trouble," she said with cool civility, and made to open her satchel. "I want to pay you for bringing you out of your way—and for having inflicted my company on you."

The landing was dim but that made his eyes more disconcertingly brilliant than ever. "Yankees think they can pay for everything, don't they? I don't want your money, Miss Alden. As I told you, save it for your ticket home."

He gave her a curt nod and was down the stairs before she could move. Dreadful nasty bigoted jaundiced misogynist Rebel!

Whatever the Mason-Dixon school board was like, it couldn't be made up of more difficult men than the two she had already met.

❋ *Two* ❋

Feeling grimy and bedraggled after three days on the train and the hot, dusty trip from Dodge City, Susanna made grateful use of the water brought up by Johnny. When she'd protested at the grizzled lame man's carrying buckets, his faded blue eyes twinkled and he grinned.

"I been rolled on by one bronc too many, ma'am, but the doggone leg don't hurt, it's just unreliable. Doc Rawdon rigged me a brace that helps a whole lot. I've got a soft bunk around here, just helpin' Cookie, so don't fret about me but enjoy yourself. Nothin' like a good bath after comin' in off a long trail."

Not only did he fill the round tin tub, but he also left two extra buckets. Susanna washed and rinsed her hair in these, and then, hair wrapped in a towel, she eased into the tub with a blissful sigh. Weariness and miles soaked gently away. She was close to drowsing when a thunderous slam made her jump. Hastily scrubbing herself, she stepped out onto a mat, toweled until her skin tingled, and pulled on a cool batiste nightgown, plain and prim as befitted an old maid schoolmarm.

Susanna grimaced. She'd never even thought about her

nightgowns before. Why did some perverse whimsy conjure up a vision of Matt Rawdon tilting his head and jeering with that provoking arrogance of his, "I was sure your gowns wouldn't have lace, Miss Alden, but is it really necessary to button right up to your collarbone?"

Good grief! Was she going to be haunted by that disturbing, completely impossible man, invent colloquies with him? Susanna pulled her comb through snarls of damp hair with a vigor that made her flinch. Setting her teeth, she had worked out almost all the tangles when a rap came at the door.

"I've brought your soup, dear," called Betty Flynn.

Hurrying into a wrapper—also plain and prim—Susanna opened the door. The housekeeper came in and somewhat distractedly set a tray on a small marble-topped table beside an armchair upholstered in rose satin to match the coverlet.

"This is a beautiful room," Susanna said, keenly aware of how out of place she was, a spinster in austere nightwear. She laughed a little at her own misgivings. "I feel like an imposter, Mrs. Flynn. Isn't there an ordinary room I could use?"

Mrs. Flynn's face turned pinker and her warm greenish brown eyes were distressed as she glanced from the gilt-framed mirror to the rose satin draperies. "You don't like it?"

She sounded hurt. Puzzled, Susanna said, "Of course I like it, Mrs. Flynn." She gave her head a small shake as she held up an unadorned sleeve. "But this room—oh, it fits someone with ruffles and frills." Someone with a man who loves her, who wants to give her nice things and have her look pretty.

"It needs a woman," said Mrs. Flynn with energy. "And please call me Betty. Ase left furnishing the house up to me. Wanted it nice for Jenny—not that Jenny gives a hoot. All she wants to do is tag after her daddy and tear around

22

on her pony like a wild Indian. That was her just banged the door fit to break windows."

"I saw her riding."

"Something she's not supposed to do by herself but Ase wouldn't let her help on the roundup." Betty Flynn's full bosom lifted and fell in a sigh. "When Ase was just getting started down in Texas, Jenny's mother got dragged to death by a bolting horse when she was helping herd cattle. Jenny was just a baby. Ase can't get over it. So he wants Jenny to have everything her mother didn't. And all Jenny wants is to be with her daddy and do everything he does. They're both mule-stubborn and I hate to think what'll happen if they keep on wrangling."

'I suppose you've talked with Mr. McCanless."

"I have but you might as well waste breath on a rock. He needs a wife who could be a mother to Jenny and sort of stand in between them."

"It doesn't sound like a comfortable position."

"It wouldn't be," Betty Flynn admitted. Again her eyes traveled around the gracious chamber. "But if somebody loved Ase——"

"You do."

"He's the son I never had." Betty's hazel eyes softened. "We were neighbors in Texas, lived on the Clear Fork of the Brazos. When my man froze to death in a storm a few months after Ase's wife died, he asked me to move in and look after Jenny. He came back from the war flat busted but in a few years he was trailing cattle north to market. He was lucky, worked like a devil, and now he's one of the biggest cattlemen anywhere. Not that it's made him happy." Betty clapped her hand over her mouth. "Here I am, rattling on while your supper gets cold! Enjoy it, dear, and just set the tray in the hall when you're finished. Johnny'll fetch it. You get a good rest and come down for breakfast whenever you're ready in the morning."

Susanna took the older woman's work-roughened hand. "You're really kind, Betty. I hope I can repay you someday."

"You will, if you just teach Jenny something besides trying to be a boy." Hesitating a moment, Betty lifted her chin
and looked Susanna in the eyes. "Try to enjoy the room,
my dear. It's not that hard to sew frills and ruffles on your
clothes."

Susanna blushed. It was clear that this generous-hearted
woman, troubled about her employer and his child, would
welcome an ally, a mistress in the house. Buried deep in
Susanna, scarcely acknowledged for fear of disappointment, persisted the wishful hope that the possibility of loving a man and being loved by him, her chance of being
a wife and mother, was not buried finally and for all with
Richard. Ase was certainly an attractive man in his rough
way, yet it was remembering Matt Rawdon's eyes that sent
a warm, expectant shock through her; it was his deep, wry
voice that resonated in her.

"If I get the school, I'll be too busy to sew on ruffles,"
she said evasively.

Betty Flynn smiled. "I'd do it for you, child." Pausing in
the door, she added, "Enjoy your meal. If you hear yipping
and howling, it's just coyotes. A body can kind of get to
like the sound."

She shut the door behind her and Susanna sat down to
her tray. The cream of tomato soup was delicious and the
moist corn muffins were still hot enough to melt butter;
there was a glass of cold buttermilk and a golden-glazed
crusted pie made of some kind of small orange fruit. After
greasy, hastily eaten food bought from vendors at train
stops, Susanna relished each bite. But this luxuriating was
ruined by her conscience when Johnny knocked and
began to carry out her bathwater in buckets. After he'd
reduced the level somewhat, Susanna dragged the tub out
into the hall.

"Hold it right there, ma'am!" An outraged Johnny hurried from the porch, clanking the buckets. "That's my job!"

"It makes me feel so lazy," Susanna pleaded. "Won't you
let me help you carry this down?"

"I sure won't!" Puffing, Johnny hustled up the steps. "Why, Ase would skin me alive—"

"I'll help." The door at the end of the hall had opened in stealthy contrast to the way it had banged half an hour ago. A brown-skinned girl with a thick braid of yellow hair raced to the stair and grasped one handle of the tub. "Johnny, I declare, you're as bad as Daddy, saying women can't do this or that."

'Jenny, you pesky little devil, get away from that tub!"

With a defiant laugh that showed white teeth and several dimples, the girl gave Susanna a challenging stare from eyes such a deep blue that in the shadowy hall they looked almost black. "Grab hold, lady, if you really mean what you said."

That close to the stairs, Johnny couldn't interfere without risking somebody's falling. Grumbling, he held to the banister as if needing support while Susanna and the child, who could only be Jenny, went down the stairs with the tub, carefully, in order not to splash.

"We'll dump it on the trees," Jenny said. "Not enough soap to hurt 'em."

Susanna hated to get her bedroom slippers dusty but she knew that avoiding it would earn Jenny's scorn. To get anywhere with this girl meant first having her respect. So Susanna only held the hems of her white gown and wrapper out of the gritty dust of the bare yard and helped pour the water into hollows dug around the cottonwood trees and another kind with very dark, narrow-ridged bark. The trunks of these had thorns, but their tapering oval leaves moved gracefully with the wind. Twisted brown pods dangled in bunches from the ends of twigs.

"Honey locusts," Jenny said. "Not many trees can live out here." Turning the tub upside down on a bench that held several others, the girl looked directly into Susanna's eyes. She was perhaps eleven, still a child but with subtle changes beginning, the budding that Susanna had watched so often these past years in the girls she taught.

"Trees have to be tough here," said Jenny. "So do people. You aren't."

Susanna concealed amusement for she guessed that Jenny could forgive anything but being laughed at. "What makes you say that?"

"If you were tough, you'd have let Johnny carry all the water."

"You didn't."

A toss of the yellow braid. "I just helped because Daddy wouldn't like it."

"If you go through life with that for a rule, you're likely to cause yourself a big lot of troubles." Susanna started up the steps to the side porch. Jenny ran ahead and turned to confront her, eye to eye, from the step above.

"Betty says you're going to start a school."

"That's why I came."

"I don't want to go. Daddy can teach me everything I care about."

"Whether or not you go is between you and your father," Susanna said coolly. "Whether you learn is your choice."

"You won't try to make me study?"

"I'll give you the grades you earn. What they are is up to you."

A jaw, firm in spite of childish contours, dropped a little. "Daddy won't like that."

Susanna took the last step. Jenny's head just reached her shoulder. "Again, that's between the two of you."

"If you can't teach me, you won't keep the school." Recovering her confidence, Jenny spoke boastfully. "The only reason Daddy helped with it was that he hopes I'll learn more that way than I did from those silly women he hired. Gov—governesses! They didn't govern me. None of them lasted more than a month."

Smothering a retort, Susanna stopped at her door. "Thank you, Jenny, for helping me empty the water. Good night."

Susanna closed the door on a tanned young face twisted with anger and bewilderment. There was the sound of pelting steps, and then, down the hall, a door slammed even more loudly than it had the first time.

To Susanna's surprise, she found that she was trembling. Had she handled Jenny properly? Should she have been gentler or harder? Susanna, in spite of her experience, had no idea, for never had she encountered a child like this. No wonder the hapless governesses had fled! *She won't be my only pupil,* Susanna comforted herself. *Some will want to study, will be hungry to learn.*

Or would they? Maybe youngsters out here were different. There'd be boys, too, and she'd never taught them or even been much in their company, though she'd heard plenty of stories about male pupils of seventeen and eighteen who beat up men teachers, defied the female, and turned classes into a brawling circus. Panic flooded Susanna.

Her pupils were bound to share the animosities of their parents, former Unionists and Confederates. She had her own feelings. She'd have to control herself before she could control her students and get along with the parents. This wasn't at all what she'd bargained for. Maybe she should ask Superintendent Morton if he didn't have a school she could take that had no patrons from the South.

Mightily tempted, she walked to the window and leaned on the sill, welcoming a breeze that at the gathering of twilight was somewhat cooler. A dusky cross-stitch of cottonwoods marked the course of a meandering stream and out on the world's rim, blue-gray prairie merged with a sky that was lighter at the horizon, darker above, showing the first stars.

Why, that was the Big Dipper, the Great Bear! Tracing a route from the lip of the Big Dipper, she located the Little Dipper by spotting the North Star at the end of its handle. "The Dippers pour into each other," her father said when she was little and he, loving the Greek myths, pointed out twinkling star groups and told her their legends: Orion and his dog pursuing Taurus the Bull and the shy Pleiades, the Hunter in turn pursued by a giant Scorpion; the Archer aiming at Scorpius; the Centaur and the Heavenly Twins, Castor and Pollux—oh, those had been lovely stories in a happy time! She no longer remembered how and when to find any but the most conspicuous constellations, but it was heartening to see the familiar heavenly lights.

Swept with a wave of longing for her father as he had been before the war, Susanna gripped the window ledge and blinked back tears. The surge of grief carried its own healing in treasured memories. When bitter regret seized her for those last terrible years, she'd try to think back to the dear companionship of those earlier times. Charles Alden had sometimes treated sick or wounded animals and had been especially interested in wild ones. He wouldn't kill snakes, not even poisonous massasaugas, saying they had their part in the circle of life. He'd read deeply in all natural sciences and taught her more, offhandedly, than ever she'd learned in school.

She smiled through tears now to remember how, till she was six or seven, she ran to greet him with the pirate cry of "Daddy! What did you bring home in your pocket?" There had always been something, a pretty rock, bunch of acorns, shed snakeskin, bright feather, a small book, candy, or, at the least, some of the horehound drops he carried in his medical bag.

She hadn't called him Daddy since before the war; after he came home, she called him Father. But now, hundreds of miles from his grave, she gazed at the stars he'd shown her and whispered into the night, "Daddy, please let me know you don't hurt anymore or need the whiskey. Let me know it's well with you."

As if he'd been waiting, she felt him near, heard him in her mind though there were no audible words. *It's well with me and very well. Where I am there's endless day, my darling, perfect peace and perfect joy.* She almost heard him chuckle. *That broken old body I dragged home from the war was no use to me or anyone. I'm glad to be out of it.*

Is mother there?

She is. So is Richard. So is everybody. It's nothing you can imagine, love; just believe it's good and get on with what you have to do before you come to us.

The awareness faded, the flow of communion ceased as gently as night deepened from dusk, but she was comforted. Maybe it was all a trick of her senses, conjured up from fatigue and feeling so apprehensive and alone in this strange place. However it came, it was the best medicine her physician father had ever given her. Any time she saw the stars they'd watched together, she could remember him, and happily. His death had given him back to her.

The wheezing, softly rising cry of a barn owl floated from the outbuildings and the familiar sound made her hope that some things closer than the stars would also be the same. Earlier, she had noticed a silver box of matches by the rose hobnail lamp, and feeling her way, she managed to light the wick which fortunately was turned up just the right amount.

Her father's favorite book had been *The Meditations of Marcus Aurelius* and the worn volume was one of the several dozen books she'd chosen to keep in place of family antiques and other cherished belongings. Till now, just seeing the book had been painful, but she opened her trunk to look for it. First, she hung up her black silk mourning dress, her best one, which she had decided she would not wear in school, the dark gray loose-woven wool grenadine and the tarlatan, once a delicate primrose, that she'd dyed to a very dark green. A utilitarian brown calico with tiny yellow sprigs completed her wardrobe except for a brown wool mantle, her mother's paisley shawl in lovely jewel colors, a pair each of high-laced brown and black shoes and black velvet slippers.

Sighing over the array's drabness as much as the wrinkles, Susanna ruefully thought of Matt Rawdon's cutting remark about a schoolteacher's being careful of her clothes, her money, and her reputation. Did he think she could be careless?

Burrowing in the trunk till she found Marcus Aurelius, Susanna, with tremendous effort, banished Rawdon's disturbing face and sat down near the lamp, opening the much-turned pages to the ribbon that marked her father's favorite passage: "Art thou unwilling to do the work of a human being? And why then dost thou not make haste to do that which is according to thy nature?"

The work of a human being. That meant more than simply work, carrying out one's allotted tasks. It meant fulfilling the duties and obligations of the mortal state, living with as much grace, kindness, and fortitude as possible. Yes, and happiness, too, for martyrs were a fearful burden. An ideal, surely, an echo of the moth-eaten credo of leaving the world a little better than you found it, but only by trying for the best could she hope to shape a life that would count for something even if she never had a lover, a husband, or children.

Again, she thanked her father, and again she felt him close. She braided her still-damp locks, blew out the lamp and fell into the deepest sleep she'd had since her father died, but not before she wished she could see Matt Rawdon's mouth tender and happy, without that twist of bitterness.

As she started to dress next morning, Susanna, with her usual reluctance, picked up her corset. It was a Warners creation, supposed to be comfortable, but alas, it wasn't. None were, or could be. Her cheeks warmed as she remembered Matt Rawdon's scandalous remark. As if to defy him, she started to hook it up, but then paused.

Betty didn't lace. Probably none of the homestead and

ranch women out here did, except for special occasions. Her dresses would fit without the thing, for, heeding her father, she never had corseted tightly. In an abandon similar to that she'd felt when taking off her bonnet and letting down her hair, she tossed the corset on her trunk and discarded the small bustle she wore as a grudging concession to propriety and fashion. This was her new life. Why shouldn't she get rid of hampering relics of fuss and vanity?

She put on her coolest dress, the tarlatan, though it was futile, even without corset and bustle, to think of coolness when wearing the three petticoats Aunt Mollie decreed absolutely essential to decency. Susanna went downstairs as the sun was rising amid shafts of gold and roseate peach. There was nothing to obstruct the glory and she stood at the open door, almost in worship, till the sun burst through the brilliant streamers and the colors ebbed.

Teased by the fragrance of coffee, she found Betty making buckwheat cakes which Johnny, seated at a red-checked oilcloth-covered table, was devouring with such speed that he seemed to breathe them in. He paused to grin appreciatively at Susanna before he got to his feet and limped around to seat her. It was nice, she thought, to be treated like something rare and precious even if Johnny was old enough to be her grandfather.

"You must've slept good, ma'am," he said. "When you got here, 'peared like you'd wintered on a hard range but this mornin' you're lookin' purty as a speckled pup and fit to settle your loop over this complete, entire neck of the woods."

Puzzled by some of his language but knowing from his jovial beam that it was complimentary, she smiled and thanked him as Betty set a stack of golden-brown hotcakes before her and poured steaming coffee.

"Try the Dutch honey," Betty urged. "It's good on buckwheats. I make it from sour cream, dark syrup, and sugar cooked till it's smooth and thick." She turned to Johnny with exasperated affection. "For you to lift your face out of the plate and start your blarney, you must be full to the gills."

"Reckon I could force down a couple more. If those poor dumb cowhands ever sank their teeth into your hotcakes, Betty, they'd use Cookie's flapjacks to half-sole their boots."

"Flattery will get you well nigh anything." Betty laughed, dropping two cakes on his plate before sitting down to her own stack and pouring cream in her coffee. "You won't find milk on most ranches, except condensed," she told Susanna. "But Ase was set on having the fresh kind for Jenny and now we're all spoiled to it, except for Ase."

"Speakin' of Jenny, where is our little gal?"

"Pouting in her room, I expect." Betty sighed. "She's hardheaded as Ase and I declare I don't know what's going to come of it."

"If Ase don't loosen his reins, she'll prob'ly run off with some cowboy when she's fifteen or so," Johnny predicted with a sad shake of his gray head. "Ase can gently a filly 'thout breakin' her spirit but he don't know how to do that with his daughter. Dang shame it is. He loves her more'n anything under the sun but he won't let her be his helper, let her tag along with him. If he hogties her into his idea of a lady, she'll be ruined but if she's strong enough to keep fightin' there's bound to be an awful smashup." He gave Susanna a weighing look. "How'd you two get along?"

"Not too well," Susanna had to admit. "She let me know she's run off several governesses and that she wasn't interested in anything I could teach her."

"Can't expect you to believe it, but at heart she's a good kid." Johnny finished his coffee and pushed back his chair in replete felicity. "Want I should saddle you a rocking-chair sort of horse, ma'am, and take you to see the school?"

"Is it far?"

"Bless you, you could go by shank's mare in twenty minutes, it's not more'n a mile. Ase built it close so you and Jenny wouldn't have to go far."

"Mr. McCanless built it?"

"Sure. It's on his land."

Susanna digested this with growing dismay. "Did he deed the building and site to the school district?"

Betty and Johnny, startled, looked at each other and burst into laughter. "Ase McCanless give up control of a piece of his land? It'll rain in hell first—beg your pardon, ladies."

"I haven't been hired yet," said Susanna, suddenly queasy and losing her appetite though the Dutch honey and buckwheats had wonderful flavor. "But I can't teach in a privately owned school that sits on private land. I'm surprised the board of trustees didn't object."

"You might say they did, ma'am, the two Yankees—'scuse me, the two who fought for the North, Will Taylor and Saul Prade. But Ase is chairman of the board and he's got two other Texans votin' with him, Luke Tarrant and Kermit Brown."

"I should think the county superintendent of schools would do something."

"Henry Morton?" scoffed Betty. "Honey, make up your mind to one thing right now and it'll save you a heap of trouble. Henry's been chewed on by both sides till he's not about to get mixed up with this school. He's sure not the man to tangle with Ase."

"Not many are," said Johnny.

"Well, it looks as if I'll have to tangle with him." Susanna, at Betty's hurt glance at her plate, made to finish the hotcakes but it was now as if she chewed sawdust. "I may not get my certificate, of course, but if I do, I won't sign a contract with the trustees unless they establish a school on a neutral location."

"Ase sure put up a dandy building, wood freighted up from his ranch in Texas," said Johnny. "Real glass windows, too, ma'am." He gave a delicate cough. "Maybe you'd ought to look it over afore you start buckin'."

"I can't and won't teach in a school controlled by one patron." Outrage blazed in Susanna, forging her consternation into absolute resolve. "I can't think of anything more detrimental to education, especially in a divided community like this—and by the way, I don't intend to have that ridiculous name, Mason-Dixon, over the door of any school where I'm in charge."

"Is that so?"

They all whirled toward the open door to the back porch. Absorbed in their talk, they hadn't heard Ase McCanless approach. He must, thought Susanna with indignation, have come up stealthily, for now, tossing his hat on a peg, he entered the kitchen, high-heeled boots coming down with his full weight so that they shook the floor, or seemed to.

Pushing sweaty hair off a forehead banded red from his hat, he sloshed coffee into a blue enamel mug, took a long swallow though it must have been near boiling, and stared at Susanna as if expecting her to sprout horns or another head.

"Sounds like I missed a mighty interesting conversation, Miss Alden. But I guess you're balkin' at the school bein' on my place."

"Not just balking, sir." Did he think she was a mule? Susanna's cheeks burned and she braced to meet the force of his eyes, a piercing blue made even deeper by the ruddy brown of his square face. "I simply won't teach in such a compromising situation."

Thick, bleached brows almost met above his rather flat, pugnacious nose, as he continued, incredulously, to look her up and down. "That's sure a nice thanks for the chance to use a clean new frame building instead of a dugout or soddie like most schools out here. Before you get all rared back on your hind legs, you'd better have a look."

"No need to look, Mr. McCanless, to see that your owning the school puts you in position to wield improper influence."

A slow smile eased the grim line of his mouth and his eyes glinted with an amusement that turned his face almost boyish. "Improper influence, ma'am? Sounds like it might be fun. But I sure don't aim to tell you what and how to teach any more'n any trustee has a right to."

"From what I hear, the trustees are likely to tell me a lot of different things. I'll listen, but let me make it clear right now that I won't take the school unless it's understood that I'm in charge of it. If the trustees and patrons don't approve of the results, they can refuse to offer me another contract."

Betty tried to diminish the tension by bustling to the griddle. "Buckwheats, Ase? Plenty of batter left."

"Thanks, Betty, but I'm plumb weighted down with Cookie's flapjacks. Tried to sneak off without eatin' but he corraled me and I had to tuck in or start huntin' another cook. You know how cantankerous he is." The cattleman turned his gaze full on Susanna again, and it struck her with almost physical impact. "Don't beat around the bush, do you?

Taut with anxiety, for in spite of her bold words, she felt sick at the prospect of having to give up this school and hunt for another, Susanna stared back, trying to keep her features expressionless. It was like confronting a searing prairie wind. Her muscles went slack with relief when McCanless threw back his head and laughed from deep in his belly.

"I'll make you a deal, Miss Alden, fair and square, and no brands blotted. Have a look at my school, think about what else is around, and I won't buck your decision. What's fairer than that?"

"It *sounds* fair," she acceded doubtfully.

His laughter rumbled again and he swung a chair to the table and settled his rangy, solid length into it. "Betty, reckon I could put away some of your good hotcakes. And

I'll call Jenny down. Her nose is all out of joint because I sent her home yesterday but ridin' along with us ought to sweeten up her disposition." He shouted his daughter's name.

Betty stoked the fire again, washed her hands, and poured golden batter on the sputtering griddle before she hurried out. "I'll get you a sunbonnet," she said to Susanna. "Otherwise you'll get that nice complexion all sunburned."

She was back with a ruffled green calico bonnet as a door opened above. "What do you want?" called Jenny's faint, truculent voice.

"Eat your breakfast and you can ride over to the school with the teacher and me."

There was a silence. "Can I use a real saddle?"

McCanless smothered a groan. "Just this mornin' on account of Miss Alden'll need your sidesaddle. But don't let it give you ideas."

The door closed. Johnny cleared his throat. "If I was you, Ase, I'd give that gal a little more slack. She's got a lot of you in her. Snub her in too tight and you'll get a hardmouthed runaway."

The rancher gave the old man a look that made him fidget unhappily though he didn't glance away. "You're not me, Johnny. All I can do for her mother is raise Jenny like a lady, and she'll be one if it kills us both."

"Pour on the Dutch honey," Betty advised, piling hotcakes on his plate. "Sweet talk gets a lot further with Jenny than spurs."

Ase glared from his housekeeper to the old cowboy. "You all spoil her rotten and then I have to clamp down for her own good and that makes me look ornery and mean. If she hadn't lost her mother——" He looked moodily out the window.

Feeling an intruder, Susanna excused herself and hurried upstairs to put on her fullest skirt since she had no riding habit. As a child, she had sometimes ridden bareback on Madgie, the gentle old mare who pulled Charles Alden's phaeton, but Madgie was long gathered to her equine ancestors and Susanna was sure the ranch horse she was about to meet would be far different. If only she didn't fall off or otherwise disgrace herself!

Even if she did, she wasn't changing her mind about Ase McCanless's school.

❋ *Three* ❋

Jenny, Levi's much too big for her belted in by a piece of cord, toed a dainty, stitched boot into the stirrup and swung astride a proud-headed pony. It danced, tail held high. Susanna helplessly studied the side-saddle cinched to a sorrel mare Johnny held by the reins. Although the horse stood docilely, the saddle seemed a formidable distance from the ground.

The awkward padded hook jutting from the left side was what a woman anchored her right knee over while the left foot, thank goodness, rested in the stirrup. But how did she get up there to start with? And, more urgently, how did she stay?

Surely etiquette required her to introduce herself to her mount—or at least this delayed the moment when she had to somehow attempt the ascent. Stroking the mare's neck, Susanna murmured, "Good morning. Are you all ready for a ride?"

"Her name's Cindy, ma'am, in case you have to holler at her," said Johnny, grinning reassuringly. "Doubt if you'll need to. The only thing that makes Cindy pick up her hoofs fast is when she's headin' home."

"Is that right, Cindy?" Susanna tried to sound confident

as she smoothed the white blaze between the mare's large, drowsy brown eyes which suddenly showed yellowish bloodshot whites as a hind hoof kicked up and the sparse tail swished violently.

"Just one of them grasshopper-sized horseflies." Johnny soothed the mare and a retreating Susanna. "Want I should give you a hand up, ma'am?"

"She needs a lot more than that." Jenny's tone was derisive. "She's not got the faintest notion of how to sit on that thing."

"Jenny!" roared McCanless.

Blood heated Susanna's face but she was almost grateful to have her embarrassing secret laid bare. Catching her breath, she managed to laugh. "You're absolutely right, Jenny. I don't know where to put my knee or foot or—"

The unmentionable part of her anatomy was perched on the saddle seat before she could protest McCanless's lifting her bodily by the waist and tossing her up as if her weight was nothing.

"There, ma'am," he said. "Trust your stirrup with your left foot while you get your knee over the horn." He nodded encouragingly as, gripping the front of the saddle, she got herself balanced. "Now then," he instructed in a perfectly civil, respectful way though she glimpsed hilarity sparkling in his blue eyes, "hold the reins up enough so they don't flop. Cindy'll stay with us so you can just settle back and enjoy the scenery."

They followed the rutted tracks leading northeast that Rawdon must have used yesterday. At first, Susanna sat stiffly, wishing there was something she could hold to except the reins. If she tumbled off, Jenny would hold her in contempt. Besides, it looked a long way down and Susanna was afraid of falling beneath Cindy's hoofs. Gradually, though, her body adapted to the mare's easy pace. Cindy, thank heaven, didn't toss her head around and prance like Ase's chestnut gelding or Jenny's spotted pony.

Cautiously relaxing, Susanna began almost to enjoy the

outing, especially when a meadowlark flashed upward, the familiar bird making her feel less alien though she wondered if she'd ever get used to this vastness, the burnished, cloudless sky curving to a rolling sea of grass. The awesome expanse, its lack of shelter and refuge, made her feel naked and exposed, but also free, unlimited by fences and walls and dense woodlands. The boundlessness invited her. If the eye could encompass so much, couldn't the spirit also reach and perceptions sharpen? Till yesterday, she'd never thought of grass as more than lush green of meadows and lawns; this grass was different, individual, tough, and colorful as the people she was meeting.

One of these tough, colorful individuals reined back. "Everybody on the board of trustees is pretty busy right now, Miss Alden, cattlemen with branding and farmers with harvest. I've sent word to the others, though, and we'll try to meet at the school this Sunday. That gives Henry Morton four days to get out here and give you your certificate. If he don't make it, we'll vote about hiring you anyway." His blunt features retained a strength that reminded Susanna of rock worn by blasts but still impregnable, and his slow grin was probably meant to be reassuring. "Like I said, we haven't had a stampede of teachers out this way. We might favor an older, stouter-looking lady, but since you're what we've got, I'd reckon there's not much chance we won't keep you."

"How very gracious of you!"

He gave her a startled glance. "No offense, ma'am. I just meant—"

"That you'd take whatever you could get."

How blue his eyes were in that weathered face! A shock, half pleasant, half hostile, wholly discomfiting, ran through Susanna and she pretended a sudden interest in the space between Cindy's ears.

"Don't you think that for a minute, Miss Alden." His voice was so soft that Jenny, a bit ahead of him, probably couldn't hear. "I'm particular about what I take."

She could think of no answer. Feeling his gaze still fixed on her, she blushed and was mightily relieved when he said in a tone of pride, "There it is, ma'am."

Except for his home, it was the first decent-looking building she'd seen in all western Kansas, a simple oblong frame structure that would have been quite ordinary in Ohio. After her glimpse of Dodge and the soddies on the way, though, Susanna valued the four glass-paned windows, all facing south, the fresh white paint, and, most of all perhaps, the roof of shingles split from logs, for she could imagine the trickles of muddy rain, the insects and roots that would sieve through a sod roof.

"I had the boys dig a well so the kids won't have to carry water from my place or Saul Prade's." Ase glanced delicately at two small white structures about twenty yards from the school. "Everything's real handy. I'll bet it's the best Kansas school west of Wichita."

"I'm sure it is." Susanna struggled with herself. The trustees had assented to this location. The children would have a clean, light, pleasant place to learn, and she, to teach in. The only thing against it was that Ase McCanless owned it.

He sprang down and trailed his reins in front of the chestnut horse that stood as steadily as if hitched to an iron post. Jenny did the same.

"Come have a look inside," said Ase. Without waiting for Susanna's consent, he took her reins and tossed them down, swept her from the saddle, freeing her skirt that caught on the side horn and billowed in the wind, and started to usher her inside.

Susanna balked, withdrawing her elbow from his hand and thinking if the wind blew like this all the time, she'd have to find some way of anchoring her skirts. "I've seen your school, Mr. McCanless. It's worlds better than anything I expected. But I won't teach here unless you deed the land and building to the school district."

Sun-whitened eyebrows jerked together before he bit

back whatever he'd started to say and gave a tolerant shrug. "Scout around the building, ma'am, and then you can have your final say."

If men weren't exasperatingly stubborn before they came here, the place must make them so. Scowling at him, Susanna lifted her skirt enough to climb the single step and surveyed what might have been her kingdom. White-washed walls added to the light from the sparkling windows. A potbellied iron stove stood in the middle of the back of the room and a bin in the corner was providently full of yellow-brown disks that had to be the dried products of cattle or buffalo which Susanna knew were used for fuel in this almost treeless region. On the other side of the door was a bench with a tin bucket and dipper. Pegs for coats and caps were set at various heights. Long plank desks of several sizes, tops tilted, with shelves beneath for books, faced a blackboard and a *real* oak teacher's desk with a barrel-backed chair.

Susanna could imagine pictures and maps on the wall, her books on that warm-grained polished desk, and children of all ages ciphering at the blackboard or standing to recite. Regret bitter in her mouth, for of course she wanted the best possible conditions for her pupils, Susanna turned her back on the oak desk and stepped out into wind that tugged at her skirts till she had to hold them down.

Noticing, the rancher grinned and said, "When Colonel Custer brought his wife to Kansas, I've heard tell her skirts flew clear over her head and you can guess he didn't like that. He cut a lead bar in pieces and had her sew them into the hems. If you'd like to try it, I'll fix you a bunch of little weights."

"You're thoughtful, sir, but perhaps I won't be coping with the local winds." His eyes narrowed and momentarily heedless of her skirts, she brought her hands together, bracing them for support as she forced herself to meet his puzzled stare. "This is a wonderful school. I can see you've used the best materials and planned it carefully. I wish I could teach in it. But I can't."

He slammed one big fist into an open palm. "Of all the confounded stiff-necked persnickety Yankee school-marms, why did we have to get one who's crazy to boot?"

Susanna whirled away from him and marched toward Cindy. Too hurt and furious to be nervous of the mare, she snatched up the reins, looped them over the mare's neck, and set her foot in the stirrup, trying to clamber up, but the impeding skirts got in her way and, gasping, she had to drop her right foot back to earth.

Before she could try again, McCanless lifted her to the saddle. By the time she hastily hooked her knee over the horn, he was mounted and riding ahead with Jenny. Susanna's head buzzed till she was dizzy with alternating waves of humiliation and outrage.

Could she have handled it better? He had gone to an immense amount of trouble and expense. Yes, but he *must* see how improper it was for him to own the school, especially in a district as divided as this one. She swallowed hard and bit her lip. Well, that was no longer her problem. Perhaps he'd be civilized enough to let her stay at the ranch till Superintendent Morton came out and gave her a ride back to Dodge. No one spoke till they neared the house.

"I'm going to the brandin'," McCanless said. "Miss Alden, I'll sure be interested to hear what you figger out to tell the trustees about turnin' up your nose at the best school-house in Ford County—hell, in this half of the whole state! Sorry, I didn't mean to cuss in front of a lady—"

"Even if I am a Yankee?" Then the implications of what he'd said struck her and she caught in her breath. She didn't know why she wanted to teach in this contentious district where she'd have to deal with former Confederates, not to mention the fractious Jenny, but it was a challenge she felt impelled to meet. If she had to give up, she'd carry a weight of failure and that wasn't the way she wanted to begin her new life. Turning to McCanless, she couldn't keep incredulity out of her tone. "You mean you want me to wait and see the trustees?"

He yanked off his hat and rubbed his forehead. "That's why you're here."

"But—"

He gave a harsh laugh. "Look, Miss Alden, we've tried for three years to get a teacher. The few who've applied weren't fit to teach hogs how to stick their feet in a trough."

"For all you know, I'm not."

"Henry sent us a letter from that lady you taught for, and your grades from normal school. Besides, I've got ears. If Jenny can learn to talk like you, I'd be plumb satisfied."

Jenny swung her pony in front of him so abruptly that the chestnut skittered. "Dad! I don't ever want to sound like a damnyankee!"

"You learn the right words, honey, and then you can say 'em the way we talk." Directing that blue gaze to Susanna, he added, "About as bad as their bein' ignorant, none of the sorry varmints—they were all men, Miss Alden—had enough spine for an angleworm. You've got too much but you're liable to need it." He replaced his hat and lifted the reins.

"Wait!" cried Susanna. "I don't know what other buildings might be used. That's the trustees' duty, to furnish a school."

"Thought I had." He shrugged. "Since you're so fussy, you better make your pick of the places on abandoned claims—couple of caved-in dugouts and an old soddie. Jenny can show you where they are." Touching the brim of his hat, he sent the chestnut trotting south.

Bemused, not sure whether to be glad or sorry, Susanna stared after McCanless till Jenny reined in between. "Want to go now or after dinner? It lacks a couple of hours till noon."

"How far are these buildings?"

"A dugout's not a building," Jenny said scornfully. She jerked her head northward so that her single thick yellow plait bounced. "There's a soddie maybe three miles that way and another one a mile-and-a-half southeast of Dad's school, and there's another empty dugout on the claim east of Prades' next to Doc Rawdon's."

The central and western part of the state had only started settling up after the Civil War, and most of the region west of Ford County was so sparsely peopled that it hadn't organized into counties. So many abandoned claims in a five-mile radius testified louder than words to the difficulty of making a living—or simply of living. With a suppressed shiver, Susanna thought of the deserted soddie she'd passed in Rawdon's wagon and the woman who'd lost her baby and been driven mad by the wind. Of the children who started school, how many would finish the term, much less complete the eighth grade?

She had to stop worrying about possibilities; probabilities were bad enough. "Could we go see the north soddie now," she asked, "and look at the other places this afternoon?"

"You may be too stiff to ride this afternoon."

"I'll ride."

"We'll see," said Jenny. Bending over the spotted pony's neck, she let out a wild yell and was off, the pony's hoofs seeming to skim the grass rather than touch it.

Cindy sighed even louder than Susanna and resignedly followed horse and rider who soon vanished in the red-brown ocean of grass. Hoping Cindy could stay on their track, Susanna loosened the reins.

Jenny looped back to her as Susanna reined up at the soddie and stared at earthen walls crumbling where the roof had fallen in on one side. Picturing how dark it would be with just one small window, still partly covered by a tattered piece of oiled skin that flapped in the wind, she shook her head decisively.

"This won't do."

"You won't like any soddie, let alone a dugout," Jenny said, turning Scout so that Cindy followed. Her lip curled. "You may decide to use Dad's school after all."

"Not unless ownership's transferred to the district."

"We'll see." Without warning, Jenny streaked off again, crouched with her face in Scout's flowing mane. This time Susanna didn't worry, confident that Cindy knew the way home and was eager to get there. She sensed that much against Jenny's will, the girl was impressed with her but she was also sure that subduing the roughest, brawniest, most recalcitrant boys would be easy compared to taming Jenny.

Taming wasn't the right word. Something in Susanna yearned to ride with that same free abandon. She could sympathize with Jenny's determination not to be forced into the mold her father believed best for her. The child needed—what was that word of Johnny's?—*gentling*. Ase should have done it but wouldn't or couldn't, and now Susanna wondered if Jenny would ever let her close enough to try.

Dinner was beans, cornbread deliciously crusty on top and moist inside, buttermilk cooled in the well house, and plump wedges of gold-glazed dried apple pie. While Susanna was freshening up, Jenny must have told Johnny and Betty about Susanna's rejection of Ase's school, for they tactfully didn't ask about it, though Johnny's eyes danced when he looked at Susanna, and Betty made small soothing sounds as she served the food. It was clear the kindly older woman was distressed for Susanna as well as for the man she regarded as a son, but to Susanna's relief, Betty didn't besiege her with all the practical reasons for using Ase's school.

"I'm glad you decided against the Schuyler place," she said. "Awful it was, Mr. and Mrs. Schuyler frozen with their little boys between them. And only a mile from home! Young couple from Iowa they were, hard-working and pleasant-spoken." She paused for a moment. "One thing you'd best consider, dear, is how far a place is from the patrons. The kiddies have to get back and forth in some pretty mean weather, and of course you will, too, boarding around."

"Boarding around?" Susanna had been so caught up in where she was going to teach that she hadn't even thought about where she was going to live. With a sinking feeling, she asked, "Isn't there a house for the teacher?"

"Land's sake, no, child. It's different in towns, I suppose, but out here teachers get part of their pay as board and room. They take turns staying with their patrons and stay longest with the families who have the most children enrolled."

"But those are the houses that'd be the most crowded."

"That's right, dear, and in a one-room dugout with three or four youngsters, it would get a little snug." Betty gave a delicate cough. "I know Ase figgered the teacher could just stay with us if she'd a mind to, since we're closest to the building."

Jenny was all ears and eyes; only that kept Susanna from blurting her thoughts aloud. He'd own the school, the land it's on, and how could anyone staying in that beautiful rose room instead of in a hole in the ground where she'd be lucky to have a cot to herself—how could anyone not be swayed by her benefactor's wishes and opinions? Benefactor? Owner!

"That would be extremely kind and generous of Mr. McCanless," Susanna said when she could trust herself. "However, living in any patron's home seems prejudicial to discipline and I frankly abhor the thought of shifting myself and my belongings every month or so. One of the reasons I left Ohio was that I had to sell our house to pay my father's debts and I didn't want to move in with my aunt and uncle, much as I love them."

"But Susanna, that's how it's done out here," Betty almost wailed.

"Then it's fortunate I haven't accepted the position. I

can understand that a very young woman away from home for the first time might actually enjoy staying with families though I think it would be exceedingly hard for her to keep order among children who might regard her as a playmate. I'm a grown woman, though, Betty. I want a place of my own, however small and crude. If the trustees won't find me something, I'll refuse the school even if they offer it."

Johnny gave a long low whistle. "Shuckins!" he lamented. "I was sure hopin' you'd stay, ma'am."

Deep blue eyes glinting with mischief, Jenny sniffed. "To hear you talk, Miss Alden, anybody'd think *you* were hiring the school board."

At that, Betty choked on her buttermilk, Johnny cackled, and Susanna, after a moment of shock, didn't try to keep her laughter from pealing out. "If the board thinks I'm too picky they don't have to hire me," she said, sobering. "But I expect some things from them just as they expect certain things from me." A sudden hope glimmered. "That soddie we're going to this afternoon, Jenny—does it have more than one room?"

"I've never been close enough to tell," Jenny said.

"That was the Madsen place," Betty frowned. "Let me think. I was there to help when Estelle had her baby. Pretty little dark-haired girl who died of whooping cough before her first birthday. Drought blasted their crops that summer, and it was just too much. They went back to live with Estelle's folks till they could make another start. Yes, there's two rooms, one good-sized and the bedroom smaller."

"Maybe the bedroom could serve as my quarters." It would be a far cry from the neat little house she had envisioned back in Ohio but compared to being shunted from one crowded soddie or dugout to another, any private, permanent domicile was attractive. Though there were things she was resolved not to compromise about, Susanna, to her bewildered amusement, found that her

desire to teach in this district seemed to increase with
each outrageous discovery. She still wondered if she could
maintain her calm if assailed by former Confederates,
especially if they accused her of bias; the chairman of the
board of trustees wanted to own the school and have her
live in his house; the other trustees expected her to board
around; and this afternoon she was eager to prowl what
was sure to be a dilapidated mud shanty in hope it might
provide both a school and home.

How would she explain all this to Aunt Mollie and Uncle
Frank? Compelled to chuckle softly, Susanna spoke hastily
to ward off Betty's protest. "I'm willing to pay for any supplies needed to fix up the room and if I boarded with families, they'd have to feed me so why can't they just give
me the same amount of food?"

"Sounds fair," Johnny said.

Betty glared at him. "Fair! What's that got to do with
a young lady straight from Ohio living miles from the closest neighbor?"

"Miles?" Susanna echoed faintly.

In her revolt against staying with trustees, she'd forgotten she wasn't in town here. There'd be no close neighbors. Ever since her father and Richard went off to war,
she'd been afraid to be alone at night, especially after dark.
She knew it was silly, knew there was no reason for it, but
in her aunt and uncle's home, she'd left her door open at
night. In those months after her father died, ashamed to
admit her fear, she'd locked all the doors tight and slept
with a lamp lit. Her dismay must have shown on her face
for Betty caught Susanna's hand.

"Please put that notion right out of your head, my dear.
I suppose you don't have to worry much about Indians,
though who knows when some might not break off the
reservations, but there's white rapscallions aplenty. And
what about tornadoes? Prairie fires? Blizzards? Or if you
get sick?"

That was a fearsome parade of dangers, and from what

she had seen and heard, Susanna knew it wasn't exaggerated. All the same, she couldn't live in Ase's house and boarding around was unthinkable. Summoning a laugh, she said, "Goodness, Betty, surely all those things won't happen. But if a tornado struck, I can't see that being close to people would help much." Betty looked so distressed that Susanna patted her hand. "It's sweet of you to care about me, but I'm more concerned about my daily living conditions than possible catastrophes."

Betty eyed her sadly and shook her head. "It makes me sick to think of that pretty room sitting empty while you try to get along in a soddie."

"Most people do." Susanna softened her words with a quick smile. "That's the best cornbread I ever tasted, Betty, and the pie was delicious. I ate so much Cindy may not want to carry me."

Jenny shoved a last large bite into her mouth and sprang up, wiping her hands on her Levi's. "Ready to go?"

"As soon as we do the dishes."

Jenny stared. "Betty never asks me to do dishes."

"Perhaps not, but I am. Betty cooked our meal."

Jenny scowled, thrust out her lower lip, glanced rather shamefacedly toward Betty, and after a moment said grudgingly, "I'll dry if you wash."

The task was quickly done with hot water from the reservoir on the side of the stove, a stove that must have been freighted in by wagon at great expense. *She* wouldn't have one, Susanna knew. Did that mean she'd have to cook in a fireplace? With cow chips? Well, she thought, throwing back her shoulders as much as possible while bending over the dishpan, hadn't she come out here to be a pioneer?

❀ *Four* ❀

The good things about the soddie were that it had two rooms, a roof, probably in place because the roots of flowers and grass had knit together to hold it to the rafter poles, and it commanded, from a gentle slope, a pleasant view of the bend in a creek fringed by cottonwoods just beginning to yellow and willows that were still green. The bad things started with the dirt floor, the mud walls, and the hairy-legged frightening creature that dropped from a dangling root in the ceiling to some litter right in front of Susanna.

Susanna screamed and stepped back, bumping Jenny, who burst out laughing. "It's only a tarantula. They won't sting unless you really pester them. Mostly they hunt at night so you don't see them out much in the day."

"Except when they drop from the ceiling!"

"Shucks, if one did bite, you'd only get a little headache or maybe sick at your stomach. A black widow or some kinds of scorpion can hurt you a lot worse."

The prospect of such co-tenants perturbed Susanna a lot more than the chance of tornadoes and other major disasters. Her father said spiders controlled flies and mosquitoes, and she'd always captured and carried them outside instead of killing them, but they made her nervous and she was glad when the four-inch-long tarantula disappeared in the weeds by the door. Jenny watched with such malicious glee that Susanna wished she had been able to conceal her fright. If the child told the other pupils the teacher squealed at tarantulas, it was all too likely that these would be turning up on her desk or creeping out of corners.

Braced for whatever might happen and determined not to show fear even if a rattlesnake challenged them, Susanna inspected the sod fireplace built in the wall between the two rooms so that it could heat both. The chimney needed repair but otherwise it looked serviceable and the center wall helped support the rafters, which was surely another reason the heavy sod roof hadn't caved in. The poles, bowed with the weight of the roof, which must have increased ten-fold when soaked with rain, were deeply sunk into the top of the walls.

The thick sod made it cool inside and that would be a blessing in hot weather. It also made the house dark as a cave. Apart from the entrance from which the door had been removed, the main room was lit by two small paneless windows which sent shafts of light to the floor. The bedroom had one little window. Fortunately, it looked toward the creek, but Susanna realized that the dim interior was going to bother her a lot more than any number of spiders.

If she were only going to be here during school hours, escaping for the rest of the time to—the rose room? Susanna gave herself an admonitory shake. These were the conditions her pupils lived under, with the exception of Jenny; in fact, most were doubtless more crowded, and from all she'd heard, a soddie was as superior to a dugout as a frame house was to a soddie. If what seemed to be a well-built soddie was this depressing, there was no use inspecting the dugout. There wasn't any place else to run, except to Ase McCanless's house, Ase McCanless's school.

So do I give up before I start? she mused. Let children grow up ignorant because I can't stand living the way they and their mothers do? Because I'm afraid of the dark and being alone? Her fears had never centered on ghosts but a baby had died here, a mother and father had grieved and given up. Checking that train of thought, Susanna sent a wish to the Madsens that things might be better for them now and that they had a baby.

"*. . . art thou unwilling to do the work of a human being?*" Now that her eyes were accustomed to the shadows, it was easier to see. In the winter, when the door would be shut, the fireplace should cast a compensating glow. Abraham Lincoln had studied by such a light, hadn't he?

Smiling at her self-exhortations, Susanna turned to Jenny whose intent expression was a blend of curiosity, derision, and—could it be hope? "It seems peculiar that no one's taken over a claim this close to a creek."

There was light enough to see Jenny flush. "Uh, well, Daddy runs cattle here and I expect nesters figure it's taken." With a little help from McCanless hands?

"How long a walk will it be for the children?"

"Walk?" It was Jenny's turn to look horrified. Then, with a contemptuous toss of her long blond braid, she said, "I suppose most of the sodbuster kids will have to walk. Some don't even have horses, just stupid old oxen." Squinting in concentration, she counted off on her fingers.

"Prades live across the creek about three miles away. There's Sarah—she's older than me and I think she's nice even if she is a Yankee—and the twins, Paul and Pauline, and Frank, who's oldest. The Taylor girls are only two miles south." She made a face. "That shiftless Cash Hardy has four kids. They live across the creek a couple of miles. Browns ranch southwest of us but Freck and Dottie have horses so they won't mind six miles." She hesitated, then burst out, "Will you let a breed come to school?"

"A what?" *Breed* was such a shocking word that Susanna had never before heard it spoken.

"You know, a half-breed. Part Indian, part white."

"Oh." Jenny sounded anxious, not sneering, so instead of her chiding her for the offensive term, Susanna said, "Any child in the district is supposed to come to school. I certainly wouldn't teach here if they couldn't."

Jenny almost smiled; and if she ever did, without that edge of spite, how charming she would be. "I hope Ridge will come. School wouldn't be so bad if he was there. But he's mighty proud. Daddy reckons when he gets a little older he'll run off to his Cheyenne relations and that'd be the best thing if it didn't break his parents' hearts." Jenny was plainly quoting Ase. "A breed can get along fine in an Indian village but he'll always have trouble around whites."

"It might help if they weren't called breeds," Susanna suggested as gently as she could.

Jenny's eyes widened. "Why, that's what they are! People say someone's a 'full-breed' or a 'half-breed.'"

"Do they say someone's a full-breed white man?"

"No, but—" Jenny chewed on that. Again, hot color showed beneath the creamy tan. "It doesn't sound nice, does it? It—it's like an animal, the way they call an Indian man a buck. I'll bet Daddy never thought about that. He likes Luke Tarrant—that's Ridge's father—and Daddy says Luke's wife is a lot better woman than most white ones, prettier, too. You ought to see her in her best buckskins. Luke calls her Millie since that's pretty close to her Indian name."

What had Millie thought about the dreadful slaughter at Sand Creek in 1864 when Colorado volunteers killed and mutilated a camp of peaceful Cheyennes, mostly women and children? With so much mutual hatred between their peoples, the Tarrants must be strong and special individuals to stay together. Jenny seemed to sense Susanna's thoughts.

"Luke was a bull-whacker on the Santa Fe Trail when the train he was with found Millie along the way. Her camp had been attacked by Kiowas, her parents killed, and her little brother carried away. If he lived, he grew up as a Kiowa brave. Millie was wounded but she managed to run away. She was only ten. A bull-whacker whose family had been wiped out by Cheyenne wanted to kill her but Luke beat him in a fight with their whips. He put Millie in a wagon, took care of her all the way to Santa Fe, and left her with a nice Mexican lady—that part of the country still belonged to Mexico then, you know. He'd go see her when he came to town, and when she was thirteen, she followed the train when it started back to Missouri. Luke put her in convent school in Saint Louis but she ran off again to track him. So he finally promised to marry her when she was sixteen if she'd stay in the school until then."

"After all that, I hope they've been happy."

"Oh, they are!" Jenny's eyes shone. "Why, the way they act, you wouldn't even think they were married. They're like—like sweethearts."

With a pang, Susanna thought of Richard. Would he have stayed her sweetheart if he'd come safe from the war? By now they'd have been married ten years—and probably have a child old enough for school. With a wave of passionate regret, Susanna wondered if she'd ever marry now, cuddle her own babies. Out here in the West where there were lots of bachelors she could surely find a husband, but she shrank from marrying a man she didn't love.

Pushing away such useless thoughts, Susanna said briskly, "This is about as central a location as possible, then. Thanks for showing me, Jenny. If the trustees do want to hire me, I'll ask them to get it ready for use."

Jenny peered in the bedroom with its single small window. "You really want to live here instead of at our house?"

Susanna didn't try to hold back a ripple of laugher. "Of course I like that beautiful rose room a lot better. But this is where I should be, Jenny, and so, yes, I do want to live here."

"Spoken like a rock-ribbed Yankee puritan," came a voice from outside. Ducking, Matt Rawdon entered. He must have been working, for his gray shirt, open at the throat and with sleeves rolled up, clung damply to him and he had a good male odor, pungent but not sour. He had bared his head and the thick mass of hair waved damply where it touched his face. Surveying the interior with a sweeping glance, he regarded Susanna with a quirk of black eyebrows. "Can I believe my ears? You're planning to live in this hovel?"

"And teach here, too, Doc," Jenny put in. "If you think Dad's not fit to be tied!"

"I can imagine."

Susanna's cheeks burned. "I can't see that it's any of your business, Dr. Rawdon. As you told me rather forcefully, you don't have children in school."

"My dear young woman, you have much to learn about this kind of community if you don't know that everything is everybody's business. My land's across the creek. I was virtuously scything hay when I saw riders stop here and linger inside so long that I came to investigate."

In this dim room, his eyes were more than ever luminous as if light shone behind the gray. He looked brown and fit and handsome, the hand ruined for surgery well able to grip a scythe. Or hold a woman? The unbidden image deepened the blush heating Susanna's face. "Your place borders the creek?"

"Don't sound so dismayed, Miss Alden. My home, such as it is, sits a good four miles east as the coyote lopes, though the creek meanders a lot to get there. As I told you yesterday, I bought several proved-up homesteads from settlers who'd had more than enough of them. Since this one only had a dugout, I decided to live on the quarter-section where there's a soddie." He eyed the ceiling critically. "Mine has a good cedar-shake roof."

"How very nice for you!"

"Isn't it?" He grinned, unscathed by her sarcasm, but his gaze searched her. "How come you're not tickled pink with Ase's handy-dandy new school?"

"Because it is his, and it's on his land."

"You told Ase this and he didn't yell loud enough to blast you straight back to Ohio?"

"He didn't like it."

Jenny chortled at that and Susanna had to smile before the doubts that had been gathering suddenly swooped and settled on her like a heavy weight. "I know it's dangerous for a school to be the property of one patron, but it's so light and clean and this is so—so—"

"Dark and dirty?"

"Yes. It'll be so much more uncomfortable for the children, so much harder for them to study. I feel as if I'm wronging them."

She broke off, turning away. Now he'd laugh, be cynically amused. Why had she exposed herself to him?

To her amazement, his tone was almost sympathetic. "Don't trim your sails, Miss Alden. Remember, Ase can always make the school over to the district and the trustees don't have to hire you."

"Of course they don't!" Why had she forgotten that, taken the whole load of responsibility on herself? Heart lifting, in spite of her anxieties about how she was going to get through the nights, Susanna took a deep breath, laughed, and caught Rawdon's hand.

It was an instinctive gesture of thanks. She hadn't thought about his maiming, but when her fingertips touched ridged scars, she glanced down. Rawdon snatched his hand away. The closeness that had been between them for a moment vanished—maybe it had been her imagination, anyway.

"I wish you luck with the trustees, Miss Alden, though your best luck would be for them to reject you so that you could find a school where you could enjoy both a decent building and your principles." He backed out the door and the sun washed over the harsh angles of his face before he put on that battered gray Confederate hat. As if against his will, he paused. "There are ways of lightening up a soddie, ma'am, and making it cleaner. You can stretch cheesecloth across the ceiling and plaster the walls with ashes mixed with clay or cover them with newspapers. And there's one big advantage it has over a frame house. Except for what wood there is in it, it won't burn. A prairie fire can warm one up, but flames generally race on before the sod even starts smoldering much."

"Splendid." Hurt by his unspoken rebuff, Susanna gave him a brilliant smile. "I suppose that means I'd better hope for a fire so that I can rejoice in having insisted on the soddie."

"You won't rejoice if you're ever caught in a fire. Goodbye, Miss Alden."

He strode down the slope. If the trustees wouldn't hire her, this would be her last glimpse of him and somehow it seemed terribly sad and wrong to part like this. Why had she made that childish gibe?

Because he'd snatched his hand away as if she'd deliberately tried to shame him. He was terribly sensitive about those scarred fingers, and not just because they kept him from practicing surgery. Had he loved a woman who recoiled from him? Wrenching her gaze from his proud figure, Susanna said, "Thanks for bringing me, Jenny. There's nothing more I can do till I get my certificate and meet with the board."

As they rode, Jenny played her morning's disappearing tricks, but Susanna scarcely noticed. She was too busy thinking up ways to improve the soddie both as a dwelling and a school, and in wondering whether to be glad or sorry that if she stayed, even though he didn't have children in school, from time to time when he worked the neighboring part of his land, she was bound to see Matt Rawdon.

* * *

"You've seen that miserable old soddie and you still want to teach there?" Three days after Susanna's inspection, the branding was finished and Ase had ridden home grimy and bewhiskered but with a triumphantly expectant look that froze into disbelief. Buttered biscuit halfway to his mouth, he stared at Susanna. As if to smother what he wanted to say, he swallowed half the biscuit, annihilated the other piece, and finally could contain his wrath no longer. "Hell's bells, girl! You must have been in the far pasture when they handed out brains."

"I'm not a girl, Mr. McCanless. And I'll be delighted to teach in the splendid school you've built—when you deed it to the district."

"You'll see blue northers in July before I deed away a square inch of my land!"

His anger beat against her with almost physical force. There was a hollow all-gone feeling in the pit of Susanna's stomach. She waited to speak till she thought she could hold her voice steady.

"You seem to think, sir, that you have principles and I have notions. That's not the case, I assure you."

Their eyes battled. Strength drained from Susanna's legs but she managed not to retreat or study the floor. After what seemed forever, the rancher grunted and attacked another biscuit. "No use wastin' our powder and shot on each other, ma'am. The trustees meet tomorrow at the school—my school—and it'll be mighty interesting what you say to one another." He allowed himself a grim smile. "They're in for a surprise. Henry Morton's sent word that he'll be there, too. If we hire you, he can give you your certificate, and everything'll be all official and proper."

Susanna shook her head in rueful amazement. "I should think the board would insist on the certificate before they hire me. And poor Superintendent Morton. What if after I'm hired, he finds I'm not competent?"

"If this board can agree to hire someone, Henry'll be so tickled that he'd certify a Georgia mule."

"What a flattering comparison, Mr. McCanless."

His lip twitched. "No offense intended, ma'am, but you've got to own up to some similarities in disposition."

"As must you, sir." With a withering glance, Susanna swept off to her room, but she couldn't claim final honors for his laughter followed her.

After years of seeing few attractive men near her age, she had encountered two intensely masculine ones, and maddening as both were, there was no denying that they made her feel alive and aware as a woman, wakening sensations that were at once frightening and delicious. The board wanted to hire a settled, sedate old maid. It was a good thing they didn't know that she felt like a tight-sealed bud just warming into flower, a rousing quite different from her sixteen-year-old response to Richard's shy wooing. She was a woman, not a girl. Even if this consciousness brought her pain, it carried with it a sort of proud strength. She was ready to meet the trustees of the Mason-Dixon school.

Ase offered to take her in the buckboard but Susanna hastily declined. She still felt a bit distrustful of the sidesaddle but it was much more comfortable than jouncing along as she had with Matt Rawdon.

The meeting was at two o'clock in the afternoon. A wedge of wild geese called from high above, wings flashing as they dipped, and a prairie chicken whirred from the grass with which it blended perfectly. The sun was hot but there was a refreshing tang of autumn in the breeze which today, thank goodness, wasn't a regular gale. Susanna, in her brown dress and bonnet, didn't care to meet the board all disheveled and windblown.

Ase McCanless, obviously resolved not to argue, told her something about each trustee. "Your Yankees," he said, "are Will Taylor from Missouri who has a passel of little gals and Saul Prade from Illinois who's kind of a strange

62

duck. Got four kids and a wife who'd be a beauty if she didn't look so tired." Ase frowned a moment and gave his head a troubled shake before he went on. "Luke Tarrant used to be a freighter. Married a pretty Cheyenne girl young enough to be his daughter but they sure seem happy, even if Luke did come home from the war with a bad limp. If anyone makes any cracks about Indians, let me handle it. Kermit Brown was a Texas Ranger who helped me chase cows out of the brush after the war and decided to trail up here when I did. He married a real nice gal, Hettie, from San Antonio, red-haired like him, and the kids take after 'em."

"Why is it, Mr. McCanless, that this board has five members instead of three?"

"Just seemed like a good idea since except for Cash Hardy, we're the ones with school-age kids." Ase shook his head. "Cash's too lazy to scratch fleas, which goes to show that hailin' from Iowa won't necessarily mean a body's not shiftless. He and his missus have three boys and a gal. Must be half a dozen Yank homesteaders south and east of here, but a couple are bachelors and the family men's kids are still boll-weevil size."

"I'm sure the mothers would appreciate that."

Ase slewed Susanna a look of aggrieved innocence. "I didn't call 'em that on account of they're Yankees, ma'am. Truth is, human young'uns aren't much to look at, much less talk with, till they're out of pinfeathers. Every other warm-blooded critter I know of looks pretty decent when it's born, 'specially a foal or calf, but babies— It's sure a good thing God gave 'em mamas 'cause if you could force a man to tell the truth, I'll bet they mostly take one look and want to bolt."

Scandalized but laughing helplessly, Susanna said, "I hope you never told Jenny that."

Ase shrugged. "She's got eyes. Maybe she was different, though. She was born while I was off fightin' and I didn't see her till she was two years old."

But he had come home, unlike Richard; and unlike Susanna's father, his body wasn't wrecked. Swept by grief, Susanna wished she hadn't come to a region where she'd have to be around Confederates. But that was cowardice. So long as children, North and South, went to school only with their own kind, bitterness couldn't heal or the Union be truly that. Mingling would be hard for everyone but that was how the wounds would finally close.

The school came in sight, or rather, grew, dark against the horizon. As they neared enough to see tethered horses and a number of men, Susanna's heart leaped into her throat and pounded hard.

What would the trustees be like? What would they ask? For all her resolve not to board around or teach at Ase's school, Susanna felt as hollow inside as if she hadn't eaten Betty's good dinner. She couldn't, wouldn't, shouldn't give in, but oh, she wanted desperately to win this contract!

So tense that the men were a blur, Susanna, as if paralyzed, sat gripping Cindy's reins till McCanless swung her down. A gangling man in a dark coat doffed his hat to reveal wispy fluffs of brown hair merging with luxuriant sideburns that contrasted with his pink bald head. His sagging lidded brown eyes had a mournful cast but he beamed at Susanna and enthusiastically pumped her hand.

"So here you are, Miss Alden. I'm glad to welcome a lady of your abilities to Ford County. Let me acquaint you with the board of trustees and then we'll move inside where we can all be comfortable."

Wherever they moved, Susanna wasn't going to be very comfortable. As Mr. Morton introduced each board member, she offered her hand, glad that Ase had told her something about the men.

Heavyset, red-haired Kermit Brown took her fingers as if afraid of breaking them. Though he must have been well into his thirties, his snub nose and freckles gave him a boyish look. "Proud to meet you, ma'am," he drawled, and his bright blue eyes were friendly even if he was a Southerner.

Will Taylor, lanky and rawboned with a kinky black beard and hair, barely touched her hand and mumbled something. If he'd speak up, Susanna thought he'd have a deep, pleasing voice. Limping forward, Luke Tarrant enclosed her hand in both of his. Gray-haired, of average height, and compactly muscled, he gave an impression of steadiness and his hazel eyes beamed at her in a fatherly way. "Glad you're here, Miss Alden, and we hope you'll be glad, too."

"She's not hired yet, Tarrant." The most striking man of all confronted Susanna, arms crossed, while cold green eyes inspected her. Tall as Ase, he was gracefully built and his features were almost too perfect. Before the superintendent could present him, he inclined his golden head. "I'm Saul Prade."

That was all. No pleasantries. He took her hand. Shock ran through her as if, in freezing weather, she'd touched iron and her flesh felt seared by a cold so intense that it burned like fire.

He was a Union man, Susanna remembered. He should have been her ally but she knew he would not be. As if sensing her uneasiness, Henry Morton said, "Come on in, folks. I don't want to rush you but I want to get home before dark."

Getting the teacher's chair from behind the beautiful desk on the platform, Ase placed it for Susanna. Then he faced the other trustees who had taken seats on the largest bench while Morton hovered nervously in the rear. "I'm calling this meeting of the trustees of the Mason-Dixon School District to order," Ase said. "But before we start askin' Miss Alden questions, maybe she'll tell us a little about herself." He paused and glanced significantly at her. "Could be some things we'd better know right off."

At least he was going to let her state her case. Rising, Susanna thanked him and, with a thudding heart, met the eyes fixed on her. She tried to smile but her lips wouldn't bend till Kermit Brown grinned at her, and then she could.

Her voice was pitched too high to start with and cracked so that she had to start over. She gave the briefest facts of her life, education, and experience before drawing in a deep breath and plunging.

"I've already told Mr. McCanless that I cannot teach in this excellent school building because it's his private property. This would give the appearance, if not the reality, of his having undue influence on the school." There was a buzz at this and Superintendent Morton's long jaw dropped as if the supporting muscles had been slashed.

They might as well have it all at once, Susanna thought, and spoke loud enough to be heard over the commotion. "I hope the soddie to the south of here can be fixed for a school, and I wish to live in the bedroom instead of boarding with patrons."

"Or staying at my house like any sensible mortal would," said Ase.

The trustees stared at Susanna, then at each other, and back to her. "Board's part of your salary." Will Taylor rubbed a floppy earlobe. "How much more money would you want?"

"None, if you'll make the bedroom habitable, give me food to cook, and supply fuel."

"Fuel?" cut in Prade. "Fuel's mighty hard to come by out here. If you boarded, it wouldn't take any extra."

"The fireplace warms both rooms," Susanna said. "It wouldn't take a lot more to keep the fire going till close to bedtime."

Taylor snorted. "Wait'll you see how fast buffalo and cow chips burn, not to mention hay twists and sunflower stalks."

"I'd be as careful of fuel as I could," Susanna promised. "And I'd collect as much as possible myself."

"Do you think you're too good to live with us?" Prade demanded. "How'll we get to know you?"

"I can't see why we need to know each other that well," Susanna said and was confused when everyone laughed except the handsome man who watched her with narrowed green eyes.

"If I herded kids all day, I'd sure want shut of 'em come night." Kermit Brown shifted a wad of tobacco in his cheek and leaned forward. "Guess what I want to know, ma'am, is what you're goin' to teach about the war, you bein' from Ohio and all."

Susanna's nape tingled. "I'll teach the truth, as best I can find it—that the South was agricultural and the North industrialized, that though the South used slaves, New England ships brought them to this country and made fortunes in the Triangle Trade, taking rum to the Guinea Coast and packing in slaves, stopping in the West Indies for molasses and sugar, and then selling the slaves to plantations in the South."

"I never heerd that before." Will Taylor frowned, rubbing his large knuckles. "But even if it's so, you can't get around the fact that the Rebs tried to wreck the Union."

"We weren't rebelling, Taylor," cut in Ase. "We were doin' what we damned well had a right to—break free of the North and have our own government."

"And keep your slaves," added Prade.

"Hell, man, I never had a slave and neither did most folks, even in the parts of the South where there were big plantations. Sight more sharecroppers scratchin' harder'n most slaves for a livin' than there were folks in fancy white houses with pillars and verandas."

Prade gave a jeering laugh. "Maybe. But I bet every last one of those sharecroppers hoped they'd own slaves someday."

"One thing's sure," Ase shot back. "Most owners treated their slaves a heap better than Yank factory owners treat the women and kids *they* work to a nub."

"If you think it's a good idea," ventured Susanna, "I'd like to ask those of you who fought in the war to tell the children something about it, how it was to be a soldier."

"Now, Miss Alden," interposed a fidgeting Henry Morton. "Do you really think that's wise?"

There was silence as Northerners and Southerners warily eyed each other. Stretching out his bad leg as if to ease it, Luke Tarrant said, "Might be a good thing, Henry. It was a Yank surgeon worked to save my leg or I'd have lost it sure even if it didn't gangrene. I reckon what we tell the kids will sound pretty much the same. War's plain old hell." He grinned slightly. "Maybe you'd better invite us on different days, ma'am."

Several chuckled at that but Prade, unsmiling, stared at the soft-spoken older man. "Since you're here, Tarrant, I guess you aim to put your boy in school."

"That's right." Luke Tarrant's voice was even softer but there was steel in it.

"Shucks," drawled Kermit, "if my kids can go to school with Yanks, it sure won't hurt 'em to share a speller with young Ridge."

"You say that now on account of Tarrant's a cattleman and a Reb—I mean, Confederate like you. What'll you say if one of these days he wants to marry that girl of yours?"

"Why," said Brown into the shocked silence, "that'd suit me better'n if your boy came courtin'. Not that I've got a thing against your kid, either. If we're down to brass tacks, Prade, I sure wouldn't cotton to you for an in-law."

Prade turned scarlet but before he could retaliate, Ase held up his hands. "Look, folks, we're not here to worry about our kids gettin' married. We want to get 'em educated. Let's stick to that. Anyone got more questions for Miss Alden?"

"What subjects kin she teach?" asked Taylor.

"The usual curriculum, Mr. Taylor." At her aunt's school, she had taught rhetoric, physiology, geometry, algebra, and Latin, as well as basic subjects, but mention of that might make these men think she was showing off. "I would teach reading, penmanship, spelling, grammar, composition, mental and written arithmetic, history, and geography—"

"Joggerphy!" Taylor stiffened his gangling frame and crossed his arms. "I've got three sweet little girls, gentlemen. I don't want their minds putrified with learnin' about a lot of heathen places across the ocean."

"Don't see how it could hurt," said Ase mildly.

"Why, if my little girls get their heads full of furriners who live in peculiar places and worship idols, it could get 'em all mixed up! Boys may be tough enough to take that kind of thing but girls—" Taylor shook his head. "Joggerphy will just discombobulate 'em."

"I wish I knew more about other countries than I do," put in Kermit Brown. "'Specially Yorkshire in Old England where my grandparents came from." His blue eyes slanted sideways at Taylor. "Unless you're an Indian, Will, your people had to come from somewhere else."

"Mama's mother came over from Germany," admitted Will. "Pa's mother was Scotch-Irish. 'Cept for that I'm pure-dee American and have been ever since the Taylors came over from England back before the Revolution." That brought chuckles, including an unwilling one from Taylor. "You got me dead to rights on that one, Kermit, but all them folks be Christian. Outside of having kings and queens, they're not so different from us, I'd guess." He appealed rather plaintively to Susanna. "Can't you hold the joggerphy down to places like England and Germany, maybe France?"

"I can't, Mr. Taylor, and feel that I'm doing my job." Susanna spoke gently but she had no intention of allowing the board to impose such restrictions. "An important part of education, I think, is to help us understand people who aren't like us and develop a view of our country as one of many nations that have to share the world."

"The sooner other countries get to be like us, the better off they'll be," said Taylor, thrusting out a belligerent jaw. "All I want my girls to learn is how to read and write and cipher a little."

"Then you'd better teach 'em at home." Impatience

edged Kermit Brown's tone. "I don't want the teacher trimmin' down what she knows to suit you. Anyhow, supposin' one of your gals wants to be a teacher or marries a man with a business where she needs to keep books and figger interest and all?" As Will winced at these prospects, Brown turned toward Ase. "Miss Alden suits me right down to the ground. You can tell by listenin' to her that she's got more book learnin' than the whole bunch of us, includin' you, Henry. I say let's give her a contract for six months at—what's fair, Henry?"

The superintendent had been looking more downcast by the minute till Brown's decisive proposal. Smoothing back his wispy hair, Morton said, "Considering Miss Alden's superior qualifications, thirty dollars a month, with fuel and food, seems reasonable."

"That agreeable to you, ma'am?" inquired Ase.

Susanna nodded. She would have stayed for twenty since she was putting the trustees to the trouble of repairing the soddie and supplying extra fuel, but if the children of these wildly differing men had any wish to learn, she was confident she could give them educations worth many times their parents' investment. She wished she had met the mothers and resolved, if she were hired, to call on them as soon as possible.

"If you'll step outside with me, ma'am," said Henry Morton, "I can give you your examination. We're not supposed to do it this way anymore, but the state superintendent don't have the faintest notion of how hard it is to find good teachers out here." As they moved a little way around the building, keeping in its shade, he added, "If this cantankerous bunch don't hire you or if they're too ornery to get along with, you just let me know, ma'am, and I'll find you a school someplace else. Now then, let's see—" Perspiring, he cleared his throat. "What's the capital of Kansas, ma'am?"

"Topeka."

"When did Kansas become a state?"

"On January twenty-ninth, 1861, Kansas was admitted to the Union as the thirty-fourth state."

Morton wriggled an eyebrow and suddenly demanded, "In what year did who bring the first herd of Texas longhorns to where in Kansas, and what's the name of the trail?"

She knew Susan B. Anthony and Lucy Stone had traveled around the state speaking for women's suffrage, and that a women's suffrage convention met in Topeka in 1869. She knew about grim, crazy old John Brown of Osawatomie, Quantrill's bloody raid on Lawrence, and the struggle between North and South to win Kansas and its Congressional votes. Humbled, she had to say, "I don't know, sir."

Morton beamed and his chest puffed out. "Joseph G. McCoy trailed longhorns up the Chisholm Trail to Abilene in 1867, and Dodge City, mark my word, is going to be just as famous a cowtown. But bless your heart, Miss Alden, no one knows everything." He reached into his pocket and produced a piece of paper. "Here's your certificate."

Unfolding the sheet, she scanned it and looked up at him. "But—it's already signed."

He looked positively roguish. "You didn't reckon I'd let you get away? From the look on Ase McCanless's face, you've got the school." Taking her hand, he shook it solemnly as a general sending a soldier on a desperate mission. "Good luck, Miss Alden. You're going to need it."

❀ *Five* ❀

As the trustees took their leave, Will Taylor looked beseechingly down at Susanna. "About that joggerphy, ma'am, I hope you'll just kind of whisk it by my girls."

"Mr. Taylor," Susanna said, "I've taught geography to dozens of girls and I assure you all those old enough are married and seem to be as happy as if they'd never heard of the equator."

"Is that gospel truth, ma'am?"

He looked so relieved that she had to quell a bubble of laughter. "It's the truth, sir."

Cheering, he tightened the saddle cinch on a gray nag as angular as he was, mounted, and said rather shyly, "Want you to know, ma'am, that I voted for you in spite of that dratted joggerphy."

"I didn't." Saul Prade had come noiselessly up beside her as she watched the Missourian jog off. Prade's sculpted mouth curved in a bleak smile. "Comical, isn't it? Those Southerners voted for you like greased lightning."

"May I ask why you didn't?"

Dilating pupils nearly covered the green of his eyes. Going to his horse, a big roan gelding that stepped nerv-

73

ously at his master's approach, Prade untied a few supple willow branches perhaps four feet long and offered them to Susanna. "These have enough play in them to raise welts and that's what you'll have to do to conquer your students."

Susanna shrank away. It was broad day and there were other men around, but this one terrified her. "I don't want to conquer the children, Mr. Prade."

He still offered the switches. She knew she was making a dangerous enemy, that there was something hidden and fearsome about this man, but outrage drove her to take the slender limbs and hurl them to the ground. They stared at each other. What gazed out from behind those chilling eyes? Something ancient and cruel. Something evil. Yet he was beautiful, if a man can be, and radiated a force that compelled female awareness of him even as she distrusted him.

He saw this. His smile broadened. He swung away from her, mounted, and rode east. Shaken by the wordless exchange, Susanna welcomed the warm, friendly handshakes of Tarrant and Brown which took away the cold feeling left by Prade's taunt. Henry Morton's handclasp was fervent. "I'll be out now and then to see how you're getting along," he said. "Let me know if I can help you."

"Textbooks—"

"Miss Alden, you'll have to make do with whatever the students can bring from home. I'm afraid it'll be some years before we have uniform texts." At her appalled look, he said cheeringly, "After all, you'll have to move at each student's pace so it won't matter a lot if they have different books." He got rather clumsily into the saddle and rode south with Luke Tarrant while Kermit Brown struck off west.

Susanna was left with Ase who helped her mount and cast a brooding glance in the direction of the soddie. "It beats me how you can be so all-fired stubborn."

"You must have voted for me."

"Sure, I did. You were the only one who applied."

"Oh."

She couldn't keep hurt from her voice and he cast her a grudgingly remorseful sidelong glance. "All the same, any fool can tell you're a good teacher though you're liable to find this is a sight different from a school for young ladies. You may wish you'd kept those switches of Prade's."

"Any child who doesn't want to learn will be sent home—and that includes Jenny."

"Fair enough. But if you can keep Ridge in school, I reckon she'll act halter-broke most of the time, though she may rear and pitch now and again. The trustees will get the soddie ready next week so's you can start up the first week in October." He cleared his throat. "I sure wish you'd think about staying at my house. The other trustees won't kick since it'd save them fuel and food. I plain don't like the idea of your livin' out here alone with your closest neighbors, the Taylors, two miles across the creek."

"It's good of you to be concerned, Mr. McCanless, but I've already explained why I can't."

He shook his head disgustedly. "Reckon I might ask you a question that's none of my business, ma'am?"

"If I don't wish to answer, I'll say so."

"How come a woman as pretty and nice as you isn't married?"

"As I explained the day we met, my fiancé was killed in the war."

"I'm plumb sorry for that. But the war's over ten years now."

"I was nursing my father till he died this spring. Besides, of the men a suitable age for me who came back from the war, the ones I had any regard for were already promised to other women." He looked at her so commiseratingly that her cheeks burned and she blurted, "I had three proposals, sir, from men of substantial means, so don't think I couldn't have married had simply achieving matrimony been my aim."

He chuckled and watched her with a warmth in his clear blue eyes that made her blush even more furiously. "Ma'am, I never doubted it for the flick of a lizard's tail and I sure admire you for makin' your own way rather than hitch up with a man just to get a missus in front of your name and have him support you." He ruminated for a moment before his gaze again sought hers. "I reckon that means you wouldn't study gettin' married unless you thought a lot of the lucky galoot."

"Exactly."

He rubbed his blunt chin. "But—well, here's another none-of-my-business question, ma'am. A man's got a free hand to swing a rope at you, don't he? You're not moonin' around over somebody so that the fence is up?"

Matt Rawdon's lean face rose from the back of her mind as if it had been there all the time, but she was certainly not going to moon over him. "My affections aren't engaged, sir," she told the rancher. "However, though I'm not wearing black, I couldn't, from respect for my father, keep company with a gentleman till a year after his death."

"That may be how they do back east," said Ase, "but, ma'am, out here I've seen a widower bury his wife and right after the funeral ask a single lady who'd attended if she wouldn't be his wife and mother his children."

Susanna recoiled. "I can understand why a man left with small children would be desperate, and their poor mother would probably agree that care for them was more important than her being fittingly mourned. I'm not under such compulsion. Further, I feel it would be a grave breach of propriety for a teacher to—to become involved with a patron or anyone who had anything to do with her employment."

"So there is a fence."

"I suppose that's one way of looking at it."

After some moments of glum silence, Ase swung toward her again. "School's out the end of March. You won't be an employee then." He didn't add, though he must have thought it, that the year of mourning for her father would also end that month.

"I would hope to be offered a contract again in the fall."

"Well, sure, but all kinds of things can happen in six months." He sobered. "Now there's one thing I want you to promise, Miss Alden, ma'am. If anyone, trustee or not, starts making you trouble, I want to know."

"It'll be best if I handle problems myself. But yes, if there's something beyond me, I'll tell you." It was only fair to acknowledge his magnanimity. She took a deep breath. "I appreciate your support, Mr. McCanless, and I hope you'll find a good use for your school."

"It'd make a fancy line camp but I reckon we'll see if some hard rains and a leaky roof don't decide you to move. Meanwhile, we'll shift the desks and benches and such to the soddie. No use makin' the kids suffer for *your* principles, ma'am."

That was a relief and she forebore to remind him that he could bend *his* principles and deed over the superior building. She had her contract, certificate, and at least the tentative approval of most of the trustees. Now she had to prove that she could teach their children.

The two Ace High hands not trailing cattle to Dodge helped haul furnishings from Ase's school over to the soddie and transplanted the frame privies on either side of a sandhill plum thicket a distance from the school that was discreet without being a formidable journey in bitter weather. They then cleaned out the well and attached a new rope to the old windlass. Will Taylor had a deposit of gypsum on his claim and brought a wagonload of the chalky substance to be crushed and mixed with creek mud to plaster and lighten the walls. Dumping this near the door, he unhitched his wagon in order to hitch his plow to his oxen and started cutting sod which Prade, with his shovel, cut into bricks two by three feet long.

When they thought they had enough of these for the fuel shed, Will unhooked the plow and the men loaded the wagon which the patient oxen pulled to where the fuel shed would be built.

Susanna still hadn't met Cash Hardy, who was the only patron not joining in the work. "Said he was down in the back when I stopped by," Will Taylor said. "Promised to fill up the fuel shed, though."

"I'll believe it when I see it," scorned Prade, catching his breath after helping Taylor lift one of the heavy bricks in place. "If he won't do his part, we shouldn't let his kids come to school."

"That hurts the kids, not Cash," objected Will, knuckling off sweat. "Besides, they're Mrs. Hardy's kids, too, and she's a nice lady. She washes for Jem Howe, that old bach on the east side of them, and he's paid her with a couple of hens. She told me, real proud, that she's going to send the teacher some eggs when the kids come for the first day of school."

"I bet Cash's back's not so crinked he can't go hunting," said Prade. "About the only food he ever puts on the table is jackrabbit or prairie chicken."

"Except for pork, that's the only kind of meat we get now the buffalo are mostly gone," returned Will peaceably.

Ase snorted. "If you don't kill a beef now and then you're sure different from most sodbusters." He looked up from nailing braces across the new plank door. "I'll talk to Cash but as long as I'm chairman of the board, Prade, any young'un in the district can sure come to school."

While Susanna tacked cheesecloth to the rafters to prevent at least some spiders, bugs, roots and dirt from falling to the floor, Kermit Brown repaired the chimney. Ase's men—if they could be called that since neither tow-headed, skinny Bert Mulroy nor brown-haired, brown-eyed Tom Chadron looked more than twenty—helped Luke Tarrant plaster the walls. They started with the bedroom where Ase, as soon as the door was finished, began to make a bunk. The cowboys were so busy stealing glances at Susanna that she was glad when they started plastering the schoolroom and she could unpack and set her room in order without being followed worshipfully by one pair of brown eyes and one pair of hazel.

The Tarrants had donated a small table and leather-bottomed chair for Susanna's quarters, Mrs. Brown supplied a dresser with a mirror, and when Susanna came in, Ase was through with the bunk and was hammering the last nails in a row of shelves against the wall next to the fireplace. Mrs. Prade, who owned a sewing machine, had sent a ticking mattress filled with corn husks.

"A helluva thing to sleep on," Ase grumbled when Susanna approached the bunk.

"It'll be fine." She covered it with sheets embroidered with her initials. At the scent of Aunt Mollie's lavender, a wave of homesickness swept over her.

What was she doing in this house cut from prairie sod, so far from familiar faces and the pretty little town where she'd spent her whole life? She thought of her aunt's mellow brick academy, shaded by great trees and softened with climbing roses and ivy, the neat classrooms, and girl students who were usually biddable and often enthusiastic.

If that's what you wanted, you should have stayed there, she told herself, struggling to swallow the aching knot that swelled in her throat, glad that Ase had moved on to help Kermit Brown with the windows. Remember how it was? What you were afraid of? Every day, every week, every month the same, slipping into years till you were middle-aged, then old, and what would you have done that anyone couldn't, what sweet, sharp tastes of life could you win there, what victories?

And what defeats can you have here? her doubts mocked. Why, you're even afraid to stay alone at night! What if the trustees knew that? Or your students?

Out of the trunk that had traveled with her so far, she

took her own down pillow and her favorite quilt, wreaths of yellow roses appliqued on yellow calico patterned with tiny green sprigs, on which she and Aunt Mollie had stitched many an evening. It had scarcely been folded into her hope chest with sachets of lavender when word came that Richard had fallen at Five Forks in Virginia only eight days before Lee surrendered. She had never brought herself to use the quilt but this was a new life. She shook it out, accepting the pang that shot through her, and breathed in the scent before she spread it on the bunk and smoothed it.

Amazing how much the quilt improved the little room. Carefully unwrapping her grandmother's teapot and the two fragile cups and saucers, Susanna sighed happily to find them intact. She arranged them on the top shelf so that the swans floated serenely against willows and sunset. Until Susanna was in a position to send for it, her mother's good china was stored at Aunt Mollie's along with crystal, a few treasured vases, and all the silverware except for four place settings she now placed in a box on the second shelf. She didn't mind the heavy ironstone plates and bowls Betty had outfitted her with, but she did like the weight and beauty of the silver with its deeply engraved acanthus leaves.

Her brush, comb, and silver mirror that had been a gift from her father went on the dresser along with the brass-trimmed sewing basket Aunt Mollie had filled with threads, needles, buttons, and other necessities. There was room for Marcus Aurelius beside the basket and she placed her other books on the shelves, each loved and often read—Dickens, Tennyson, the Brontë sisters, Whitman, Kipling, Longfellow, Browning, Mark Twain, and George Eliot as well as an assortment of textbooks.

By then it was noon. Though the men had gone about their work divided North and South, Susanna had supposed they would eat together. They did not. After washing up at the tin bathtub that would usually be kept on a big cottonwood stump the men had hauled up from the creek, the cattlemen, who were also the former Confederates, sat on the west side of the soddie while the Union homesteaders leaned against the wheels of Taylor's wagon. Resolved to avoid any appearance of taking sides, Susanna sat at the table though she would have preferred being out in the bright air to breathing in the smell of drying plaster while she consumed biscuits, cold beef, raisin pie, and buttermilk.

How stubborn these men were. Grudgingly civil, but no more, they spoke to the "other side" only from necessity, joking only with their own kind. What if the children were as mulish, or even worse? Grimacing at the thought, Susanna went back to work.

Undergarments and shawls in the dresser, shoes neatly arranged beneath it; sheets, the other quilt, and some blankets loaned by Betty in the trunk; dresses and cloak spread on the bunk to go on pegs as soon as the plaster dried; lamp on the table; cast-iron Dutch oven, skillet, water kettle, and cooking pot, all with legs to keep them above the fire, ranged on the clay hearth near the fireplace with a broom and ash shovel and bucket in the corner. As she accomplished each chore, Susanna felt increasingly at home. Ase had supplied a wood box with a tight-fitting lid, which held flour, cornmeal, rice, and dried corn from the Tarrants, and a little precious sugar. For sweetening, she'd mostly use the sorghum molasses contributed by the Prades. Under the bunk were stored a bushel of potatoes, onions, and a box of beans from the Browns as well as a keg of sauerkraut brought by Will Taylor who had also supplied some fat bacon. Ase was responsible for the tin of Arbuckle's coffee, cans of tomatoes and peaches stored on the shelves, and raisins, dried apples, and prunes in jars to protect them from mice and other scavengers. A leather bag suspended from a rafter held jerked beef prepared by Millie Tarrant. Salt, pepper, baking soda, and a can of lard completed the supplies, which would be replenished as needed and according to whatever the patrons had.

Surveying her home with considerable satisfaction, Susanna frowned as she noticed the bare window. It was glass, thank goodness! Kermit Brown had measured the windows and from Dodge City had fetched sashes fitted with panes for the soddie's three windows. She was grateful for that since she knew that improvident Cash Hardy's house was far from the only one with scraped, oiled skins instead of glass. Still, the window looked so naked.

Dismay turned to anxiety when she realized that at night any passerby could peer right in at her, and though she supposed there wouldn't be many such nocturnal travelers, curtains for at least this window changed from a luxury to a necessity. Banishing the thought of the lavish satin drapes in the rose room at the Ace High, Susanna decided there was nothing for it but to sacrifice a sheet till she remembered the embroidered tablecloth at the bottom of the trunk. Worked with cheerful yellow pansies, it would match the quilt and make lovely curtains, which she needed much more than an occasional covering for the table.

Getting out the tablecloth, also made years ago for her hope chest, Susanna measured it to the window, took scissors from the sewing basket, and winced as she cut into the linen. The hems, fortunately, would save her considerable time and the window was so small that even after gathering the curtains she'd have enough of the cloth left to make runners for the table and dresser.

Moving the chair so she could see through the window to the creek, Susanna hemmed till her neck and shoulders hurt, and then, stretching, went to look at the classroom. The men were through with it and were all working to get the roof on the fuel shed, the first task shared by North and South.

Bless Ase! He had brought over the blackboard and teacher's desk as well as the students' desks, which were arranged to get as much light as possible. The recitation bench was close to the fireplace facing the teacher's desk on the other side of the bedroom door and the blackboard was attached to the wall which had dried to a creamy pale brown. There was a fair amount of gypsum left outside; surely it could be used to make something educational, perhaps relief maps, even a globe? Thanks to Ase, she had a real blackboard. That would be a tremendous help, but she was going to have to invent ways to keep the children interested and learning. What had worked with town-bred Ohio girls of thirteen to sixteen might earn the derision of these frontier youngsters.

To make the room seem really hers, she got out her hand bell and clock and set them on her desk. A large world map, packed carefully folded in her trunk, now added color to the wall by the blackboard. Getting out the small flag rolled around its rod in the bottom of the trunk, she thrust it securely in a crack where the walls joined.

It was four days till school started next Monday. If Ase would let her ride Cindy, she'd visit her patrons and meet the women and children—

"Do you have to stick that up there?" Ase's disgusted voice made her whirl, but she faced him defiantly.

"Yes, I do. Whether you like it or not, sir, it is our country's flag."

"Yours, maybe." Shrugging, he glanced around. "Outside of that, it looks a sight better in here than I reckoned it could." Ase blocked the door a moment before he ducked and entered. Crossing to her room, he glanced inside. "Comfy," he admitted. "But just wait till it rains. It'll drip muddy water in here two or three days after it's dry outside. Better let me loan you a tarp to spread over that pretty quilt. And you'll need an umbrella to hold over your head while you cook and eat and—"

"Mr. McCanless!"

"Ma'am?"

"Except for you, doesn't everybody around here live in a sod house?"

"Sure, but Luke and Kermit have plank floors and good roofs. Makes a lot of difference."

"Well, in time perhaps the trustees will give this building a sound roof and floor."

"Not while you're turnin' up your nose at a perfectly good frame house a mile up the road."

He didn't, of course, want to make her too comfortable. He still thought that real experience in the soddie would drive her to *his* school, even his house. It was too late for that. Having put the trustees to all this trouble, she *had* to make it through the school term in this building.

Meeting Ase's quizzical blue eyes, she said in her starchiest tone, "Even if I am from Ohio, sir, I'm sure I can live under the same conditions that my other patrons do." Fairness compelled her to add, "I appreciate the school furnishings. Whether you care to admit it or not, Mr. McCanless, I'll wager now that it's fixed up this is the best rural school in any county west of wooded country where lumber's plentiful and cheap."

He looked half-flattered, half-annoyed. "It may be that, ma'am, but I guess I'll still drop by the first time there's a soaker and hear what you say then. I'll pound in some pegs for your clothes and that'll about do it."

Exaggerating his crouch, he entered her room. Susanna took a last sweeping glance around the school—her school—and gathered up the curtains to finish later. Then she went out to thank the trustees and say that in the next few days, she'd come to visit their families.

"It'll be fun to take you to the Tarrants and Browns," said Jenny, eyes shining before she made a face. "I'm not going to visit any damnyankee sodbusters, though."

"What you say at home is your father's worry, but let me

tell you now, Jenny, there'll be no such name-calling at school."

"Why, they are damnyankees. They are sodbusters."

"How about Northern farmers? Or settlers? Or homesteaders?"

"That doesn't sound like what they are."

Susanna couldn't repress a chuckle. "Perhaps not, but I won't let them call you what they undoubtedly think you sound like."

"If it's Reb, I don't care! I'm glad we bucked when the Yanks started spurring us and if we'd had more factories, we'd have won!"

"We'll study about that, Jenny, but we aren't going to keep fighting the war." Susanna tied on her bonnet. "If you're not going with me, I'll see you at supper."

As she passed through the kitchen, Betty thrust a tin box at her. "Here's something to eat, dear, just in case those"—she checked herself with a merry twinkle—"those Northern homesteader settler farmers don't invite you to have a bite."

Strange. Ten days ago, she'd been nervous of gentle old Cindy and deathly afraid of falling beneath her hoofs. Today, she'd mounted alone by stepping on a stump Johnny had placed in the corral. Nothing would ever make a sidesaddle feel like a truly secure perch to Susanna but she no longer rode filled with anxiety. Nor was she troubled about riding by herself across the prairie. According to Johnny, all she need do to find the Hardys was to cross the creek beneath its bend near the school and follow the stream south a few miles. To reach the Taylors, she'd leave the Hardys, tracing wagon tracks across Matt Rawdon's property, and travel north till she struck the Missouri family's homestead. After that, the rutted way led to the Prades.

That was the encounter Susanna dreaded more than a

fractious horse. No matter how she chided herself for cowardice, she hoped Saul Prade wouldn't be at home. She couldn't understand, rationally, why the handsome green-eyed man disturbed her so. Ase had said things much more offensive, but she knew that Ase, beneath his gruffness, was a kindly person, and was equally sure that Prade was not. It was hard to imagine living with so daunting a man. What would his wife be like? And his children?

Those were cranes overhead! Johnny had pointed out to her how the swift upstroke of their wings sent them into a glide till they flapped their wings again. Their call was a low-pitched, melodious rattle that carried surprisingly well. Flocking prairie chickens scattered at Cindy's approach and a meadowlark flashed its yellow breast as it captured some insect stirred up by the mare.

It was a glorious day, the wind gentled to a breeze just crisp enough to make Susanna's blood effervesce as if she'd had champagne. When the school came in sight, grass and sunflowers on the roof blending it into its surroundings, she felt a rush of possessiveness.

Her school, her home. Winter would come, snow, rain, and relentless wind, but she would be touching young lives, opening the world of books and learning, and by coming together to study, the children should learn to be neighbors, heal in their time the festering wounds left from the war.

An insistent creaking penetrated her reverie. Shielding her eyes, she saw a horse and wagon labor up the slight rise from the creek and draw up by the soddie. A thin boy, all arms and legs, jumped down, followed by two smaller ones. Without waiting for Susanna to come near, they attacked the load heaped in the wagon bed, hurling and cramming armloads of sere brown grass, weed stalks, and cow and buffalo chips into the shed.

Not till Susanna reined in did the oldest boy stop and pull off a tattered straw hat that revealed tangled light brown hair. The smaller lads imitated him exactly and, gazing into the three pug-nosed faces and three pairs of eyes more golden than brown, Susanna thought she could see in the smallest flaxen-haired child how the eldest had looked at seven or eight, and in that elder who might be fifteen and must stand close to six feet tall, the pattern to which the younger ones would grow, features roughening as their hair darkened. All were burned brown and wore no shoes though their garments were neatly patched.

"Hello," Susanna greeted, smiling. "I'm the teacher, Miss Alden. Are you the Hardy brothers?"

All three nodded. "I'm Dave," said the tall one, and jerked his head to indicate each brother. "Ethan's twelve. Georgie's seven." His tone softened. "Our sister's Rosie and she's nearly ten. Now if you'll excuse us, ma'am, we got to rustle. Need to fetch another load to finish filling the shed and we have to get through today so we can finish up the field work before school starts."

Straightening his thin shoulders, he turned to the wagon. Like shadows, his brothers did the same and began scooping up variegated combustibles.

"Thank you, boys. That should be enough to keep the school warm for a long time."

"You'd be surprised how quick it burns, ma'am." Dave evidently knew all too well and didn't pause in his labor.

"Good-bye," called Susanna, giving Cindy a slight touch of her heel. "I'm going to visit your mother."

Dave stopped long enough to flash a sweet, slow grin. "Why, ma'am, she'll like that. Mama gets lonesome. Says with all us men critters to take care of she can't get off the place. Miz Taylor's too poorly to visit and Miz Prade—" He broke off, flustered, and started working even faster.

Susanna, as she rode toward the creek, thought there was a man in the Hardy family, but from all she saw and heard, it wasn't Cash.

❀ Six ❀

Margaret Hardy was glad indeed to have a woman visitor though she was embarrassed to be caught barefooted. She hastily laced on black boots so scarred and worn that carefully applied polish couldn't disguise the marks. Though she was probably only five or six years older than Susanna, exposure to sun and wind had grooved lines at the corners of her gold-flecked brown eyes, and the faded blue calico dress was so loose that she had clearly lost weight since it was fitted to her. But she was still a pretty woman with a pert nose, dimpled chin, and a mass of curling yellow-brown hair that escaped a severe bun to cluster at neck and forehead.

"It's dark inside," said the woman with an apologetic glance at the half dugout burrowed into the side of a slope, extended in front with sod blocks and roofed with sod. Two windows were covered with scraped, oiled hides and the leather-hinged door hung open to cast an oblong of light on the swept-earth floor. "Why don't we sit out here and I'll bring you a glass of beverage? Rosie, fetch the chair for Miss Alden."

Rosie, with taffy-colored eyes and bouncing pigtails, dragged out a cane-bottomed chair, bobbed her head shyly at Susanna's thanks, and brought out a wooden box. Digging the bare toes of one foot beneath the instep of the other, she held out the skirt of her green plaid gingham dress, much too big for her, and confided, "Aunt Madge sent this and two other nice dresses my Cousin Marilyn outgrew. It's a shame she doesn't have some boys so she could send my brothers things—"

"Rosie! I declare, honey, your tongue's fastened in the middle and wags at both ends." Margaret Hardy gave Susanna a glass of faintly tinted, aromatic fluid, settled on the box, and positioned her daughter in front of her. "I hope you don't mind my altering the dress while we talk, Miss Alden, but she's set on wearing it the first day of school."

"Mama, you can't let my red dress out any more and you said the blue one's so patched you can't find a place to sew a new one to!"

Margaret flushed but laughed good-naturedly. "Can't take on airs when there's little pitchers with big ears around. Rosie, if you don't stop wiggling, you'll jab into a pin! Now, Miss Alden, just let me tell you how glad I am you're going to have a school. Dave and Ethan got some schooling before we left Iowa four years ago but Rose and Georgie haven't had any."

"I can read Dave's third-grade reader," protested Rose. "And I can spell better'n Ethan and know my multiplication tables up to the tens."

"I've taught them all I can in the winter," Margaret said. "Dave's good to get the others to study, makes it a game." Her eyes grew wistful. "My sister Madge and her husband wanted Dave to stay with them and finish his education but with him the oldest and with Cash not able to do much heavy work because of getting his back hurt in the war, we just had to bring Dave along." She brightened. "If he can finish eighth grade, Miss Alden, can't he go to the teachers' summer institute, take the examination, and get his teaching certificate?"

"I don't know the Kansas regulations but that sounds very likely, Mrs. Hardy."

Her sympathetic tone led her hostess to glance around as if to make sure the audacity wasn't overheard. "What Davie dreams about is going to college. Can't get enough learning, that boy. But I don't see how he ever could."

"Why not?" The instant the question was out, Susanna would have recalled it if possible. The answer was all too evident in the glassless windows and a veritable cave instead of the comparative comfort of a soddie. A few red hens scratching around the yard were the only hint of more than the barest necessities. The cornfield with its drying ears, other fields of cane and oats, and a large patch of ripening pumpkins were, she was sure, the result of Dave's work. He would be needed at home, at the very least till his brothers and sister were grown. The most he could aspire to was to improve his certification by attending summer institutes that ran less than a week, teaching at a three- to six-month school, and, from spring to autumn, farming the homestead. Still, Susanna couldn't accept this for the serious brown-haired boy she had met only that morning.

"There's a state university at Lawrence, in the eastern part of Kansas," she said. "Maybe when Ethan and Georgie are old enough to take over the farm work, Dave can work his way through there. If that's what he wants to do, Mrs. Hardy, don't you think we should encourage him?"

"He's—he's such a good boy." The mother's lips trembled. "I'd hate for him to be disappointed."

"Isn't it better to be disappointed in trying for what you want than just giving it up?"

"Who's to say?" Bitterness, for the first time, edged into the other woman's voice. "Cash worked on the river docks before the war but he couldn't do that with his bad back and didn't like the other jobs he tried because they were indoors. We thought homesteading was the answer. A hundred and sixty acres just for the taking! We'd grow all our food and from selling crops, we'd buy cows and a good team. In a few years, we'd be doing fine."

She pulled the dress over Rosie's head, took a threaded needle from a pincushion, and began stitching. Her words muted and Susanna ached as tears dropped on the green gingham, glittered a second, and disappeared. "Turned out that plowing hurt Cash's back. I know, we should have thought of that, but we didn't, and it took every cent we had to buy a wagon and team and what we needed to start, so there wasn't any going back. I washed and baked for Jem Howe, though, and he broke enough sod with his oxen that first year so we could plant corn and he plowed a little more each year till Dave took over spring before last using our horse that didn't freeze in the blizzard of 'seventy-one. He can plow what Jem already broke, but even a team of horses isn't strong enough to really break virgin sod. Takes oxen. We had beautiful corn and wheat a year ago but in July the grasshoppers came—I guess you've heard about that. Ate the stalks right into the ground, cleaned leaves off the trees and bark off the young ones. I swear the sound of them in the corn was just like cattle feeding. I covered up my garden with quilts and blankets and they ate through them to the onions and potatoes and turnips. Just like that plague of locusts that Moses called down to scourge the Egyptians! Those 'hoppers feasted from Nebraska to Texas. Lots of settlers gave up and we would have, too, only we didn't have anywhere to go."

Rosie was staring at her mother as if she'd never heard such things, light brown eyes wide with alarm. Margaret caught her close and gave her a hug before she released her with a little swat. "Don't just stand there in your shimmy, dear, put on your dress. Don't worry your head about those 'hoppers. Haven't we had nice roasting ears and dried a lot of corn on top of having plenty for corn-meal and popping this winter?"

As the child skipped off, Margaret said, "I'm ashamed

of myself, taking on like that, and when you were sweet enough to come see me. Doc Rawdon's done all he can for Cash—brings him medicine and won't take a cent. When Georgie broke his arm last year, Doc set it, and when Rosie had pneumonia, he sat up with her three nights to let me rest. Jem Howe's been mighty good to us, too. I certainly shouldn't complain."

"Sometimes it helps to talk," Susanna said. "Especially to another woman."

"Well, dear, if you ever need to get something off your chest, just come to me," Margaret invited. "I'm sorry Cash missed you, but Jem Howe took a load of corn to Dodge and Cash went with him to buy shoes for Davie if he can sell the eggs for enough." Susanna could well imagine how much Margaret would have enjoyed the trip but there was no complaint in her deep-pitched voice which quickened with pride. "As long as the hens lay, I can send you three or four eggs a week, and when you need cornmeal, we'll bring some. There'll be oats, and after the cane's cut, we'll send molasses. When I told Mr. McCanless we wouldn't have any cash money to give toward your salary, he said it'd be fine to make it up in food and fuel."

"That's as good as money," Susanna said.

"I'm just so grateful that we have the food," Margaret said and her eyes were haunted for a moment as if she remembered those hard months when she must have seen her children go hungry. "Can I get you some more beverage? We'd love to have you stay to dinner, just cornbread and beans, but you're mighty welcome."

Susanna had sipped all the beverage even after deciding it was water flavored with vinegar, but thought that was enough for courtesy's sake, and rose with a smile. "Thank you, but I have to be going. I need to call on Mrs. Taylor and Mrs. Prade today. Please, though, don't feel too discouraged about Dave's prospects. You see, I'm twenty-seven but I'm only starting to live my own life." She explained and Margaret Hardy exclaimed in sympathy.

"Well, we're mighty glad you've come. I can't tell you how it cheers me up, having a school for the children. What with the good corn crop, it seems our luck's turning. If we only had a church—" She laughed at herself and again her eyes were merry. "Some folks are never satisfied."

Susanna laughed, too, but this visit starkly underlined the isolation of these prairie women, the hunger for another woman to talk with. Though she'd planned to wait till her pupils could make a good showing and she had them well under control before setting plans in motion to bring the families together, Susanna decided not to delay. "Every Friday afternoon, parents are invited to come to school," she said. "We'll have spelling bees and ciphering matches and perhaps some of the children will want to give poems they've memorized."

"A program? Every Friday?"

Taken aback at the delight in Margaret's tone, Susanna said, "Not a real program, but we'll have those, too. Fridays will just give parents a chance to see how their children are progressing and give a little time to visit."

"That's wonderful! Cash might even come—" Margaret's voice trailed off. "Of course, the Confed—I mean, the Southerners, those big cattlemen, they'll come."

"I hope so." Susanna grinned to take any sting from her words. "Presumably they care as much about their children as Northerners."

Margaret colored. "It was Ase McCanless got the district together and pushed for a school," she admitted. "He's got every right in the world to be there—but so will I be." She added softly, "Another thing, Miss Alden. That must be an awful fine school Mr. McCanless built on his land but I'm glad you moved the school to the soddie. Otherwise, the rest of us would feel like beggars, or anyway too beholden. And there are some who'd say you'd have to favor his daughter and act to suit him." Rising, she gave Susanna a shy, swift embrace. "Good luck to you, dear, and if you ever have a speck of trouble with any of my children, let me know and I'll talk it out with them."

Quite a change from Saul Prade's switches. "I'll look for you next Friday," Susanna promised. As she róde over the slope, she waved back at Margaret Hardy who stood beside her dugout and flourished her apron till Susanna was out of sight.

Passing through Matt Rawdon's hayfield, Susanna scanned the rolling land to the east but saw no sign of his dwelling. No protruding chimney, nor did a shingle-roofed soddie catch the eye from a distance. What would he think when he learned she'd been hired and would, moreover, be teaching at the soddie, that she wasn't, as he'd so condescendingly predicted, retreating to Ohio? And why should it matter to her what he thought since *he* certainly had retreated, letting his medical training go to waste because his injured hand could no longer perform with the deftness necessary to a surgeon?

It did matter, though, however often she fought away a sudden flash of those strangely luminous eyes or felt a treacherous melting in remembering how he'd lifted her into the buckboard and as easily helped her down. But something female in her also responded to Ase McCanless's strength and closeness when he helped her mount and dismount. He was attractive, single, and in spite of his domineering ways, she liked him.

Back in Ohio, if she'd met a man half as eligible as Ase, she would certainly have allowed him to call, would have given him a chance to win her affection, if not her love. She was years past the age when she should have experienced all that followed the sort of magnetism that coursed between her and Rawdon. That must be why it affected her so powerfully. Thank goodness she'd be too busy teaching to think much about him.

Susanna saw what must be the Taylor house, sheltered

from at least some of the wind by a gentle knoll. A saddled clean-limbed gray horse waited in front. The Taylors must have a visitor.

This soddie had a shingled roof and glass windows. In a distant field, a man, probably Will Taylor, was scything grain. As Susanna approached, she heard voices, one high-pitched and querulous, the other a deep masculine tone that she recognized even before Matt Rawdon appeared in the door.

"I'd advise lacing only for special occasions, ma'am," he was saying. "If you'll take a brisk walk each morning, your appetite will improve. And I think it would be wise, in view of your heart palpitations, to limit yourself to one cup of coffee a day."

"It's the one thing I enjoy, Dr. Rawdon," said the woman with pale blond hair, so aggrieved that she didn't notice Susanna. "As for lacing, a corset helps support my back. And walking on this dismal prairie! I had hoped you could give me some real help."

"I'm sorry, Mrs. Taylor, but no one can give you health, like a pill. It's made up of your inherited constitution and your habits, which only you can control." His gaze moved to Susanna. "You have a visitor, ma'am. Good morning, Miss Alden."

"Good morning, sir." After the way Margaret Hardy had sung his praises and the overheard advice which could have come from the lips of her own father, Susanna smiled at him but his nod was barely polite. He fastened his medical bag behind the saddle, swung up, and rode down the track.

Mrs. Taylor, pouting, turned to Susanna. Three girlish faces peered around her. "You must be the new teacher." The woman had classic features, very fair skin, and cool blue eyes. She wore a pretty black wrapper with a watered floral design and white tatting making a V at the neck. Kid slippers showed as she stepped outside. "Do come in and excuse the house. I'm not well—I suppose I should have known a Confederate doctor wouldn't believe a Northern woman can be delicate! And a soddie! You'll soon learn that you can't keep one clean."

Dismounting, Susanna trailed Cindy's reins where the mare could get the meager shade of a honey locust and followed her hostess inside. In spite of three windows, the interior was dim but the floor was wood and a squill-patterned carpet covered the end of the room graced by a piano, a chaise longue, and several polished chairs. Sinking onto the chaise, the woman said, "Please do sit down, Miss Alden. I'm Delia Taylor, and these are my daughters, Charlotte, Berenice, and Helen. Charlotte, love, bring us coffee if there's some left in the pot, and don't forget the sugar. Berenice! Go brush your hair, wash your face, and pull up those stockings! Helen, fetch Mama her fan."

From the way they carried out their tasks, Susanna concluded that they were used to performing them. Charlotte had her mother's eyes and hair and looked about thirteen. Berenice, perhaps eleven, had dark brown eyes and hair that was straight except for some tangles. She also had her father's long face with too much jaw and nose for a girl and moved as if she were all knobby elbows and knees. Helen, about six, was dark but had inherited her mother's oval face. All the girls wore shoes and stockings and their dresses, though a bit faded, had no obvious patches. Will, it was clear, did his best for his womenfolk, and it struck Susanna that he probably had to do the whole outside work of the homestead.

"If you're not feeling well, Mrs. Taylor, I can call another day," Susanna said.

"Oh, it's chronic." Delia Taylor lowered her voice. "I wouldn't take anything for my precious girls but they cost me my health. In town near my doctor I might have recovered in time, but Mr. Taylor was set on coming out here though he drew a good salary in my father's haberdashery. I try not to let my parents know how wretched it is but when they heard I was burning—well, those disgusting animal leavings, they had a hay-burning stove freighted to us." She gestured, giving Susanna leave to turn and admire the ingenious invention that had two large cylinders inserted at the side of the stove beneath the oven. "The springs at the end of the cylinder push the hay into the firebox, and Will keeps the other cylinder packed full and ready to use. A load burns for an hour or two, convenient in summer when one only needs a fire to cook, but in the winter—oh, my dear! Serve the teacher first," she instructed Charlotte, who, with an appraising look, offered a tray with coffee in delicate china cups with saucers.

Susanna thanked her, declining sugar, and wondering why this woman, so scornful of conditions that were luxurious by the standards of the region, had married Will Taylor, who must have felt as awkward as he'd have looked while trying to help affluent men select their attire.

"If my fiancé had lived," Delia Taylor began. "But he gave his life for his country at Wilson's Creek that first awful summer of the war. Mr. Taylor, who served with him, was wounded in the same battle and sent home to recover. He brought the sad news and a letter." With a lacy handkerchief, Mrs. Taylor blotted a tear. "I visited Mr. Taylor while he was recuperating. In wartime, all that's important to a womanly heart is to cheer our brave soldiers. I married Mr. Taylor before he went back to the front."

Her tragic glance left it to Susanna to picture the martyrdom of a refined woman mismatched with a crude farmer but what Susanna saw, though usually she never thought of such things, was that Charlotte didn't look a bit like Will. Threatened with disgrace, Delia might well have preferred marriage with an otherwise unacceptable suitor.

"The war hurt everybody," Susanna said, but she didn't feel like sharing her griefs with this woman. Her natural impulse was to sympathize with suffering but it occurred to her now, for the first time, that though selfish and wicked people grieved and felt pain, that didn't make them likable or better. The funny-sad thing was Will Taylor's worry about "joggerphy" corrupting his girls when their mother and the whole family would have been much happier had she learned to care about the wider world instead of concentrating on her own body.

"I hate sending the girls to school with those rebels." Mrs. Taylor frowned. "If my health was good, I'd teach my darlings at home where they'd be protected from Confederates and that bunch of rough, ragged Hardys, not to mention that half-breed Tarrant boy——"

"He's part Cheyenne, I've heard," said Susanna firmly. "Mr. McCanless speaks highly of his mother."

Having the grace to flush slightly, Delia went on in her high-pitched voice that carried the hint of a whine. "Mr. Taylor's taught the girls to read and cipher a little—he has the patience though unfortunately the poor dear man only had a few years' schooling. I've taught Charlotte piano but Berenice drives me mad with her blunders. She's surprisingly good at knitting, though Charlotte's better with crochet. Just what subjects will you teach, Miss Alden?"

Susanna told her, and then, rising, thanked her for the coffee and said that Friday afternoon would be visiting time for parents.

"I doubt that I can come." The blond woman sighed. "Jolting along in the wagon puts me in agony no matter how well Mr. Taylor tries to cushion the seat. I'm sure he'll come, though. He dotes on the girls."

Berenice could use that, poor little ugly duckling, though in the long run she might be luckier to have Delia Taylor's hostility rather than the smothering affection lavished on Charlotte.

"I do hope you can come at least for special programs," Susanna said. "That means so much to children."

"I'll try." Delia Taylor rose and walked with Susanna to the door. "I'd ask you to stay for dinner but it's such poor fare compared to what you get at Ase McCanless's that I'm sure you wouldn't enjoy it."

Though that didn't sound like much of an invitation, Susanna decided to treat it as one. "Thank you, but Mrs. Flynn packed me a lunch."

Her hostess didn't come into the yard. "My girls have been well-brought up, Miss Alden. I trust that you'll watch carefully to make sure they're not abused." She lowered her voice, giving Charlotte a significant glance. "You'll need to be extra careful about Charlotte. She's thirteen and those older boys—well, Miss Alden, although you're not a mother, I'm sure you understand what I'm worried about."

"While the children are at school, they're my responsibility. On their way back and forth, I'd suppose that concern for their behavior and safety would be shared with me by the parents and trustees. Of course, if you have any problems, please let me know."

Delia Taylor didn't return the offer.

Halting in the shade of a giant cottonwood where crows were holding a raucous convocation, Susanna loosened Cindy's saddle cinch and let the mare graze in the deep grass along the creek bank. Both to let Cindy enjoy the grass and because she rather dreaded going to Saul Prade's, Susanna loitered over her lunch and tried not to think about Prade and his frightening malevolence. Instead she mused over the two very different women she'd just met and their children, who would be her pupils. She must try to be impartial but that was going to be hard, and she could almost prophesy that Jenny and Charlotte would detest each other. Rosie might befriend Berenice. But heaven forbid that Dave Hardy succumb to Charlotte!

Goose! She laughed at herself. Next thing, she'd be pairing them off. In sober truth, though, most of the children were likely to marry schoolmates or at the least be neighbors their whole lives long, so friendships and enmities forged in school would have consequences when these students had grandchildren. Would they be mixed then, farmer with cattleman, Unionists and Confederates?

For a moment, Susanna permitted herself a dream. A white frame two-room schoolhouse in the soddie's place, the Stars and Stripes floating in the breeze, acknowledged by all the children as their flag, not seen by one side as that of the oppressor. The children playing or at their desks resembled Jenny and those she'd met today, but the swiftest runner among the boys was one who had Matt Rawdon's brilliant eyes . . .

You're a double goose! Susanna told herself. Leaving some biscuit crumbs for the gossiping crows, she gave Cindy a few dried apple bits and tightened her cinch, fervently hoping that Saul Prade would not be at his house.

He wasn't, but his personality seemed to permeate the sod house which, like the Taylors', had two rooms with the bedroom divided by curtains. Unlike the Taylors', it had a sod roof and a fireplace, but the windows were glass and the inside was as comfortable and attractive as a woman's thrift and work could make it, though there were none of the crocheted doilies, scarfs, and antimacassars so fussily evident in the Taylor home.

Instead there were braided rag rugs, curtains, bright quilts on the beds, patchwork shuck cushions on the homemade chairs. Family portraits hung on the clay-and-ash-plastered walls, and on the scrubbed wood table a blue glass vase held a bouquet of grasses and wildflowers. In spite of all this, though, Susanna's gaze fixed immediately on the heavy braided whip, coiled like a rattlesnake, that hung from a peg above a massive homemade chair draped with a buffalo robe. Small, dainty Laura Prade would be lost in that chair and Susanna was sure that when Saul was enthroned there, his quiet children grew quieter and his wife didn't sing as she had been doing when Susanna rode up.

Singing and sewing. Laura's treasure was the Singer sewing machine placed where it caught the best light from one of the two living room windows. "I'm getting the children ready for school," she explained, after welcoming Susanna very sweetly and making sure that she had eaten. Bending, Laura put an arm around a boy and girl who looked a little older than Georgie Hardy and who had their mother's violet eyes and hair of pale silver. "These are the twins, Paul and Pauline. Sarah, their big sister, has got them through her Second Reader and they can do easy sums. Go get the cow chips now, children, and stop by the well house to tell Sarah to bring Miss Alden a glass of cool buttermilk."

As the twins slipped out the door, their mother smiled after them before something shadowed her eyes. "Sarah's thirteen and a wonderful help to me. She's churning out in the well house because it's cooler there and she's at that age when she needs to get away sometimes from her brothers and sisters. Frank's helping his father cut cane." That darkening again of those clear, lovely eyes. Did Laura know the side of her husband that Susanna feared and shrank from? "Frank's fourteen. He can read through the Fourth Reader. It's hard for him. Seems he changes letters around and then he gets nervous. I hope you'll be patient with him."

"I've had students with that trouble before. We'll just move along at his best rate. It'll help, of course, if he practices at home."

"He'll do that but—" Laura broke off and the shadow left her eyes as a girl as tall as she was came around the house. "Thank you, dear," said the mother as her daughter handed Susanna an enameled cup of buttermilk. "If the butter's made, why don't you sit with us a while?"

Laura introduced them and, taking Sarah's firm brown hand, Susanna fairly ached at the girl's beauty. She had golden hair and green eyes with brows that winged upwards in a face whose pointed chin and widow's peak gave it a heart shape. She had a gentle voice and hesitant smile which, with encouragement, deepened and spread to her eyes.

As they sat and talked, Laura worked buttonholes on a shirt and, without being told, Sarah mended stockings of various sizes. Laura was a comfortable person to visit with for she was interested in Susanna without prying and the conversation flowed easily back and forth with Sarah now and then asking a question or adding a bit to what her mother was saying.

"We proved up on our claim last year," Laura said with pride that Susanna by now understood was justifiable. "Of course, when the grasshoppers ate our crops right into the ground, we weren't so sure that our homestead was any great prize. My husband got a job freighting supplies from Dodge City to Camp Supply down in Indian Territory while the rest of us kept things going here, and this year we've had good crops. With luck, Saul won't need to go freighting again, but those cash wages certainly rescued us last year and in 'seventy-one when a blizzard froze our milk cows and oxen. Saul built a good barn after that but the storm of 'seventy-three came so fast that we couldn't get our cows in and lost them again though we saved our oxen and pigs." She gave a wry little laugh. "It seems we're always starting over. But by planting and watering forty acres of cottonwood cuttings, we've proved up on our timber claim so we own three hundred and twenty acres, and every year we've broken more sod and planted more grain. When my husband gets discouraged, I tell him that even if we lose a crop to drought or 'hoppers every four or five years, we should do well enough in good seasons to save up for the bad."

"I suppose farming always is that way." Susanna nodded. Her father's family had produced doctors for three generations and her mother's people had been teachers and storekeepers for about the same period, so she had no ties to the soil. From all she heard, farming in this region was a gamble of time, hard labor, and money that dwarfed any cash stakes laid out by card players. "It must be terrible to see fields withering or devoured by grasshoppers. But it must also be wonderful to harvest the grain and know it grew from a tiny seed you planted and took care of."

"It is for me but I grew up on a farm. Father was a minister but got such a small salary that it scarcely counted. It's different for my husband. He grew up on army posts and ran away when he was fourteen because his widower father was—severe. Saul was big for his age and hired on with a freighting company. When the war broke out, he enlisted and worked his way up through the ranks to captain. I met him when he came home on leave with my brother who was in his company." Laura's voice wavered and her eyes misted. "My brother was killed shortly after that visit. Saul wrote us about it. He'd been wounded, so we asked him to convalesce with us and we were married that spring of 'sixty-two." Laura paused. That shadow was in her eyes again as she sifted out facts and finished briefly. "After the war, there was an—unfortunate partnership. We lost everything. We moved to Fort Hays about sixty miles northeast of here where Saul freighted supplies to Fort Dodge till we saved enough to"—here flashed laughter— "grow broke homesteading."

How did Laura see her husband? Again, here was a war marriage between young people caught up in the urgency of the threat of death to the young man, a reckless disregard of the future that might not come. Susanna's father had pityingly called it nature's way of replacing the young men who were going to die. It sounded as if Saul had been gone much of the time till they took up the homesteading.

Was it possible that even now Laura didn't know her husband all that well? Had Susanna herself misjudged him? She would have been glad to think so, but remembering how he had looked when he held out the switches, the cold flame of his eyes, Susanna repressed a shudder and knew in her bones that the evil she had sensed in him truly existed.

Just as instinctively, she felt Laura's goodness, a simplicity that would puzzle over her husband, but unless brutally crushed, was incapable of seeing him as Susanna did. Her gaze involuntarily going to the bull whip, Susanna thought of the boy out in the field with his father. Did he know Saul in a way the rest of the family never would?

More disquieted than she'd been at either the Hardys' or Taylors', though she liked Laura Prade, Susanna stayed only a short while longer. Before she left, she invited Laura to the Friday afternoon activities.

"I don't think you'll have trouble with our children," Laura said, resting her hand on Sarah's as they came out to see their visitor off. "If the twins or Frank should act up, Sarah will set them straight." It plainly never occurred to Laura that her eldest daughter might need discipline and although she had to stifle a laugh, Susanna didn't think so, either.

"I'm sure I can use all the help I can get," she said. "Sarah, I'll see you at nine o'clock Monday morning, and Mrs. Prade, I'll hope you can come on Friday."

"I'll surely try." Laura's eyes lit. "It'll be fun to have an outing and get to know our neighbors. Mrs. Hardy came to help when I was having a hard time with my last baby three years ago, bless her. Saul was off freighting and I might have died if she hadn't sent Frank for Dr. Rawdon when she saw something was wrong. The cord——" Laura broke off, coloring. "It doesn't offend you, Miss Alden, for me to speak this way?"

"I'm a doctor's daughter," Susanna reassured her. In spite of his refusal to practice, Matt Rawdon seemed to have been involved with almost everyone she'd met. It would be amusing if he weren't so stubborn about wholeheartedly pursuing the profession for which his skills and inclinations clearly fitted him so well.

"The cord protruded beneath the baby's head," Laura

went on so softly that the children couldn't hear. "That cut off the flow of blood to the baby. The poor little thing was dead before she was born. With Mrs. Hardy's help, the doctor nursed me through milk fever."

While Susanna added one more credit to the account of the irascible and unwilling physician, Laura Prade looked rather shamefaced. "After all that, you'd expect Mrs. Hardy and me to be great friends—and I would do anything for her, but there's no church or store and hasn't been a school, any place to meet, and Lord knows we both keep busy. Saul's dropped the children and me off to visit a few times when he was going to town with the wagon, and we'd walk home in time to do the chores since he wouldn't come back till next day. But the long and short of it is that the men trade work and get to town now and then but women mostly stay home with the youngsters. The school, though, it's not so far that we can't walk if the men can't bring us in a wagon. I'll be there as often as I can." She tilted her head in a birdlike manner. "Do you think the ranchers' wives will come?"

"I hope so. They're sure to be interested in their children's progress and they probably get lonesome, too."

Laura considered that a moment. "I expect they do. When you say *ranchers'* wives, it sounds like there's a lot of them, but come to think of it, there's only Mrs. Tarrant and Mrs. Brown. I haven't laid eyes on either of them. I just hope the children don't choose up sides and fight the war all over again."

"They won't do it more than once," said Susanna though she had no clear idea of how she could prevent it. Laura must know one of the ranchers' sons was part Indian since Prade had objected to him, but Laura didn't mention it.

Cautioning Susanna to watch out for rattlers and gopher holes, Laura stood in the door with Sarah, and again Susanna was waved out of sight. Susanna followed directions and forded the creek above the next bend, struck west toward the lowering sun, and soon encountered the trail looping back to the Ace High.

She'd met the homesteader women and most of her pupils. She was concerned for the Hardys, was resigned to some problems with Delia Taylor, and was afraid she could never like Charlotte. Such things were to be expected and she'd have to deal with them as best she could. What wasn't ordinary, what she couldn't philosophically dismiss, was the menace emanating from Saul Prade, and this disturbed Susanna the more because she had at once warmed to Laura and Sarah and felt protective about them both, oddly, more for mother than daughter.

Laura was . . . Susanna groped for a word. Innocent. Yes, she was, in spite of years of marriage and hardship and motherhood. Hers was a trusting nature that should bring out the best in most men. But Prade?

A chill fingered Susanna's spine as she thought of the coiled whip. Well, Saul had worked as a freighter and might again. Naturally he had a whip. But hung in the main room? Surely most men kept such things in a barn or shed.

Forcing away the ugly image, Susanna pondered the two days left before school started. Tomorrow, Saturday, she'd visit the Tarrants and Browns, an all-day undertaking since the Browns lived three miles from the Ace High and the Tarrants were at least eight miles southeast of them.

That left Sunday. Again her spine prickled. For all her bold words to Ase and Matt Rawdon, Susanna was fearful of being alone at night in the soddie. Because of that, she decided that she'd forego spending Sunday night in the Ace High's rose room. Instead she'd move over on Sunday, spend the day accustoming herself to the place while it was light and she could investigate any suspicious sounds. And the curtains! Before night fell, they had to be in place.

Imagining what might prowl around the soddie sent a flood of panic through her but she invoked her father, Marcus Aurelius, Aunt Mollie's quilt, and her grandmother's tea things. There was no way to retreat from her resolve to live at the school, no way at all, so the sooner she gritted her teeth, laughed at her own nonsense, and got used to it, the better.

Thinking of the three women she'd met that day, wives and mothers who were none of them ten years older than she, Susanna couldn't keep from feeling robbed and wistful. Margaret, Delia, and Laura shared at least one thing besides being married to homesteaders who were former Union soldiers. They had been old enough to marry before or during the war; they didn't fall in that awkward gap where Susanna had found herself, too old for boys grown to manhood since the war, and too young for the generation old enough to escape fighting.

Stop looking back! Firmly, she set her mind on school and all she had to do.

❀ Seven ❀

Ase and Jenny escorted Susanna to the soddie. At her insistence they left early in the morning, for she knew that was her bravest time whereas ever since her father went off to war, she'd been nervous at night, even at Aunt Mollie's. If awakened once she'd gone to sleep, she usually spent till dawn fighting off anxieties and worries she could control during the day.

Tied behind three saddles or tucked into saddlebags were the rest of Susanna's belongings and Betty's contributions, fresh-baked wheat bread, cinnamon rolls and pie, butter, cottage cheese, and a carefully wrapped jar of sourdough starter. Susanna didn't aspire to Betty's artistry with hot cakes, biscuits, and other baked goods, but she'd been making bread for years, so with Betty's training in the use of this tangy sort of leavening, Susanna expected the results to be at least edible.

"No one better make fun of Ridge because he can't read," Jenny burst out as they came in sight of the school. "He can already track and hunt and ride better'n Daddy, even. The only reason he's coming to school is that his folks want him to so much. They won't force him." She shot her father a reproachful glance. "That's not the Cheyenne way."

"Pete's sake, Jenny, you're not a Cheyenne," said Ase. "Or a boy, either. And just as soon as Miss Alden's through with it today, you go back to sidesaddle."

"Miss Alden," Jenny appealed, whirling around so that her thick yellow braid jerked. "Are you sure you won't keep Cindy, and that dad-blasted old saddle?"

"I won't have time to ride during the school week." Susanna repeated her earlier response to Ase, though the nearby presence of any living creature would have been a comfort. The soddie looked so *alone*. "I'll hope to see the parents at school often enough not to need to pay visits, and from all I hear about blizzards, I'd rather not be responsible for a horse when there isn't a barn or shed."

Jenny's glum expression was a laughable contrast to her animation of yesterday when she'd accompanied Susanna to the Browns' and Tarrants'. When thirteen-year-old Freck Brown muttered that he was only coming to school to look after Dottie, his nine-year-old sister, who, like Freck, had molasses-colored hair, a snub nose, and bright blue eyes, Jenny pointed out that he'd get to see Ridge nearly every day instead of once in a coon's age.

She'd used the same argument on Ridge, a handsome thirteen-year-old who had hazel eyes, black hair, and skin the shade of a copper-blushed peach. Jenny's importunity may have weighed a little with Ridge, but from the way he looked into his parents' hopeful eyes, sighed, and assented, Susanna knew it was their wish that moved the boy on a path he would not choose of his own will. At least he had several friends, and if some taunt from the Northern children didn't wound him, perhaps in time he'd come gladly to his books. He wouldn't learn much by Friday's demonstration, though; she'd have to think of a way to preserve his pride.

Dismounting before Ase could help her—glad that she'd learned that much—Susanna untied a bundle of clothes from behind the saddle. The door had no lock, but thank goodness, Ase had insisted on fitting it with a stout bar inside.

As she stepped into the school room something rattled, flashed in the oblong of light, and vanished in the shadows by the fireplace. Susanna screamed and jumped back, bumping into Ase who caught her and held her a few breaths longer than necessary. Putting down his load on the nearest desk, he said, "Wait outside, both of you. I didn't wear my Colt but I can kill the thing with the poker."

"Don't!"

He stared at Susanna. "You sure don't aim to make a pet of that old rattler?"

"No, but—" Susanna didn't know how to put it in a way that wouldn't earn his derision, and, worse, Jenny's, but she had always hated the almost universal practice of killing snakes, even harmless ones. People who'd rescue an injured bird or pity a trapped mouse killed snakes as if engaged in some primeval struggle that knew neither reason nor compunction. "Let me chase it outside," she volunteered.

"Outside?" roared Ase. "Are you daft, woman? Maybe you want to cozy up to snakes, but what about the kids?" Before Susanna could interfere, he grabbed the poker from beside the fireplace and slashed it down on the weaving, triangular head.

"Kill him, Daddy!" Jenny shrilled.

Susanna buried her face in her hands, sick and faint at the crushing, pulpy sounds and desperate thrashing. She shrank away when Ase, panting, went past her with the rattler's five-foot-long body impaled on the poker. In spite of the awkward gait of his high heels, Ase carried the creature a long way off before getting rid of it. By the time he returned, Susanna had quit trembling and walked to meet him, hands clenched, confronting him while they were out of Jenny's earshot.

"Mr. McCanless, we need to have something clear. I'm employed by the board of trustees and can be discharged by majority vote. I want suggestions and, if need be, criticism. But so long as I'm the teacher, I must have final authority in the schoolhouse."

He rocked back on his heels. "You're mad on account of I killed that rattler for you?"

"You didn't kill it for me. You can't kill every snake on the prairie, sir, so though beating this one to death may have gratified you, it hardly accomplished much."

"He sure as hell won't bite anyone now, ma'am." He set his hands on his muscular hips and gave her a long, incredulous stare. "If I'd have known you had such damnfool notions, I wouldn't have voted to hire you."

"You can always call a meeting, tell the trustees I'm crazy, and vote to get rid of me."

"And go through all the mess of huntin' a teacher again?" He took off his hat and scratched his head disgustedly. "Nobody's perfect and I guess we'll just have to put up with your notions long as they don't harm the kids. No one expects a lady teacher to kill snakes anyway. That's a job for the bigger boys."

"I'll take care of the snakes." She didn't know how but she'd find out.

"Will you?" He looked her up and down and grinned. "Tell you what. Lots of times, snakes come in pairs. Let's have a good hunt to make sure there's not another inside. If we find one, you can take care of it—sprinkle salt on its tail or sing it to sleep or whatever you think will work."

To Susanna's vast relief, a thorough search into nooks and corners yielded only a few bugs and spiders which, to Ase's mocking astonishment, Susanna carried outside on a piece of paper and released.

"You a Quaker?" he demanded. "I hear they've got real funny ideas."

"Peace? Doing good? Yes, I suppose that is peculiar, and

no, I'm not a Quaker. But my father taught me never to hurt harmless creatures that are only trying to live."

"Rattlesnakes harmless?" Ase snorted.

"My father said they had a part in the chain of life. They control mice and rats and—"

"Songbird babies and anything else they can sink a fang into!"

"That's their nature."

"Well, ma'am," Ase retorted hardily, "it's my nature—and most folks'—to kill each and every damn snake they come across. Sorry I'm cussin' but you sure do drive me to it. You goin' to stuff this applesauce down the kids?"

"It's not a subject, Mr. McCanless, but of course I hope some of them may learn something from the way I act." He looked so grim that laughter suddenly bubbled from her. "Is it going to ruin the children if they stop to think whether they really need to kill a snake or spider?"

"Hell's bells, woman! That's not the kind of thing people think about!"

"It's my job to teach children to think."

Their gazes locked. "You just remember this, ma'am," he said quietly. "You have authority in the school, that's only fair. But you're responsible for the children. If you put 'em in danger with your high-falutin' ideas, you'll be out of here so fast your head'll spin."

"That's fair," she said. "But I could argue that trying to kill a snake with a lot of children around is more dangerous than moving it."

"Just so you're the one does the moving."

The rest of Susanna's things were quickly unloaded. Ase drew up enough water from the well to fill coffeepot, hot-water kettle, and the bucket on a crate by the wash basin. Then, to Jenny's mutinous groan, he switched the sidesaddle to the pinto pony and swung his daughter up before he walked a little way back toward the school with Susanna and spoke only for her ears. "I'll bring a board over tomorrow and raise that threshold so a snake can't wiggle under the door the way that one must've." He added sarcastically, "That is, if you got no objection."

"I'd be delighted." Having established her autonomy, she gave him her sweetest smile. "I don't want snakes and tarantulas inside any more than you do."

"They get into a soddie without much trouble." He cleared his throat. "You can move back to the rose room anytime. Betty's going to miss you."

"She says she's coming to the Friday afternoon exercises," Susanna said. "Will you?"

"Why, ma'am." He grinned. "I wouldn't miss it for worlds."

Whistling, he mounted in an easy swing, lifted his hat in a final good-bye, and, leading Cindy, rode off, looming large beside his rebellious daughter. Watching them out of sight would make her feel more alone and deserted, so Susanna went inside, after some internal debate leaving the door open.

Soon enough, weather would compel her to keep it shut. Till then, she'd prefer the risk of undesirable callers to the added darkness. It was so quiet. It would have helped greatly even if gentle old Cindy were grazing somewhere in sight. She knew the Hardys were only two miles across the creek, but she felt immeasurably far from any human being. She could walk to the neighbors in less than hour, draw comfort from Margaret Hardy's redoubtable presence, and still be back in time to plan the week's lessons.

She had one foot out the door when she jerked it back. No sneaking off, she scolded herself. If Ase McCanless knew! She knew she was a cowardly cat but no one else needed to know. Since childhood, perhaps because she had no mother to do it, Susanna had chided herself as if divided into two people. Sometimes it helped. *March yourself right in there—and make yourself at home, because that's what it is!*

* * *

She put away the things she'd brought, securing the baked goods in a big lard can, and, as Betty advised, set the sourdough starter in a crock of cool water. Betty had sent enough cooked food for the day and a cinnamon roll would do at noon but Susanna thought that building a fire and cooking supper would be a good way to help make herself feel that she belonged here. Sorting out bits of stubble and shriveled or broken beans from the sound ones, she put several cups of speckled rosy brown pintos to soak. Then she set to work finishing the window curtains, with paper and pencil close at hand so she could jot down ideas about her students and curriculum.

She knew which readers some of them should be able to get through. Except for the first-graders, Ridge Tarrant seemed the only one who couldn't read at all. How was she going to handle that without humiliating a sensitive boy who didn't want to be in school in the first place? There'd be a wide range of knowledge of arithmetic. Probably all the children would need lots of drill in spelling and penmanship, and, except for the oldest children who might remember something from Eastern schools, history, geography, and grammar would start from scratch. Putting down the curtain for a moment, she made a chart with the children's names grouped according to their professed reading ability. Delia Taylor's vagueness gave no hint of where her girls fitted, and Jenny had scornfully declined to read aloud from any of Susanna's set of McGuffey's readers though Susanna suspected she read well above the sixth-grade level she'd have attained at age eleven in a regular class.

With a sigh, Susanna resumed her sewing. There wasn't going to be much connection between a pupil's age and the reader he or she would use and that could be disastrous should someone like Ridge be jeered at for sounding out the primer with the "babies." She might have to have almost as many classes as there were pupils. There was no use trying to set up a schedule till she'd had a few days to determine where each child stood in every subject, but she could already see that even if she held each class to fifteen or twenty minutes, she'd be hard-pressed to cover every subject daily for every level.

Overwhelmed at the prospect, so different from teaching proper young ladies who, on the whole, fitted into proper classes, Susanna mechanically made the last stitches on the curtains, scarcely seeing the happy-faced yellow pansies.

North and South, cattleman and homesteader aside, this was going to be hard. *Marcus, Marcus! I'm willing to do the work of a human being but this would scare even you, I'll bet!*

She shook out the curtains, wide enough to fall in pretty gathers, and measured the distance between the pegs Will Taylor had pounded in to tilt slightly upwards. Now to find a slender branch to use for a curtain rod. She had no hatchet—after all, there was no wood to chop, but she took a formidable heavy-bladed butcher knife from the divided shallow box Betty had filled with kitchen necessaries, shut the door against invaders, and started toward the creek.

Yellow-headed blackbirds, who, according to Ase, would soon be flying south, croaked from cattails growing in a little marsh produced by the bend of the creek, and a great flock of their red-winged cousins, who lived here the year around, rose from the willows at her approach and swarmed to the opposite side, muttering hoarse imprecations. She didn't alarm the crows, though, who hopped about the golden cottonwoods and made jocose remarks.

"If you don't leer and cackle just like old men on the courthouse lawn!" she told them. Their cheeky behavior and the beauty of the blackbirds lifted her heart. People weren't the only living things on the prairie; she'd have to learn more about her wild neighbors—including rattlesnakes.

How glad she was that Ase had kept people from cutting down these big cottonwoods. Their wood curled and warped too much for building lumber and though they'd yield fuel for a season, their shade would gladden animals, birds, and people for many years. The limbs were too high for her to reach, but she found a willow branch of just the right length and thickness, cut it, and returned to the house well pleased.

Pushing the rod through the folded-over and stitched tops of the curtains, she fastened the ends of the rod securely to the pegs so that opening and closing the curtains wouldn't jerk it loose. Arranging the embroidered folds on the sides of the window so they didn't obstruct the light, Susanna viewed them with satisfaction and relief.

After they were pulled tonight and the lamp lit, she'd make tea in Grandmother Alden's pot and read—well, not Marcus tonight, but perhaps Charlotte Brontë's *Jane Eyre*. Though published nearly thirty years ago, it was the novel Susanna had reread most, each time sympathizing with Jane and thrilling to the brooding, unpredictable Rochester. Yes, after writing a letter to Aunt Mollie and Uncle Frank, she'd indulge herself, read till she was so sleepy that she'd drop right off.

Using dry grass and weeds as a starter, she built her first fire with the chips plainsfolk called prairie coal. They smoldered, took some time to catch, and smoked more than wood, but she knew from watching Betty cook that their worst drawback was constant need of replenishment. The Hardy children had filled the fuel shed full to top and corners, so perhaps, since October shouldn't be cold, the supply would last through November.

It was past noon when she set the beans on to cook and went outside to enjoy a raisin-studded cinnamon roll with the jar of milk Betty had sent. Geese were flying south, wings glinting in the sun. When they came back next spring, would she greet them from this same doorway? What would happen in the months between?

Going into the schoolroom, she arranged all her texts between bookends in a row across the front of the desk, the full set of McGuffey's readers, Webster's spellers, Clark's grammar, Ray's *Mental Arithmetic,* Montieth and McNally's geography, and several histories and other volumes. Sitting at the desk, she made up an attendance chart, writing in the names of the students, and roughed out a plan for the next day, getting up as necessary to build up the fire. About midafternoon, she set the teakettle at the edge of the coals.

Toward the back of her ledger, she wrote each child's name on a separate page with spaces for grades. As she learned about them, she'd make notes on their interests, problems, and any ideas about how best to teach them. She paused over Frank Prade's name. He was the only one of her pupils she hadn't met. What would he be like? Irrational fear chilled her as it always did when she thought of anything connected with Saul Prade. To calm herself as she had learned to do after her father's death, Susanna took long, slow, even breaths and tried to banish the thought of that Lucifer-handsome man by gazing out at the big, medium, and small desks and benches and picturing the room full of eager, laughing children, the future of this country.

Glancing at the flag hanging from a staff planted in the crack between sod bricks, she hoped that in this little room North and South would gradually come to be simply American.

Light slanting through the western window was so orange a gold that she looked and saw the sun touching the horizon. Though it would be light for perhaps another hour, she got up quickly to bring in what she considered an ample supply of prairie coal before shutting and barring the door. To discourage snake, lizard, rodent, and insect visitors, she rolled up a braided rag rug Betty had loaned her and stuffed it snugly in the space beneath the door. She hoped Ase would remember to fix it.

Standing by each schoolroom window, she peered at her quarters and decided that she couldn't be seen through the bare panes as long as she wasn't near the door in the dividing wall. She also decided that she needed a curtain to screen off her room and would rig up a sheet, right now, to serve till she could get suitable heavy cloth.

She lit the lamp, turned the wick down, and carefully adjusted it to burn as brightly as possible without blackening the clear glass chimney. Then she pulled her curtains, saying goodnight to the cottonwoods along the creek and the creatures sheltering in the roots and branches.

Maybe she wouldn't be so nervous if she were outside, she thought suddenly. Maybe it was being in here alone that was scary. But that was ridiculous. She certainly couldn't sleep out in the grass or perched up in a tree. She laughed out loud to think of what the trustees would think if they knew her weakness, but the laughter seemed discordant, hung mockingly in the air.

Goodness, this wouldn't do! Getting a sheet from her trunk, she drove the stoutest weed stalks she could find on either side of the bedroom door, strung cord across, and draped the sheet over it. Now, cowardy cat that she was, she could walk back and forth without worrying about some chance night traveler glimpsing her.

After stoking the sulky fire, she washed her hands, mashed a cup of nearly cooked beans, and mixed them in the kettle for thickening. Then, following Betty's directions, she set the spider, a three-legged frypan, over some coals and put in a tablespoon of lard. While it melted and the pan heated, she mixed a sort of spoonbread batter with cornmeal, salt, and the rest of the milk, and poured it in the spider to bake, setting a cast-iron lid over it.

How aggravating! What she'd considered an abundance of fuel was nearly consumed. If she wanted crisp-crusted bread, well-done beans, and water at the boil for her tea, she'd have to venture out to the shed. And now it *was* dark.

She couldn't, wouldn't, give in to absurd fears! Surely it was just a mouse she heard skittering among the desks. Picking up her fuel basket, she slipped past the sheet, shoved the rug aside, and unbarred the door. The stars shone for their own splendor, not to light distant humans, and there was no moon.

Remembering the snake, she thumped the basket several times on the mounded stalks and chips before she set it down. Then, reaching gingerly into the shed, she began to fill the basket.

"Good evening, ma'am."

Susanna jumped almost out of her skin. She hadn't heard a sound, but as she whirled around she saw a large shape blacker than the night and heard the chink of a bit as the horse snatched a mouthful of grass.

After that first heart-stopping second, she'd known Matt Rawdon's voice and gone limp with relief but now anger flared up, the hotter because she'd been so frightened.

"What do you mean, sir, sneaking up like that?"

"I didn't sneak," he said equably. "You were just making so much noise that you didn't hear me." He finished filling the basket, lifted it, and said, "Aren't you going to invite me in?"

"Why didn't you come in the daytime?"

"I didn't know you'd moved in till night fell and I could see a light."

"You can see it from your place?"

He laughed softly. "After dark, in this country, light shines a long way. I could say the same for a pretty woman."

Did he think she was pretty? Annoyed at the way she felt herself melt at the caressing note that crept into his voice, she held open the door. "Since you're here, you may as well come in though for propriety's sake you surely understand that—that—"

"Indeed, Miss Alden, I understand perfectly. Following the cardinal precept of schoolmarms, you're guarding your reputation. It would hardly do for people to think you chose to live alone in order to entertain gentleman callers."

He stepped inside. Longing to kick his shins, Susanna closed the door and rearranged the rug.

"Why are you doing that?" he asked.

She explained about the snake.

"If you have a board," he said, "I'll fix the threshold."

"I don't, thank you very much anyway, and besides, Mr. McCanless will do it tomorrow."

"Of course he will. How could I have thought otherwise?"

"You don't need to try to be obnoxious. By nature, you're offensive enough." In the dim light, she could see that he was grinning at the sheet. Flushing, she snatched it down, breaking the weedstalk pegs.

With one long stride, he reached the fireplace and set the basket down. Taking the poker, he expertly shoved and bullied the fire into showing a little spirit, added some chips, and lifted a dark eyebrow at the sheet she still gripped like some kind of protection. "Tell me, ma'am, was that up as a second barricade against varmints?"

"Since one got in, it wasn't very effective." Childish, but he made her too angry to care.

"Nice curtains," he said lazily, lifting one and fingering the material. "Tight, strong line. Hard to see through."

"That's why they're up," she retorted, stung past caring what he thought. "And why I hung the sheet, and a good thing, too. If I hadn't you might have—"

She broke off at the sudden chill in those gray eyes. "Looked in your windows?"

"You sneaked up behind me."

An exasperated breath ripped from him. "You couldn't have heard a tornado, the way you were banging your basket and rooting around in those weeds and chips." Crossing his arms on his chest, he stared at her. "Now if I had seen you feeding the fire or whisking back and forth, do you think it would so enflame my senses that I'd break down your door?"

"Get out!" she blazed, cheeks burning. "Get out and don't you come back again!"

"So vehement?" He caught her hands but though his fingers were like steel, he held her more with his searching, mocking gaze. "It can't be that you're like the virgin lady who peeked under her bed each night quite terrified—that a man wouldn't be there?"

An unforgivable taunt, especially when he knew about Richard. Outraged hurt made her go absolutely still. She silently watched him till he reddened and dropped her hands.

"I beg your pardon."

"You wouldn't have said that had I been a Southern lady."

Laughing again, he took the butcher knife and tried to give it to her as he made to unbutton his shirt. "Take your pound of flesh, Miss Alden. Got some scales handy?"

Her lip twitched in spite of herself. "Let's cry quits. Have you eaten supper?"

"Hours ago, but if that teapot's out for a reason—"

Maddening as he could be, she was strangely glad that he'd be the first person in this new life to drink from her grandmother's china, take hospitality. "I'm making tea and you're welcome. Do have the chair. I can sit on the trunk."

"So can I, but first I'll fetch in what I brought you." He raised a hand as she started to protest. "It's not a personal gift, not even eminently respectable bonbons or a book. It's something for the school."

"But you don't have any children."

"No, but I am—was—a doctor. I doubt if it's occurred to you that you're far from help and will probably have to treat all kinds of cuts, sprains, and the other things youngsters do to themselves and each other."

He was right. She hadn't thought of it at all. Some of the older young ladies fainted now and then from having their corsets laced too tightly and loosening them had been the only treatment Susanna had ever had to give. Students who got sick were sent straight home, never a matter of more than ten or fifteen minutes. This was different, children of all ages who had to come miles on foot or horseback in a region of snakes, ferocious storms, and heaven knew what else. She should have thought of this and come prepared.

She said, "It's kind of you to be concerned, Dr. Rawdon. But I'd like to pay for whatever medicaments you've selected." A whole alarming new problem yawned before her and she appealed, "You will come, won't you, if there's an accident or something serious?"

He hesitated, then gave a brusque shrug. "I will if I can be found, but it's close to three miles to my house, Miss Alden. Many injuries need immediate treatment." Again he hesitated and when he spoke she wasn't sure whether he was grudging or diffident. "It might be a good idea for me to give you some advice."

"I'd be forever grateful. What about a rattlesnake bite, for instance?"

"I'll let you in on a secret, ma'am. The best thing to do is probably nothing except to keep the victim quiet."

"Nothing!"

"Quite a lot of the time, the fangs don't carry venom at all. When they do, it can make a person mighty sick but a bite usually kills only frail or little people."

"Like children!"

"Well—yes. But warn the children not to pester snakes. I'd reckon a good half of bites happen when people are bothering the rattler, trying to pick it up or kill it. Their nature is to scoot, fast, when they can—"

"That's all very well but what can I do if one of my pupils is bitten?"

"Calm the child, have him or her lie down with the bitten part—it's usually a hand or foot—lower than the heart, send for me. If you don't have sores in your mouth, or a hollow tooth like the poor girl in 'Springfield Mountain,' you could sterilize a very sharp knife by holding it over flame, cut very lightly, no more than an eighth of an inch deep, lengthways in the direction the fangs entered, and then suck out as much poison as you can. Never give whiskey. That's the popular remedy but it only pumps the poison faster to the heart."

Her face must have betrayed her dismay. He laughed and said cheerfully, "Snakes scare people but in my experience with bites, no patient's died yet, whereas I have lost several to bee and wasp stings and an infant to a black widow. You would do well, ma'am, to keep a sharp eye out in the schoolroom and your quarters, and also to check the privies every morning. More than one person's been bitten on an embarrassing spot because they didn't look before they sat."

He went out, leaving Susanna with burning cheeks at such plain talk but he *was* a doctor and these were things she needed to know. The teakettle was boiling. She tipped a little water into the teapot to heat it, dumped that into her wash basin, and then poured steaming water over tea leaves. Rawdon came back with a wooden case which he set on the table and opened.

"Eat your supper, Miss Alden, and I'll explain what's here. Yes, please, I'd enjoy a cup of tea. Haven't had any in years."

Susanna wished she knew more about his past, who had served him tea, who had made him so touchy about his hand. Not daring to look at him lest he sense her awareness of him, Susanna poured tea into Grandmother Alden's cups and then served herself beans and a generous portion of spoonbread.

"At least you'll have one of Betty's cinnamon rolls," she said, trying to sound natural.

He must have felt the tension, for he said heartily, "No need to ask a man who's baching a question like that."

She brought him one, regretting that it wasn't of her making, but even so there was something delightfully intimate about sitting at the table, sharing food, and sipping from the tea cups which had been in her family for so many, many years.

Their eyes met. The dim yellow lamplight darkened his eyes but not the glowing in their depths. Flame, sweet, wild, and intoxicating, leaped through her. It's what comes of being an old maid, she scolded herself, and wrenched her gaze from his. It would probably amuse him to know how he affected her.

Willing her hand not to tremble, she poured more tea for him and said in her most dry, deliberate tone, "Please, Dr. Rawdon, will you show me what you've brought and how to use it?"

❀ *Eight* ❀

Bandages, including a triangular one that Rawdon showed Susanna how to tie for a sling to support a broken arm; a muslin-padded splint; adhesive plaster; tincture of iodine—these were her armory against the host of accidents that might befall her students.

"The body's its own best healer," Rawdon said. "If a wound bleeds freely, it'll cleanse itself so don't wash a cut unless it's dirty. Then use warm water and soap. Don't bandage unless necessary to keep the wound clean or hold its edges together." She'd heard this from her father. When she gravely nodded her understanding, Rawdon considered for a moment and produced from his coat two small jars filled with packets. "Don't administer these unless the child's in serious condition and I can't be found. The Dover's Powders are ipecac and opium for pain or dysentery. The calomel and quinine are for ague. I've written instructions on the bottles. But any child who's sick enough to need these should be sent home immediately."

"And what happens to them then—if you refuse to practice?"

"I'll come in an emergency," he said, mouth as grim and

stiff as his voice. "But I was a surgeon, not a dispenser of pills, so kindly spare me your high-minded preachments."

He shut the case with an abrupt click and got to his feet. "Good night, Miss Alden. Thanks for the refreshment."

She longed for him to use his training and satisfy the need there must still be in him to heal. "Thank you for the kit," she said. "I hope I don't have to use it often but it makes me feel better to have it." Deliberately, risking a repulse, she added, "It's a comfort to know I can send for you in real need."

"Make sure it's real," he warned. At her surprised look, he said with a bitter laugh, "I can almost hear your mind whirring, Miss Alden, trying to salvage me for the benefit of my neighbors and my own recalcitrant soul."

"It—it seems such a waste." Of a man and his power to live, not only of a doctor.

He shrugged and picked up his hat. "Miss Alden, you've idealized your father as a modern Hippocrates, and perhaps he was, but the abilities of doctors are grossly overrated. The best ones make it possible for the patient's body to heal of itself. In spite of my sister's sacrifices and urgings, I'd never have made it through medical school if I hadn't become intrigued with surgery after seeing one of my teachers remove a tumor the size of three hen eggs from the right side of a young man's neck. It was interfering with his breathing. The scalpel saved him. A surgeon has the chance to save those who would otherwise most surely die."

"Laura Prade thinks you saved her life when her baby was born dead," Susanna pointed out. "Johnny walks better because of the brace you made for him, and Margaret Hardy won't forget how you sat up with Rosie when she had pneumonia. Why isn't that kind of medicine as important as taking off arms and legs—which is what my father says comprised most surgery in the war?"

"Anyone with a little experience could do the little I have for my neighbors, Miss Alden. They're overly grateful because there wasn't another practitioner." He hesitated, then burst out, "Do you know what I really hoped to specialize in? Abdominal surgery, repairing hemorrhaging organs, suturing perforated intestines. As you know, drains may be placed in such a wound to drain suppurations, but patients usually die from blood loss. In several cases where death was otherwise certain, I did open the abdomen and sew up lacerations, checking the hemorrhage. I lost two patients, but a then-seventeen-year-old Tennessee boy may be alive today because of me."

"That should give you satisfaction."

"When I can't go on with what I was learning?" He held up his scarred hand, the splayed fingers ridged with scar tissue. "Would you like to have this clumsy hand use a scalpel near your arteries, try to manipulate forceps or probes in your delicate innards?"

She flinched at his words, not his scars, but he misinterpreted. With a jeering, cruel laugh, he raised his hand, brushed those fingers across her face, let them linger on the throbbing of the large vein in her throat.

When she didn't shrink away, the smile died on his lips. She bent her head and kissed the wealed fingers.

He jerked them away. "Damn you!"

She thought he would strike her and awaited the blow, eyes steady on his blazing ones. Without a word, he turned to the door. A horse whinnied, was answered, and he froze.

"More company." He scowled. "Were you expecting someone?"

"No more than I was expecting you." Susanna flushed but as she heard the nearing creak of leather and clop of hoofs, she was grateful for Rawdon's presence, whatever damage it might do her reputation. A glance at the clock showed a quarter till nine, much too late for a respectable caller. Rawdon had been there two hours. That, she well knew, was not respectable, either.

A loud knock came at the door. "Who is it?" Susanna called.

"Saul Prade."

Grateful indeed that Matt was there in spite of potential gossip, Susanna unbarred the door. "What brings you this way, Mr. Prade?"

"I was over at Hardys' and thought I'd drop by to make sure you were settled in." Tall as Matt but heavier, gold hair catching the tremulous light, Prade smiled at Rawdon before he looked down at Susanna. "There's nothing in your contract about callers, Miss Alden but—and no offense to you, Dr. Rawdon—you know how folks talk. I'd suggest you—entertain during the day."

"I brought Miss Alden a medicine chest," Matt said. "If there's any talk, Prade, I'll know where it started."

"A fight to defend the lady's honor?" Prade chuckled as if he found the prospect amusing. "That would certainly quell rumors, wouldn't it?"

"I'm not an eighteen-year-old who requires a chaperon." Susanna was more than ever glad that she hadn't been forced to deal with this man by herself, alone in the night. Matt, guessing her absurd fears, had teased but she'd believed him sympathetic. Prade, she was certain, would study any weakness he spied in her and use it if he could. It was like being stalked by a great cat, patient, soft-footed, till the prey was trapped and the hunter sprang like lightning.

Sure that fear would draw Prade as blood attracts predators, Susanna spoke decisively. "It's not my intention, sir, to have gentlemen stopping by at night, though when there's a reason like Dr. Rawdon's kind errand, I trust there'll be no colorful speculation. Let me also make it clear that trustees are no more welcome after dark than any other man of the district. Any concerns can be discussed with me after school hours or at a properly called board meeting."

"Ma'am," said Rawdon swiftly, "that sounds like just the

policy I'd count on from a Yank . . . I mean, Ohio teacher. Far be it from me to tarnish your reputation. And just so you won't, Prade, let's leave together."

"I have some questions for Miss Alden."

"I'll wait."

Prade glanced around the darkly shadowed room, his hair the only brightness, and again primeval dread chilled Susanna's spine. "How do you intend to enforce discipline, Miss Alden?"

"I won't enforce it, sir. I'll send home pupils who don't want to learn."

"'Want to learn.'" he echoed. "It's your job to teach them, whatever they want."

"I'm not a jailer."

"Or much of a teacher, from your birdbrained notions. Children, especially boys, are young animals who only learn through their hides. My sincere best advice to you is to take the first student who gets out of line and thrash him till he begs."

Susanna had to swallow before she could trust her voice, and then it was frayed. "If that's your best advice, I'd hate to hear your worst. Kindly give me a chance to teach, Mr. Prade, before deciding my ways won't work."

"You'll learn." The green eyes, catching lamplight, for a moment were as incandescent as a beast's. "I hope I'm there to see it when you find out this school isn't like your young ladies' academy."

Turning, he ducked his head to pass through the door. Defiance ebbing, Susanna felt terribly afraid, not only of Prade but of the possibility that he might be right, that she would sink to his methods.

"Good night, ma'am." It must have been an accident but Matt Rawdon's hand lightly brushed her hair. Bending his head close to hers, he whispered, "Give 'em hell!" and was gone, closing the door behind him.

As Susanna barred it and stuffed the rug under the crack, she heard the horses moving off toward the creek.

She couldn't imagine the two men would ride far together though she somehow felt confident that Rawdon would make sure Prade didn't turn back.

Turn back? Of course, Prade wouldn't. He must know if he harassed her further without cause, she'd appeal to Ase. All the same, her heart contracted at the thought of how badly Prade's visit would have shaken her had Matt not been there. Matt's had shaken her, too, but in a different way.

Her private room, as she hung up the sheet again, was filled with his presence. Here, he'd built up the fire, now winking embers. There, he'd lounged on the trunk while she made tea. There was the cup his lips had touched, and beside it the chest, his gift to her and the children. Along with regret for his refusal to practice medicine and aching hurt for the way he loathed the hand that could no longer serve him with deftness, Susanna felt again the touch of his fingers on her throat. It had been without conscious volition that she'd bowed her lips to his hand. And he had cursed her for it.

Reciting aloud all the Marcus Aurelius she could remember, she did the dishes, banked the coals, and though she didn't think they would last halfway to morning, she filled the teakettle and nestled it against them. Spoonbread and beans were covered and would serve for tomorrow's supper.

Turning back the quilt and sheet, she examined her bed for creepers and crawlers while savoring the familiar scent of Aunt Mollie's lavender. Homesickness, a longing for the people and place she'd always known, seized her as a whirlpool suddenly grasps an unwary craft. For moments, she gave in to it, standing in the little room with her aunt's quilt in her hands. But then, while affirming her loving gratitude to her family, she said, defying Prade, "I can make a difference in this place. I can teach the children. Whatever lessons are here for *me,* I will try to learn them."

This resolve was mocked at once as she paused by the

lamp, its mellow light a companion in this isolation. What would it hurt to let it burn all night, just this once? Should she have trouble going to sleep or wake in the darkness, the light would be so welcome.

Kerosene was expensive and though the flame would probably gutter out if the wick burned too low, it was dangerous to leave a lamp unattended. These were good reasons but the real one was rooted in her fears, and it was daunting, the way her dread of Saul Prade was meshing with that senseless, humiliating old fear of darkness.

She blew out the lamp. Her feet wanted to run to the bed, but she made herself walk slowly. Undressing, she hung her garments on pegs. As she removed her slippers and set them on the foot of the bed, where they would, she hoped, be less likely to harbor scorpions and such, she caught the red wink of the embers. Indeed, as her eyes got used to the dark, it was lightened considerably by the muted glow from the fireplace.

It has to get dark for little lights to show, she told herself. She lay down and her tired body gratefully relaxed. The shucks crackled and yielded to her weight. It was cool enough for the quilt, and with it pulled around her and the smell of lavender permeating her senses, she was too drowsy to summon up the willpower to banish the memory of Matt Rawdon's deep voice which seemed to vibrate in her ears. However gruff he was, it was kind and thoughtful of him to bring the medicine chest. Snuggling deeper into her pillow, she melted into sleep.

Mercifully, none of the creatures that might have dropped on her from the ceiling did. She slept sound till dawn glowed through the curtain, dressed quickly, built the fire, set on the coffeepot, and checked the privies for black widows and snakes. A box attached to the wall of each building held squares of newspaper donated by Ase who subscribed to the *Topeka Daily Capital* and the *Wichita*

Eagle, brought to the ranch in bundles when someone picked up the mail in Dodge.

Her other outside chore, done after stoking the fire, was to fill the two drinking-water buckets—two at Will Taylor's insistence because he didn't want his girls drinking after any boys who'd been chewing tobacco.

"Do some of the boys chew?" Susanna had asked.

"Dunno," returned Will darkly, "but a man with daughters cain't be too careful."

Susanna had suggested that each student bring a cup and fill it from the dipper, but that had been rejected as persnickety and she hadn't insisted, realizing that the Hardys probably didn't have four cups, let alone extras for school. She was, however, going to insist that the children wash their hands before lunch and she set her wash basin and soap on the bench between water buckets with their shiny new dippers. On pegs above the basin, she hung a towel for the girls and one for the boys.

The aroma of coffee filled the soddie. Susanna put the pot to one side to settle the grounds while she made her bed and opened a can of Borden's milk. Pouring it liberally into her mug of coffee, she took the last cinnamon roll and went outside to breakfast to the call of meadowlarks and the high, faint hailing of a migrating squadron of sandhill cranes.

What a beautiful sparkling day! It felt wonderful just to be alive. Susanna treated herself to a second cup of coffee. The prairie wasn't flat, she decided, so much as it was round; the curve of the plains met the dome of sky. Here were no landmarks of hill or cliff, no encompassing woodlands. The trees of the prairie were individuals, never a tribe. Orientation came not from impressive monoliths or ridges but from the sky, the courses of sun and moon, the unfailing North Star, and these directions were plotted from where a person stood, not from a mountain. Insignificant on the boundless grassy sea, each person was his or her own landmark. Susanna's father, with his passion for stars, would have been entranced with the infinite night sky of the plains. And how he would have breathed in a morning like this, even in those last years of pain ...

Blinking back tears, she heard distant shouts and laughter. Goodness, it was almost time for school! Hurrying inside, she made a swift tour of the soddie, peering into dark corners and scanning the cheesecloth ceiling. A lizard disappeared into a crack between wall and earthen floor and a nondescript gray spider was starting a web under the water bench. She scooped it up on a piece of paper and was depositing it outside when a spotted pony streaked past, yellow-braided rider crouched low. The pony swept to circle back at a trot to Dottie and Freck who were mounted on buckskin mares, Freck's tugging at the bit and tossing her head in evident frustration while Dottie's mare ambled along, snatching mouthfuls of grass.

"Scout won!" yelled Jenny.

"Wouldn't have if I'd let Dusty run," said Freck. "But you know doggone well, Jenny, that Dottie cries if I get ahead of her."

"Mama says not to race," choked Dottie. "And so does your dad, Jenny."

"Tattletale if you want to." Jenny leapt down. "That'll just prove you're a baby. Cry, baby, cry! Stick a finger in your eye—"

"Stop that, Jenny!" Freck boiled out of his saddle and orange spots seemed to stand out on his sunburned face. "You can't make fun of my sister even if she is a baby."

Jenny stuck out her tongue and led Scout closer to the creek, having managed not to look at Susanna or greet her.

"'Mornin', Miss Alden." Freck swept off his old hat in a surprisingly courtly gesture and in spite of her determination to be impartial, Susanna had to admit that ranch menfolk, even as young as Freck, had undeniable style. His boots, well worn and battered, were fancily stitched and the high heels gave him that inimitable cowboy gait as he helped his sister down. At nine, she rode astride, and, unlike bareheaded Jenny, she wore a pink chintz sunbonnet that didn't go very well with her yellow calico dress. Her laced brown boots were new and when she took off her bonnet, sausage-shaped finger curls jounced around her thin freckled face.

"Teacher!" she cried, hugging as much of Susanna as she could. "Oh, you do look pretty! Do you think my hair might turn like yours when I grow up? Red hair's awful!"

"My hair used to be red," Susanna assured her truthfully. Rummaging in his saddlebag, Freck produced two tin lunch pails and the Brown library, an old Peter Parley geography and a tattered McGuffey primer and speller.

"Take care of these," he charged his sister, "while I look after the horses." Vaulting to the saddle, he led the old mare toward where Jenny was hobbling Scout, having tossed the saddle over a stump.

The Hardy youngsters were walking up from the creek. They had two lunch pails between the four of them, several books, and Rosie, in her green-checked gingham, carried a small parcel as if it were Magi treasure. With a sinking heart, Susanna saw that though his younger brothers and Rosie wore shoes, Dave was barefooted. All the brothers wore bib overalls, clumsy, baggy garments, especially when compared with the faded Levi's fastened around Freck's waist with a wide silver-buckled belt.

It's not fair, Susanna thought rebelliously. What could have happened about the shoes Cash Hardy was supposed to buy for Dave with the hoarded egg money?

Suddenly, then, the three Taylor sisters came from the northeast, walking with Sarah Prade who was shepherding the twins. All the girls wore sunbonnets and the Taylors' matched their dresses. Some distance behind trudged a strongly built boy with silvery hair. Frank Prade? And the rider on the black horse trotting from the south must be Ridge Tarrant.

So here were the children, assembling from very different homes and parents—Susanna's children now for a good part of the days till April. A tug at her skirt brought her gaze down to Rosie, who handed her a small basket in which seven eggs nestled in dried grass. "Mama sent you these, teacher."

"Thank you, dear," Susanna said, smiling into light brown eyes. "They'll be delicious."

Rosie watched with a solemnity that made Susanna hope Margaret Hardy hadn't deprived her children of eggs in order to send these, as Susanna put them on the shelf near the kitchen side of the fireplace. Nodding satisfaction, the taffy-haired child moved from the door and stood admiring the flag and map.

Time to begin. Though she'd been teaching for nine years, it hadn't been like this. In many ways, she was starting over and Susanna's mouth felt dry as she picked up the hand bell, walked to the door, and rang it in a welcome.

Ten minutes later, they were all inside, seated at desks according to size, older boys directly in front of Susanna, younger children at the low desk to the side, with the bigger girls behind them. Though she was grateful there were desks at all, Susanna wished each pupil had one, preferably one that fitted. Dave and Frank, close to man-size, were cramped at the desk that was high for Ethan though it suited Ridge and Freck physically. Ridge was like a tethered hawk, one moccasined foot in the aisle as if poised to bolt.

And what a message in that row of feet! Next to Ridge's fringed, handsomely beaded moccasins were Freck's scuffed but aristocratic boots; then Dave's bare feet, toed together as if trying to hide; Ethan's heavy work shoes, laced above the ankle, surely hand-me-downs and obviously too big for him; and last, Frank's similar new shoes, polished as were all the Prade children's, the Taylor girls', and Rosie's too-big fancy laced boots, which must have been more largesse from her cousin.

Fifteen pairs of young eyes were fixed on Susanna; this was no time to look at shoes. "Good morning," she said, trying to meet each child's gaze briefly as she smiled around at them, reading in various faces trepidation, excitement, curiosity, or suspicion.

Frank Prade's expression was mask-like. He had his father's brilliant green eyes and his mother's silver-blond hair but his features, delicate for a boy, were like neither parent's. Susanna felt as if he watched the world from behind an invisible wall, a different kind of remoteness from Ridge's, which was more that of a confined wild creature. With a rush of near panic, she knew that teaching these youngsters to cipher, read, and write was not her only responsibility. As much as was humanly possible, she had to create conditions where they'd learn to live in a community, get along with people very different from themselves. An overwhelming task, seen as a goal. She could only strive toward it one step at a time—and be prepared when some of those steps were backward.

"We'll start each day with a few songs," she said. While planning the schedule, she'd seen the danger of songs evoking the war and the division between North and South, and hit on the idea of working in some history with the music, stressing common roots. "I think all of us have some ancestors who came here from England or Scotland, and they brought their songs with them. Do you all know 'Weevily Wheat'?" Most of the girls' hands went up, so Susanna launched into the song.

> *"I don't want your weevily wheat*
> *And I don't want your barley,*
> *I need some flour in half-an-hour*
> *To bake a cake for Charlie.*
>
> *Charlie, he's a fine young man*
> *and Charlie, he's a dandy . . ."*

By the time they finished, the littlest children were lustily coming in on the chorus. Ridge and Frank abstained but Susanna felt that if anything should be voluntary, it was singing. "That song's about Bonnie Prince Charlie," she said. "His Highlanders were crushed by the English at Culloden in 1746. That broke the Scottish clans and after that, more and more Scots came or were sent to Australia, Canada, and the colonies—remember, at that time there was no United States. Willing or unwilling, some as indentured servants, some driven from their crofts or farms by landlords or even their own clan chiefs, the Scots became Americans. Charles Stewart died in exile but we still have the song."

"Daddy's great-grandfather fought at Culloden," said Jenny, without putting her hand up. "I reckon those British redcoats were almost mean as the Yankees."

"My mam's great-grandfather fought there, too," retorted Sarah. "But I guess the British couldn't have treated folks crueler than the Confederates did my uncle in Andersonville prison. They starved him to death!"

Clamor broke out. "My father—" "My uncle—" "Grandpa—"

Susanna rang the bell. "Children, we're going to study the war, and talk about it, but not till we've gone back to the beginnings of our country and learned how a miracle happened." Scanning mutinous faces, she added slowly, "It was a miracle that we came to be. There've been bad things since then, sad things, terrible things, but remember, all of our forebears helped make this country. We're making it today and you'll go on making it when you grow up. Perhaps a good thing to do each morning would be for one of you to tell something about your ancestors, where they came from and why. Who'll do it tomorrow?"

Again, the girls' hands shot up. "Do we have to?" Frank Prade grimaced.

"No," said Susanna pleasantly. "And you don't have to sing." She paused. "I do expect you to get your lessons, hold up your hand, and wait till I call your name to speak so that we don't sound like the Tower of Babel, and do your best to get drinks and take care of private needs at recess and lunch hour. Once we get your classes sorted out, I'll write assignments for the day at the top of the blackboard so you can prepare in between recitations. I don't mind if you talk about your studies and help each other while I'm hearing another class, but please be as quiet and courteous as possible. When your lessons are prepared, you may help the younger pupils or read. There are some books in my quarters and you're welcome to read any of them that interest you. If you're tardy or absent, your parents should write a note saying why, but if you're sick, it'll be much better to stay home and make up your work when you're well."

She smiled at the bewildered looks of Georgie, Helen, and poor little Berenice. "Don't worry, I don't expect you to remember everything all at once."

She read then from "Leaves of Grass": "'Give me the splendid silent sun with all his beams full-dazzling . . .'" The children paid more attention when she got to "fresh corn and wheat" and "serene-moving animals."

Dave's hand went up. His light brown eyes shone and his bare feet had quit trying to hide themselves. "Could I read that book, Miss Alden?"

"I'm sure you could, and you certainly may in your free time. Perhaps you can find a part to read during Opening someday. Berenice, will you give the devotion tomorrow? Jenny, would you tell something about your ancestors and where they came from, pointing out the countries on the map? Now which of you older students will help Georgie and Helen with their primers while I hear the rest of you read?"

Sarah and Dave volunteered and, at Susanna's suggestion, sat down with Georgie and Helen on the recitation bench. That was where Ridge belonged, but Susanna couldn't bear to humiliate him. Jenny tugged at her skirt.

"Miss Alden," she said under her breath, "will you let me help Ridge?"

"How well do you read, Jenny?"

Jenny's tanned skin went rosy. "I was 'most through the Second Reader when my last old governess quit. I brought all my school books so I've got a primer."

Teaching Ridge might inspire Jenny more than anything and even if she didn't remember much of her reluctantly acquired skill, it would get this aloof boy started. "All right. I'll start with the older boys so you may sit in Freck's place for a while."

Making sure each child had a book, Susanna told them to read till she called them, and asked Freck, Ethan, and Frank to read from whatever book each had. Freck stumbled at the start of the Third Reader so she reviewed him on the last selection of the Second, and told him to have it ready for that afternoon. Ethan breezed through the end of the Third and in the Fourth's first lesson met with only a few unfamiliar words he sounded out, so she assigned that piece and the next. Frank almost scornfully said he was in the Sixth Reader, and he was, for when she picked pages at random for him to read, he was halfway through the book before he missed a word.

It was noon, with time out for a fifteen-minute recess, by the time Susanna had heard all but the primer students. Five children were in the Second Reader—Dottie, Rosie, the Prade twins, and, to her chagrin, Jenny, for she was a year older than Rosie and three years older than Paul and Pauline. At thirteen, Charlotte almost cried at being placed in the Third Reader, but sulked less when she learned that Freck would share her recitation period. At twelve, he was a year younger than she, and barely as tall, even in his boots, but it was clear that in her eyes he was a dashing figure. Her chagrin manifested itself again when Berenice easily read in the book her older sister had yet to master and went into Fourth Reader with Ethan. Dave, Sarah, and Frank were in the Sixth Reader.

While she was listening to her pupils, Susanna was amusedly surprised at the way Sarah enforced order with the younger children. "Twins," she said, "don't hunch over that way." Later, it was, "Georgie, don't pull Helen's hair." "Dottie, get your feet off Berenice's skirt." "Rosie, don't chew on the end of your sash."

Should she intervene? Susanna wondered. None of the reprimanded children seemed to mind and all obeyed, so Susanna decided to be grateful for her unofficial aide.

Ringing the bell for attention, she said, "Line up to wash your hands and get your lunch pails, youngest children first. Stay close to the school. When you've eaten, you may play till I ring the bell. That gives you five minutes to get drinks and be ready for arithmetic."

She felt as if the morning had lasted a week.

❁ Nine ❁

The easiest way to supervise the playground was to play, so Susanna, after a hasty snack of bread and preserves, caught Helen and Berenice by the hands and cried, "Let's play Drop the Handkerchief. Georgie, you can be 'it' to start with."

"That's for little kids," scoffed Frank, giving the older ones, who stood undecided, a challenging smile. "Who's not scared to play Crack the Whip?"

Dave, Freck, Ethan, and Ridge apparently felt they had to prove themselves, and formed a chain linked by tight-clasped hands. Jenny scrambled into the dangerous position of last in line. From her circle, where Pauline hotly pursued Georgie, Susanna watched in apprehension though she wanted to leave the play period as free as possible, a time for the youngsters to work off their pent-up energy after unaccustomed hours in class.

Frank, at the head, ran across the field, surprisingly quick in his heavy work shoes, dragging the hapless Freck whose boots weren't suited to a sprint, and then, when momentum was carrying them all along, Frank veered abruptly to one side, halted, and cracked the whip by giving Freck a yank that almost jerked him off his feet. Dave, next in line, held tight, as did Ridge and Ethan, but Jenny was snapped loose and went tumbling headfirst into the dry grass. Dave and Ridge hurried to help her, but Jenny was up and laughing though the impact must have hurt her knees as much as her pride.

"Let's do it again!"

That time, she clung like a burr and it was her turn to be the head while Frank went to the bottom. Jenny, weighing perhaps eighty pounds, about half Dave's or Frank's weight, didn't have the strength to snap the column, but when she stopped, Dave, who was next to her, cracked so hard that Frank went sailing. Frank didn't snap off alone next time; Ethan went with him. On the next crack, Dave broke loose, taking the other boys with him in a scrambling, yelling heap.

Coming out from under, laughing, Dave shouted, "Teacher! Let's play Blindman's Buff. Everyone can do that."

Everyone did except Frank who disappeared in the direction of the creek. After a time, Dave, too, slipped away, but Susanna didn't know how he'd spent the rest of his free time till she came in to ring the bell and found that he had refilled the water buckets, emptied the ashes from the fireplace, and heaped the fuel basket high.

She thanked him quietly. "Shucks, ma'am," he said, blushing as if caught in a misdeed. "I'm glad to have school again, 'specially for Rosie and Georgie 'cause they never got to go in Iowa."

That afternoon, while ascertaining that Dave knew his multiplication tables through the twelves, was swift at long division, and could do simple fractions, Susanna spoke under the hum of those who were practicing their spelling aloud. "David, I could use someone to help clean the school and do chores. If you will, I could pay you two dollars a month."

His eyes lit but after a wistful glance at his feet, he shook his head. "I'll be glad to help you, Miss Alden. Be only right, since there's four of us, and we—well, I reckon we can't give you much food but cornmeal and molasses and some eggs now and then."

"That's good food and the eggs are a real treat." Susanna respected his pride, but his poor feet—"Listen, David, how about this? I'll give you a dollar a month." When he started to argue, she said firmly, "You'll more than earn it, and if you won't let me pay you that little bit, I won't let you do the chores."

The light was back in his eyes and Susanna followed up. "I want to pay you in advance each month, and you have to promise me something."

His brow furrowed and he shoved back a handful of sun-streaked light brown hair. "What's that, ma'am?"

"That your first money goes to buy you some shoes."

He winced and went crimson. "Pa was going to get me some but—something happened."

What? More than a few of Susanna's girl students' fathers had, according to Aunt Mollie, drunk more than they should have with harsh results for their families, and after those last sad, hopeless years with her father, Susanna connected many ills with alcohol. How wretched if Cash Hardy had used his wife's egg money for whiskey instead of shoes! Don't blame him too soon, she warned herself. There may have been some good reason. But Dave's embarrassment betrayed shame for his father.

"Wait after school and I'll pay you for the month," she said. "Do you suppose your neighbor will be going to town soon?"

"Jem goes 'most every week," Dave said eagerly, and returned to his seat with a buoyant tread that made Frank's green gaze fix on him in a speculative fashion that Susanna didn't like.

Soon or late, these two biggest boys would probably have a fight and Susanna, after less than a day, had to admit she wasn't impartial. She wanted Dave to win.

* * *

Ase McCanless appeared as, after filing decorously to the back of the room to get their lunch pails, the children exploded from the soddie and pelted off in all directions while those with horses went to saddle their mounts.

Catching Jenny as she streaked by, Ase scanned his daughter, evidently liked what he saw, and grinned. "Had a good day, honey?"

"Oh, Daddy, I cracked the whip! You should have seen the boys go flying—big boys! And I'm helping Ridge and—" Her face fell. "But I'm only in Second Reader! It's not fair after the way I had to study with those old giver ... governess ... ess!"

"I reckon it's fair enough," Ase drawled. "Run on and saddle Scout while I fix the doorsill." She dashed after Ridge and the Brown youngsters. Ase stared after her, glanced at the other racketing children, and, cocking his head, crossed his arms and looked at Susanna. "Well, teacher, looks like you made it through the first day."

"I guess I did." She couldn't restrain a long sigh, but smiled at the end of it. "It took more out of me than a month at the young ladies' academy, but it was more fun, too." Remembering that he was after all the head of the board of trustees, she gave him a brief report.

Ase nodded satisfaction and went to get the board and hammer he had tied behind his saddle. He drove the sill tightly in place and tried the door. Stepping inside, he surveyed the writing on the blackboard, the desks with books stored on the shelves beneath, the flag in the corner, and the extremely soiled hand towel by the wash basin. "Got everything you need?" he asked. "Except a decent building?"

"When we start penmanship, we'll need pens with steel nibs, ink, and ruled paper. It would be a big help, since some families don't get to town often, if someone bought enough for all the pupils and let the parents pay him back."

Ase gave a careless wave of his hand. "That won't amount to a hill of beans. Got enough books?"

"They're mixed up but I think we can manage."

He nodded toward her room. "Need anything for yourself?"

"If Betty could spare some old material, anything, for a curtain to hang between my quarters and the schoolroom, I'd really appreciate it. Otherwise, I'm quite comfortable, thank you."

He frowned. "I still don't like your bein' out here by yourself."

Susanna chuckled. "Actually, I had rather a lot of company yesterday evening." She told about Rawdon's gift of the medicine chest and passed lightly over Prade's visit. In case Prade spoke to Ase about Matt's being with her after dark, it was just as well to provide her account first.

"By grannies," complained Ase, rubbing his ear. "If I'd have known you were entertainin' the whole district, I'd have come, too. But that was nice of Doc. Shows he's got some normal feelin's no matter how standoffish he acts."

"Come on, Daddy!" Jenny shouted, loping up.

He looked at her with love. "So long then, Miss Alden," he said, touching the brim of his hat. "I'll stop by pretty often to see how you're gettin' along, but if you have any problems, let me know. By the way, Betty's hopin' you'll spend the weekend with us. She misses you somethin' fierce."

Behind his back, Jenny pulled a face. Susanna just smiled at her. "I'll see. It may take me all weekend to catch up for Monday."

"You don't have to go at it that hard," he said, swinging easily into the saddle and waving as he rode after his daughter. Susanna wondered if Jenny would study her reader that night. Not to mention her spelling and arithmetic. Most first-graders knew more than she had learned from those governesses—but that was scarcely the fault of her teachers.

Susanna turned to find that Dave, having washed the blackboard, was sweeping the floor. Trying to clean a dirt floor struck her as humorous but he was, with the broom donated by Betty, amassing considerable debris. Disuse had softened the earth but it wouldn't take long for the children's feet to pack it stone hard again. Dave scooped the sweepings into the ash shovel and tossed them out the door. "I filled your water bucket, Miss Alden. Anything else I can do?"

"You've thought of everything." She smiled. Going to her room, she took a dollar from her little hoard in the top dresser drawer. "Now, remember, Dave, this is for shoes," she said as she handed it to him.

"Yes, ma'am!" He touched the money as if it were a strange, wonderful, and possibly dangerous thing, folding it carefully before he put it in his pocket. "I'll get here early enough in the morning to fill the water buckets. Shall I start your fire?"

"Thanks, I'll do it later. I'm just warming up food tonight."

Collecting his reader and arithmetic book, he glanced longingly at the books on her desk. "Miss Alden, could— may I borrow the geography?"

"That's what the books are there for."

Smiling after him as he went happily off, books under his arm and the crisp dollar in his pocket, Susanna thought what a pleasure her work would be if all students were as nice and as eager to learn. On the other hand, the not-so-eager ones were certainly a challenge. Anyone could teach Dave or Sarah or Berenice. An average teacher could have fair success with most of the children. But to capture wayward Jenny; vain, supercilious Charlotte; restless Freck; and Ridge, stoically determined to endure this schooling as he might have taken part in the self-torture of the Sun Dance—well, that would take all of any teacher's skill, fortitude, humor, and ingenuity. Frank was a different problem and by far the most alarming. He had an excellent intelligence but his nature was warped. He'd taken real delight in snapping Jenny off the end of the column. It wasn't his mind that needed education, but his heart. Saul Prade had possessed his son for fourteen years and something there was very, very wrong, something that made Susanna's skin crawl worse than it had at the rattler.

Sitting at the desk, she opened her ledger, and beside each name, where she'd already recorded the pupil's position in various subjects, she added anything she'd observed that day that might help her deal better with that child. Tomorrow, each class would write the week's spelling words and she'd start the little ones at printing. The middle and older students would have geography two days a week and history for three with grammar every day. She wanted to work in nature study, perhaps as an after-lunch activity to get all the children settled down after the excitement of playing. Oh, there was so much to teach, and not enough time to do it!

As she closed the ledger, the slanting evening sun called to her, to tensed nerves and muscles aching from the strain of the day. A walk to the creek would do her good, a glimpse of the blackbirds, a chat with the crows, who, like the meadowlark, were old Ohio neighbors.

Shutting the door behind her, she was reassured at how snugly it fitted now to the sill. With luck, there'd be no more snakes in the soddie. As she approached the creek, the nearest red-winged blackbirds rose in a flurry but the yellow-headed ones continued to perch in the reeds and cattails of the little marsh. In the fine sand at the crossing, she could see the tracks of the Hardy children, including Dave's barefooted ones, and a whole museum of damp hieroglyphs.

The dog-like ones were doubtless coyote, and those three- and four-pronged ones must be birds, but what were the long, plain, pointed ones? What were those graceful loose spirals? And these like tiny hands with pointed nail tips? Here was perfect nature study—if she could find a teacher. The children would probably know some of the prints, but since Ridge was part Cheyenne, she immediately wondered if he might not be their track expert. If he could teach the rest of them something, that would be good for everybody.

Intrigued, Susanna followed some curious tracks through the sand, pushing willows aside. There was a small irregular round print and above it, slightly to the side, five tiny marks. Then, descending from the bank, were shoe tracks. They blotted out the odd, delicate prints, and then—

Susanna stopped, freezing. A beautifully patterned yellow-green shell was caved in, the bloody pulp buzzing with flies and insects. But the turtle hadn't died quickly, by an accident. The legs had been torn off and the head, tossed under some willows, looked as if it had been yanked off the body.

Frank had been off in this direction most of the noon hour. That shot through Susanna's reeling thoughts as she whirled to run, get away from the horrible sight. Retching, she leaned against a cottonwood tree, shuddering, sickened, unable to believe what she had seen. To deliberately— It was too awful.

Clammy face pressed against the rough bark, she wept. How could anyone be so cruel? If Frank had done it, and he almost certainly had, how could she bear to look at him, how could she try to teach things that he mocked by his very existence? She was still sobbing when she heard the rumble of a wagon.

Who could that be? Of all the wretched times for someone to come along! In her shocked flight, she'd splashed and muddied her shoes and skirts. Her impulse was to hide, but whoever it was might be coming to her place. After making her way through the willows, she reached the crossing as Matt Rawdon's buckboard rattled down the opposite bank.

Then she wished she had hidden, but it was too late now to do anything but give her face a swift wipe on her sleeve and wait while the team splashed across.

"Been having a wade?" he asked, staring at her draggled skirts. Then his gaze came to her face. "What on earth?"

Reaching over, he swung her up on the seat beside him. She was instantly welcomed by a wagging plumy tail and fervent licks from a red tongue, both belonging to a large black dog with cinnamon trim on face, chest, and feathery forelegs, a white patch on his chest like an old-time courtier's neckcloth, tulip-leaf ears, and a broad forehead. "This is Hank," Rawdon said. "I thought he'd be better protection than a door curtain, and lots better company. But what's the matter? Were the little devils that bad?"

She shook her head, unable to speak. Rawdon clucked to the horses and they moved up the bank. When they reached the soddie, he hitched the team to one of the posts supporting the well windlass. She scrambled down, followed by the dog who set off on a sniffing tour of the premises. Rawdon didn't touch Susanna but barred the way in front of her while the wagon was at her back.

"All right, teacher. If it's not the kids, what is it?"

It was a relief to let it pour out, though what would he, a battlefield surgeon, think of her squeamishness? "Why would he do it?" Her voice broke, and seeing the sadistic ugliness again, she turned away to grip the wagon in an effort to quell the sickness that again scalded her throat. "Why?"

"You could spend your life asking that," Rawdon said. "Why does a baby die at birth? Why did boys only a few years older than some you're teaching get blown to pieces or crippled in the war?"

"That's different. I certainly wondered why my father had to suffer as he did after he'd spent his life trying to ease others. I asked why the man I loved was killed. Those are the whys one asks God. But this—it wasn't fate and it wasn't war. There was absolutely no reason. Frank or whoever it was just did it to torture something."

"So there's your why."

"No. Why did he want to? How could he? And what can I do about it?"

"Talk to his parents?"

Susanna shivered. "I'd hate for his mother to know. And Saul Prade—he'd cut me some more switches."

"What will you do?"

"I don't know, except that I won't let Frank leave the playground again."

Rawdon watched her with a strange expression that made her intensely uncomfortable. Was this the way a physician scrutinized a hysteria-inclined patient? His eyes changed, lit by the inner glow that penetrated to her depths and then, like sun warmth in her veins, suffused her every nerve. Shaken like a tree swayed by an imperious wind, Susanna broke the spell by moving past him and looking at the dog who was still investigating the surroundings with now and then a judicious lift of his leg before he trotted on, ruff, tail, and the fringes of his forelegs giving him a jaunty, gallant air that reminded her of a cavalier, all frothy lace and plumes.

"Are you really giving him to me?"

"If you want him."

"He's wonderful! But I can't take your dog."

"He hasn't been mine long and from the way he greeted you, I think he'll consider it a good swap. He belonged to an old lady who died a few months ago. She asked me to take care of him but I don't need him."

The dog rejoined them, lifting his muzzle adoringly to Rawdon and lavishing dog kisses on his hand. "I think you do need him," Susanna said, caressing the smooth domed space between the pricked-up ears. "Oh, he's lovely!"

"I'm not afraid of ghoulies and ghosties, long-leggety beasties and things that go bump in the night." Rawdon laughed. "Don't be so rock-ribbed, Miss Alden. Hank's used to ladies. Besides, he thinks it's great sport to chase my horses and that's likely to get him kicked in the head."

"If you'll let me buy him—"

"*Buy* a dog, ma'am? How can you buy a wagging tail and that glad heart? If you hadn't taken to each other, I'd have whistled him home and never said a word." Going to the wagon, he tossed a rug off an object and lifted it out. "Mrs. Slade, Hank's mistress, didn't have any close kin and since I sort of took care of her, she left me her belongings. I don't need this rocking chair, or the hooked rug, either."

"You don't need a dog. You don't need a chair. You don't need a rug." Susanna shook her head in exasperation. "Is that a point of honor with you? Not to be human like the rest of us and need or want?"

"Take the confounded chair or I'll use it for kindling."

She gasped. The chair, maple burnished by years of use, was carved at the top and on the arms with birds and flowers. It wasn't just a chair. It had been crafted with love and as its mellow, waxed grain testified, cherished as it was used.

"Kindling! That would be—be wicked!"

"Then you'd better rescue it."

"You have to let me pay something—"

"Is that your point of honor?" he asked roughly. "Always to pay?"

She threw back her head. "Yes, it is and I don't see what's wrong with that, Dr. Rawdon."

They glared at each other. After a moment, his mouth curved down as if he were trying not to grin. "Would a highly educated lady like you take offense at being asked if she can sew on buttons?"

"She would not, sir, and she is, in fact, quite practiced at it for both her father and uncle were notable shedders of buttons. But it wouldn't equal the value of the chair if I sewed on buttons for you for the rest of our lives."

Too late, she realized how that sounded, how domestic, how—married—and she colored hotly. He must have, too, for a smile lurked in his eyes though his tone was serious. "Ah, you haven't seen the shirts I've been stuffing in a bag when they lost their buttons, ever since poor old Mrs. Slade got too blind to sew three years ago."

"Three *years*?"

"Disgraceful, isn't it?" He displayed his coat cuffs and shook the front of his dark gray coat. "Nary a button left, ma'am, and winter's coming on."

She frowned. "Did you know one of your elbows is worn almost through?"

"No!" He twisted his neck in order to see. "Dratted poor material!"

"I think I can darn it so it would hardly show." Susanna longed for the chair and he would scarcely have cut off all his buttons in order to fabricate a job for her. "The chair's an heirloom, worth at least five dollars. My wage works out to about fifteen cents an hour. I'll keep track of how long your sewing takes and when I've put in thirty-three—no, thirty-four hours, I'll feel I've earned the chair."

"Yankees," he said, shaking his head.

"Now, about the rug—"

He fended her off. "Those yellow roses are fine for ladies but I turned it upside down for Hank to sleep on. Mrs. Slade would much rather have it appreciated."

She could well believe that he was just that philistine and argued no further. After all, Hank—that was an awful name and if he was agreeable, she was going to change it—could still sleep on it, right side up by her bed, and it would go perfectly with Aunt Mollie's quilt and the curtains. She got it and followed Rawdon as he carried the rocker into her room.

"That'll give you the best light in the day for sewing on my buttons," he teased, situating it near the window. "And this winter, you can pull in close to the fire." Hank had come after them. When Susanna spread the thick, cushiony rug by the bed, he lay down, nose between his paws, and thumped his tail.

"He approves of the arrangement," Rawdon said.

Probably because he thinks you're staying, too, along with rug, rocker, and him, Susanna thought.

Their eyes met. Her heart caught, stopped, then beat like the frantic wings of a trapped bird. "Let's go outside." His voice was rough, husky. "I want to hear how the first day went, but God knows we'd better not be inside if one of your trustees comes snooping around—though I see by the doorsill that Ase McCanless has already been by."

"He's chairman of the board," returned Susanna stiffly. What right did he have to almost sneer about any male visitor she might have? "It's his responsibility to see that the building's in good repair."

"I'm sure he'll do that." Hank had padded after them and now, in puzzlement, nosed at Rawdon's hand as if to say, What's the matter? I thought we were all cozy and comfortable. Absently stroking the dog, Rawdon stared at where the sun was lost in streamers of red, gold, and purple clouds that blazed across the whole western horizon, painting the grass a ruddy bronze. "Tell me. No battles between North and South? No jeers at homesteader kids' bare feet from high-heeled, booted ranchers' sons?"

"Freck Brown's the only one in boots," Susanna said. "But, oh, Dr. Rawdon, of all the children, it was Dave Hardy, the oldest, who didn't have shoes. After Margaret Hardy saved up eggs enough to buy him a pair."

"Damn Cash! Him and his bottle!"

So that was what had happened. "I'll get the kid some shoes," Rawdon said in a tight, angry voice.

"And lose the buttons I sew on so Mrs. Hardy can sew them back?" Susanna said. She laughed at his sheepish grin and went on to explain that Dave was working for her. "Which will give me more time to do your mending," she finished merrily.

He chuckled but there was a twist of bitterness to his mouth. "Makes you wonder why a scamp like Cash got such a bunch of good kids. There's no harm in him but he's too lazy to scratch fleas and that shrapnel he caught gives him an excuse for both loafing around and drinking."

"My father drank to numb his pain," she said defensively.

"Sure. I did, too, till the worst was over." She was sure he was talking about more than his hand, or even the war. "But if I had any one of those Hardy kids—" He broke off. "Well, they're Margaret's pride and I reckon they'll look after her—and Cash, too—when they're grown. How did you fare with the redoubtable Jenny?"

She told him about Jenny's poor scholastic rating and how gamely she'd been the tail of the whip. Then, since he seemed truly interested, she told him about the rest of the day's perplexities and small triumphs.

"At least there weren't any fights." She gave him a challenging smile. "I may not need my fare back to Ohio."

"Too soon to guess about that," he warned, but he chuckled. "What if some trustee comes along and finds you playing Ring Around the Rosie?"

"I'd ask him to join us," she retorted.

"That'd be a sight for sore eyes! Ase McCanless or Will Taylor hoofing it with the primer class!" The sun disappeared, colors flaming in a last wild glory before they began to ebb. "I've got to get along and do my chores. You don't have to worry much about feeding Hank. When he's hungry, he'll hunt up a rabbit. Good night, Miss Alden."

Unhitching the reins, he climbed up. The dog lingered, looking hopefully from Susanna to Rawdon, but when Rawdon spoke to the horses, Hank, with a regretful glance at Susanna, prepared to jump into the wagon.

"No, boy," Rawdon said. Reaching down, he patted the black head. "I'll bring you a bone sometimes but you're to stay with the lady. Stay." He said the last word emphatically and started the team.

As the wagon swung around, the dog watched, head atilt, ears up, tail drooped, and made soft little whimperings that sounded odd coming from his husky body. Susanna bent to hug him. "If you miss him too much, I'll send you back to him. But I'm so glad to have you. Not just because I'm a scaredy-cat at night, but because you're so beautiful and friendly. Would you mind if I called you Cavalier? Cav, for short?"

He kissed her hands but gazed after the wagon till it crossed the creek and rumbled out of sight. Susanna watched, too, suddenly feeling very lonely, wishing Matt had stayed for supper though she had much to do in preparation for the next day.

Suddenly cold in the gathering twilight, she stroked her new companion, scratched him behind the ears, and started for the soddie. "Come, boy!" she invited. "Come, Cavalier!"

He followed, head and tail lowered dejectedly, and she felt a qualm. It wasn't fair that animals were so at the mercy of people. She eased her conscience by thinking that if he wanted enough to disobey, he could run after Matt. Anyway, if the dog grieved and wouldn't eat after the first few days, she'd insist his master take him back.

Cav at once took up his place on the rug, pointing his nose between his cinnamon paws. His eyes, mournful now, watched Susanna as she built the fire and put the teakettle and her supper on to heat. Even if Cav was self-supporting—she felt sorry for the rabbits but knew there was no reasonable way to keep him from hunting them since he was used to it—she wanted to feed him something; but what? In Pleasant Grove, Mr. Meigs, the butcher, had always saved bones for her beloved spaniel, Tip, who'd died of old age three years ago. Longing for another pet, she hadn't gotten one because her father was in no condition to look after a dog while she was teaching and he loathed cats.

"How about some spoon bread, Cav? With some of Mr. Borden's milk?"

That brought a tail thump. She dedicated one of her two serving bowls to his use, filled it, and set it down, calling him. He wolfed it, assiduously licked up every crumb, and waited.

"That's all for now, boy." Recognizing finality in her voice, he resumed his usual pose, but later, after Susanna had eaten and done the dishes and pulled the rocker near the lamp so she could prepare next day's lessons, he forsook the rug and came to lie at her feet, this time crossing his paws and resting his muzzle on them.

What a difference his presence made! As she worked, Susanna talked to him, and, depending on her tone, he gave her a consoling look or let his tail thud agreement.

Thankful as she was to have him, what she had seen that afternoon along the creek kept rising between the ledger and books and her gaze. The best exorcism was to relive the time with Matt, remember the way his long, straight mouth quirked downward in that half-smile that was beginning to tug at her heart. But that was a dangerous solace when he seemed so determined to avoid attachments, even to a dog. It was interesting, though, that he'd tended old Mrs. Slade despite his protests that he no longer practiced.

She bent and stroked Cavalier, talking to him the while, praising him so extravagantly that he got up and pressed his head on her knees, whisking his tail. When she went to bed, he lay on the rug.

It was a blessed mercy that he was there for the crushed turtle haunted her, the sight wresting her from near sleep and bringing back the worry of what to do about it. Touching Cavalier helped, knowing he was there, and there because Matt Rawdon, for all his cynicism, had wanted her to feel safer and not be alone.

Bless him, she thought. No matter how stiff and difficult he could be, he had a good heart and she wished him happy. With that in her mind and her hand on Cavalier's back, she at last drifted past that threshold where a flash of horror could rouse her, and fell into sleep.

❀ *Ten* ❀

Dave's merry whistling accompanied Susanna's breakfast the next morning. Cav had heralded his coming with a throaty growl. Susanna, peering out the window, saw it was Dave inspecting the privies. She quieted the dog with a word and let him out to make friends. They raced and tussled as Dave went about his chores, Cav ecstatic at the roughhousing.

"So Doc Rawdon gave you his dog," said Dave as he brought in the water buckets. "We had one, Rover, but a rattler bit him in the nose last year and it killed him." At her dismayed look, Dave added as he tousled Cav's ears, "Generally a bite won't kill a full-grown dog and having a dog around helps keep snakes away." His smile was pure joy. "Miss Alden, Jem's going to town tomorrow. He'll get my shoes. Mother was so tickled she didn't know what to say when I told her about my job but she sure does thank you."

"You're earning every cent," Susanna said with a smile, and began to write the day's assignments on the board.

Jenny came in with a bundle which she thrust ungraciously at Susanna. "From Betty," she said. "She got out the sewing machine last night and sewed the dratted thing up instead of making me molasses candy."

"Maybe she'll make the candy tonight," Susanna said. "Thanks for bringing it."

"I had to," Jenny shrugged. "Oh, there's Ridge!" She ran out, leaving Susanna to wonder if the badly spoiled child was ever going to get over her hostility.

However that might be, Susanna was glad to have the curtain, especially when she unrolled the paper wrapping and found it was a pleasing shade of silvery green chintz. She could scarcely wait to see it in place but it was time already to ring the first bell. When school took up, Cav settled himself as guardian of the door, near enough the water buckets for children to give him a quick pat as they went for drinks. That morning they sang songs of the Gold Rush, "Sweet Betsy from Pike" and "Oh, Susanna!" which gave an opening to talk about how the nation had spread westward, not only in quest of riches as in 1849, but just as their parents had, in a steadier, quieter search for homes.

"We were already west," Jenny boasted, when Susanna called on her to tell where her people had come from. "We came up here to get away from Reconstruction. My great-grandfather was in Texas before Stephen F. Austin, and grandpa helped whip Santa Anna at San Jacinto and two of his brothers died at the Alamo. Way, way back, Daddy told me, not long after the English cut off Charles the First's head, that bloody old Cromwell beat the Scots at Dunbar. A McCanless was one of the soldiers he kept locked up for almost a year and then sent to slave in the Carolina plantations. He married an Irish girl who'd been shipped over as a bond servant, too, after Cromwell took Drogheda. They worked off their indentures and worked and saved till they could buy a farm. A bunch of their great-grandsons fought with Washington against the British and we won that war! Some of the family settled early in Tennessee and some of them came to Texas." She glanced around in proud and challenging fashion, yellow hair garnering such light as there was. "And now we're here!"

"That's a history in itself, Jenny," Susanna said. "As a year-long history and composition project, some of you might like to write down all you can find out about your families. It would make a wonderful gift for your parents and be something to treasure. Wouldn't you like to have a family book written by your great-grandparents?"

That brought a chorus of excited yeses. Berenice gave the devotion, the Twenty-third Psalm, and after writing down names of volunteers for the next day's opening exercises, including Freck who wanted to bring his guitar and sing a Texas song, Susanna started the primer class at printing their names. Then she heard the large Second Reader class. The twins, Dottie, and Rosie had obviously studied and they read their paragraphs without a bobble, but Jenny floundered through, snagging on a number of words and not knowing how to sound them out.

"Sarah," Susanna said, when the lesson was over, "do you have time to help Jenny for a while?"

"I'm supposed to help Ridge!" Jenny protested.

"You can't help anyone much till you learn more," Susanna said equably.

Dave, without being asked, was already working with Ridge. Jenny sulked, but Sarah, used to shepherding the twins, firmly took charge. Without such help, there was no way Susanna could possibly teach all subjects to all grades, but she resolved to make sure Dave and Sarah got plenty of instruction for they had bright, inquiring minds and perhaps might go on to higher educations. Even if they couldn't, she wanted to teach them as much as possible so that whatever their occupation or circumstances, they would go on enjoying the pleasure of learning.

The morning flew, but as she flashed multiplication cards, showed little hands how to shape the lines and circles that comprised printed letters, heard reading classes, gave out spelling words, and began Ethan and Berenice in division, Frank's cold-eyed, watchful presence, and what she was sure he had done, tormented her.

Should she confront him? She decided against that since she had no hope of shaming him or making him sorry. He knew his lessons perfectly, reciting in a bored manner that stopped just short of insolence but he never offered to assist the younger pupils, not even Paul and Pauline. Susanna noticed that the gentle, tow-haired twins seemed to keep out of the way of their older brother though they frequently appealed to Sarah.

It was a wonder to Susanna how the kind, sensible girl could be born of the same parents as Frank. All they had in common was intelligence and unusual comeliness. Even though Charlotte was charmed by Freck's cowboy glamor, she missed no chance to parade archly past Frank. As for Sarah, Dave blushed every time she looked at him and Ridge watched her with a sort of wonder.

At noon, Susanna rang the bell for attention. "Most of you prepared your lessons and have done very well this morning," she said. "Remember, your parents are invited Friday afternoon and though they won't expect a lot this first week, wouldn't it be fun to surprise them?"

Jenny scowled, Frank looked superior, and Ridge like a tethered, long-suffering hawk, but the rest of the students cheered and clapped. As they rose to file to the wash basin and lunches, Susanna said, "I'm responsible for you during school hours. No one is to leave the school ground. That means to stay in plain sight."

Frank stared at her, a taunting glint in his eyes, and when he passed outside, she heard him say under his breath to Dave, "Next thing she'll want us to play with the babies."

"I like my little brother," Dave returned good-naturedly and Susanna thanked her lucky stars that Frank seemed to have no aiders or abettors.

As if he recognized this, too, Frank, after lunch, played Red Rover with the bigger children. No linked hands could keep him from breaking through, not even those of Dave and Ridge, but that was how the game was played. However, Susanna noticed that Dave, who also repeatedly broke through the human barrier, moderated his charges so that he didn't knock smaller playmates sprawling and though he held fast against Sarah when she was called to "come over," he gave way suspiciously to Rosie or Jenny or Berenice. Even with that tempering, all the girls except Jenny soon had enough of the rough game and joined Susanna and the younger children at London Bridge while the older boys turned to playing leapfrog.

That excluded Jenny who couldn't, because of her skirts, set her hands on a kneeling person's shoulders and vault over. Snippily refusing to join the other game, she stood around till Cav approached. The next time Susanna looked, Jenny was tossing a piece of knotted rope for the dog to retrieve. When he pranced back with it, Jenny's laughter shrilled as she tugged and tussled with him for the rope. After a time, good humor restored, she slipped into the circle to play Go In and Out the Window quite happily till the five-minute bell.

For nature study, instead of coming inside, Susanna had them stay in the shade of the building while she read part of Whitman's *Leaves of Grass:*

> *"I guess it must be the flag of my disposition, out*
> *of hopeful green stuff woven.*
> *Or I guess it is the handkerchief of the Lord..."*

"Grass is all around us and we take it for granted," she said. "Without it, though, life on this earth would end except for that in the waters. Every blade of grass performs a miracle no chemist can. A man named Stephen Hales found out about the magic of grass over a hundred years ago. He learned that plants turn sunlight into food and produce the green that scientists call chlorophyll. Other chemists continued his work, including Justus von Liebig who wrote on artificial fertilizers. Von Liebig also discovered chloroform, which has been such a blessing for people undergoing operations."

She would have liked to add that the Queen of England, Victoria, allowed her physician to give her chloroform during the birth of Prince Leopold, which assured the anesthetic's acceptance, but childbirth was not a subject to discuss with children. Indeed it was a matter spoken of only among married women, although growing up with a blunt doctor father had made Susanna cognizant of a great many facts respectable ladies either didn't know or pretended not to.

Freck's hand went up. "I don't know anything about chlor . . . whatever that green stuff is, but I can sure tell you bluestem and grama and buffalo grass are good grazing while dropseed and wiregrass ain't—I mean, aren't."

"Maybe everyone but me knows the grasses and prairie plants," Susanna said. "Why don't you all go see how many kinds of plants you can find in five minutes, and then *you* can teach me for a change."

All the children, even often-tearful dark little Helen Taylor, knew some of the assembled specimens. But, except for Dottie, the ranch children were experts, differentiating between six kinds of bluestem, sideoats grama, blue grama, and woolly grama, and an amazing number of other plants that blended into the prairie.

"This one ought to be pulled out by the roots when anybody sees it," warned Freck, holding up a plant with drying seed pods and stems and leaves covered with thick, fine whitish hairs. "It's woolly locoweed. Some horses get so they won't eat anything else and it'll give them the staggers. It poisons cattle, too, if they get enough of it."

Thanking Freck and the others for the lesson, Susanna led the way inside and wove the history-geography lesson around how ancient the practices of herding and farming were, how civilization was cradled in fertile lands along rivers, and how there had been disputes about grazing ranges as far back as Abraham and his nephew, Lot, and doubtless much earlier than that.

There followed a round of classes—grammar, composition, and more reading. Before Susanna knew it, the clock hands showed four. As she saw the children off and Dave went about his tasks, Frank loitered behind his sisters and the Taylor girls. When Susanna was alone, he strode back to her.

Wild thoughts streaked through her head. He was taller than she, heavier, and without a doubt, much stronger. But he wouldn't dare, surely, to offer her violence. In spite of knowing that, and having Dave within calling distance, she felt true physical fear as he halted only a few feet away. It was as if his father gazed mockingly out of those brilliant green eyes, as if his father animated him.

"Teacher." His tone, though soft, was just on the edge of impudence. "May I ask you something?"

"Of course, Frank." What else could she say?

"Did you take a walk along the creek after school yesterday?"

"I did. And I think you know what I found."

He smiled and shrugged. "Thought you must have, the way you told us to stay where you could watch us."

Too horrified to refrain though she knew she was feeding something sick and dreadful in him, she caught his shoulders and barely kept herself from giving him a shake. "Why did you do it?"

Her intensity took him aback. Sounding more like a child, he shrugged again. "It was just a turtle."

"It was alive! And you killed it, tortured it, for no reason! How could you do it, Frank?"

He pulled free of her. "You want to see something messy, teacher, come over next month when we butcher a hog." As she stared at him, wordless, he chuckled. "You'd hate that, too, teacher, but I bet you'll eat the bacon and ham we bring you."

"There's a big difference in killing for food and for fun."

"Doubt if it makes much never-mind to the hog." Dave came out to fill the fuel basket. Frank turned away. "Goodbye, teacher," he threw over his shoulder.

Susanna stood as if rooted till Cavalier pushed close to her, licking her hand, demanding with an insistently waving tail that she now pay him some attention.

Automatically stroking him, she told herself she could not, must not, be afraid of one of her pupils. But she was. Of him, and for him. Cold to the heart, she went inside and picked up the green curtain.

"Dave," she called. "Will you help me hang this, please?" It would shield her from the chance peering-in of nocturnal passersby; but what protection was there against the cruelty she sensed in Prade and saw manifested by his son?

Susanna, a little breathless because of her corset, which seemed even more intolerable after a blissful week without it, was still playing Fox and Geese with the children when the first wagon appeared on Friday afternoon. "Hurry, children!" she called, cupping her hands to reach the big boys (and Jenny), who were playing ball with one Dave had made by stitching leather around a grass-padded rock. "Get your drinks, tidy up, and let's be ready for our visitors!"

The Taylors rolled up first in a buckboard fitted with a canvas shade and Delia's side cushioned with pillows. When Will helped his wife down, she ignored Cavalier, who'd trotted out to meet the guests, put her hand to her back, and by way of greeting said accusingly to Susanna, "That jarring and jolting will give my back miseries for days, but the girls begged so hard that I had to come."

"I'll have Dave bring my rocker for you," Susanna said,

wishing she could suggest that lacing as tightly as Delia did must have dismal results on anyone's internal organs. "That'll be more comfortable."

"Nothing will help much." Delia sighed. She untied her ruffled sunbonnet and touched her light blond hair with a graceful hand so white and well kept that Susanna had to wonder if Will did the washing. "I only pray God gives me strength to live till my precious girls are grown."

This, coming from a woman only six or seven years her elder, dumbfounded Susanna and then exasperated her, especially when Will, gazing at his wife with worried adoration in his black eyes, helped her sit in the chair as if she were an invalid.

Susanna thought, maybe she does have a painful spine, but it's too bad for three little girls to think that's what it is to be a woman. With relief, she hurried to embrace Betty who entered ahead of Ase. He was scratching Cav behind the ears before he straightened, saw the flag in the corner, and frowned. Next came the Prades, Laura in a violet dress that matched her shining eyes, Saul filling the door. His smooth, hard face was unreadable though his eyes, as he nodded slightly to Susanna, fixed on her with the vigilance of an eagle sighting prey.

Susanna tried to disguise the discomfort he roused in her by moving the recitation bench closer to the wall and to the water bench, which had been cleared to accommodate guests. With Susanna's desk chair, that made enough seating for those crowding into the soddie. Margaret Hardy, unlaced but slender and pretty in her clean, faded, pale green dress, introduced the graying man with her as their neighbor, Jem Howe.

"Cash isn't feeling good," she said. "Jem was interested and Dave thought it'd be all right for him to come."

"Everyone's welcome." Susanna at once liked this older man with keen gray eyes who *had* brought Dave the shoes he now wore so proudly. The Browns arrived just then, Hettie patting her bonnet-mussed brownish red hair into place, and Kermit, as Ase had, scowling at the flag before, with obvious effort, he spoke courteously to Susanna.

The men all knew each other at least by sight but the ranch women had never met those from the homesteads. Hettie, taking Betty in tow, went over to meet Margaret Hardy who introduced them to Delia Taylor and Laura Prade.

"Glad we're gettin' more womenfolks," boomed Hettie. "When we first came, there wasn't another white woman in miles—"

She choked off, coloring as Luke Tarrant limped in with a woman whose proud head wore no bonnet. Carved cheekbones emphasized by the way her lustrous black hair was drawn back in a coiled loop secured by silver ornaments, Millie Tarrant was straight and graceful as a young cottonwood. Her dark eyes tilted slightly upwards and her sweet red mouth and creamy warm brown skin made the other women, except for tanned Margaret Hardy, look florid or too pale. She wore a high-necked beige poplin gown patterned in buff stripes alternating with small yellow roses, and trimmed with dark brown braid. The skirt stood out as if reinforced by the requisite petticoats, but she wore no bustle, not even the small pad Susanna had tied around her own waist that morning for this special day. Every feminine eye in the room went from that lovely face to moccasins peeking from beneath the skirts. As Luke introduced her, Millie Tarrant put out a shapely hand and pressed Susanna's.

"I am happy, Miss Alden, to make your acquaintance," she said in perfect though accented English. Of course! She'd gone to convent school in St. Louis while Luke waited for her to grow up; she'd probably had a better education than any woman here except Susanna. She added so softly no one else could hear, "Thank you for being kind to our son. School he cannot like yet but you make it tolerable."

"I hope it'll get better than that for him, and soon," Susanna replied as quietly.

She introduced the Cheyenne woman to the homesteaders' wives. Millie bowed and spoke with civility but didn't offer her hand, nor did any of them, though Laura Prade and Margaret Hardy smiled in friendly fashion and exchanged pleasantries. Delia Taylor sat stiff as a poker, hands gripping the arms of the rocking chair. Luke ushered his wife along the recitation bench to sit by Ase who rose to greet her. Though the women were chatting, largely through Hettie's and Margaret's efforts, the cattlemen and farmers, after brief acknowledgements of each other's existence, conversed with their own kind, ranchers about cattle, homesteaders about crops. What they had in common, Susanna detected, was a wish for rain and the hope it wouldn't be a harsh winter.

Going to stand by her desk, Susanna smiled around at the visitors who hastily took seats if they hadn't already, and, yes, they were divided, ranchfolk on the recitation bench, homesteaders on the water bench, rocker, and teacher's chair.

"Welcome to our school, and thank you for coming. As I explained when I called on you, these Friday afternoons aren't programs, but a review of some of the week's work along with a little fun. To begin with, we'll have the week's devotions and the songs we've sung. If you know the words, please join in."

The devotions ranged from Dave's choice of "Tiger, Tiger" by William Blake to Rosie's Twenty-third Psalm. How glad Susanna was that Dave, like the other children, had on shoes as he stood up in front. Freck began the singing by strumming his guitar as he sang a song that had plenty of Texas geography in it, for it named most of the rivers. It had caught the fancy of even the Northern children and they, and the former Texans, sang along in spirited glee.

"I crossed the broad Pecos, forded the Nueces,
Swam the Guadalupe and followed the Brazos,
Red River runs rusty, the Wichita clear.
Down by the Brazos I courted my dear.

La la la lee, give me your hand—"

By the time they finished all the verses, all the home-steaders except Prade and Delia Taylor were joining in on the chorus. That warmed everyone up for the songs they all knew, and for twenty minutes the soddie was filled with voices that didn't blend too well but to Susanna's ears sounded sweeter than any choir she'd ever heard. If the Mason-Dixon school patrons could sing together, it was a start.

Next, the children who'd talked about family origins that week went to the map in turn to point to the countries their forebears had hailed from. All had at least one ancestor from Scotland, Ireland, England, or Wales, but Sarah and the twins pointed also to France while the Taylors added Holland and Denmark. Jenny touched Sweden as well as Orkney and Scotland, and Freck and Dottie had a Hessian soldier in their ancestry.

Smiling especially at Will Taylor, Susanna said, "In geography and history this term, we're going to study the countries our people came from, and why they did, so that when we begin American history next term, it will mean more."

Spelling came next, the students standing in a line while Susanna gave each one a word studied that week till every pupil had spelled five words. The primer class—dark little Helen Taylor, ebullient Georgie, and Ridge—had learned the alphabet, long and short sounds, and were printing and spelling easy words like *cat* and *dog* which Susanna now gave out to Helen and Georgie. Looking ahead to this performance, she'd asked Ridge if he wouldn't like to learn some harder words.

"Like *eagle*?" he asked, sudden interest lighting those hazel eyes, so startling and attractive in his brown face. *"Hawk? Warrior?"*

"You tell me words you want to learn. I'll print them, and I'm sure Dave will help you practice." So now, only four days later, Ridge stood between Ethan and Frank and, to his parents' evident astonishment and delight, spelled words suitable to his age.

Charlotte, flighty and excited, missed words she'd spelled that morning. Freck and Jenny also did poorly, Freck because he had trouble, as he put it, bending his mind to books, and Jenny because she simply wouldn't study. Susanna had resisted the temptation to give the two easier words. If Ridge, with no reading background at all, could spell *coyote* and *honor,* Jenny and Freck, with more effort, could have mastered their lists. Berenice Taylor's plain little face glowed, and so did Will's, as she spelled the hardest fourth-grade words. She also distinguished herself in solving multiplication problems at the blackboard. Ethan, the other fourth-grader, was just as accurate, but he was slower.

In sixth-grade long division, Sarah, Dave, and Frank were evenly matched as they were in most subjects. Freck, because he saw a use for it, worked at arithmetic and was already so far ahead of Charlotte that Susanna thought he'd eventually catch up with Ethan and Berenice. That was a great advantage of a school like this. It wasn't necessary to wait till the end of the year to advance a pupil, nor was any real problem created when, like Freck, one read and spelled at high second-grade level but was close to fourth-grade arithmetic. It was a boon, though, to have two grades where a number of students could do the same assignments and recite together as did the twins, Jenny, Rosie, and Dottie in second and Sarah, Dave, and Frank in sixth.

At five till four, Susanna told the last cipherers to take their seats. "Why don't we close with a song or two?" she asked the assembly.

"Let's sing a Kansas song." Will Taylor grinned and looked at Freck. "Young man, if you can play 'Beulah Land,' we're all set. Bet most everyone except the teacher knows 'Kansas Land.'"

Freck strummed and Will, in a rich tenor, led a song that was indeed new to Susanna but familiar to the others, even the ranchers. Saul didn't sing, nor did Delia Taylor, whose mouth had been set in vexed tightness ever since Charlotte fumbled her spelling.

> *"Oh Kansas land, sweet Kansas land,*
> *As on your burning sands I stand,*
> *I look away across the plains*
> *And wonder why it never rains,*
> *We do not live but only stay,*
> *We are too poor to move away!"*

There was more, and when the song was finished, Jem Howe called, "How about 'Government Claim'? Sing it with Ford in front of the county name, and it fits like a glove."

Again, everyone but Susanna knew the words.

> *"Hurrah for Ford County, the land of the free,*
> *The home of the bedbug, grasshopper and flea,*
> *I'll sing of its praises and boast of its fame,*
> *While starving to death on my government*
>   *claim!"*

By the end of the many verses, though, she could join

in on the chorus. She'd have to write down the words and send them to Aunt Mollie and Uncle Frank.

"Next time," said Ase good-naturedly, "we're goin' to sing 'Get Along, Little Dogies' and 'Chisholm Trail.'" He stretched, rising from the recitation bench which had surely cramped his legs. "Thanks for havin' us, Miss Alden." He glanced around at the other visitors. "Think we hired the right lady?"

Saul Prade did not join in the applause. Delia, on her way out, paused long enough to give Susanna an aggrieved look. "Some children, like my Charlotte, are high-strung and sensitive, Miss Alden. I don't think they should be forced to perform in front of a lot of strangers."

"Would you prefer she stay at her desk, Mrs. Taylor?"

"That would be worse," snapped Delia, red spots burning on her cheeks. "It would look as if she were in disgrace or stupid or ... or ..."

"Lazy," blurted Will, coming in from hitching up the wagon. At his wife's indignant glare, he ducked his head a little, but he held his ground. "Charlotte won't study, wife. Berenice does, even little Helen, and I don't reckon it hurts a bit for there to be a time like this when they show what they can do." As she stared at him, open-mouthed, Will took her arm and gently but firmly steered her toward their wagon.

Margaret Hardy clasped Susanna's hand, amber eyes sparkling and dimples showing. "I'm just so proud of my young ones," she said. "They bring home their books every night and study like a game, they're so tickled to have a school and nice teacher. Ethan reads better than me or Cash and Rosie's catching up." Lowering her voice, she murmured, "I can't thank you enough for giving Dave that work, but he'd be glad to do it anyway, you know."

"He helps so much with the younger children that I sometimes think he deserves half my salary." Susanna laughed.

Jem Howe was waiting. Tipping his hat in smiling farewell to Susanna, he escorted Margaret to his wagon with an attentiveness that made Susanna think it a shame that he wasn't her husband instead of Cash, the only one of the whole community that Susanna hadn't met.

"It was lovely, dear!" cried Betty, hugging her. "It did my heart good to see all those children showing what they'd learned. Now you will come home with us, won't you? Ase or Johnny'll bring you back Sunday evening." She patted Cavalier. "Your dog can follow along."

"I'd love to visit," Susanna said. "But I haven't caught up all week so I'd better stay here and do that. Thank you so much, Betty, for sending that curtain."

"Glad to do it, honey, and you let me know if there's anything else you need. We'll count on you coming home with us in a week or two." She chuckled at the sight of Jenny tucking books into her saddle bag. "Our young lady didn't like havin' her daddy see that everybody in her class can outspell her and do sums faster."

"No," said Ase, between chagrin and hope. "I watched her when Ridge spelled all those words. My guess is she'll figger if he can study, she can, too." His blue eyes studied Susanna, admiring, puzzled, and a bit rueful. "I don't know how you manage to teach this many kids so many different things, let alone that they're split between ranchers and homesteaders, but I'm mighty glad we hired you."

As his buckboard creaked off in Jenny's wake and Betty kept turning to wave, Susanna waved back, feeling that on the whole the afternoon had been a success. "At least," she said, bending to hug Cavalier who had enjoyed his usual meed of farewell caresses, "I don't need to wear this wretched corset again. Only Delia Taylor and Laura Prade wore theirs and I don't think anyone would dare call Hettie Brown indecent! And no one got into a fight, or even an argument, and they sang together."

All except for Prade.

❊ *Eleven* ❊

Rescued by Cav from her night terrors, busy from dawn till her eyes would no longer stay open as she read or worked by lamplight, her day filled with eager young faces, and some not so eager, Susanna felt more alive than she had in years. Except for the wind, to which she was becoming more accustomed, the weather was perfect, sunny and brisk by day, cool at night. When she looked out her window for the last time before drawing the curtain, she could see her shy, lifelong friends, the Pleiades rising, and by now she rather enjoyed the shrill nocturnal chorus of coyotes though Cav growled deep in his throat at their insolence when they came too near.

Intent on giving the children all she could in six months, Susanna launched her pupils into penmanship with the pens Ase had brought from town, devised arithmetic problems that had to do with farming and ranching, encouraged progress on the family histories; and in nature study, she often learned more than she taught. Ridge, growing up solitary, had spent his time outside watching other creatures, those that flew, burrowers beneath the ground, and those that ran upon it. At one time or another, he'd had a pet coyote, gray wolf, black-footed ferret, and badger, but presently had only a prairie dog and crow.

"My mother, when she was a little girl, met a grizzly bear when she was picking berries along the Smoky Hill River," he said. His English reflected the convent correctness of his mother's. "But it is a score of years since one has been found in what the whites call Kansas. The mountain lions are going, too, and there are not as many wolves. All of them ate buffalo as well as pronghorns, smaller beasts, and the bear loved tender plant shoots and berries. I think Coyote will last, though. He is very clever and will eat anything."

Along the creek, he showed them the X track of a roadrunner, perhaps the same jaunty-crested bird that pursued lizards sunning or hunting insects on the soddie wall; the three prongs in front, one longer behind, of the crows that reviled them in jocular fashion from the branches; leafy, fragile tracks of a lizard; twin marks the shape of elongated pears made by a pronghorn, the front ones a bit over three inches long, the hind ones a bit shorter, a distinctive track. Ridge could tell by the compression of the two parts when the pronghorn broke into a run. There were oval cottontail tracks and the larger, more-toed ones of jackrabbits; tiny hand-like prints of prairie dog; the five fingers with claw tips some distance above and the "palm" below of a badger; the dog-like track of coyotes; and when Ridge pointed out the delicate, blurred trail of a box turtle, Susanna glanced inadvertently at Frank to find him watching her.

Not with shame. With cool curiosity. In a horrid flash, she saw him, with that same expression, tear off the turtle's extremities, crush in its lovely polished shell. What was the matter with him?

Rising from where she had knelt to examine the tracks, she said in a tone so sharp that the children looked at her in surprise, "We have to get to geography and history. Thank you, Ridge. That was very interesting."

"Breeds know that sort of stuff," she heard Frank tell Ethan.

"He learned it himself," Ethan protested. "Ridge never lived with his mother's people."

"Doesn't matter a particle. It's in the blood, just like sneakiness, thieving, and——"

Fortunately, the other children were too far ahead to hear. "Frank! That's not true and I won't have that kind of talk at school."

He didn't speak but looked at her with his lip curled and a jeer in his eyes. Susanna longed to shake him, slap that silent taunt off his face. She even wished for a keen, limber switch, the satisfaction of lashing it across his shoulders, hurting him as he hurt other things.

His gaze told her he knew her feelings. "Going to whip me, teacher?" There was almost triumph in his voice.

If she did that, if she let him goad her into physical punishment, she knew she would have lost some secret and, at least for her, bewildering battle, and it wasn't simply that she'd have succumbed to Saul Prade's idea of discipline. It had to do with this boy.

"I don't whip, Frank. If anyone causes that much trouble, I'll just send him home."

"You might as well have a crack at me first, teacher, because if you ever send me home, what you could do's nothing to what Dad would. I've never cried, though. I don't want him to be ashamed of me."

Susanna's stomach twisted. It was commonplace, even in Ohio, for fathers to whip boys with razor straps or leather belts. Once her father, called by the mother, had treated a boy whose back was crisscrossed with bloody weals. Charles Alden had told the man what he thought of him but there was no law broken. Most people believed children needed rigorous punishment to correct an inborn tendency to wickedness.

"I won't whip you, Frank," she said.

He smiled in disbelief. It was as if slow black quicksand

177

tugged him down till only his head was above its murky depths. Susanna hurried on and called the first class but as Berenice and Ethan recited the names of the states and their capitals, Susanna knew that whatever she taught the others would enrich their lives but whatever happened between her and Frank was a matter of his soul—and hers.

On the third Friday afternoon, Ase and Betty lingered till the other visitors were gone. "Get your things," Ase commanded. "You're comin' home with us. You need a change from this soddie. Live in it, teach in it—I'd think you'd go crazy!"

"I'm too busy for that."

"Well, school's out till Monday," he said, crossing his arms. "You don't have chickens to shut up, hogs to slop, or cows to milk, and your dog can come with us."

"But I have papers to grade, records to fill in, and lessons to plan," she retorted.

"Bring what you can along, dear," Betty urged.

Ase grunted approval. "Sure. And if you're set on it, I'll bring you back Sunday evening."

"After breakfast?" Susanna haggled.

"Right after dinner. Have you here by two o'clock."

Truth to tell, Susanna was beginning to feel somewhat confined, and had in fact contemplated walking over to see Margaret Hardy on Saturday or Sunday. Much as she enjoyed the children, teaching all subjects to all grades was demanding. Betty's hopeful face settled the question.

"All right. I'll just be a minute." Hastily collecting overnight things and the composition papers she had to grade, Susanna asked Dave to be sure to shut the door tight, said she'd see him Monday, and called to Cav as Ase helped her into the wagon beside Betty.

"That dog's fine company for you, dear," remarked Betty, smiling as he trotted to one side, happily excited.

"He's wonderful with the children," Susanna said. "They

bring him bones, mostly rabbit, so he has caches all over the place. And the boys can run with him which Mrs. Slade couldn't, of course."

"Mrs. Slade?" Betty frowned.

"Why, yes. The old woman Dr. Rawdon took care of. Cav belonged to her."

"In a pig's eye!" chortled Ase. "Why, I was in Dodge the day he took that dog away from a barber who was kickin' him around for gettin' in the way. Must be anyhow a year ago."

"But he told me that Mrs. Slade—" Susanna broke off and bit her lip. "He—he *lied* to me!"

Ase gave Susanna a mirthful glance. "He must be another man who finds you tough to do anything nice for."

"I don't think you could call it a real lie," soothed Betty.

"Then what is it? Of all the sneaky tricks! He's let me get fond of Cav and now—" Give Cavalier back? Oh, no! Though that was what she should do. Smoldering, remembering the rug beside her bed, Susanna asked, "Was there even a Mrs. Slade?"

"Of course, dear. Dr. Rawdon did look after her, though he claims he won't practice medicine anymore. That was one reason he left Texas, because his sister kept pestering him to treat her society friends in Dallas. She's been up here a couple of times trying to get him to go back to what she calls his 'rightful place and calling.' I wonder what happened to all those beautiful rugs and things Mrs. Slade used to make."

"One's in my room," Susanna said briefly.

"Takin' quite an interest in you, isn't he?" Ase's tone was dry.

Susanna flushed. "That evening he brought the medical chest, I—I was rather startled. I suppose that made him think I needed a dog."

Heaven forgive her the mendacity. Without Cav, goodness knows how she'd have managed the nights, the long weekends. Her wrath cooled a trifle, then blazed again.

Damn him! She ought to make him take Cav back, but she couldn't, just couldn't. "I don't need a dog," he'd said, in that infuriatingly superior way. And he hadn't! He'd been able to give Cav away. She wasn't. But after all, what could you expect from a man who'd name such a beautiful dog Hank?

"It was nice of him," Betty said stoutly. "That's the main thing, dear—how something's meant."

That was just the trouble. Rawdon meant that *he* could get along without his dog, that wonderful affection and company; *he* didn't need fripperies like comfortable rocking chairs and rugs; and he seemed intent on proving that he didn't need a woman, either.

Ase said into Susanna's grim silence, "That's a good song the kids made up about Kansas rivers even if one of 'em is named the Republican."

"They had fun with that," said Susanna, and the rest of the way home they talked about the afternoon's exercises and the children.

It would have been a relief to discuss Frank with other adults. Several times, Susanna started to, but checked herself. Somehow, she shrank from letting anyone else know what the boy had done, giving him that kind of reputation. If there was a chance at all for Frank, she sensed that it lay in the outcome of the struggle between them. The easy thing would be to brand him publicly and wash her hands of any responsibility except his formal education, but that would be a defeat almost as fateful for her as it would be for him because through the boy she confronted Saul Prade and a darkness in him she felt rather than understood.

Johnny, limping out to meet them, squeezed Susanna's hands. "Doggoned if you're not purtier than when you left three weeks ago!" he vowed. Squinting at the back of the buckboard, he sighed. "No trunk! Hoped you'd be movin' back with us."

"Wait'll it rains," said Ase.

*   *   *

After the cave-like soddie, it was so light in the frame house that it seemed unnatural. Jenny, none too pleased at Susanna's visit, pouted through supper, and after Susanna had retired to the rose room, a peremptory rap came at the door.

"I want to ask you things," Jenny said as Susanna opened, and she came in without being invited.

Susanna dispensed with a lecture on etiquette though it was sorely needed. "What things, Jenny?"

"How come you don't let me help Ridge?"

"Ridge is doing quite well, as you know."

"But he was *my* friend before. Now he likes Dave and— and even that ole Sarah."

"Isn't that good? Do you want him not to have any friends but you?"

Jenny dug her toe into the rug. "I want him to like me best. And I don't see why I can't help him, the way I did at first."

"How many words did you miss in spelling today, Jenny, after having the whole week to learn them? You've had the whole week to do your composition but you waited till this morning to dash it off and I'll wager it's full of mistakes and scrawled so that I'll have a hard time reading it. You can't help Ridge because you need the time to get your own lessons." At Jenny's belligerent scowl, Susanna couldn't keep from adding, "At the rate both of you are going, Ridge will be able to help you before you're ready to help him."

"You—you're just a mean old maid!"

That hurt but it was also funny. "My marital state has nothing to do with your lessons, Jenny."

"What if I tell Daddy I won't go to your silly old school anymore?"

"Try him and see."

"I already did," Jenny muttered, glaring. "He—he said I could go to your school or he'd send me to a convent like the one Millie Tarrant stayed at. But I can run away."

"So you can," agreed Susanna. "If you do, you'd better go soon before bad weather sets in."

"I hate you," hissed Jenny, deep blue eyes fiery in the lamplight. "The other girls go on about how nice and pretty you are, but I don't think you are! I—I wish you'd die!"

With that, she bolted. Upset at the child's spiteful fury though she told herself it sprang from jealousy over Ridge and Ase, Susanna graded papers a long time that night before she felt like sleep. And sure enough, Jenny's smudged, nearly illegible composition was full of misspellings and errors of grammar and punctuation.

Withal, it was eloquent, for Jenny's governesses had taught her, more or less, the use of a number of words she couldn't spell. The gist of it was that women who taught were those who were too ugly or mean to get husbands and the main reason they taught instead of doing something useful like taking in washing or running boarding houses was that, having no children of their own, they wanted to boss other people's.

Compelled to laugh in spite of being hurt, Susanna corrected the errors and wrote at the top: "You get an A for strong writing that makes a point. For punctuation, spelling, penmanship, and grammar, you get an F."

Tired as she was, Susanna had a hard time getting to sleep. A late-rising moon, in spite of pulled draperies, made the room disturbingly light after the soddie, and she missed Cav close by her bed. Jenny's distorted face rose before her and the hateful name echoed in her ears. Old maid! Old maid!

Matt Rawdon, with his opinion of Yankee schoolmarms, could have written that composition. Rawdon, who had lied to her with utter shamelessness. Rawdon, who set himself above the needs of ordinary mortals. When she next saw him . . .

Yet for all his maddening ways, his gifts to her were woven into the fabric of her life: the chair that made her evenings comfortable, the rug that welcomed her feet when she rose mornings, and the dog who was such a dear companion as well as a sentinel against long-leggity beasties and all those night dreads that seemed so ridiculous by day.

Most of all, he made her feel like a woman, roused her out of a dormancy enforced before she had ever fully bloomed. Painful, yes, since he seemed to have renounced women, but she couldn't regret the sweetness. Surrendering at last to the softness of the mattress that seemed too silent and yielding after weeks of rustling corn shucks, she finally fell asleep in this room where she'd begun her venture as the teacher at Mason-Dixon.

The next morning, Susanna went riding with Ase and a morose Jenny, visited with Betty and Johnny in the afternoon, and after supper, retired to her room to finish going over the compositions. Grading these papers took time, and she required one at the end of each week from every child above primer class, convinced that no other assignment called for so many skills or so directly developed independent thinking.

To her relief, Ase didn't bedevil her about moving back to the rose room and his schoolhouse. As, after a delicious Sunday dinner, he and Jenny escorted her home on horseback, the child's presence prevented any personal remarks.

That didn't control the puzzled, wistful look in his eyes, however, and Susanna thought that, much as she enjoyed Betty's mothering, it wasn't wise to spend many weekends in Ase's home. She was in no danger of succumbing to its luxuries; she slept more soundly on her shuck mattress with Cav at her bedside than she had in the rose room these past two nights. But when Ase lifted her to the saddle or helped her down, that suppressed woman-being that Rawdon had awakened, responded to the warm strength of Ase's hands, the virile force that radiated from him.

That, irrationally, made her feel guilty, almost sinful, as if she'd been unfaithful—unfaithful to Matt—and that was lunacy. Matt made it plain that he didn't trust women, didn't want one in his life. Ase did.

So what will you have, Susanna? The frosted half-loaf or nothing? Forced to smile at what Ase would think of being compared to even a whole loaf, Susanna glanced toward him and encountered his eyes, blue as the prairie sky. He was a big man in every way, big of heart not to hold it against her that she declined his rose room and frame school, and it warmed her to know that he'd turned a deaf ear to Jenny's complaints though he couldn't enjoy seeing his daughter perform so poorly at the Friday visitors' hours.

Someday, maybe—if he hadn't married some sensible woman long before Susanna recovered from whatever it was that drew her to Matt. But as Ase watched her with a slow, caressing smile, the primeval female in her, denied so long, responded to him, his sheer male vitality, with frightening power. If ever he reached for her at such a moment . . .

They were nearing the school, squat and earth-colored, the roof still sporting among the sere grasses white splashes of prickly poppy and a few sunflowers. It was her world, her domain. She was glad to be home.

Ase smothered something and grumbled, "I'm betting after one hard rain you'll get some sense and move to a good building. But if you don't, we got to have a barn raising before too long. Come a blizzard, the kids' horses need shelter and feed. Worst storm we ever had was mid-November of 'seventy-one, though the Easter storm of 'seventy-three was almost as bad. Livestock froze and so did some people. Somethin' like that happens again, the best thing is to keep the kids at school but I reckon it'd get a mite crowded with four horses, fifteen kids, one teacher, and a dog."

The prospect struck dread into Susanna's heart. She was glad that in the tell-tale instant it might have shown on her face Ase was squinting toward a large bird that was alighting in the cottonwoods. Dark against the sun, another bird was circling. "Red-tailed hawks. They'll help Cav keep down snakes next spring when they'll have young'uns to feed."

Dismounting in his effortless way, he set his hands around her waist, helped her down, and went ahead of her into the soddie, leaving the door open as he inspected both rooms.

"No snakes, tarantulas, or scorpions as far as I can see," he teased. "So long, Miss Alden, ma'am. See you Friday." Jenny was already off at a canter.

Monday morning, Ridge, who had not yet told about his forebears, said he would like to. Standing by the map, the deer-like, darkly handsome youth touched the British Isles. "My father's grandparents came from Scotland and England," he said. "Their stories weren't too different from those you've already heard. I want to tell you about my mother's people, the Cheyenne." In one corner of the world map was an inset of the United States and on it Ridge located Minnesota.

"Long ago, my people, over a number of generations, traveled from here westward across the Missouri River, past the Sacred Mountain called Bear Butte into the Black Hills and wide plains watered by the Tongue, the Yellowstone, and the Platte. Blackfeet, Crow, and Gros Ventre also ranged these lands and, like the Cheyenne, disputed them with the Sioux. Many Cheyenne wandered the plains east of the Rocky Mountains to where the forests begin. Sometimes they fought Comanche and Kiowa. My mother's uncle, Mouse's Road, was one of a party that set out to steal horses from the Comanche and Kiowa who were camped on the South Platte. It was considered braver to take horses from an enemy camp than to attack. The Cheyenne passed through the camp by night, took fifty or sixty of the best horses and quietly drove them away. Next day the Kiowa and Comanche caught up with them. The Cheyenne fought bravely but at last all were killed except my mother's uncle. His bow was broken and he was on foot but he killed many chiefs with only his knife till he took a lance from one and fought on with that. The enemy saw he had great power that day—one man against a hundred. They wished to spare him and in sign language told him to take a horse and return safe home."

Pausing, Ridge's hazel eyes flashed. "My mother's uncle signed back that his friends were dead and he would not go home. This frightened his foes and they started to run. He ran after them. Two Kiowa with guns—this was before many Indians had them—got off their horses and waited. When he was close enough, they fired. He fell with a ball in his hip, but sat up to fight so they shot him in the back and all the others swarmed in. Someone cut off his head." Ridge's voice dropped. "When they did that, Mouse's Road sat upright, blood spurting from his neck. The enemy jumped on their horses and raced to camp, afraid he would follow them. They and their women caught up a few things and fled, leaving most of their lodges standing."

"That's a lie!" Frank sneered. "Except for your uncle being a horse thief!"

Ridge sucked in his breath and started for Frank who jumped up and raised his fists. Dave got between the two. Girls shrieked.

Susanna caught Frank's arm. "Frank, we don't talk like that here. Apologize."

"I won't!" Frank wrenched free of her. "It's bad enough going to school with a gut-eater but—"

Rising, Sarah stood with Dave between the two furious boys. "Stop it, Frank," she cried. "Stop right now!"

"Apologize, Frank, or go home," Susanna said.

His face went white. "Scared to whip me?"

"I've told you I won't. Go home and stay there till you can behave."

Braced for physical resistance and wondering what she could do if he refused to leave, for he was stronger than she, Susanna was relieved when he turned, face set in a snarl, and started for the door. Sarah caught Susanna's hand.

"Oh, Miss Alden, please whip him! Don't make him go home!"

Green eyes, the same color as the girl's father's and brother's, watched Susanna with a distress that made her remember what Frank had said would happen if she sent him home from school. With a swift horrid vision of the bullwhip, though surely Prade wouldn't use that on his son, Susanna winced, but she couldn't let Frank get away with such behavior.

"Frank may stay if he apologizes, Sarah."

Sarah ran after her brother. Her voice could be heard, pleading. After a little while, she came back, put her head down on her desk, and wept silently, shoulders heaving. When she lifted her face, rubbing it on her sleeve, Susanna left the primer class and gave Sarah a handkerchief, touching the bright hair. "I'm sorry, dear."

Sarah shook her head in woe. "It . . . it wasn't your fault, Miss Alden. What he said to Ridge was awful. I'm sorry, Ridge. I . . . I think your great-uncle was mighty brave and I bet he did sit up like that, just like you said. But—" She bowed her head and sobbed.

"For your sake, I will not kill him." From Ridge's tone, Susanna knew that he had intended a killing, not just a fist fight. "I was a fool to speak of my mother's people," he added bitterly.

"No!" Sarah scrubbed her eyes dry and something in the look that passed between the two children made Susanna catch her breath. Lord, what would Prade do if his daughter and the Cheyenne boy ever— "I'm glad you told us how the Cheyenne moved to the plains and about Mouse's Road. He was braver than—than Horatius at the bridge or any of those heroes in the books."

"My people have no books," said Ridge. "If we don't tell the stories, they will be forgotten."

Sarah smiled at him, tears making starpoints of her lashes. "You can write them down, Ridge."

He looked startled but then he smiled, too. "Maybe I will."

Susanna called the next class but she was haunted all that day by Frank's scared but defiant face. Laura Prade might not know how severely her husband punished their son, but Sarah evidently did. Susanna tried to assuage her regret by recalling the turtle and Frank's insolence to her, but she still felt guilty.

She passed a restless night, oppressed by recurring images of Prade and Frank, and rose early, unable to sleep. She was eating breakfast without her usual joy in the fresh morning when she heard a grating sound as the door was pushed open. She had unbarred it to let Cav out and, since dawn was breaking, hadn't barred it again. She sprang to her feet, looking around for a weapon, and snatched up the poker as Saul Prade ducked his head to enter, shoving Frank in front of him.

Unlike Will Taylor and Jem Howe, Prade wore trousers, not overalls. He unbuckled a broad leather belt and thrust it toward Susanna. "Whip this boy till he's ready to do what you say. That's part of your job. Don't send him home."

Did that mean he hadn't—? Relief flooded Susanna along with outrage. "My job, Mr. Prade is to keep order. If you don't like my methods, talk to the other trustees."

"You've got them twisted around your little finger." Prade seemed to loom. "You've got a choice, woman. Lay on good and hard, till the blood runs if need be, or I'll whip him for you, right here."

"No, you won't!" She raised the poker. Where was Cav?

Far up the creek, probably, on his morning jaunt before the children came.

Saul Prade laughed. "I can take that away from you. If you blubber to Ase McCanless, I'll say you went sort of crazy. And you are crazy, to egg that gut-eating redskin into spinning a bunch of lies. I am going to talk to the trustees about that. Now, teacher, you take this belt and don't quit till he's crawling."

"Get out of here, Mr. Prade!"

Shrugging, he yanked Frank's shirt open and peeled it from his shoulders. Susanna gasped. Faded weals and some still healing scarred the boy's entire back and shoulders. Prade raised the belt.

She threw herself in front of Prade, blocking him by putting her arms behind her around Frank, holding his rigid body desperately, determined to cling so tightly that Prade couldn't lash his son without hitting her.

A convulsion ran through Frank's body. "I—I'll apologize," he choked. Turning, he set her aside and faced his father. "I'll mind the teacher, Dad."

Saul's eyes were green fire. "And beg that dirty Indian's pardon?" He struck his son so hard the boy staggered, slamming against the wall. "That's for getting yourself in a spot where you have to eat dirt. Mind you don't do it again or you'll wish you'd never been born."

He stalked out with a crack of the belt that reminded Susanna of a rattler's strike. Dazed, scarcely able to believe what had happened, Susanna turned to meet a gaze that was at once fierce and anguished.

"Why did you do that?" Frank cried. "Why didn't you let him whip me?"

Susanna's flesh crept. "Frank—"

She put out a hand. He evaded it. "Dad's ashamed of me!"

"Ashamed of *you*?" Susanna echoed, bewildered. "What in the world's the matter with you, Frank? You wish I'd let him beat you—the way he has before?" The horror of what she'd seen overwhelmed her and she blurted, "How can your mother let him do that?"

His face closed. He buttoned his shirt. "Mother doesn't know."

"Doesn't know?"

"Dad whips me in the barn or in the field. Bandages me up if there's blood. Sarah saw us once, though. Last night, when Dad had me in the barn and was fixing to start, she had to bust in and say she'd tell mother."

"Why haven't you?"

Pride and a kind of worship flared in his eyes. "I'm his son."

"You're your mother's son, too."

He shrugged. "She mustn't ever know. If she did—well, teacher, what could she do, what'd happen?" His voice hardened. "Don't even think about telling her. I'll do what you say because it looks like you won't whip me the way you ought to, but if you say anything to Mother—" He shook his head. "Don't do it, teacher."

Dave's whistle floated from the creek. Frank gulped, suddenly a boy again after that eerie maturity. "About apologizing. Can I say it just to Ridge?"

Susanna resisted the impulse to let him off easy. "Where did you insult him?"

Frank clenched his hands, glared at her, and then sighed. "All right. Let me do it first thing and get it over with." He went out, greeting Dave, and Susanna sat down to finish her cold coffee and pat the jubilantly returned Cav with an edge of rue.

"Where were you when I needed you?" she asked.

Cav pressed closer to her knees, eyes full of the adoring love she'd seen in Frank's when he spoke of his father.

"Oh, Cav!" Suddenly overcome, she buried her face on his neck and sobbed as if her heart must break. Should she tell Laura? How could she not? Prade was taunting her, compelling her to know his cruelty, gambling that she wouldn't tell his wife.

And he was right. Doing that would break faith with Frank though she hadn't promised in words. Frank was back in school and had chosen to obey her. She must take comfort and hope in that.

As she washed her eyes to lessen their redness, she would have given anything to pour out the whole wretched story to Matt. Her unspoken pact with Frank forbade that. Only belatedly did she remember that she was supposed to be angry with Matt for lying to her about Cav.

Again she asked herself, should she tell Laura? Susanna shrank from that although she knew that by letting her see how he treated Frank, Saul Prade was daring her to expose him. The appalling thing was that he'd done nothing illegal. Perhaps it wasn't quite as bad as ancient Rome where a father had the right to put his children to death, but Susanna remembered her father's anger over cases where he was sure a man had severely beaten his wife though these women usually insisted that they'd fallen or bumped into something. Divorce was a stain on a woman's reputation, often difficult to get, and it was hard for a woman with children to find a decent way to support them. If knowledge of what she had thus far managed to avoid knowing was thrust on Laura, if she confronted her husband, what might happen then? He might extend his viciousness to the whole family.

For now at least, Susanna decided to hold her peace, but as she prepared for the day's classes, she felt more exhausted than ever she had when she waved the children off.

✾ *Twelve* ✾

Rain doesn't pitter or patter, pound, or drum on a sod roof. It beats. What doesn't sluice off soaks in, seeks crevices, permeates the traceries of roots, the tiny homes of insects, and begins to drip. "Fortunately, it doesn't exactly rain inside," Susanna wrote Aunt Mollie and Uncle Frank. "The torrents find channels and drip through them, so the trick is to set kettles and buckets beneath these conduits and remove them before they overflow. The older children help with this duty in the classroom. I've gotten fairly adept at it so the floors aren't truly bogs but I've put my rug, the lovely quilt you gave me, and my dresses in the trunk till things dry out."

She nibbled on her pen, casting a rueful glance around the room where muddy trickles, after three days of wind and bright sunshine, continued to plash in every vessel she could use, including the ash bucket. "I can see why women who live in soddies say what they do—that it rains one day outside and four more inside. I chose to use this building, so I can't complain but I do hope the trustees will someday put on a shingled roof. All my patrons save one have them and I'm assured it makes a great difference."

Save one. Thinking of Margaret Hardy whose floor in the half dugout must be a bog and who struggled valiantly to send her children clean to school, Susanna was ashamed of herself and put the letter aside to finish later.

Thank goodness the drips were abating, and by afternoon, when parents came, for this was Friday, most of the receptacles could be put away.

Ase arrived during lunch hour, mounted on Rusty, for Johnny had taken to coming and driving Betty in the buckboard. Grinning, he reined in beside Susanna who was hastily pinning up ringlets that had tumbled loose during a vigorous game of tag. He directed an appraising glance at the roof with its flowers basking innocently in the sunlight.

"Well, I see it didn't cave in the way they can when it rains three or four days instead of one. Still drippin'?"

"No!" It was none of his business that the ash bucket still awaited a hesitant, occasional drip in one corner of the bedroom.

"Guess it was pretty dark inside the day it rained," he continued hopefully.

Dark! She'd had to light the lamp by the blackboard so the pupils could see it and had moved the recitation bench near the window so the children could read. To Ase, Susanna said lightly, "Oh, we did a lot of spelling and memory work that day. The worst part was that the children couldn't play outside at recess or noon. Of course, they got restless so I cut lunch hour in half and made each recess fifteen minutes longer."

Ase stared. "What, for the love of mud, did you do with these kids for three half-hours?"

"We played hopscotch and Simon Says, the girls jumped rope and the boys played mumblety-peg and spun tops." She had to chuckle. "When everybody got the squirms, I had them stand up and do stretches."

"Better'n yellin' at 'em." Ase studied her. "Ready to move?"

"Are you ready to deed the school to the district?"

"Stubborn as a bowlegged mule!"

"You or I, Mr. McCanless?"

He glared and then he laughed. "Reckon it's a tie, ma'am." He waved a hand at the smiling sky, sparkling brighter than ever after the rain. "Time of year you can't count on much more of this. I'll talk to the other men, see when we can get a barn built."

The barn raising wasn't the community work gala that it might have been. Saul Prade said his children walked to school and he wasn't building a barn for those that didn't. Cash Hardy's back wasn't up to that kind of work. But Will Taylor plowed long, straight furrows with his oxen, and since it was Saturday, Dave tried to fill his father's place in helping the ranch men cut the sod bricks and load them on Jem Howe's big low sled which carried the blocks to the building site about fifty yards from the school.

The site was a compromise. In winter, especially in case of a heavy or prolonged storm, it would have been best to have the barn attached to the school for ease of getting back and forth and caring for the animals. In warmer weather, though, the horses would draw flies, and there were already enough of those.

Delia Taylor hadn't come or sent food; most likely she had scolded poor Will for helping. But Margaret Hardy drove over at noon in the wagon, bringing the younger Hardys and a kettle of beans to add to the array the ranch women spread on planks laid across the back of the McCanless buckboard.

After dinner, the men went back to work, the children dashed off to play, and the women did the dishes before settling down again to mend or sew as they chatted, sitting on benches and two chairs brought out of the soddie. Though Millie Tarrant beaded moccasins while Margaret Hardy patched overalls and Hettie and Betty mended

Levi's, the conversation centered on children and home-making. Those homes ranged from the Hardy half dugout to the McCanless two-story frame but the women clearly enjoyed each other's company.

Since Will Taylor, Dave, and especially Jem Howe had helped with something of no benefit to them, the men hadn't separated at dinner the way they had when building the fuel shed and repairing the soddie, but homesteader and rancher still found little to talk about except the weather. Dave, tall as the two of Ase's hands who'd volunteered to help, must have envied their Levi's and boots though the boots were a drawback for this kind of work. Tom Chadron, whose laughing brown eyes sobered when he looked at Susanna, and tow-headed, sunburned Bert Mulroy had eaten with the men, but watched Susanna so avidly that she felt like the peach cobbler Betty had brought. Poor things, they were scarcely more than boys, and there seemed not to be any young women their age for miles around.

By late afternoon, the barn was finished. Kermit Brown had supplied some old lumber for the mangers which divided the haymow from stalls partitioned by cotton-wood poles. There were four extra stalls in case some of the homesteaders acquired animals their children could ride or drive. The ranchers would take turns filling the haymow.

"And when that's done," said Ase, "we'll have the school as set for a blizzard as it can be. Of course that fuel shed's got to be kept full."

"I'll do it next," said Will Taylor. "We supplyin' fuel accordin' to how many kids we got, Ase?"

"Aw, let's leave the long division to the kids," said Ase. "Let's just take turns. That'll even out the warmer months with the cold ones." He turned to Susanna with a coaxing grin. "Might as well come home with us."

"Thank you, but I have too much to do."

"Never saw such a fool for work," he grumbled. "Thought it was the kids supposed to work in school."

Susanna gave him a sweet smile. "Maybe you'd like to help me grade compositions?"

"You know durn well I can't. My mother taught me to read and write a little but when I have to write a letter, I throw a wide loop at the spellin' and as for all those funny little marks—" He shook his head.

"Why don't you tell Jenny she can write your letters when she learns enough?" Susanna suggested. "If she thought she could be useful to you, it might make her try to do better."

"I don't write that many letters," Ase began. Then he chuckled. "Reckon I could start. Hell—excuse me, ma'am—you might just wind up rubbin' off a little education on us old mossyhorns, too."

After everyone was gone, it seemed lonely till Cav frisked up to her. "What a fine dog you are," she told him with a hug. "I don't know what I'd do without you."

He wagged agreement with her praise. "Do you miss your master?" she asked under her breath. She did, even if he had lied to her about Cav.

The first week of November brought a frost that browned the gold of the cottonwoods, bleached sideoats grama and dropseed white, and painted the various bluestems rich tones of red and purple. The yellow-headed blackbirds had flown south but the redwings still had kindred for they were now neighbored by a sort whose black plumage showed green iridescence in the sunlight. The red-tailed hawk could be seen circling as he searched for prey. Susanna had located the tree where he usually roosted. Since he hunted by day, he had no territorial strife with the great horned owls a little distance up the creek, for they were silent hunters of the night. Once at dusk, though, Susanna watched in amazement as several crows harassed an owl, screaming and swooping toward it.

Though the sun quickly dissolved the fine glittering diamond dust of frost that most mornings now covered the prairie, Susanna sat close to the fire at night. Feeding it during the day was added to the tasks, like filling the water buckets and bringing in fuel, that older pupils took turns doing.

Thanksgiving was approaching, and the Saturday after the barn raising Susanna took her bowl of cornbread crumbled into beans outside to eat, enjoying the sun while she pondered whether to celebrate the holiday with a program for the community. President Lincoln had proclaimed it a national holiday in 1863 which made many Southerners feel it was a "Yankee" occasion, but its official origin went back to the Massachusetts Bay Colony.

Hadn't George Washington run into trouble from states' righters when he'd made it a holiday? Susanna had to smile at that remembered wisp of information. Fine. Tracing the day's history could also sketch in the country's. She'd bring it up to the trustees who were meeting at the school tomorrow afternoon.

Though most of them attended Friday exercises, this was their first formal session since hiring her. Would Prade carry out his threat of objecting to Ridge's being encouraged to talk about the Cheyenne? Beyond a curt greeting, the man hadn't spoken to her since that terrible morning he'd tried to make her beat Frank.

Her problems with Frank were far from solved. He didn't watch her derisively anymore, on the verge of sneering, but he was remote, reciting when called on but volunteering nothing. He no longer took part in the games at noon and recess but played solitary mumblety-peg or whittled. Cav didn't stay with him as he did with any other child who for one reason or another wasn't playing. There must be a war inside Frank but Susanna could think of no way to help.

Cav gave a soft bark, ears pricked toward the crossing. Susanna looked that way to see riders coming up the bank. Two jolted up and down on workhorses, as if they were unaccustomed to riding. A third was mounted on a small white mule. And the fourth was Matt Rawdon on his fine gray gelding. Cav, with a joyful bark, bolted for his perfidious master—who was certainly going to get a piece of Susanna's mind if she had a chance to give it.

Choking on the last bite of her meal, she fled inside to put down the bowl and see if her hair had strayed from the pins she'd thrust hurriedly in place that morning. The clustering brown mass was more down than up but there was little she could do about it now. Desperately anchoring the most rebellious curls, she rolled down her sleeves, buttoned her stand-up collar, and went out to greet the cavalcade.

Even before Matt introduced them, she was sure the three strangers were foreigners. They wore cloth caps, long vests buttoned to the throat over full-sleeved shirts, and as they awkwardly dismounted, Susanna saw that their trousers had ample gathers. All wore a kind of sturdy sandal. Holding their caps in their hands, they gazed hopefully at Susanna.

Caressing his one-time dog who pressed against him in such rapture that it gave Susanna a pang, Matt said, "My new neighbors have school-age children so they've come to talk to you. This is Frederick Krause." A solid man in his forties with a dark brown beard and hair inclined his head. "Peter Krause is his brother." At this name, the older man with graying hair and keen gray eyes smiled and nodded. Matt turned last to the big yellow-haired blue-eyed young stranger who surely wasn't old enough to be the father of a school child. "Jacob Reighard is betrothed to Frederick's eldest daughter. He worked on a Pennsylvania farm for a year so he speaks a lot of English. I came along, though, in case there were any difficulties. They bought their land from the same Dodge City man I found mine through. He buys from settlers who couldn't make it here and sells to those who want to try." Indicating Susanna, Matt presented the strangers who all bowed and spoke politely.

"Good day, miss," said Jacob, bashfully averting his eyes. "Is it possible that to you the children come to learn? Four they are, in age twelve, ten, six, and seven. Only German are they speaking though I have taught them a few words."

Susanna spoke and had taught schoolgirl German and French but she only caught the gist of what Frederick said and allowed Jacob to translate. "The Krauses will pay, gladly, if you will so kind be."

"Since the children live in the district, of course they're welcome," Susanna said though she was by no means sure what the trustees would say and expected trouble at the least from Saul Prade. "There's no need for special payment, though of course you'd join with the other families in supporting the school. You are from Germany?"

"A hundred years ago from Prussia." Jacob smiled. "Catherine the Great, German she was, knew Mennonites for good farmers, and invited them to the Russian steppes and the Crimea. Roamed by Tartars and Cossacks, the Wildlands were." He searched for a word. "Frontier. Like this."

He went on to explain what he obviously often had before. Catherine had offered the settlers free transportation, 175 acres of land per family, no taxes for ten years and after that only a small fee for land lease, freedom from military conscription, and the right to practice their religion, often so savagely punished; and she guaranteed that they could maintain their own schools and speak their own language. In fifty villages surrounded by fields, orchards, and pastures for their livestock, they had flourished, governed by village burgomasters and an elected chief burgomaster.

In 1871, however, the czar determined to make them Russians. It was proclaimed that in ten years the special privileges would be revoked. Appreciating the Mennonites' husbandry, Czar Alexander II tried to persuade them to remain and, knowing their religion prohibited bearing arms or fighting, the government even offered to substitute time in the forest service for years in the military.

Some Mennonites chose to stay, especially rich ones who found it hard to leave their fertile lands, sell their comfortable houses, herds, and belongings at a great loss, and undertake the long journey halfway round the world. Most, however, feared that they would eventually be forced into military service. Delegates traveled to the United States to look for land in a region where they would be exempt from conscription. From the first, the Kansas state constitution provided for exemption for those with conscientious scruples against bearing arms. Till last year, these people had had to make a yearly affidavit and pay thirty dollars into the public school fund, but in 1874, to encourage such desirable settlers, the legislature repealed the money payment.

Some villages emigrated as a whole. Thousands of acres of land were bought from the railroads, and already there were settlements around Newton, the nearest town to the east, which only a few years ago had been the end of the Texas cattle trail and as wild as Dodge City now was.

The Krauses and Jacob were the only emigrants from their village on the lower Dnieper. Rather than try to find land near an established settlement, they had decided to come farther west. "Villages, for this country, are not the best way to farm," Jacob said. "Our religion we keep, but Americans we wish to be, citizens. To live apart, as in Russia we did, we do not think a good thing."

"They bought two homesteads north of me," Matt said. "Moved in three weeks ago and they've already plowed the sod twice and planted rye and a sort of hard red winter wheat they brought from Russia. If it does well here, it should be a lot more reliable than the spring-planted soft wheats we have now because it can usually be harvested before drought blasts it."

"Well it must do." Jacob smiled. "Like our steppes they are, these plains. This soil already we know. Also grasshoppers. When in Russia they came to us, we built smudge fires in the fields close enough together that grasshoppers the whole crop could not destroy."

Susanna looked at them with new respect. They seemed to know the natural adversities they'd have to contend with. In Russia, apparently, they had learned how to deal with tribulations that had crushed so many inexperienced homesteaders from kinder climates.

"Welcome to Kansas," she said. "I'm a stranger here myself. The children may start school Monday. It would be good if you could make a desk and bench for them, and of course you'll help supply fuel like the other patrons. If the children ride, you'll need to put some hay in the barn."

Jacob translated. The Krauses nodded and smiled as Peter spoke and Jacob explained. "Freddie and Magdalena, the youngest, they will Flora ride, the little white mule. Cobie and Valentine, walk they will."

Susanna invited them to look around the schoolroom. In response to their questions, she assured them that religion was not taught in school and no attempt would be made to turn the children away from their faith or imbue them with warlike attitudes. "Aren't Mennonites similar to the Amish?" she asked. "There are many Amish in Ohio, where I came from, and they're known as the best farmers in the state."

At this, there was frowning and discussion. At last, Jacob said that the Mennonites sprang from the Reformation, starting first in Switzerland though their faith was named for Menno Simons, a priest who taught the simple creed in Holland where the Krauses' forebears had been early converts. Jacob Amman was a Swiss Mennonite who taught rigorous "shunning" of any person, even by his or her family, if they flouted the religion's precepts. This caused a split in the Swiss Brethren. Those following Amman's strict rule became known as the Amish, and many of them came to Pennsylvania in 1711.

"You might say the Mennonite religion is a tree with many branches," said Jacob, with a wry shrug. "We do not agree on using buttons or washing of feet as Christ did that of his disciples, and other such things. But fast we stand on the chief principles. We will not take oaths, fight wars, baptize infants, or receive sacraments, and we do not believe the government should support and thus control the church as is done in so many countries. As to the rest——" He smiled. "Well, vowed to peace we are, but we have our arguments."

"There are many religions in this country," said Susanna. "Right from the start we've had separation of church and state."

"We know," said Jacob. "Your constitution, we have studied it."

Susanna exchanged a startled glance with Matt. That was more, she suspected, than the Mason-Dixon board of trustees could boast.

Thanking her, the Mennonites started to depart. When Matt would have followed, Susanna said, "Dr. Rawdon, I need to speak with you."

With a lift of a dark eyebrow, he murmured, "My pleasure, ma'am." Trailing the gelding's reins, he called to Jacob, "I won't be riding with you, neighbors. Miss Alden wants to confer with me. I'm the school's—uh—medical and health adviser."

Saluting with their caps, the three rode toward the creek. "Medical adviser." Susanna sniffed. "You, sir, are an accomplished prevaricator."

"I gave you a medical chest."

"Yes, and you gave me *your* dog. Mrs. Slade, indeed!"

"That," he said, "wasn't a lie because you were bound to find out."

"Of all the Machiavellian nerve! You—you counted on

my not learning the truth till I was so fond of Cav and depended on him so much that I wouldn't send him back!"

"I almost took him when you dropped an honest name like Hank and stuck Cavalier on him."

"I might have known no woman would give such a beautiful dog a name like that."

Matt knelt to ruffle the dog's ears and hold his muzzle between his hands, an endearment that sent Cav into such ecstasy that he slathered his tongue across Rawdon's cheek. "How about that, Hank?" inquired his erstwhile master. "It's a good thing you're as big as a calf or she'd make you into a lapdog."

Seeing the love they had for each other tugged at Susanna's heart, made her feel guilty. "How could you give him away?" she asked. "He must have thought you didn't want him."

"We had a talk." Matt rose but kept on scratching the dog behind his ears. "I asked him if he didn't think he should look after a Yankee lady with lots of enterprise but not much common sense. He allowed that was his duty. Besides, where do you think he goes on those runs he takes every morning?"

Susanna stared. "He goes to you?"

"Sure. We have a little visit and then he says he's got to go meet the kids. In fact, I think he's looping past Hardys' and coming with Dave, isn't he?"

Now that she thought of it, they usually did turn up at the same time. Gazing at Cav, she shook her head. "So you're duplicitous, too. All the same—"

"Forget it." Matt's tone changed abruptly from teasing to brusque. "You need him. I don't."

The arrogant words roweled Susanna like one of the huge, many pointed Mexican spurs Kermit Brown wore though he never seemed to use them. "Are you proud of that?" she demanded. "Are you glad you can get along without anyone or anything to love or love you? You're like a wall built around a bare, empty place!"

A muscle jerked in his cheek and his eyes were like storm clouds with sun behind them. "Would you care, Miss Alden, to make any other observations on my nasty character?"

The anger in her died, leaving sadness. Tears stung her eyes. Bowing her head, she whispered, "I'm afraid of the dark and snakes and scorpions and a lot of things, Matt Rawdon, but that's better than being afraid of life."

He gave a harsh, startled laugh. "You think I am?"

"Aren't you? Hiding away out here by yourself, refusing to use your gift of healing and your training because you can't do fancy surgery?" In this far, she couldn't stop. She cared for this stubborn, difficult, lonely man, and she hated to see him deny the essence of his nature. Taking a deep breath, she looked up at him and cried in a voice that trembled, "I'd rather be afraid of all the things I am than be afraid to live."

The blaze of his eyes flashed through her. Transfixed as if by lightning, she could do nothing as he caught her in his arms, swept her against him, and took her mouth with a bruising kiss, hard and punishing till his lips softened, moved sweetly, ardently on hers while his hand found the nape of her neck and fitted her even more closely to him.

When at last he drew away, Susanna would have staggered if he hadn't steadied her. The grooves carved from cheekbone to mouth seemed deeper and tighter.

"Shall we go to your bed, Miss Alden? Or would you prefer an elemental tumble in the grass?"

She lifted her hand as if he'd struck her. "You want to," he pursued. "If one of your assorted fears is that of becoming pregnant, I assure you I can prevent that."

Hurt and humiliated, scarcely able to believe he was acting like this, Susanna clenched her hands. "I don't think I've done anything to provoke such an insult."

"What's insulting about being considered a healthy woman with healthy needs?" He shrugged. "We can be discreet." His smile made his face even more a mask. "Assuming your fiancé left you virgin when he went off to war, I'll wager you've maintained that state, charming in a young girl, dreary in a woman of an age to need physical fulfillment."

"Sir—"

"For my part," he went smoothly on, "I have no wish to marry, and no taste for Dodge City harlots or seducing honest married women, which is inconvenient as well as dangerous. Even if the few fathers with attractive daughters living within a day's ride didn't also have shotguns, I boggle at taking advantage of some innocent."

"But *I'm* an old maid."

He made a deprecating motion. "Let's just admit that you're no tender babe." His voice grew ironically caressing. "Come now, Miss Alden, how can you say you're not afraid to live when you shy away from what has to be one of the most pleasurable, well-nigh necessary, parts of living?"

The incongruity of formally addressing her while making an improper proposal sent Susanna into almost hysterical laughter. "I can't believe a man with any pretensions to decency would make such an offer," she said when she could control herself. "I suppose I should slap you or swoon away or cry." Her cheeks flamed at the enormity of it, not only that he would speak so to a woman with no male protectors, but that she was actually tempted, wished it were possible to have that much of him since apparently she could never hope for more. "Forgive me that I don't know your Southern idea of how a woman should answer such an insult. While we're having this extraordinary conversation, I'll concede that I might yield to love—I'm human and I do have feelings. But I'd die before I—" How did one say it? "Before I went to bed with a man as a matter of ... of ..."

"Hygiene?" he suggested.

"Yes! The way one eats a meal or—or visits the outhouse!"

He stared and burst into laughter even as she bit her lip and blushed at what she'd said. "For a proper Yankee schoolmarm, you say some shocking things, Susanna Alden."

"You drive me to it!"

His eyes kindled. He turned up her chin, only for a moment, before he moved back and put his hands behind him. "A nun has the consolation of being the bride of Christ. What's your comfort, Susanna?"

After all they had said and what he had done, what did it matter if for now he used her name? "My comfort is my work." Let him mock if he would. "And Cav and books—blackbirds, meadowlarks—just being alive. And I am alive, Matt Rawdon, whatever you may think!"

The twist of his lips faded, leaving him suddenly haggard. For a moment, pain was almost palpable between them. He inclined his head. When he raised his eyes to hers, he was masked again. "All true, Miss Alden, and commendable." They were back to formality which both relieved and jarred on her. "As a male, though, I deplore the waste of a lovely woman." With a last caress for Cavalier, he started for his horse, then turned with a wicked chuckle. "As a one-time doctor, let me congratulate you on discarding your corset even if the stays are still laced tight around your formidable Yankee rectitude."

He was in the saddle and away without a backward glance.

❧ *Thirteen* ❧

No matter how sternly she applied herself to grading compositions and reviewing her German in order to communicate a little with the four new children, Susanna's treacherous body kept melting as it had in Matt's arms. Richard's boyish kisses had done nothing to ready her for a man's embrace, not that anyone at all could have prepared her for the—the ravishment of Matt Rawdon's kiss.

He *had* ravished her, seizing by storm some inner citadel. She had tasted his mouth and with it the fruit of knowledge. Cruel as it had been to long for unknown raptures, it was devastating to hunger for the strength of his arms, the hard length of his body, the imperious mouth that made hers yield, open to him as the secret depths of her yearned to do.

Had he meant his cold-blooded proposition? At first she hadn't questioned his intent, but now she wondered. Not that he would have declined had she acquiesced—he was a man, virile and unmarried—but had it been a way to chastise her for accusing him of hiding from life and its responsibilities?

What if he hadn't meant the kiss at all, except as humiliating punishment? She writhed inwardly at that thought but honesty forced her to acknowledge that in spite of the turbulence sweeping her, she was glad that at least once, however slightingly he intended it, the man she now realized she loved had held her, set his mouth to hers. A taste of honey to mock old Charon, even if it was the last she'd ever get.

The words of Heine swam before her as she turned them into English: "Röslein said, 'I'll hurt you so you'll always remember . . .'"

And though Matt had been the wild lad on the heath who carelessly plucked the rose, it was Susanna who would ache and think of him. Trying as the board meeting threatened to be, she was glad she wouldn't have to get through Sunday by herself.

Ase and Saul Prade arrived early, fortunately at the same time because, for different reasons, Susanna didn't want to be alone with either. Deciding to get it over with, she told them about the Mennonite children.

"You said they could come?" Prade demanded. "I don't want my kids going to school with a pack of dirty little Dutchies! Let 'em start their own school."

"They want to learn English. They want to be Americans."

"What kind of Americans can they be when they won't fight for the country?"

"They're supposed to be excellent farmers and feeding the country's surely as important as fighting for it which I hope won't ever happen again. From what they say, they're used to drought and grasshoppers. They brought this special winter wheat they grew in Russia—"

"They can keep their damned wheat and lunatic notions. I'll go over there after this meeting and tell them you had no business agreeing to let those flat-headed Dutchies come."

"Hold on, Prade." Ase, brow furrowed, spoke for the first time. "That's for the whole board to decide. I'm not plumb crazy about havin' 'em in school. I was in Topeka last year when a bunch of 'em were camped there, funny lookin' crowd for sure. But they seem to be workers. I don't want to see more farms here—by rights, it should all be cattle country—but if we got to have 'em, I'd a sight rather have ones who know what they're doin'.".

"You're saying you'd just as soon have foreigners farming here as men who fought for the North."

"Oh," said Ase, and grinned. "I'd a damn sight rather." He turned to Susanna. "The boys were in Dodge and picked up the mail. You got a big bundle from your aunt, and a letter." He smiled at her delight as he took a parcel and envelope from his saddlebag. "Why don't you read your letter, ma'am, before the rest of the board get here?"

Thanking him, she put the heavy package inside and swiftly opened the letter, three pages of Aunt Mollie's elegant slanting Spencerian script and a few paragraphs of Uncle Frank's blocky, straight up-and-down writing.

Skimming it, though later she would savor every word, Susanna learned they were well and the school was flourishing, though the girls missed Susanna and hoped she'd return. "We all do," wrote Aunt Mollie, and Susanna felt a rush of grateful love for this woman who had been almost a mother. "My gracious, darling! Rattlesnakes, dirt floors, and living and teaching in a house of prairie sod! Your students sound worthy except for that Jenny snippet, but you're not a missionary." Susanna grimaced at the news that Benjamin Harris, the lawyer who'd paid a substitute to fight for him, inquired after her every time he met her relatives and wondered about prospects for a law practice in Dodge. "Judge Henry gave me stacks of old *Atlantics* and *Scribner's*," Aunt Mollie continued. "Knowing your admiration for Miss Charlotte Brontë's works, I'm sending some magazines that tell about her schooldays and later life. There's also a most diverting account by a Welsh governess about her tenure at the court of the King of Siam. At least, my dear, you haven't gone that far away though it sometimes seems like it."

Will Taylor's Missouri twang came from outside, and Kermit Brown's lazy Texas drawl. Pensively tucking the letter beneath the parcel, Susanna glanced around the cave-like dirt-floored room, for a moment seeing it as her aunt and uncle would, and felt a wave of homesickness. This passed, however, when her mind's eye placed children, *her* children, at the desks.

Ohio had plenty of teachers. The prairie didn't. Here, she made a difference, for the children she taught would be the builders and shapers of this raw new region. She pinned a straying curl in place and went out to greet the trustees who, having all arrived, entered the school, Northerners sliding into the big boys' desk, Southerners occupying the recitation bench, Susanna sitting near the blackboard, hands folded in her lap, knees pressed together to keep from fidgeting.

What if a majority sided with Prade against admitting the Mennonites? Would he persuade most of them to forbid Ridge to talk about the traditions of his people? Compared with these problems, about which Susanna was determined to resign if necessary, what they decided about a Thanksgiving celebration seemed unimportant.

Ase called the meeting to order. Susanna gave a report and asked what they thought about holding a special Thanksgiving program, presenting it tactfully as a holiday going back to colonial times before Washington, a Virginian, made it a national celebration.

"Well, if Washington thought it was all right, I guess it is," said Kermit grudgingly.

"Reckon it won't hurt." Ase shrugged.

Luke Tarrant nodded as did Will Taylor but Saul Prade stood up. As always, such light as there was caught and shone on his hair which almost brushed the sagging, stained cheesecloth ceiling. "Before we talk about what happens the last Thursday of the month, we need to talk about tomorrow and something that's been going on that I'm dead against. Taylor, did you know you've got a bunch of Russians east of you? Want those little girls you're so careful of going to school with a pack of dirty Dutchies?"

Will's dark eyes widened and his long jaw dropped. "Can't say's I did know. But if they're Roosians, how come you call 'em Dutchies?"

"They speak German," Susanna interposed, "and their people have lived in Russia a hundred years, but a long time ago, this family came from Holland."

Will scratched his head. "Sound doggone mixed-up to me. They Mennonites like those around Newton?"

"Yes," said Prade. "And these should've stayed with the rest of their kind. We can't keep them from buying land since they've got the money but we sure don't have to let them come to our school."

"We're pretty mixed-up as it is," said Kermit. "From what I hear, those folks are honest, work hard, and don't cause any trouble. Can't see it'd hurt to have the kids."

Prade looked at Will. "How'd you like one of your girls to marry one of them?"

"Well—" began the lanky Missourian.

Ase cut in. "Far as I'm concerned, if Jenny's goin' to hitch up with a farmer, I care more about his makin' her a livin' than where he or his folks came from."

"Me, too," said Kermit, trying unsuccessfully to flatten his red cowlick. "Anyhow, some of Hettie's folks are German and they're good people."

"Kiddies ought to go to school somewheres," Will said unhappily.

Luke Tarrant's hazel stare fixed on Prade. "They're in the district. Can't see why we even have to talk about it."

"*You* wouldn't," Prade gritted.

"You're slurrin' my wife." Tarrant was on his feet in one continuous motion. "Looks like you haven't got a gun. Would you know how to use one if Ase loans you his?"

"Bet I killed as many Rebs in the war as you did Yanks." Far from showing fear, Prade smiled and his eyes were green fire. "But you were a bull-whacker, same as me. Anyone can point a Colt and pull the trigger. Let's have it out with bullwhips—if you're not too old."

"When and where?"

"Cut it out," growled Ase. "We're here to do school business, not get into fights." He looked hard from one to the other. "How are our kids goin' to go to school together if their fathers have at each with whips? You both think about your families and simmer down."

"I'm thinkin' about his family or he'd already be dead," said Tarrant.

Prade's teeth flashed white. "Or you might be."

Ase got to his feet. "Men, we agreed to have a school. We don't have to like each other but we got to get along, and Prade, that means you don't demean Luke's wife and son—or the Mennonite folks, either—on account of everyone but you says to let 'em come. You give your word you won't make any more of this kind of trouble, or we'll throw you off the board right now."

Slowly glancing round, Prade saw agreement on every face, even Will's uneasy one. After a tense silence, he hunched a powerful shoulder and sat down. "Guess I don't have much choice. There's no other school. But without demeaning anyone, I'd like to know if you're supporting this school so your kids can hear about some Indian who sat up after he got his head hacked off." His gaze skewered Will. "Nice story for your girls, Taylor?"

Will squirmed but said doggedly, "Guess it's no worse'n David and Goliath or what one of them English kings did to a bunch of his wives." He looked mournfully toward Susanna. "Once you start joggerphy, there's no way of stoppin' a lot of this stuff. But the girls like school even if Charlotte don't get as good marks as her mama thinks she should." He cleared his throat so that the big Adam's apple bobbed. "I move we leave what's taught and done in school up to Miss Alden even if we don't like every single thing."

There was a chorus of assent. Prade sent Susanna a stare of such venom that she braced herself to keep from wincing. He sat like stone through the rest of the meeting. "I had my doubts about hirin' a Yank—I mean, an Ohio teacher," Ase concluded. "But it looks like we got a mighty good one. If she'd just see sense about the buildin'—" He broke off at Susanna's frown. "Guess there's no reason we need to meet as a board for a while. Don't forget Thanksgiving."

"I'll send word home with the children," Susanna said.

Except for Prade who strode out immediately, the other trustees shook her hand and had some word of praise. "Mr. Tarrant," she began as he came up. "I understand how you feel but please—"

He pressed her hand between both of his and grinned. "Bless your heart, if there's any trouble, it won't start with me. My family needs me alive a lot more than dead, and Prade's in the same boat." He turned to Ase. "Thanks for callin' a halt. There's nothin' I'd like better than to work that guy over with a bullwhip but his wife's a real lady— been sweet to Millie, and that oldest gal has sure been nice to Ridge."

Lingering, Ase said, "Reckon I'd better ride over to the Mennonites and tell 'em about their share of supportin' the school. You can handle four more students? Who don't speak English?"

This was a legitimate question though Susanna was glad he hadn't raised it during the meeting. "Dave and Sarah— most of the older children, in fact—help with the others, and I speak a little German. It'll take the youngsters time to learn English but I'm sure Jacob will help them study at home." She smiled at a sudden thought. "We talk in school about how our ancestors came from Europe. Now we'll have a living history lesson."

Ase shook his head in mingled resignation and wonder.

"You just feed any and everything into that teachin' mill of yours, don't you? Jenny still bucks and rares some that Ridge's not her private property, but she works right along on that family history. Even uses that dictionary she'd never touch before."

"Really?" That surprised Susanna for Jenny was still often sullen and ill-prepared for class.

"Really." Ase's grin turned to disgust as he stared up at the bedraggled cheesecloth. "But how in the world a smart lady like you can——all right, all right! I'm goin'."

Because of their Netherlandish origin, Susanna had expected flaxen-haired little strangers to appear on Monday. Instead, the only one with yellow hair was the small girl riding bareback on the plump white mule, hanging tightly to a slightly older boy with red-brown hair and solemn gray eyes. These were six-year-old Magdalena and her cousin, seven-year-old Frederick who had already become Freddie to the younger Hardys with whom they had joined forces. Similarly, Magdalena's twelve-year-old brother, Valentine, slim, dark-haired, and gray-eyed, had received the name of Val, which Susanna judged it wisest to use. Cobie, whose black hair peeked from beneath the triangular kerchief tied, like Magdalena's, snugly under her chin, had brilliant green eyes and was ten years old, she and Freddie being the youngest of Peter Krause's brood. Susanna would learn later that the elder three, all young men, had decided to hire out to Mennonites around Newton till they found wives.

Under their coats, the girls wore dresses of identical green-sprigged black cotton. Val and Freddie wore the same baggy trousers, blouse-like shirts, and high-buttoned vests their fathers wore. All had homemade leather sandals and knitted black stockings.

Val pulled off Flora's halter, spoke to her softly, and gave her a pat. She ambled off and began to graze. Leading his cousins and little sister forward, Val swept off his brown cloth cap. "Good morning, our teacher."

Jacob had been busy. "Good morning." Susanna smiled. That was when she learned their names and ages, for it developed that all of them could count to twenty and Val and Cobie to a hundred.

The pleasant surprise engendered in Susanna by this auspicious beginning faded as she tried to talk with the children, along with her hopes of being able to communicate in German. She had heard of Plattdeutsch, the dialect spoken in the lowlands of northern Germany along the Baltic, and now she discovered these children spoke this soft language with many vowels that sounded quite different from the High German she had learned.

Even so, they understood her better than she could them and as the day passed, with their bits of English, what they puzzled out of her German, and many gestures, they were sounding out words and copying their spelling. Arithmetic showed Val to be working at sixth-grade level with the oldest pupils, Cobie to fit with Ethan and Berenice in fourth, and Freddie and Magdalena to add and subtract with the second grade, which chagrined Jenny considerably though Rosie was proud of her young new neighbors, Dottie didn't care, and the Prade twins were close enough in age not to feel particularly bested.

Till the Krauses delivered a desk and bench, the new pupils had to crowd in with the older. Fortunately, Magdalena and Freddie had sufficient room with the four younger children who were, also fortunately, uninclined to tease their seatmates.

Cobie did have to squeeze for there were already six big girls. Jenny and Charlotte rolled their eyes at Cobie's apparel but Rosie and Sarah made room for her between them and at recess Rosie and Berenice took her off with them to see the playhouse they'd constructed with the barn for one wall and the other boundaries defined by dried stalks. Imagination turned piles of weeds into beds and chairs and made doll-children of corncobs and cottonwood roots.

Ridge got up to motion Val to a place between him and Freck. Dave worked with the younger boy that day, patient and kind as he always was, but it was aloof, reserved Ridge who took Val in hand, helped him with his studies, and brought him into the games at recess and noon. Here was someone more different than he, someone he could teach and protect.

Frank simply ignored the newcomers. Increasingly withdrawn, he worried Susanna more than he had when contemptuously mocking her, but her attempts to bring him into discussions failed. He would answer a direct question but that was all and his green eyes, once smoldering, looked dull and lifeless. With a sense of defeat, Susanna could only hope that time would bring him out of his apathy and she prayed that his father wasn't beating him.

Val accepted Ridge's friendship gratefully but it became apparent in a few days that he would happily have spent his play time talking to the horses and caressing them. The children who rode were supposed to rub their mounts down after unsaddling but Dottie shirked this chore and Val eagerly took it over from Freck who'd been taking care of it for his sister. A shame, Susanna thought, that a boy who loved horses so didn't have one, but surely in this range country, sooner or later he would.

The overcrowding lasted only until Wednesday morning when Jacob Rieghard drove up behind Flora with a desk and bench almost the length of the small green, flaring-sided wagon bed secured by much intricate ironwork. Val and Cobie, on the seat beside him, jumped down and helped him carry the desk and bench inside.

Smoothly sanded and polished to a sheen, they were much better made than the other classroom furnishings. Susanna complimented Jacob and asked him to tell the elder Krauses about the Thanksgiving program.

"They will come. To meet the teacher, they are eager." Jacob's tanned brow furrowed. "Except for Grandfather Anselm. The father of Peter and Frederick, he fears the children will forget their religion. To ourselves he thinks we should live. Often we have been forced to this. Here, his sons and I want it to be different." When Susanna mentioned the Friday afternoon exercises, though, he regretfully said Grandfather Anselm would consider such a weekly outing so frivolous that the others wouldn't dare to come. With rare exceptions, worship, keeping the Sabbath, and serious illness were the only acceptable reasons not to be working.

That creed should make them the most successful of farmers but it made Susanna sorry for this earnest, good-natured young man. However, if he and the young woman he loved could have a home and children, live together all their days, wasn't that the greatest happiness anyone could hope for on this earth?

Matt's face rose before Susanna. Knees and spine melting at the memory of his kiss, she envied Jacob his simple, straightforward courting, and then, as she told him good-bye, she smiled grimly at her own self-pity. All Jacob had done to be with his love was leave a prosperous village and all his kindred to spend six months traveling halfway round the world!

She redistributed the children by placing the five eight-to ten-year-olds—Dottie, Cobie, Rosie, and the twins—at the new desk, which fitted across from the big girls and behind the youngest pupils. Even though the older boys' desk was the longest in the room, it was somewhat crowded with the addition of Val but Susanna knew it would create endless problems to move him or any of the bigger boys back with the four older girls, so she left him beside Ridge.

All the Krause children were fascinated by the map, finding the Dnieper and tracing their journey to Odessa on the Black Sea and then to Lvov in the Ukraine, Wroclaw in Poland, and the great German port of Hamburg—this in itself a weary and arduous journey. The voyage to New York on an old coaling vessel took eighteen days. On the inset map, Susanna showed them the railroad route that had brought them to Topeka.

This odyssey impressed even Jenny and Charlotte and startled Susanna into realizing that she knew practically nothing about Russia, that vast country, twice the size of her own, spreading between Europe and Asia, except that the Russians—and winter—had driven Napoleon from their country in 1812, that the country lost the Crimean War to Turkey and Great Britain in 1856, that the ruling czar had liberated the serfs in 1861, and that in 1867 Russia had sold Alaska to the United States.

Delving in her histories provided only tantalizing glimpses which she passed on to her students. Viking traders, faring south along Russian rivers to trade furs and amber for the spices, silks, and jewels of the Orient and the luxuries of Constantinople, established trading centers at Kiev and Novgorod which grew into powerful city-states ruled by a Norse line that merged with native Slavic nobles. Converting to the Byzantine Christianity that was still Russia's state religion, Kiev's princely family married with the royalty of England, France, and the Germanic and Scandinavian kingdoms. Then in 1237 came the Mongols, pillaging and destroying, and for over two hundred years Russian princes ruled only if acknowledged by the khan to whom they paid heavy tribute.

By the time of Ivan the Terrible, Mongol power had decayed and could be defied. The czar assumed total power, ruling through church and state. Peter the Great forcibly tried to turn Russia's estranged face back toward Europe. His grandson's German wife, the redoubtable Catherine who invited the Mennonites into steppes still roamed by descendants of the Mongols, corresponded with Voltaire and Diderot though she ordered rebellious Cossack leaders to be quartered alive and encouraged the introduction of serfdom into southwestern Russia where it had been unknown. It was her grandson, Alexander I, who rode in triumph through Paris after Napoleon's defeat, and his grandson was the present czar.

All this, Susanna saw, could lead to many topics: Viking explorations and conquests; how a small Greek trading city on the Black Sea became the center of the immense Byzantine Empire whose power and territories had fallen to the now declining and embattled Ottoman Turks; the cultures of China and India and the ancient trade routes that brought their wares to the West—after all, hadn't the Americas, first discovered by Vikings though only briefly colonized, been encountered by Europeans seeking a water route to the fabled lands of spices and silk?

It was such a colorful, interwoven pageant that Susanna had to tear herself away from history-geography which the children loved, too, for as Rosie said, "It's like a long, long fairy tale."

Meanwhile, much time went into the Thanksgiving program. The children decided to tell a little about the countries their people had come from and the reasons, if known. They would trace the holiday from colonial times and conclude with songs.

Arriving early for that Friday's exercises, the women united in asking Susanna if they couldn't all bring food and begin the celebration with a shared meal. "Do you suppose Tom Chadron and Bert Mulroy could come?" asked Betty.

"And Jem Howe?" inquired Margaret. "Dr. Rawdon? And there are two or three other families living east of us with children either too big or little for school."

"Several bachelors live north of us," put in Laura Prade.

"Let's bring plenty of food and invite the whole dang shootin' match," urged Hettie, her warm brown eyes sparkling. "We might even get that fiddler from Ashy Creek and have us a dance."

"Fiddling's of the devil," Delia said, primming her

mouth. "We won't allow our girls around that sort of carrying on."

Hettie swelled up, but Margaret said quickly, "My church doesn't believe in dancing, either—we're Methodists—but we used to have play parties. That's all right."

"That's what we'll do," said Betty heartily. "That's not against anybody's religion that I know of, to sing and march."

"Fine, if that suits everybody," said Hettie. "But we're having a fiddler at our Christmas ball and anyone who thinks that's sinful is welcome to stay at home."

That was the closest the women had come to a clash but it was quickly smoothed over by planning. This was the first fragile shoot of community spirit extending beyond the school. With trepidation and delight, Susanna slipped out the door and rang the bell to call the children in.

❀ *Fourteen* ❀

It snowed the week before Thanksgiving but the snow melted so that the school ground wasn't muddy on the day of the celebration. Shortly before noon, horses and wagons brought everyone Susanna knew in that region, and many whom she didn't. Matt Rawdon accompanied two quaint, sturdy Mennonite wagons and was already introducing the Krauses to their neighbors when Susanna hastened to welcome them, shaking their hands as she carefully avoided Rawdon's hooded eyes. Cav, joyful at seeing his master, frisked like a puppy, bringing smiles from everyone.

Anna, Frederick Krause's wife, had skin almost as smooth and fair as that of her daughter, Catherine, Jacob's betrothed. They both had clear blue eyes fringed with long dark lashes. Beneath a plain, close-fitting black cap that tied beneath the chin, Anna's hair was light brown. Catherine, taller and slimmer than her mother, wore a black kerchief that revealed the bright hair shared with Magdalena, her little sister.

It would seem the Krauses had purchased a tremendous bolt of that green-sprigged black cotton worn by Cobie and Magdalena, for all the women's dresses were made

223

from it, neat, simple garments, buttoned high, that made not the slightest concession to style or femininity except for a small ruffle at Catherine's throat. That throat was so creamy and graceful, though, it needed no adornment.

Peter's buxom wife, Freda, had red cheeks, graying black hair, and the almond-shaped green eyes she'd bequeathed to Cobie. Less shy than her sister-in-law and niece, she beamed at Susanna and the women Susanna introduced to the newcomers.

Jacob had evidently taught the elder Krauses to say, "Good day" and "How are you?" but when this was done, Americans and Mennonites could for the most part only look at one another with good will and embarrassment though Jacob did his best to act as spokesman. Susanna was glad that Matt seemed to have appointed himself the Krauses' sponsor for he stayed near them and talked affably with those who came up to meet them and then didn't know what else to say, with glances and smiles to include the Krauses in the exchange even if they couldn't understand it.

There were other strangers to Susanna and with a smile of temporary farewell to the Krauses, she hastened to meet the group clustered around Margaret Hardy, Laura Prade, and Delia Taylor. Could the lanky man with tobacco-colored eyes and sandy hair and drooping mustache be—at last—Cash Hardy?

He bobbed his head as Margaret happily presented him. "Sure appreciate havin' you here, ma'am. Sorry this durned back keeps me from pullin' my weight for the school district, but I reckon Dave does his best to make up for it."

"Indeed he does," Susanna said. Maybe Cash did have back troubles, but it was strange that his first appearance was at an occasion where he could be reasonably sure of food much tastier than that Margaret and her sons managed to put on the table.

Mary and Jack Harris, blond and blue-eyed as their baby girl, didn't look more than twenty and, coming from Iowa, had just filed on their homestead last spring. Plump, brown-haired Sally Wright, and her husband, Ben, a skinny red-haired young man, each held a red-haired twin of perhaps a year and a half while a sturdy little boy of about three peeked from behind his mother's skirts, at first afraid of Cav but then venturing forward to hug him. Their claim lay between the Hardys and Harrises.

"We got here in time for the Easter blizzard of 'seventy-three," said Ben, "and we hung on last year after the grasshoppers, but if we hadn't made a good crop this summer, we'd have had to give up. You might say we're ready for Thanksgiving and we better have it before something else happens."

"We came out here for Shell's health," said the gaunt older gray-haired woman introduced as Mavis McGuinn. "Sold our store in Independence, Missouri, and gave our children everything we couldn't pack in a wagon. We thought farming would be a good way to spend the rest of our life, not too hard, plenty of fresh air." She snorted. "Let me put it this way: we're not asking our children to move out here."

Shell, gray-haired and sunburned, had hazel eyes that twinkled behind thick spectacles. "Well, Mavis, the wind's scorched whatever was making me cough all the time clear out of my throat and I feel better than I have in years." He winked at the others. "She's finally got some roses growing and a couple of apple trees we covered with rugs and tarps and saved from the 'hoppers. Don't think I could haul her out of here if I wanted to."

"Try me and see," said Mavis dourly, but then she smiled at her husband and her long-jawed sallow face lit with affection.

To share a life like that . . . Turning to welcome two strange men who were talking with Will Taylor, Susanna's eyes found Matt Rawdon. He was watching her. As their gazes met and shock went through her as if she'd touched

225

something freezing cold or searing hot, his mouth curved down in an ironic smile.

Had he meant his indecent proposal or had it been his way of keeping her from asking him disturbing questions? Blood rushed to her face as she remembered. How dare he behave as if he had nothing for which to apologize, as if nothing had happened? She turned her back on him and thought she heard soft, mocking laughter as Will introduced her to bachelors with claims north of the Prades, short, compact Nate Steele, whose smooth pink skin indicated that his thick white hair was no sign of his true age, and husky brown-haired Jeff Morrison who almost crushed Susanna's hand and let go of it only with reluctance.

Ase and Kermit had started laying planks across the wagon beds and the other men joined in this chore while women hurried to arrange the food. No boards were spread across the Tarrant buckboard for two huge iron kettles sat at the rear, one holding stewed antelope, the other, beef in a thick gravy.

Ase and the Browns set out great pans of roast beef, so there was plenty of meat for the crowd though the rest of the food ran to corn prepared in every way desperation and ingenuity could devise: parched corn cooked with milk, corn pudding, hominy, corn muffins, cornbread, pumpkin loaf made with cornmeal and molasses, baked Indian pudding, corn dumplings, and apple cornbread. There were pots of beans, several bowls of turnips and cabbage, and hoarded white flour had gone to make crusts for an array of pies—rhubarb, sandhill plum, elderberry, mince, and dried peach and apple, which were hungrily eyed by the children.

Jem Howe's contribution was a bowl of pale rosy tan hard-boiled eggs that created as much anticipation as the pies. There were pickled buffalo peas, gleaned from the prairie, crisp green watermelon-rind pickles, and jelly made from the ubiquitous sandhill plums. When Anna,

Freda, and Catherine Krause fetched their crocks and platters from the little green wagons, they flushed with pleasure at the unmistakable enthusiasm manifested at the
sight of balls and rounds of cheese, several kinds of sausages, and large seed-spinkled loaves of bread, which if not
made of white flour, were of some grain other than corn.
There was a large kettle of rice and currants cooked with
milk, smelling of cinnamon, and a tray of assorted buns
and rolls, again redolent of spices and dotted with currants.

The supercilious pity with which Delia Taylor had
regarded the Krauses changed laughably to amazed envy,
and everyone viewed them with new respect. Frugal and
odd their attire might be, but if this was a sample of their
regular fare, they ate better than anyone here unless one
shared Ase's conviction that all anybody needed was
plenty of beef.

Johnny had brought the giant chuck wagon coffeepot
full of brewed coffee which he set down at once to reheat
at the fire where Susanna also had coffee brewing. They
brought the pots out to sit on the laundry bench with
buckets of water. Everything was ready but Susanna had
forgotten to ask someone to say the blessing.

As head of the school board, Ase was the logical person.
She'd never heard him say grace but surely he knew one
or could improvise. Susanna rang the bell, and glanced
around the gathering as talk faded away and all faces
turned to her. These were her children; her people, with
the exception of Prade, even those she had just met. This
was home, as Ohio could never be, for she'd chosen this
place and it was here she carried out her work as a human
being, the teaching that was according to her nature.

Then Matt Rawdon's gray eyes pierced her quiet exul-
tation, made it almost a mockery as a shaft of pain and loss
twisted through her. Loving a man was certainly according
to her woman's nature, and she loved him. *What then,
Marcus?* she gibed at that stoic philosopher-emperor.

Shall I make haste to make a fool of myself over a man who might take me to bed but won't speak of love?

Rawdon's lips quirked as if he guessed her feelings. Wrenching her gaze away, she tried not to sound flustered. "Mr. McCanless, will you please say the blessing?"

Ase jumped as if he'd been shot. Betty Flynn smothered a giggle in a feigned cough, Jenny tittered, and the ranch people watched him with interest. Casting Susanna a look of reproachful anguish, Ase searched the skies for deliverance.

When none came, he swept off his hat, ducked his head, and cleared his throat. "God bless the grass. Amen."

That was all. After a moment, people began peering from beneath lowered eyelids. A few cautiously raised their heads. Will Taylor took a tighter clutch on his straw hat. "No offense, Ase. That may be enough of a prayer for a cattleman, but I reckon us homesteaders need a little more."

"Hop to it," said Ase, and ducked his head again.

Will made up for Ase's brevity. He thanked God for everything bad that hadn't happened as well as the good things that had, implored a like benevolence for the coming year, and wound up with, "Most of all on this day, Lord, we thank you for our school and this good teacher You sent us, and our neighbors, even them that—" He broke off. "I mean, thank You for our neighbors and bless this food to its intended use. Amen."

There was a chorus of Amens. Everyone had utensils, plates, and cups, mostly of tin. Hettie helped Millie Tarrant serve from the big kettles and Ase and Kermit sliced off beef while Betty ladled out beans. The Krauses held back, but Susanna urged them into line. No one else needed coaxing. Soon women were perched on the desks and benches that had been carried out. The children sat on the grass and men hunkered on their heels or stood.

Last through the line, Susanna moved from group to group, chatting and complimenting the women on whatever it was each had brought. Though she'd been admonished not to cook anything, she'd saved up eggs for two weeks and concocted a kind of pudding with cornmeal, evaporated milk, and molasses. In spite of the proliferation of corn dishes, she took satisfaction in finding there wasn't a speck left when she reached the bowl. She got one small bit of Mennonite cheese and the last spoonful of rice pudding, but she secured the crusty end of a loaf and one of the currant buns.

When she stopped with the Krause women who sat with Margaret Hardy, Sally Wright, and Mary Harris on the recitation bench while their men stood nearby, Susanna truthfully praised the nutty flavor of the bread and bun.

"From Turkey Red wheat our flour is made," said Jacob, keeping a proud, watchful eye on Catherine who was attracting wistfully admiring looks from the cowboys and bachelors. "Enough the Krauses brought for milling this autumn as well as for planting. If God grants to us a good harvest, gladly will we give seed wheat to our neighbors."

Saul Prade had ignored both Mennonites and Susanna, but otherwise seemed to be unusually affable that day, talking especially with the men of the community who weren't on the school board, and at the same time making conversation with Jack Harris and Ben Wright.

"It'll be a cold day in July before I need some foreigner telling me how to farm," he remarked, keeping his back turned to Jacob.

The young man colored. Dismayed, Susanna tried to think of something to say that wouldn't make matters worse. To her relief, Matt Rawdon said carelessly, "I'm sure going to ask them how, Prade. The kind of luck you men've been having, I wasn't figuring on fooling with trying to grow grain, but this Turkey Red sounds like it's worth a try."

So he *could* be nice. Why wouldn't he do it more often? A sudden dreadful thought struck Susanna. Could he be drawn to pretty, soft-voiced Catherine? Was that why he was going out of his way to be so friendly to the Krauses? True, with the young woman betrothed, nothing could come of it. All the same, the possibility rubbed salt in Susanna's wound. She visited a few more minutes and moved on.

When, amazingly, most of the food had disappeared, the children were playing, and kettles, pans, bowls, and eating things were being stowed into wagons, Susanna rang the bell. Seats and desks were carried in and occupied by the women and younger children. Everyone else stood and the overflow peered in the door and windows.

The history of Thanksgiving was traced from February 22, 1631, in the Massachusetts Bay Colony through Dutch New York and George Washington's proclamation to Abraham Lincoln's setting it on the last Thursday in November. Only Northerners clapped the Lincoln part but at least there were no catcalls.

Each group of children, then, was warmly applauded as they told about their ancestors' countries and their reasons for coming here over the ocean. The momentary silence following Ridge's account of the Cheyenne migration burst into clapping led by Ase.

The Krause children stood last by the map, cherubic little Magdalena smiling confidently while Freddie, as much as he could, got behind Val and Cobie. Susanna had asked them if they wanted to take part. They had, so she and Dave and Ridge worked with them on what they wanted to say and they had pretty much memorized it.

Finding the Netherlands, Cobie traced their family to Prussia. "In Prussia, as in Holland," she said in her lilting accent, "our people used dikes and canals to make good farms on swamplands. For a long time, the kings gave us freedom of worship and our men did not fight in wars."

"Frederick the Great confirmed these rights." Val, slender and dark, took up the story. "But even before he died, we were made to support the Lutheran state church and pay much money to escape military service. In 1786, Catherine the Great invited us to Russia."

Gypsy-like with her green eyes and dark hair, Cobie moved her finger from the Vistula to the region of the lower Dnieper. "Here our people came, again seeking a place where we could keep our faith. It is plains, like here. Once there were bison, like the buffalo."

"It seemed our people could stop their wandering," Val continued. "All was good for nearly a hundred years. Then the czar revoked his grandmother's promises." He showed the way to Hamburg and across the ocean.

On the small map, Magdalena's chubby finger traveled from New York to Kansas. "Now we live here. In Kansas, the United States of America," she said so blithely that everybody smiled.

Still half behind Cobie, Freddie took a deep breath and blurted, "We give thanks for good land and a country where we can worship."

"As we did a hundred years in Russia," Cobie said.

"Two hundred years in Prussia," said Val.

"And a hundred years in Holland," chimed Magdalena and Freddie.

The boys bowed and the girls curtsied. The cheering was thunderous. The program finished with singing. Freck, with his guitar, led off with the song they called "Kansas Rivers."

"We crossed the Arkansas and forded the Saline,
We swum the wide Smoky Hill, followed the Kaw;
The Verdigris runs rusty, the Little Blue clear,
But 'twas down on the Cimarron I courted my
    dear. . . ."

After a few old favorites shared by North and South, everyone moved outside, and while the children played their own games, their elders formed a double circle for Jolly Is the Miller Boy. Sarah and Charlotte were swept into the line by Tom Chadron and Bert Mulroy as Cash Hardy led the singing in a rich deep tenor. Though Susanna didn't know these play-party numbers, she was about to let Jeff Morrison pull her into the circle when she saw the Krauses moving toward their wagons.

Hurrying to catch up with them, she called their names, and as they turned, regarding her with a sort of resigned sadness, Jacob, blushing, said, "Dancing is against our religion."

"Oh, this isn't dancing." Susanna explained the difference though, to be truthful, the distinction made little sense to her.

Jacob shook his head. "We do not say your way is wrong, but to us, dancing this is."

"I'm sorry."

He smiled. "Do not be. Expect others to be like us we do not. Grateful we are if we are not expected to be like everybody else."

Peter spoke, his shrewd gray eyes resting on Susanna, and the others nodded as Jacob said, "A wonderful day this is for all of us. To hear the children speak well the English and tell of our journey was very good. Our neighbors we have met. Most are kind. Enough we cannot thank you for helping the little ones."

"I'm glad you've come," Susanna said truthfully. "The children try hard and never cause trouble. Besides, your story makes history and geography more real and helps us all understand better the good things about our country."

"I wish there were a school for us, too, the grown ones," Jacob said wistfully. "So many things we would like to know. Is it true that in five years we citizens can become?"

"Yes, but I'm not sure if it requires an oath of allegiance to this country."

Jacob's face fell. "Oaths we cannot swear."

Susanna searched for comfort. "Children born here are citizens."

"Full citizens? Like you?"

"Absolutely."

Eyes lighting, Jacob said, "Waiting we are used to."

Susanna's thoughts had been racing. "If you wish and can spare the time, I would be happy to come to your homes when the weather's good and hold a class either Saturday mornings or afternoons." It was four miles each way but she enjoyed walking and after all Cobie and Val did it every school day.

"You would?" So overcome that his eyes moistened, Jacob gulped. "Too good you are! But we will pay—"

"No. I want to do it. Talk it over and let me know."

"We will," Jacob promised. When he spoke to the Krauses, Freda caught Susanna's hand and bore it to her cheek. Frederick and Peter exchanged a few words and Anna Krause looked imploringly at her husband while Catherine's fair skin flushed with excitement. After a few questions, Jacob, grinning, turned back to Susanna.

"If willing you are, we invite you to have dinner on any Saturday that you can come and then we will have school. If you send word by the children on Friday, one of us will call for you with a wagon."

"I hate to put you to that trouble."

"Miss Alden! We to you are putting the trouble."

"Supposing I walk over? That way, if the weather or something changes you won't have a trip for nothing. Then I'll be very glad to be driven home. I'll try to come this Saturday if that's all right."

"More than all right it is!" Beaming, Jacob pumped her hand as the Krauses delightedly thanked her. "Very lucky we are to have settled near your school."

"It's your school, too," Susanna said.

She waved them off and turned to find Saul Prade watching her. He alone hadn't joined the couples who had now linked hands behind themselves to walk to the singing and scramble hastily when it was time for the women to step forward and the men to fall back, for this was the "miller boy's" chance to get out of the center by capturing some man's partner.

"We're not paying you to teach Dutchies, Miss Alden."

"Indeed, you're not. What I do on Saturday is surely my own affair, so long as it's not immoral or illegal."

His lips thinned. "It ought to be illegal, foreigners crowding in and taking over the school! You can't even try to deny that the time you spend on those squarehead brats isn't stolen from ours."

"Yours are learning things they wouldn't have if the Krauses hadn't come, things that aren't in books." Susanna trembled with indignation. "The other trustees agree the Krause children belong."

He laughed fleeringly. "They'd agree with anything you said. I'll be glad when they see what comes of this soft-headed slush you're teaching. Let in an Indian and look what happens!"

"To Millie and Ridge Tarrant, we're the foreigners," Susanna retorted.

"Well, you be damn sure that breed doesn't make up to Sarah, because if he ever does, I know how to fix him so he won't be a problem to any white woman—any woman, for that matter."

Stunned that he could think of such a thing, Susanna stared at him for a disbelieving moment and found nothing to which she could appeal, nothing to shame, in those hard green eyes. "What's made you like this?" she whispered.

"My father taught me early the truth about people and the world. What he didn't show me, the war did. You're a fool, woman, and I'll see the day when these other fools want to get rid of you as much as I do."

The first song had ended. Ase McCanless was striding toward them. "Why don't you blabber to him?" Prade sneered. "I'd like an excuse to see if his Colt can outmatch my whip." He lounged off to talk to Nate Steele and Jeff Morrison, who'd had to partner each other since there weren't enough women to go around.

"What's he saying to you?" Ase demanded, staring after Prade who gave him a cool smile.

"Nothing important."

"Your cheeks are mighty red for 'nothin',' Miss Alden, and your eyes are sure a-flashin'. Tell me what he said or I'll go ask him."

Susanna caught Ase's arm. "Don't! What he said doesn't matter—he's still complaining about the Krauses—and think how it would upset Laura and the Prade children if you men got into a fuss."

Ase glanced at Laura, his blue eyes softened. "Reckon you're right. But if he causes any real trouble, you've got to let me know. Promise?"

Almost overwhelmingly tempted to confide in Ase, tell him about Prade's savage treatment of his son, Susanna forced back the poisonous facts it would have been a relief to share. A teacher shouldn't discuss one patron or trustee with another. Besides, with Frank and her own spirit at stake, no one could fight her battle with Prade for that would give him victory. It was a struggle in the dark, one she couldn't clearly define or understand, and more terrifying because of that.

"I'll tell you if Mr. Prade makes problems at school," she said, and then explained her arrangement with the Krauses.

Ase whistled. "Mighty nice of you, ma'am. But you'd ought to let me bring Cindy over so's you could ride."

"It won't hurt me to walk four miles every other week."

The rancher shuddered with the aristocratic repugnance to walking felt by men who'd saddle a horse to go half a mile. "When you change your mind, ma'am, don't be too stiff-necked to say so. But I came over here to pick a bone with you."

"Really?"

"Askin' me to say the blessin'. I felt like I'd all of a sudden fell into a bog!"

"You did beautifully." Susanna chuckled.

"You might at least have warned me."

"I didn't think about it till the last minute. But if I upset you, I apologize."

"Not good enough, Miss Alden, ma'am. Only thing that'll square it is for you to spend the Christmas holidays with us. Betty won't hear to you stayin' in this dark old soddie by yourself those four days, and neither will I." Before she could speak, he went on, "It's plumb ridiculous the way you already spend weekends at this dump. The Tarrants, Browns, and me have talked it over. If you won't stay at the Ace High, you're goin' to be with one of them."

Despotic as he sounded, it was kindly meant and Susanna was touched at this concern for her. "I'll be delighted to stay at the Ace High," she said demurely.

His jaw dropped. "You're not goin' to pitch and buck about it?"

"Not for a minute. I *do* have work to do on weekends, but, even with Cav, it would be lonely to pass Christmas by myself."

Ase's eyes held hers. "So you're human like the rest of us," he said. "Sometimes I've wondered." Grinning boyishly, he took her arm, his big, callused hand warm, protective, and insistent. "Well, while your Yankee starch is a mite wilted, let's get in on some of this Presbyterian waltzin'! Sure looks like a Virginia reel to me, but if it makes everybody happy to call it a singin' game, that's fine too!"

It was fine with Susanna as well, this happiest, proudest day of her whole life, but when Matt Rawdon swung her in the center between the rows formed for "Weevilly Wheat," her body melted at his touch while a yearning so acute that it was physical pain made her feel faint and weak.

Why had he done it, why had he held and kissed her,

when he meant it to punish her? What had happened to make him like this? He must have been terribly, terribly hurt but why couldn't he put it behind him?

"The program was a great success," he said rather stiffly as they linked arms.

"Thank you," she said, even more stiffly.

The Harris baby had started crying and at the end of the game, Susanna went to quiet the little blond girl so Mary could enjoy this rare pleasure. As she held the soft, warm little body against her and swayed in a lulling motion, Susanna knew she had much to be thankful for that day, and truly she was. Would she ever have a husband, though? Rock her own baby?

❋ Fifteen ❋

The first Saturday in December dawned bright and chill, frost glittering in the sun. Putting on her warmest dress, the gray wool grenadine, over both her red flannel and two cambric petticoats, Susanna had breakfast standing near the fireplace for warmth. Then she banked the fire which was just starting to heat the room, and put on her brown mantle. She started to put on her brown bonnet but cold ears won over vanity and she wrapped a wool scarf around her head, tossing the ends over her shoulders.

The Krause children had taken home a speller, primer, and American history book that Jacob was reading to them, so Susanna needed to carry no books. Pulling on her mittens, she unbarred the door, laughing at Cav's joy that she'd be walking with him. She hadn't let him out earlier for fear he'd race off to Matt's. The track ran past the Hardys' and forked at their east boundary, the right-hand road running to Jem Howe's and on to the Wrights', McGuinns', and Harrises', the left traveling past Matt Rawdon's and on to the Krauses'. She would almost certainly see Rawdon and no matter how she chided herself, that filled her with anticipation.

To bridge the creek, shortly after school started, Dave had felled a dead cottonwood, trimmed off its branches, and leveled the top enough to make a surface about a foot and a half wide. Susanna, skirt and petticoats swaying, still found it difficult enough, though had she slipped, she'd only have gotten a thorough dunking. Cav had dashed ahead, glancing back encouragingly.

"It's fine for you," she grumbled, catching a breath of relief as she stepped onto the bank. "You've got four feet." To the crows and blackbirds who were clattering in raucous amusement, she called, "Have you heard about the four-and-twenty blackbirds who got baked into a pie?"

They cackled merrily, so impudent that Susanna had to smile as she walked on. As she neared the Hardy dwelling, Rosie scurried out, taffy braids flying. "Mama says you've got to stop for a cup of coffee, teacher! You will, won't you?" Her face fell. "'Course it's not really coffee, just corn meal and molasses cooked to a powder."

"Of course, I'll stop," said Susanna though she hadn't intended to. Realizing what an affront that would be to Margaret, she saw that she'd just have to work in a short visit. Besides, after walking two miles at a temperature not much above freezing, her nose and feet and hands were cold and chill air had found its way up her many skirts.

The fire glowed cheerily in this home partly dug into the slope but there was scarcely room to move around since Margaret and the four children took up most of the room not occupied by several shuck mattresses rolled into a corner, a table, a trunk, one chair, and several upended boxes that served for seats. Though she had seen her only the day before, Margaret clasped Susanna's hands, kissed her cheek, and made her sit on the chair Dave brought closer to the fire.

"Sorry I can't come out, Miss Alden," came Cash's voice from behind a curtain made of burlap sacks. "This dadgummed old back's got me flat again."

"I'm sorry about that, Mr. Hardy," said Susanna, but affa

ble and harmless as he was, she couldn't like a man who didn't seem to try to do better for his family than this, drinking up Margaret's egg money while they lived in a virtual cave.

That Margaret hadn't given in to these conditions was a marvel. The faded oilcloth on the table was wiped clean, the lamp chimney glowed, and everything was neat and in its place. Just washing for this family with the scrub board and tubs that leaned against the wall outside was a prodigious feat and an equal wonder was that Margaret could be so cheerful.

They chatted over the makeshift coffee, which was not unpalatable and did spread a welcome glow through Susanna as her toes, fingers, and face warmed. "I wish we had a riding horse to lend you," Margaret said when Susanna insisted that she had to be getting on her way. "But you just stop off here and warm up."

Susanna thanked her, put on her outdoor things, adjusting the scarf this time to cover her nose, and resumed her journey, accompanied by Rosie and Georgie who'd begged permission to "walk teacher to the road fork."

They bounced along beside her, playing with Cav and chattering all the way. When they turned back, waving and calling good-byes, it seemed very quiet. As several sod barns and a sod house with a shingled roof came in sight, Susanna's heart beat faster and she strained to see everything she could about this place where Matt lived though she still writhed inwardly when she remembered his cynical proposition.

Perhaps a score of horses, among them gray Saladin, grazed around an earthen tank where a few brown-orange leaves still clung to several big cottonwoods. A number of leggy, half-grown colts raced off at her approach, manes and tails flying. Lovely creatures, snorting in joyful fright.

They would feed well this winter. Behind two long, low barns that must have log supports inside to hold up the heavy sod roofs, hay was stacked higher than the buildings and the haymows inside were surely full. Matt took better care of his horses than Cash Hardy did of his family.

Averting her eyes from the house, which had several glass-paned windows and a lean-to fuel shed, Susanna was somewhat past it when she heard the creak of a door and Matt called her name, catching up with her in a few loose strides.

"When I saw you coming, I thought you'd decided to accept my eminently sensible proposal," he said in that hatefully superior and amused way he often had. "Alas, you marched right past my abode though I noticed that you paused to admire my horses."

She unmuffled her nose. "They, sir, deserve admiration."

"And I don't?" He shrugged and chuckled. "Too true, I'm afraid. But where are you going?"

When she explained, he said almost angrily, "You can't walk this far in the middle of winter! I never heard such nonsense!"

Her toes were so numb that she was prone to agree but she said defensively, "It's too much trouble for the Krauses to drive me both ways. Mr. McCanless offered me Cindy but it seems silly to keep a horse when I can only ride on weekends."

"It's a good deal sillier to plan to walk that distance when you could get caught in a storm and freeze to death."

"If it looks threatening, I won't leave home and if it clouds up while I'm at the Krauses', I'm sure they'd want me to spend the night. Besides, if a storm did catch me on the road, I could shelter at the Hardys'——or even at your place, if things were really bad."

"Thank you, ma'am." He bowed. "Salutary as it might be to see you grovel up through snowdrifts to my door, I can't say I'd care to find you frozen stiff a few feet from it and, believe me, in a blizzard that can happen. Men have lost the way and died while trying to get from their house to their barn."

Hard to credit, yet it sent a shiver down Susanna's spine. "I'll be careful," she said.

He groaned with exasperation. "Here on the prairie, those last words could be engraved on many a tombstone."

Aching with the fiery pleasure-pain that being near him caused in her, Susanna tried to ease it with a joke. "If that fits on my tombstone, I should think you'd call it good riddance to a Yankee school teacher."

"For that you deserve a damned fine spanking, Susanna Alden, and I'd give it to you if you weren't so bundled up that it wouldn't do much good."

She halted, glaring at him. "If—if you ever try that, Matt Rawdon, I—I hope Cav bites you!"

At his name, Cav dashed up and inquiringly wagged his tail. Matt threw back his head and roared. When, choking, he could speak, he stroked Cav and gave Susanna a look from those strangely deep-lit gray eyes that completely melted her, fool that she was.

"Reckon it wouldn't be fair to put the poor fellow to that kind of choice. Would it, Hank?" The dog ecstatically agreed, pressing close to his former master's knees and slathering worship on his hands. "Go your way, most dutiful of teachers, you who seem to think it's your calling to educate everybody in sight." He turned serious. "If a storm does loom when you're near my house, don't hesitate but come in. Make yourself at home if I'm not there. If I am, I promise to behave." His eyes laughed. "At least till the storm's over and you can run away if you feel so inclined."

"That's kind of you—I think." Tucking the scarf back over her frigid nose, she said in muffled tones, "Good day, Dr. Rawdon."

He pulled his tousled forelock in mock obeisance. "Farewell, pretty lady." Their eyes caught, held as if locked.

Lightning swept between them. Susanna's body felt weighted, heavy; she almost closed her eyes.

With a smothered sound, he swung away. Cav started after him, paused unhappily, and glanced at Susanna with an imploring whimper. "Go, Hank!" Matt said roughly, not looking back.

Wordlessly, Susanna bent to give the dog a hug, brushed away tears that were icy fire on her cheeks. "He doesn't need you, Cav, and he certainly doesn't need me. Come on, old fellow. Magdalena and Freddie will be thrilled to play with you and I'll bet Val or Cobie will save you a piece of sausage from their dinners!"

After three hours of spelling and reading in English and another hour of informal United States history and government with Jacob translating the Krauses' questions and Susanna's answers, they all gathered around the big table in Peter's house. The patriarch, Anselm, whose weathered face made his white hair and beard look even snowier, sat at the head and intoned a very long and heartfelt prayer.

From his manner with her, correct but guarded, and his absence from the study group, Susanna gathered that he didn't approve of his family's wish to learn the language and customs of their new country, as much as was compatible with their religion. His piercing gray eyes, shepherding his descendants from beneath fleecy eyebrows, need only touch a squirming Magdalena to quiet her. There was no levity at the table but voices were calm and amiable as twelve people applied themselves to tureens of steaming soup—borscht, Jacob explained—delicious crusty wheaten bread, succulent dumplings stuffed with white cheese, and the rice pudding with currants that had been so popular at the Thanksgiving feast.

There was butter and the children had milk to drink, for the Krauses had bought the best livestock they could find and had six Holstein milk cows, two of which had not gone dry. On a low cupboard steamed what Jacob called a samovar, a gleaming copper urn with an ornamented lid and a spigot from which tea could be drawn. Beside it was an exceedingly large coffee mill.

The floor was packed earth but, late in the year though they had come, the sod roofs had been torn off and replaced with shingles and each house boasted an ingenious brick stove built into the wall partitioning the two rooms Frederick and Anna had and the three in the larger soddie shared by Peter and Freda's family, Anselm, and Jacob. These large thick-walled stoves, designed on the steppes of Russia to burn hay and grainstalks, only needed filling morning and evening. Heat permeated the bricks which stored the warmth and radiated it for hours.

"That's perfect for the plains," Susanna marveled. "But there must be many things you miss."

Jacob shrugged. "Too luxurious perhaps we were. Tea we got from China overland, and the best Brazilian coffee by way of Hamburg reached us. What we miss most, except of course our village and friends and relatives who chose to stay—what we miss is fish. There were many kinds in the Dnieper. But learn we will to eat jackrabbit instead."

He went on to say they had already planted trees they'd brought with them, mulberries, cherries, apples, peaches, apricots, and pears. Winter was no time to build, and spring to autumn next year would be spent tilling, planting, and harvesting, but between harvest and the onset of winter, they planned to build frame houses, incorporating the brick stoves and reusing the shingles.

"For Catherine and me, there will be also a house," he said with shy pride, stealing a swift look at Catherine whose blue eyes sparkled as their glances met. "Then we marry." He gave a chuckle so soft that Anselm didn't frown. "Mennonites usually in winter marry in order not to interfere with the farm work."

Very practical, Susanna thought. It gave the young couple time to adjust to marriage before the round of work began that could keep both man and woman busy from before dawn till after dusk. In summer heat, resting in each other's arms might be uncomfortable, but in winter— No! She must not think of Matt and her own cold and lonely bed.

Peter asked Jacob something and while they were conversing, Susanna could unobtrusively look around this largest room which was kitchen, dining room, and living room. A kind of brick bench was built adjoining the stove. This, Jacob had explained, was Anselm's bed, for in spite of his erect posture, he was, at seventy-eight, assailed by rheumatism and prone to take a chill.

Table and chairs were plain and handmade, probably here, but a tall, carved cupboard of golden oak looked as if it had been lovingly polished by many generations. It displayed burnished copper platters and cookware, colored glass and china. A high chest, where a brass lamp stood by a big, well-worn Bible, looked similarly cherished, and the handsome old wall clock that hung above it must have told time for Krauses in Prussia, the Ukraine, and now all of Europe and an ocean away.

Susanna had considered the rice pudding dessert but Catherine and Cobie cleared away the big floral-patterned plates and replaced them with bowls of a sort of date cake lavished with cream before refilling everyone's teacup.

The clock, with its revolving sun, moon, and stars, was striking a sonorous two in the afternoon when Susanna thanked her hostesses, accepted thanks from all the adults save old Anselm, and prepared to leave.

A basket covered with a linen towel was pressed upon her and, smiling, Freda lifted the towel to reveal a firkin of butter, a ball of cheese, date cake, and two loaves of the good-smelling bread.

"It's too much," Susanna protested, but Jacob said, "We grateful are. Let us show it."

Again except for Anselm, everyone stepped out to wave

good-bye as Jacob helped her into the shiny green wagon. Val, who'd been holding the horses, handed Jacob the reins. Jacob clucked to the team and they were off.

As they rumbled along, Jacob told Susanna more about their homes on the Dnieper and how the Krauses had sold theirs with most of their furnishings and farm implements for less than half their value though their excellent cows and horses had brought close to fair prices. "Still," he said, "glad we are that God granted us a refuge. For Catherine and me, it is easier than for her parents and aunt and uncle. We are young, our children here will be born, and here we will make our lives."

Marcus Aurelius, Susanna thought, would have approved their steadfastness. They hadn't emigrated, as most peoples had, in hope of becoming prosperous, or to escape grinding poverty or persecution. Indeed, the czar had entreated these most successful producers of food to remain in his realm. Though they were much better off than the homesteaders around them, the Krauses had sacrificed much to reach this prairie and Susanna hoped they would be rewarded and never regret their choice.

As they passed the Rawdon place, Matt seemed to be training a rambunctious sorrel colt to obey the lead of a halter. In order not to frighten the dancing youngster, he gave the slightest gesture of greeting.

Touching the edge of his cloth cap, Jacob gave a rueful smile. "Our Valentine, to Mr. Rawdon he is always coming when he is not at home needed, so that he can help train the horses. Always, horses he has loved. A neighbor in the Ukraine gave him an Arabian colt that grew into a very good saddlehorse. We could not bring him. Valentine was not much comforted that the burgomaster bought him. With our work horses, Val is good, but his heart is with the fleet ones."

Could Mennonites be cowboys? It didn't seem too likely but neither could Susanna imagine dreamy, artistic Val being much of a farmer whether here or in the Ukraine.

That led her into musing on the probable fates of all her pupils. The ones she worried most about were Ridge, Jenny, Berenice, and Frank. Frank most of all; his apathy was almost more distressing than his earlier malice. It was as if he were empty. She could only hope that when his spirit filled again, it would not be with his father's malevolence.

She spent one more Saturday morning with the Krauses before Christmas. As she approached, Cav at her heels, Val was out by one of the barns, watching and advising Catherine as she rode sidesaddle on a clean-limbed blue-gray mare with a mane and tail like spun moonbeams.

The mare was so beautiful that even though she knew little about horses, Susanna halted in admiration and understood something of the feeling for the animals that Val and Matt evidently shared. When she was ready to leave, instead of a basket of good things, she was given a plump bundle and Jacob, grinning, said, "Please do come out and see Valentine's surprise."

Thin face aglow, Val held the bridle of the blue-gray mare. Susanna stood astonished while Jacob took her bundle and slipped it in the saddlebags. "Please, our teacher," Val said proudly. "This Schatzie is. Mr. Rawdon has—to me gave—" Floundering, he appealed to Jacob. The children were all making swift progress in their English but sometimes had trouble finding the right verb forms, especially in excitement.

"Mr. Rawdon has to Valentine the mare given in return for his helping train the horses for three years in his spare time." Jacob laughed. "Unnecessary it is. Valentine for this would pay if he could. But to Frederick Mr. Rawdon came and it was agreed. First must Valentine work here. During the busiest times, he cannot with the horses be, but Mr. Rawdon says he would rather Valentine have for the hours he can spare than anyone else the whole time."

"That's wonderful, Val," Susanna praised. "But I still don't see—"

"Now, our teacher," cried Val joyfully. "You—to us you need not be walking. You will ride. On my horse, *mein Schatz.*"

My sweetheart. Confound Matt Rawdon! Of all the sneaky tricks! Sneakier even than his way of giving her Cavalier, for how could she possibly dash that proud delight from the boy's face? Susanna's brain whirred and suddenly she had at least a partial solution, which might be the best she'd ever do when that infuriating man decided *she* needed something. And, of course, beneath her resentment at his high-handedness, she was touched at his concern for her.

"Val," she said, speaking slowly and clearly so he would understand, "I will be glad to ride Schatzie back and forth to your home, but during the week I have no time to ride or care for her. It would be best if you rode her home on Mondays and then on Friday left her with me. That way, she won't miss you so much."

His eyes shone and he pressed his cheek to the mare's. "You are sure?"

"Very sure."

Val thought a moment. "The saddle, when I tell—told Mr. Rawdon what I do, he loan it. Cobie behind me can ride on—on a blanket." Jacob helped Susanna mount, unlike Ase, not touching her waist at all or cupping her foot a second longer than was necessary. Val caressed the mare's neck and whispered as he pressed his cheek to hers, "Monday, little horse. I will see you then."

As the beaming assembly waved her off, Susanna sat a little stiffly, well aware that this mare was no placid old Cindy who sometimes seemed to go to sleep as they ambled along. Schatzie had an easier gait, smooth as the proverbial rocking chair, and responded instantly to the reins, which prompted Susanna to pay close attention to how she used her hands. By the time they had gone a mile,

Susanna relaxed and began to enjoy the swinging pace. With a horse like this, she might someday become a reasonably good rider. She still intended to give Matt Rawdon a piece of her mind, and when they neared his place, she looked for him, but he was not to be seen.

Coward! He knew perfectly well she'd be coming by about this time. He couldn't be far away for a thin dragon of smoke rose from the chimney. He could be inside, gloating. Had she been sure she could get back on without demoralizing Schatzie, Susanna would have dismounted and rapped on the door but, sweet-tempered as the mare seemed, Susanna didn't dare try her patience by awkward clambering to get her leg positioned back over this ludicrous hook. The only prudent thing to do was ride on.

As she neared the Hardys', the youngsters all ran out and stared in awe, Dave and Ethan with such wistful admiration that Susanna's heart misgave her. How she wished these good, bright children had more than they did! And yet, when she pondered her pupils' futures, she had no worries for these except that Dave get the education he craved and Rosie not wind up married to an attractive layabout like her father. But why, why, couldn't they and Margaret have a little more comfort?

At least Dave had the tiny wage she paid him but she knew where that would go——for necessities and shoes for his brothers and little sister. Susanna just hoped Cash wouldn't inveigle it from him to spend on whiskey.

Explaining that she'd have Schatzie only on weekends, Susanna invited them to come over Sunday and ride for a while if Schatzie didn't mind. That brought Dave's slow smile and glee from the younger ones.

The creek didn't reach Schatzie's knees so Susanna didn't get splashed. As they trotted up the bank——Susanna hoping she wouldn't be clumsy in getting off saddle and bridle——the mare lifted her head and nickered. Susanna gasped.

Two gray horses were in the schoolyard. They whinnied

and the loose one cantered toward Schatzie though the saddled gelding stayed ground hitched. Matt Rawdon came forward, grinning like the Cheshire-cat, not a whit afraid to face her.

"Fine horse you've got there, ma'am."

"A lot finer than the deceitful man who gave her away!"

He shook his head. "I didn't *give*, Miss Alden. I do need a helper and Val is a rare, natural-born horseman. Makes me think somewhere in these last hundred years, a Tartar was grafted to the Krause family tree. Anyway," he added with bland innocence, "it was the boy's idea to lend the mare to you."

Susanna didn't try to restrain a snort. "A lot of good she'd do him if I kept her all the time! Well, you guessed right that I couldn't hurt him by refusing to ride, but at least he can pick her up Mondays and have her till Friday."

"Clever lady!" Matt twinkled.

Deflated as she wondered if he'd expected that, too, and if what she'd deemed a partial thwarting of him had only followed his expectations, she glanced at the mare who'd run to meet them and who looked much like Schatzie except that her mane and tail were dark and she was heavier. "May I ask why you're here?"

"Can you dismount from a spirited horse, Miss Alden?"

"I—I don't know."

"Ride over by this stump and try. Keep a grip on the reins but be sure you don't jerk them. Weight on the stirrup foot, knee easy off that damned hook and foot on the stump—that's the way."

Standing on the stump, Susanna looked straight into his eyes. That was so disconcerting that she quickly scrambled down. "That's one reason I came," said Matt. "Now lead your horse to the barn and let's see you unsaddle and take care of her."

He had come to make sure his horse was properly tended. A bit piqued, but glad that he had that much concern for animals, Susanna led Schatzie inside, tossed hay into the manger, slipped the crownpiece of the headstall over the mare's ears and took the bridle off, Schatzie helping to get rid of the bit. The mare lipped up hay while Susanna pulled on the cinch to make enough slack to unbuckle it. She pulled the saddle off, placing it on the top pole of the waist-high stall divider.

"Glad to see the kids are keeping the barn cleaned out and fresh straw on the floor," Matt said. He produced a piece of old blanket. "Now you rub her down and I'll show you how to groom her. I see the kids have a brush and currycomb here but I'll leave these, too. You won't use the currycomb on Blue Girl's—I mean, Schatzie's coat except to work off dried mud and clean the brush, but you will need this hoof hook that's attached to the back. If you don't thoroughly clean out the cleft of the frog—that's this triangular horny pad here in the middle of the foot—and clean well between it and the shoes, thrush can get started, which is mighty nasty." He squinted up at her. "Better take off that mantle or by the time we're finished, you'll need a currycomb yourself."

After demonstrating on one hoof, working from heel to toe, he handed Susanna the hook. She was a bit nervous about lifting Schatzie's foot, but the mare obliged at first touch, and after several admonitions from Matt to bear down harder, she cleaned the hoof to his satisfaction. He then did a rear hoof and supervised her on the other.

Next, starting on the left with neck, breast, withers, and shoulders, Matt, standing back from the horse and keeping his arm stiff so that his weight was on the brush held in his left hand, used quick, sure strokes, stopping every few sweeps to clean the brush with the currycomb held in his right hand, working to back, belly, croup, and down to the hoof. He groomed the right side in the same swift, expert manner, and brushed her head, talking gentle nonsense to her in a way that made Susanna envious as she had already been, wondering what it would be like to feel those strong, skilled hands on her.

Matt did mane and tail by starting at the ends and working up to the roots. "Her mane and tail don't really need this. Val must have given her a good grooming before he saddled up, but I want you to know how. Now you use the grooming cloth to clean her face, with special care to ears and nostrils, and give her a final polish."

When Susanna had done this to his satisfaction, he cleaned the brush, shook out the cloth, and hung it on a peg. "Reckon you'll manage," he said with a doubtfulness that stung after Susanna had gotten herself covered with gray hairs in her efforts to follow his instructions. "After all, there's only Sunday that Val won't be checking her."

"I didn't ask for your horse," Susanna snapped, brushing without much success at the hairs embedded in her wool grenadine before she gave up and got her bundle out of the saddlebags. "Do take her home if you're so worried. Tell Val I'm too pigeon-brained to be trusted with a horse even if most people seem to think I can look after their children." His startled expression broadened to a grin which further exasperated her. "Most mothers don't fuss that much over their children and I'll wager you wouldn't, either."

His tone was unruffled. "I may have been a doctor but I always felt that once delivered, babies were mysteries best left to their mothers."

The older gray mare approached and as he stopped to stroke her, Susanna demanded, "Why did you bring her?"

"To keep Schatzie company." At Susanna's stare, he said, "Don't you know horses are very sociable critters? They hate being alone. Zuleika's retired and out to pasture so she might as well be over here with Schatzie, her last colt. It won't hurt if she comes along with you to the Krauses'. If Schatzie was here alone, unless you kept her tied in her stall, which would be a shame in good weather, she'd take off mighty fast for my place."

He made sense. He always did, to her disgust. "I'll bring

over some hay," he said. "And in case of a storm, they'll head for the barn of their own accord."

"You say Zuleika's retired, but would it be all right for her to carry children around a little?"

"What children?"

She told him how the Hardy youngsters had run out to admire Schatzie. "I hope it was all right to invite them over tomorrow for a ride," she concluded.

"Schatzie's Val's horse now, but I don't think he'd mind. Schatzie's gentle but she's not used to small kids. Zuleika, now, is a kid horse. I bought her off a man whose kids rolled on, off, and under her. Put a halter on her and she can take Rosie and Georgie on a ride. If one fell off, she'd stop." He thought a minute. "Dave and Ethan are used to workhorses but maybe I'd better ride over and give them a few pointers."

He gave her a wry smile and she couldn't tell whether he was amused or annoyed. "You're hell-bent on education, aren't you, ma'am? First, it's Saturday school for the Krauses and now it's a riding class. If someone's not learning, you'll put them to teaching."

"Teaching's a good way to learn," she said. "Besides, Dr. Matthew Rawdon, you're the one who started this horse business. I didn't ask you—"

"Quite right," he sunnily admitted and raised a dark eyebrow. "Surely you're going to offer me a cup of tea or coffee."

"I'd have to build up the fire and get the water boiling," she evaded.

More than anything in the world, she wanted to be with him, yet feared what might happen if he ever really made love to her. The way her bones melted along with her will, common sense, and morality, it didn't bode well for her being able to resist a forceful onslaught. That left him the keeper of their honor—and could she trust him when she couldn't trust herself?

"I took the liberty of stoking your fire and setting the

kettle on," he said. "One cup of tea, Miss Alden, and I'll be on my way."

She took that as a promise. "Come in, then, and I'm sure Anna Krause sent some ginger cake."

It was pleasant to be greeted by a fire instead of a dark, chill interior. Matt fed the flame and perched on the trunk as she got out the ginger cake and put the wonderful fresh bread in the Dutch oven to protect it. When the water boiled, she poured it into Grandmother Alden's teapot.

As the fire warmed the room, Matt's presence made her glow inside, feel as if her secret darkness were filled with soft, delicious light. It was such happiness to be with him that she desperately wished they could just spend time like this if he could never learn to trust her enough to love her. She would rather have his company than every-thing—children, marriage, a shared life—with anybody else. Then, as she handed him his tea, their hands brushed and sweet, dizzying flame leaped between them.

No. It was impossible. Besides, even if she, an inexpe-rienced woman, could accept such a tantalizing bargain, it was ludicrous to think that a virile young man would. She retreated to the rocking chair and her tea.

Silence deepened. Her heart thudded till she thought he must surely hear it. Indicating the magazine on the table, she swallowed and said in a high, tinny voice, "This *Atlantic* my aunt sent me has a most diverting account of a Welsh governess who was employed to teach the countless children of the King of Siam—"

"Hang the King of Siam!" Rising abruptly, Rawdon loomed over her a moment before he reached the door in a single stride. "There you sit prattling, sipping your tea while— Never mind! You were quite right to try to send me on my way, Miss Alden. I'll take it now. I'll shut the mares in the barn so they won't follow me off."

Feeling as if he'd struck her, Susanna got to her feet. "I—I can do that, sir."

"No, stay here and keep warm." His tone gentled. "I'm

sorry, Susanna. It's not your fault. I should know myself better." An ironic note crept into his voice. "Have a pleasant evening with the King of Siam."

He patted Cav but when the dog would have followed him, he said sternly, "Stay here, Hank."

"His name's Cavalier!" Susanna fought back tears. "Now go ahead, Matt Rawdon, and tell him you don't *need* him!"

Matt's gaze plunged into hers. He took a step forward. Susanna closed her eyes. There was a harsh intake of breath, she heard quick steps moving away and then the door shut hard. Cav whined softly.

Susanna stood smoothing his head and tulip ears and then the tears came.

❀ *Sixteen* ❀

Surrounded by the Hardy children, Matt rode up Sunday afternoon. Tied behind his saddle were two bridles and a couple of pads and surcingles or cinches to hold them on the horses. Schatzie and Zuleika, whickering, raced to greet Saladin and Matt. Matt gave each child a handful of oats to feed the mares and after they were acquainted, Dave and Ethan bridled and groomed them before strapping on the pads.

Observing from the window, Susanna felt abashed at her impulsive invitation. She had thought Dave and Ethan could each have a nice hour's ride and then supervise Rosie and Georgie on loops around the yard. Matt was indeed teaching.

After Dave was up on Schatzie and Rosie was boosted onto Zuleika, Matt swung up on Saladin and was clearly instructing them in posture and the use of the reins. Georgie and Ethan trotted along behind as they rode out on the prairie. Susanna, a bit nettled that Rawdon hadn't even glanced toward the soddie, went back to grading compositions and, an hour later, when she went to fill the fuel box, Ethan and Georgie were just setting off with Rawdon for their turn.

Dave hurried to get the fuel for Susanna, light brown eyes sparkling. "Doc sure knows horses, Miss Alden. He says we can ride every Sunday when the weather's decent."

"Yes!" cried Rosie, dancing so that her yellow-brown braids jounced. "And when he stopped for us today, he told Mama that if she'd wash and iron for him, and bake him some bread every week with the wheat flour he traded for with the Krauses, he'd swap us a nice gelding."

At this rate, Matt wouldn't have any horses left to sell. Susanna felt a little guilty at causing the situation he'd responded to so unexpectedly but smothered it with the reflection that being with children was good for him; it was time he rejoined the human race.

If he weren't so stubborn about practicing medicine! It seemed wicked to refuse to start a practice though he did help when he was needed. A week seldom passed that Susanna didn't use his medical chest. So far, thank goodness, there'd been nothing serious.

When he returned with Ethan and Georgie, the horses were groomed again and the riding gear stowed in the barn. Matt rode off without even stopping for a moment to say good-bye, though all the children did.

Was he angry? Blaming her in some curious male feat of illogic because he'd fled the house last evening? Even if, like her, he'd scarcely slept, was that a reason to ignore her existence? And just look at him, sending back poor Cav!

Eyes smarting, Susanna opened the door for the big dog whose tail wagged dejectedly. She stopped to pet him. "I hope you don't mind being with me too much, boy," she murmured. "*He* evidently does!" She rushed in to poke at the fire till it sputtered and smoked in protest, and forced herself back to her work.

The Christmas program was a great success but the skies

were lowering, and when feathery snowflakes began to float by the windows, the carol singing was cut short. Amid holiday wishes and compliments to Susanna and the children on the entertainment, people bundled up and started home.

"Don't forget our Christmas ball!" Hettie Brown called. "The fiddler's coming and we'll dance all night!" She ignored Delia Taylor's sniff of disapproval. "If it storms so you can't get home, we'll put you ladies up in the house and send the men to the bunkhouse where they can yarn and spit tobacco to their hearts' content. Ase, mind you bring Miss Alden."

"You bet I will," he said.

Jenny rode ahead with the Browns who promised not to let her take the fork to the Ace High if there was any question of it being safe, while Ase hitched up the team and Betty helped Susanna set things in order for her absence.

"What a lot of sweet presents the young'uns brought you," Betty said, admiring gifts heaped on the desk—embroidered handkerchiefs from Sarah, molasses candy from the Taylors, and from Berenice a mat woven with many knots in its wildly assorted yarns. There were beaded moccasins from Ridge, a tin of fudge from Freck and Dottie, and from Rosie, Ethan, and Georgie a winter bouquet of dried stalks, plants, and pods displayed in a tall container Dave had whittled from cottonwood root. The Krauses had sent a large, beautifully carved wooden box filled with frosted cookies and tiny cakes.

Val's gift was a pencil sketch of Schatzie, mane and tail flying. "That child's a proper artist," Betty said in awe.

"Yes." Susanna put on her wraps and picked up her satchel. "I'm afraid the Krauses don't quite know what to do with him." Cav rose up from beside the door, shaking off the snow, as they stepped outside and shut the door tight.

"Honey," blurted the older woman as Ase drove up with

the buckboard, "I'm sorry Jenny didn't bring you something. I tried to get her to but—well, you know how she is."

"I know."

No point in distressing Betty further by saying that Jenny had left on her desk, unopened, the small gift Susanna had been able to give each child, thanks to Jem Howe's being willing to shop in Dodge for hair ribbons for the girls and pocket combs for the boys. In addition to a cozy afghan, a flannel nightgown, dark blue skirt, several shirtwaists, and two novels, Samuel Butler's *Erewhon* and Thomas Hardy's *Far from the Madding Crowd,* Aunt Mollie's Christmas box contained a mouth-watering array of toffees, bonbons, fruit drops, and mints. She had thoughtfully included a parcel of peppermint sticks "for your children" and with these, assorted candies, and the ribbons and combs, Susanna had wrapped nineteen little parcels in the tissues taken from her own gifts.

It hurt more that Jenny had disdained the gift than that the girl hadn't brought her some remembrance. What was the use, though, of insincerity? Jenny didn't like her and was as sullen in class as she dared be. She found small, cutting ways to spite Val for whom she'd conceived a jealous dislike because Ridge had befriended him, and she was hateful to Cobie who had already gone through the primer and who, because she studied, could spell better than Jenny. Instead of being spurred to greater effort by the Krause children's rapid improvement, Jenny sulked, and since none of her schoolmates seemed to notice, she glowered and pouted the more. As Ase helped Betty and then Susanna on the seat, she could only hope that Jenny wouldn't be so rude to her in front of Ase that he'd punish her and ruin the holiday.

Jenny was cleverer than that. She stalked by Susanna when they met in the upper hall but, though she was far from gracious when they were with the others and didn't speak to Susanna if she could avoid it, Jenny wasn't overtly rude, just as, at school, she always stopped just short of behavior that would earn a public reprimand.

Snow stopped falling before Christmas morning and wasn't deep enough to keep people from attending the ball that night, so young Tom Chadron and Bert Mulroy were especially full of high spirits when, with Johnny, they joined the family for a holiday breakfast of Betty's sourdough hotcakes, Dutch honey, bacon, canned peaches, and cup after cup of steaming coffee.

While they gathered near the stove after Johnny had stoked it. Jenny handed out the presents—new Stetsons for the hands, a gown of misty gray satin for Betty which Ase had paid Laura Prade to design and sew, a watch fob Jenny had made her father from Rusty's hair, Betty's colored knitted slippers for everyone, Susanna's gifts of fruitcakes, Aunt Mollie's candies, handkerchiefs, and lilac perfume for Betty, and from the cowboys, a fantastical vase with raised tiger lilies for Betty, a braided horsehair lariat for Jenny, a hatband for Ase, and for Susanna a very long horsehair rope.

As she stared at it in puzzlement, Johnny explained, "A horsehair rope outlasts every other kind and is sorta purty, too. We got to thinkin' you need a rope long enough to run from the school to the barn in case there's a bad storm. This'll do it."

Jenny retired to the heap of gifts her father had bought her and Ase stepped into the hall and came back with a beautiful big globe in a brass floor stand. "This is for you and the school, ma'am," he said, and turned the sphere slowly. "Didn't know there was that much water in the world. And see, here's the mountain ranges all wrinkled up, and the deserts sand-colored with green for the jungles."

"It's the best, easiest to read one I've ever seen." Susanna, delighted, turned it to the western hemisphere

Jeanne Williams

and located Kansas. "This is so much better than a flat map. The children will love it. Now they can see how the Vikings sailed to North America, how Columbus came— and how the Krauses did. The children already love history and geography but this will teach them a lot more."

"You'll teach them," Ase said, gruff with pleasure. "Would you like it up in your room so you can get acquainted with it over the holidays?"

"It's so heavy—"

"You know what they say." Ase chuckled. "Weak brain, strong back."

Tom and Bert fell over each other getting up. "I'll take it, boss," they chorused.

"Thanks, boys, but I've got a little private school business to talk over with the teacher." He glanced at Johnny. "If you want to ride the buckboard to the Browns', we better leave around three."

"I'll be ready," Johnny said, blue eyes twinkling. "If'n I don't spavin myself ridin' over there, maybe I'll be spry enough to jig some."

"Sure hope there's some girls," Tom said and blushed as Bert kicked him. "Beg pardon, ma'am," he stammered. "You're purtier'n any young girl but—" Bert kicked him even harder and poor Tom subsided.

"No need to apologize, Tom." Susanna laughed though she had felt a pang. "I'm not a girl." She couldn't resist a sober-faced tease. "If you'll wait four or five years, Sarah and Charlotte will be courting age."

"Four or five years!" Tom moaned.

Jenny, holding up a coral necklace, said importantly, "In four or five years, I'll be grown up, but it's no use you boys waiting on me. I'm going to marry Ridge."

"In five years, young lady, you'll still be a damn long sight from marryin' anybody," Ase said grimly. "You just put them fool notions right out of your head."

Jenny sprang up. Eyes the same deep heaven blue flashed stormily and Ase's hard jaw found its finer, smaller

262

counterpart in Jenny's. "You . . . you don't want me to marry Ridge 'cause . . . 'cause he's a half-breed!"

"No such a thing!" roared Ase. "If he's crazy enough to take you, he's welcome—the day you turn eighteen!" Suddenly, Ase threw back his head and chortled. "Ridge is goin' to have somethin' to say about this. He's quiet and peaceful but he's got a mind of his own. You can't just toss a rope on him, missy, and drag him to the preacher." He gave his daughter's yellow hair a clumsy pat. "Don't get all worked up about it, sugar. Settle down and enjoy your play pretties—"

"Play pretties!" Jenny hurled the necklace at the wall. "You . . . you think I'm a baby! But you make me use that awful old sidesaddle and horrid nasty skirts!" Her venom switched to Susanna. "And you . . . you're always telling me to act like the teacher. She's mean and hateful and gives me bad grades. And . . . and she won't let me work with Ridge. He likes that stupid, dirty Dutchie boy better than me and it's her fault!"

"Jenny!" Ase thundered, but she had already bolted through the door and stood there, gripping the woodwork in passionate fury. "Well, you just better not marry her or I . . . I'll run away!"

She whirled and as, dumbstruck, they all stared at each other, the sound of her running feet echoed from the stairs.

"Er—uh—we'll bring the buckboard up before we start for the ball," Bert mumbled, and picked up his new fawn-colored hat.

He and Tom hustled out. Johnny decided the stove needed stoking. Betty picked up her dress, murmuring something about trying it on. Mortified, Susanna fought back tears. Ase moved toward her. She stopped him with a raised hand.

"I . . . I think you'd better take me home. I don't feel like going to the ball or . . . or staying here."

"Damned if I blame you." Ase's broad, honest face was

so distressed that she felt sorrier for him than herself. "But, look, Miss Alden, ma'am, don't let a contrary little filly ruin your Christmas. Shucks, you handle nineteen kids five days a week. You can't let one throw you."

Jenny shouldn't be rewarded for her outburst with Susanna's fleeing. Further, Susanna knew if she insisted on going home, it would cloud the holidays for Ase, Betty, and Johnny. Besides, though she couldn't dance—she would wear her black silk mourning dress to the Browns', alleviating its somberness with her mother's paisley shawl— she hated to miss this greatest festivity of the year. Much as she enjoyed school programs and visiting afternoons, she was in charge and couldn't relax.

Ase smiled, reading her face. "Come on, Miss Alden, let's get this contraption up to your room."

The cowboys' horses had broken the way to the fork where other wagons and horses had already passed. Johnny sat in back on a pile of blankets, where he said he could smell the pies—peach, apple, and mince—that Betty had packed carefully in boxes. Susanna sat bundled between Betty's comforting body and Jenny's rigid one— the child had stiffly jerked out an apology, under compulsion, Susanna was sure.

Stifling a sigh, she thought how nice it would be to be able to put an arm around the little girl, share warmth and anticipation, but Jenny kept as far from her as possible on the crowded seat. No one seemed inclined to shout conversation over the rumble of the wagon and each traveled with his or her own thoughts. Susanna was glad that the bricks tucked at their feet held heat till, two hours later, they pulled up to the Browns' spacious shingled soddie. Johnny helped the women down and handed them boxes of pies and baskets of bread, climbing out himself with a great enameled kettle of beans. Ase drove off to unhitch by the other conveyances and put his team in one of the long sod barns.

Hettie, brown eyes dancing, ample figure corseted and bustled in a velvet maroon dress trimmed with scrolls of braid, embraced them at the door and led the way to the table against the wall where they set down their offerings with the bounty already there. Greeting neighbors as they maneuvered through the crowd, they followed Dottie to a bedroom where coats were already heaped high and several babies, nestled in blankets, were barricaded by heaped pillows to keep them from falling off the bed. Fair-haired Mary Harris, blue eyes shining with pleasure, came in and found a place for her sleeping little blond infant. The wiry, red-haired Wright twins and three other toddlers were being shepherded by Rosie Hardy as they watched Georgie, Freck, and Ethan shoot marbles in a corner.

Venturing with Betty into the big living room-kitchen warmed on one end by a stove and at the other by a fireplace, Susanna saw that not many people shared the Prades', Taylors', and Krauses' conviction that dancing to a fiddler was wicked, or if they did, they'd decided to risk it. She was greeting Margaret and Cash Hardy (his back seemed to recover for parties), the young Harrises and Wrights, and gray-haired Mavis and Shell McGuinn, when husky Jeff Morrison and Nate Steele, whose pink face and white hair made him look like Santa Claus, came in and joined Jem Howe. The cowboys, some from outfits fifty miles away, congregated in another corner, though Kermit, Ase, and Luke Tarrant moved back and forth between homesteaders and several other cattlemen who ranched to the north and west.

The women mingled more freely, including Millie Tarrant, striking in a gold satin gown that set off her dark peach skin and coiled black hair adorned with a matching double bow. The company overflowed into the three bedrooms though there was some effort to keep out of the one where the babies slept so that mothers could have privacy to nurse them and change their napkins.

Susanna didn't realize she was searching for Matt Rawdon till she felt bitter disappointment that he wasn't there, a disappointment that grew deeper with each new arrival. By the time Kermit banged the poker against the stove to get everyone's attention a coppery taste filled Susanna's mouth and she had to force herself to pay attention to Mavis McGuinn who was advising Mary Harris on ways to soothe her teething baby.

"Folks," bellowed Kermit, whose slicked-back red hair and freckled snub nose made him look boyish. "We're mighty glad to see you all. Seth Riley's rode forty miles from Crazy Creek to fiddle for us so don't slight the food the ladies have fixed for us but don't dawdle over it, either. Grab your plates and dig in!"

Susanna must have been the only person in the house who had no appetite even though the food was delicious, each household having supplied its best. Bert and Tom heaped their plates three times, and they were far from the only wolf-hungry bachelors to feast on woman-cooked provender. As other dishes were cleared away, what was left of the pies and cakes stayed on the table and two chuck wagon coffeepots emitted aromatic odors from the stove.

Seth Riley, a gnarled little man with skin like shriveled rawhide, a wild mop of kinky gray hair, and brilliant green eyes, climbed up on a high stool. His bow struck the strings and men—homesteaders, ranchers, and cowboys—swarmed to capture a woman, for these were in short supply even when Dottie, Rosie, and Jenny were whisked into the line forming for a reel. Susanna, Betty, and a northern rancher's white-haired mother, were the only single women. As what looked like a mass of eager males bore down on her, Susanna fled into the "baby" room but Ase followed.

"'Case you don't know it, ma'am, you're supposed to partner first with the man who brought you."

"I can't dance with anyone, Mr. McCanless." Her hand went defensively to the throat of the high, ruched neck of her black silk and his eyes widened with comprehension.

"Beg pardon, ma'am, I plumb forgot." He started for the door and then, changing his mind, marched back to her. "Listen here, Miss Alden, how long was it you looked after your daddy when he came home all smashed up?"

"Ten years."

"Since you were what—seventeen?"

"Yes, but I don't see what—"

"Just this. I reckon you mourned your daddy then. Mourned him every day, when you knew he wouldn't get better. Seems to me you've mourned enough."

She gasped at this startling view and he continued relentlessly. "What would your daddy tell you if he was here tonight?"

"That's not the point, Mr. McCanless."

"You bet it is. You sashayed around at the Thanksgiving singing games and you're no Methodist, Baptist, or Presbyterian, so what's the difference?"

"That wasn't the same as dancing at a ball. Besides, at school, I was rather the hostess."

"Bullfeathers! You don't have to partner me if you don't want to, but hell, it's Christmas, begging your pardon, ma'am. You goin' to disappoint those cowboys who rode all day just to have a whirl with you?"

Susanna laughed. "You can't blackmail me, Mr. McCanless. I've been here long enough to know cowboys would do that just for a piece of pie."

Ase folded his arms. "How's this for blackmail? If you won't dance, I'm just goin' to stay right here and talk to you."

Something in his tone flashed warning through Susanna.

"That seems a waste of the evening since you can talk to me at home."

"In front of Jenny? Or Betty and Johnny? You sure vamoose the minute it looks like you might accidentally be with me alone for a little while." One of the babies whimpered and the rancher walked over to peer down at it. With remarkable deftness, he tucked the blanket more snugly around the Harrises' little girl. "Well, Miss Alden, looks like you've got customers comin' on, but from the looks of the calf crop, I can see this won't be cattle country much longer."

"What do you mean?"

"Not a one of these yearlings is from a ranch family and just look at your school. Four ranch kids to fifteen from homesteads." He rubbed his ear pensively. "You can sure see who's goin' to inherit this range though I'd reckon that even with the Indians on reservations and this damn bob-wire that's spreadin' around, the Neutral Strip in betwixt Kansas and the Texas Panhandle and West Texas itself will get left to cows for a mighty long time. Truth is, most of it's no good for much else. Not enough rain for crops and water so scarce a coyote packs a canteen."

He moved toward her and again, strongly aware of him as a man, Susanna felt that rush of warning and stepped back though he made no move to touch her. "Miss Susanna, though I don't see Christmas dancin' as a slight to your daddy, I respect your waitin' for a year before you let anyone come a-callin'. I just want you to carry this in your mind, though, when you're usin' that globe." Slow and deliberate, he dropped each word. "If you'll have it, I want to give you my world." Moving aside from the door, he chuckled. "Miss Alden, ma'am, you'd be safer dancing."

He held out his arm and on the same kind of impulse that had made her, with Matt Rawdon, pull off her bonnet and let down her hair, she slipped her hand through the crook of Ase's arm. He was right. She had done her mourning. And though the face she longed for was not there, she was going to enjoy this holiday as much as she could.

Above the cry of his fiddle, Seth was shouting for a new dance. "Come on now, prance lively! Swing your lady, swing her sweet! Paw dirt, doggies, stomp your feet!" Laughing breathlessly, Susanna didn't need to puzzle over the peculiar language for the men grabbed her waist and hand and swung her. "Swing and march, first couple lead! Round the room and then stampede!"

Polkas, reels, quadrilles, waltzes, Susanna danced till she collapsed. Tom Chadron brought her coffee and a piece of pie, hovering near in hopeful fashion, and it was so much like stoking a fire that she had to smile into her cup. Since there weren't partners for all the men, the extras either went outside for a while and returned smelling of cloves which didn't quite conceal the whiskey that, except for the fiddler's, was forbidden inside, or they clapped and shouted from the sides, alert for the end of a number when they could dash in and catch a woman.

All of the men got to rest. Not so the women, except during brief interludes when Seth had to stop to soothe his throat with something from his jug and Kermit, who had a rollicking bass, would sing while Freck strummed his guitar.

> *"Whiskey's whiskey anyway you mix it,*
> *Candy's candy anyway you fix it—*
> *While other good folks are a-lyin' in bed*
> *Devil is a-workin' in a Texan's head."*

But the one that brought the most applause and a couple of Rebel yells from everyone but the Union homesteaders was a song that had, Kermit boasted, been sung by the Duchess of Manchester for Queen Victoria and the Prince of Wales.

> *"I'm glad I fought the Yankees,*
> *I only wisht we'd won,*
> *An' I don't want no pardon*
> *For anything I've done . . .*
>
> *"Three hunderd thousand Yankees*
> *Lay dead in Southern dust,*
> *We got three hunderd thousand*
> *Afore they conquered us . . .*
>
> *"I will not ask their pardon*
> *For what I was and am.*
> *I won't be reconstructed,*
> *An' I do not give a damn!"*

Susanna's breath constricted and she burned as if with fever. One of those three hundred thousand Yankees was Richard, her Richard, dead at twenty! And her father—he'd have been better dead. Springing up, she was starting to scream at the laughing, cheering "Rebels!" when her father's face rose before her and she heard his voice, truly heard it, though it might have been a trick of fatigue and passion.

"Better sing than fight, darling. They lost and they were brave and suffered and saw their homelands overrun. Leave them their songs, Susanna, but give them one of ours."

Several had noticed when Susanna leapt up. Ase, close by, caught her arm with a contrite, "Susanna, wait!" She broke free and made her way to the center of the room.

"Aw, Miss Alden," Kermit began, going crimson. "Damn my tongue, I plumb forgot."

There was no mistaking his sincerity but she was determined for Richard's and her father's sake, and for all the brave dead men in blue, to have a song for the country they had died to keep united.

"One good song deserves another, Mr. Brown," she said, and smiled at the Hardys and the other uneasy Northerners. "Cash, I'd think you know 'The Battle Hymn of the Republic.'"

"Bet your life I do, every single verse."

"Let's sing it."

They did, the homesteaders, though only Cash knew the whole stirring song. The Southerners, all ranchers and cowboys, endured it, but when the last marching chorus ended, Kermit said dryly, "If you're goin' to holler 'Glory, hallelujah!' for the Union, ma'am, I reckon we're entitled to 'Bonnie Blue Flag.'"

Susanna smiled at him and said what Charles Alden had just whispered to her from beyond the grave and all his battles. "Better sing than fight, Mr. Brown. I think we've just stumbled on the way to teach the war."

She laughed with a happiness that made him blink in puzzlement. With singing that song, honoring her dead in the midst of former enemies, her mourning was over.

❊ *Seventeen* ❊

As soon as they came in sight of the school, Ase shaded his eyes against sun glare on melting snow. "Somethin' different," he frowned. "What is that?"

Susanna peered, too. As the buckboard jounced closer, she said, "It looks like sort of a roof running from the door to the fuel shed."

"Now, who did that?" Ase wondered. They could now see that cottonwood branches formed a roof thatched with grass and rushes, supported on the outer edge by two poles. "It's a good idea," he admitted with some chagrin. "It'll help keep snow from mounding hard against the door so you can't get it open—that has happened—and it gives cover on the way to the fuel shed."

He hitched the team to one of the windlass uprights and swung Susanna down. "Looks like while us sinful folks were dancin', the other trustees kept warm puttin' this up." Squinting up at it, he added grudgingly, "Did a good job."

Susanna didn't for a second believe that Prade would so exert himself for something that would help her, though of course his children would also benefit. Will Taylor, with no sons to help at home, couldn't have spared the time.

273

It was the kind of thing Dave Hardy would think of, but the dance, with coming and going, had used up most of two of the four holidays. That left the Krauses—and Matt. Susanna was positive that Matt had thought of the shelter, though he might have enlisted aid.

That conviction sent a glow radiating through her along with unutterable frustration. Cavalier, the rocking chair, the rug that met her feet chill mornings, Schatzie—now this! If his only interest in her was carnal, surely he wouldn't show such care for her, but that made her feel all the more thwarted. Why, oh why, was he so bitter? Why couldn't he believe that a woman who loved him wouldn't care at all that his hand was scarred?

Shadowed by Jenny who had ridden all around, behind, and ahead of the buckboard, Ase carried in the globe and built a fire before he asked Susanna's opinion on where the globe should stand, moving it from one window to another, by her desk, and in front of the recitation bench.

"Beside the desk is probably best," Susanna decided. "It gets some light from the fire, and on really dark days it'll catch the lamplight." She clasped her hands, delighted afresh at seeing the beautifully colored and designed globe that would greet the children the next day. "It changes the whole room. I think we'll just study history and geography for a week, Mr. McCanless, because there won't be any use trying to turn the children's minds to anything else. I can't thank you enough."

"You can but you won't," he teased, restored to good humor by her praise. "Before I go, I'll hammer in a strong peg to hold that horsehair rope. I brought a plain old manila one to hang in the barn just in case anyone ever gets caught out there in a bad storm." He shrugged at her skeptical glance. "I know you can't believe it but I've been caught in blizzards where I couldn't see my hand in front of my face. Just had to give my horse his head and pray he'd get me out of it. A blizzard's not snow, ma'am. It's powdered ice with an awful wind behind it."

Shivering at the thought, Susanna said, "I'll take your word for it, Mr. McCanless. If it looks like a storm, I'll keep the children here."

He fixed the pegs, filled the fuel box, and set off. Thanks to Jenny's vigilance, he hadn't had a chance to say anything personal and Susanna was glad of that. She had come to like and respect him, he was intensely masculine, and if she had any sense, she'd welcome his courtship once school was out.

The trouble—and sweet, wild, forbidden joy—was that she loved Matt Rawdon.

Even after several days of intensive history and geography, the children were still so enchanted by the globe that Susanna rewarded those who finished their lessons early by allowing them to study it in groups of two or three. Taking advantage of this enthusiasm, she built spelling lessons around it—the youngest children could soon spell meridian, hemisphere, latitude, and longitude—and devised arithmetic problems. "If a Viking ship with twenty-four oarsmen needed four cups of water a day for each man and a water bag held two hundred cups, how many bags would they need for a ten-day voyage?" "If an ox team averages two miles an hour, and travels eight hours a day, how many days will it take to haul freight from Dodge City to Tascosa down in Texas, two hundred and fifty miles away? A mule team averages two and a half miles an hour. How long will the trip take them?"

The Krause children had obviously studied hard during the holidays. Since their parents were learning English, too, out of the hearing of old Anselm, they all practiced as much as they could with Jacob to help them, and the youngsters were improving vocabulary and pronunciation at an astonishing rate, which made teaching much easier.

Susanna had dreaded teaching the war—to her, there was really only one—in her American history class, but she had spent about as long as she could explaining the Missouri Compromise and how Kansas, years before the war, had become a battleground between Free Soilers and proslavery forces. Now, purged by the songs sung at the Christmas ball, she was at peace enough with her own feelings to think she could arrange a fair presentation. There was no way to "teach" a war so recently over, but having shown the reasons leading to the conflict as honestly as she could, she instinctively believed that singing the songs of both sides would bring festering bitterness into healing openness. So she sent notes home to the men who had fought, asking them if, on the next Friday visitors' afternoon, they'd tell the children as much as they deemed fitting of their memories of the war—and come prepared to sing.

Prade was the only one whose eyes glittered as he spoke of killing. The other men spoke huskily of comrades wounded or slain, of grief and shock over some men they had killed, of hunger, filth, terror, of battles that were horrible whether won or lost, the relief at finally coming home, even as the Southerners did, to defeat and vengeful Reconstruction.

Union or Confederate, except for Prade, the men choked up and blinked at tears. When Will Taylor, the last, stammered to a finish, Ase said, "You know, if it wasn't for the way we talk, wouldn't be a way to tell who fought on which side. It was all the same—killin' before they killed you, hatin' when your friends died, crampin' with dysentery and shakin' with ague."

"That's the gospel truth." Will nodded.

Glancing from Will to Cash and Jem Howe, Ase finished. "I guess the ones of us who fought have a lot more in common than them as didn't." And then they sang.

When she rode to the Krauses next day, Susanna didn't see Matt and no smoke rose from his chimney so she wasn't able to thank him for, as Val had told her, suggesting to the Krauses that they help him build the roof from school door to fuel shed. She hadn't, in fact, seen him since the Sunday before Christmas when he'd given the Hardy youngsters another riding lesson. At that, she'd seen him from the window, for he hadn't come to the house and she hadn't gone out.

Cav sniffed fruitlessly around Matt's soddie, tail ceasing to wag when he couldn't find his former master. The place looked so abandoned that Susanna felt a surge of panic before she reminded herself that the horses were around. Matt might be gone for a time, but as long as the horses were there, he'd be back.

The Krauses explained that he'd stopped by the day before and asked Val and Jacob to keep an eye out for his horses while he made a trip to Texas. Val, of course, was to go on working with the colts.

Texas! Susanna felt as if a giant hand crushed her chest till she couldn't breathe. She told herself there were many reasons he might have gone there, buying or selling horses, visiting relatives, or settling old business, but what if he'd gone to make arrangements for moving back to Texas? What if he'd gone to see the woman—Susanna was sure there had to be one—who had flinched from his maimed hand?

Oh, what was the use in guessing? Susanna only knew he was gone and that made her feel as if the sun had left the sky.

Monday morning was unusually mild, so clear and bright that it seemed almost like spring. By noon, the sky was overcast and a piercing wind howled out of the north. It had happened so quickly that Susanna was afraid to send the children home. At the frigid onslaught, the horses and little white Flora mule had refuged in the barn. Susanna sent the older boys out to fill the mangers, secure the guide ropes from the barn to the school, and shut the heavy barn door. Sarah, Rosie, and Cobie drew water from the well and filled all the buckets and the tub while the other children brought in fuel which they heaped along the walls.

By the time these chores were finished, razor-edged sleet cut into exposed faces and Susanna hustled the children inside, including a furious Jenny who had started to saddle her horse and go home, but been restrained by the boys. Her wrath was especially hot at Val who'd finally told her in his halting English that she had no right to endanger a fine horse whatever she chose to do herself.

"That's enough, Jenny," Susanna decreed, stoking the fire and lighting the lamp, for the soddie's usual dusk had deepened to night. "No one's going anywhere till this storm's over. We have plenty of food and fuel, the horses are safe, and we'll just study and play and sing. Right now, wash your hands and let's eat our lunches."

She hoped to goodness they had all used the privies; that would at least postpone what would be a problem if they had to stay all night, and from the way the wind shrieked and the sleet began to bank on the window ledges, she hoped it would only be one night they had to endure.

She was tremendously thankful that the storm, which she didn't want to call a blizzard, had struck before the children could start home and be caught in it. Except for Frank, who sat staring into the fire as he ate his cornbread and fried pork, the older students, Susanna was glad to see, joked with the younger ones and reassured Magdalena, Freddie, and Helen, who were frightened. Planning ahead to supper, Susanna ate while setting the large Dutch oven of beans to cook and put on a kettle of rice to which she'd later add cinnamon, raisins, evaporated milk and molasses. Fortunately, she had only used a few slices of the two loaves given her Saturday by the Krauses, and there was soft white cheese and a ginger cake that would go around

if cut small. Such delicacies should go a long way to turning an ordeal into a sort of party. Above all, she must show
no fear herself—and she was afraid, though they were as
well prepared as possible. She was feeding the fire when
she heard a snuffle from the doorway to the schoolroom.

It was little Helen Taylor, dark eyes tearful as she twisted
the hem of her skirt into a spiral. "Teacher, what—what
if Mama makes Daddy come after us and he gets losted?"

Susanna knelt so that Helen could look straight into her
face. It must be awful to be forever peering up. "I'm sure
your mama won't do that, dear." What she really hoped
was that Will would have the gumption to refuse any such
hysterical pleas. "Your mama and daddy know that you'll
be right here, safe inside."

"What if the wind blows off the roof?"

"We'd take blankets to the barn and cuddle up in the
haymow," Susanna said. She couldn't be certain the roof
wouldn't fly off and she had made a vow long ago never
to tell a child something that wasn't true. "Come now, let's
play I Spy."

At one o'clock, Susanna rang the bell for classes, which
proceeded as usual. She allowed a half-hour recess and
when the children were through playing, she told them
to put on their coats for the room had chilled greatly in
the last few hours. She kept classes going till four-thirty
at which time she served ginger cake and weak tea.

The windows were totally covered with wind-packed
sleet which had forced itself through the cracks and built
up inside and on the floor beneath. In a few places where
the storm had found a crevice or chink in roof or wall,
tiny particles had collected. Tightly though the door fitted
the sill, fine, powdery ice had sifted underneath and at the
sides which made Susanna wonder what it would have
been like without that roof outside. The ice didn't melt,
except the piles beneath the window nearest the fireplace.

Where was Matt? She devoutly hoped he was safe, wherever he was, even if that happened to be in another wom-

an's embrace. This anxious reverie was broken by the burrowing of Magdalena's head against her and an embarrassed whisper.

Susanna pulled the curtain and got the chamberpot from beneath the bed. While Magdalena found ease, Susanna quietly asked the other little girls if they needed relief. Sarah, bless her, took charge of emptying the rose-patterned "thunder-mug." Dave escorted the smaller boys out while Ridge, Freck, and Val shielded them from the ice whipping beneath the roof to the fuel shed. Without that roof, the door would be blocked by now and the way to the fuel impassable.

For once, there was plenty of time for globe games. In their favorite game, the child at the globe had a minute, timed by the desk clock, to locate countries, oceans, rivers, mountains, and major cities called out by the others in turn. Dave devised a new game. A blindfolded pupil set a finger someplace on the globe and then tried to identify it by the relief features, if any, and clues shouted by the watchers. Frank didn't join in but read in the flickering firelight, and Jenny sulked, repulsing Dottie's efforts to draw her into the fun.

While Susanna stirred lots of raisins into the creamy rice, she pondered sleeping arrangements. The ten girls *might* be able to snuggle together by lying across the bed with a bench for the feet and legs of the taller ones. Their body heat should make it possible to give up two quilts and there were two extra ones in the trunk. Everyone, of course, would sleep in clothing and coats, removing only shoes.

By clearing the desks from in front of the fire, the recitation bench, water bench, and three remaining seat benches could be aligned to make a bed eight feet long by about six wide. It could be padded with magazines, the rug, the divider curtain—anything to give a little softness before one quilt went beneath and the other three over.

If the smaller boys lay at the feet of the medium-sized ones, the nine should all fit.

Now there was practical arithmetic! Probably no one could sleep too well. Susanna, wrapped in her mantle and shawl, would sit in the rocker and keep the fire going. How she hoped that morning would bring the sun! But thank heaven, oh thank heaven, the storm had blown up while the children were still at school.

Mustering all her dishes and pans, Susanna, with the help of the older girls, served beans and chunks of the delicious wheaten bread to the younger children first, then the others, and then, again, in shifts, the children had their fill of sweet rice pudding full of plump raisins and smelling of cinnamon.

Sarah washed dishes and Cobie and Rosie dried while Susanna sat in the rocker, cradling a sleepy Magdalena in one arm and Helen in the other while Georgie and Freddie sat on the rug at her feet and used Cav for their pillow, and the rest of the children pulled benches near the fireplace where they could hear Susanna's stories.

Dave kept the fire fed while she told all the fairy tales she knew and wonder tales of King Arthur, Rustum, El Cid, Roland, Siegfried, Joan of Arc, Judith of the Old Testament, wrapping these children, her children, in the magic of what can be remembered though we forget so much. Though she felt the weight of total responsibility for the children, Susanna realized she had never been happier.

Jenny stayed in the schoolroom, still in a pout, but Frank, Susanna noticed, though he stayed on the school side of the fireplace with his book in his hands, didn't turn pages so she thought he listened, too.

Magdalena and Helen were sound asleep. Sarah took Helen while Val lifted his small sister, and they tucked them in bed beside Pauline and Dottie who had cuddled up with each other an hour ago. The boys' bed was put together, the bench that would later go under the big girls' feet left for sitting. Freddie and Georgie, asleep against the patient Cav, were put to bed by Dave and Val, and then the older children gathered close for more stories.

At midnight, Susanna sent them all to bed, but after a few hours, Sarah insisted on taking her place and Susanna managed to arrange herself in a sort of curve at Rosie's feet with her shoulders and head on the trunk.

Amazingly, she did sleep and woke to find Dave in the rocker. The wind keened like a pack of disembodied wolves. It was five o'clock. No hope for a bright morning.

Susanna sent Dave to rest and drowsed in between stoking the fire. Close as she huddled to the fire, feet drawn up under her skirts and mantle, shawl over head and shoulders, her back was still cold. She thought of the horses and Flora mule, praying their natural heat would keep the barn tolerable.

The children might as well sleep as long as they could. There might be another day or two of this. Plenty of time for lessons. How long could a blizzard howl before it wore itself out? Susanna tried to remember. The storm of 1871 lasted three days and two nights; the Easter storm of 1873 she wasn't sure about, but it must have been several days. Better expect that and rejoice if it stopped sooner. Even then, the drifts would likely be too deep for travel.

About six o'clock, Val got up and whispered that he was going to follow the rope to the barn and see about the horses. Dave swung off the bench-bed and said he'd go, too. Ridge silently joined them. They had to push hard against the door to get it open, shoving back drifted snow and ice. When they returned twenty anxious minutes later, they reported that sleet had sifted in several inches deep but that the animals were getting moisture from it and were fine. Dave shoveled from door to shed and he and Val brought in more fuel.

By then, other children were getting up, yawning and rubbing their eyes. Susanna had put on coffee and a big kettle of mush, improving it with chopped dried apples, and when the mush was cooked, she set on beans that had soaked overnight.

The mush, lavished with diluted Borden's and molasses, disappeared to the last scraping. The small children had warm milk flavored with molasses and the older ones drank coffee. Sarah presided over the gingerly washing of faces and hands, while Dave, Ridge, and Val helped tie shoes and comb hair and encouraged the little boys to scurry outside before they burst. Desks and benches were restored to their proper places and while the storm raged and no light came through the obscured windows, Susanna rang the bell for classes.

Turning recitations over to Dave and Sarah, Susanna put a mixture of dried apples, peaches, and raisins to stew before she stirred up cornbread and put it to bake in the Dutch oven. Jenny was in a surly mood. As Sarah patiently corrected her mispronunciations in the reading lessons, Jenny imitated her in a sneer. Susanna was about to call a reprimand through the fireplace when she heard Ridge say in a tone of quiet disgust, "Jenny, be ashamed."

"She's not the teacher and neither are you!" cried Jenny in a voice quivering with outraged hurt. "Well, what do I care if a half-breed likes nesters and Dutchies better than me?"

"Jenny!" Susanna had to exert every ounce of willpower not to grab the girl and shake her till her teeth rattled, and she might have done it had she not caught a strange, intent flicker in Frank's green eyes. "You can apologize to Ridge and Sarah or come sit in my room by yourself. The rest of the school shouldn't have to put up with your nastiness."

"I won't apologize! I—I'd rather die!" Jenny screamed, staring at Susanna with hating, defiant eyes.

"Bring your reader and speller and sit in here," Susanna ordered. All the days, weeks, and months of trying to win this stubborn, jealous, spiteful girl boiled up and exploded. Though she knew she shouldn't, Susanna said,

"I'm going to tell your father that he'd better send you to the convent. You won't let me teach you, Jenny, and I'm sick and tired of trying."

Jenny paled, then flushed scarlet. Jerkily rising from the bench, she got her books and stalked into the bedroom. She refused to eat at noon and Susanna, feeling herself an abysmal failure, didn't coax her. For Jenny to lash out so viciously at Ridge whom she adored—it was hopeless.

At some time during the noon hour, Jenny disappeared, evidently darting out when someone went for fuel or a call of nature. In spite of the cold near the wall, she had pulled Susanna's desk chair into the corner between the bed and dresser and hadn't got up though her eyes followed Susanna with a fury that was appalling.

It wasn't till Susanna rang the bell and watched the students take their seats that she noticed Jenny wasn't in hers, remembered, and glanced at the corner.

There sat the chair, but not Jenny. "Jenny!" Susanna called. She swallowed and asked the startled youngsters, "Have you seen Jenny?"

The one possible hiding place was beneath the bed. It only took a second to show she wasn't there. Where, then? As the schoolroom erupted, Susanna fought for control. "Sit down, children! Sarah and Dave, you take charge and keep everybody inside. Maybe she's hiding in the barn." Dave caught Susanna's arm as she started for the door.

"Let Ridge and Val and me look, ma'am. It's easier for us to bear into the wind than for you in those skirts. Most likely she's with her horse and hidin' in the hay."

Sick, Susanna leaned against the bedroom door as the place whirled around her, the frightened children's faces. Jenny's cry echoed through her brain: *"I'd rather die!"*

No, please, God, no! Susanna scarcely breathed during the eternity before the boys returned. "She's not there," Dave said heavily. "Her horse is. She's not in the shed. We took one rope loose from the barn and headed for where we reckoned the privies were. Stumbled into them. She's not there." He made a helpless gesture with hands that were man-sized but appealed now like a child's. "She—she just isn't anywhere but out in that storm."

Susanna felt as if she were slipping into blackness, caught at the wall. Death was in that blizzard. Death had Jenny. And what could they do?

"What we must do," said Ridge, "is knot the ropes together and go out as far as they'll stretch, moving in a half-circle. Freck and I have ropes on our saddles. They can be added on."

Throat choked with dread, Susanna breathed, "What if they came loose?"

"They won't," he assured her.

Each moment was agony as Dave and Ridge battled their way to the barn, returning with two lariats and the ropes. Their hands were so numb they had to rub and warm them but while they did that, Freck and Val tied the ropes together. The combined lengths made a line about a hundred and twenty feet long. If Jenny wasn't within that distance . . .

"We'll space ourselves out along the line," Dave said, taking hold of the end. "That way, if Jenny's down, we're more likely to run into her."

Frank, without a word, came forward and picked up the rope. Ridge came next, then Val, Freck, and Ethan. "Children, mind Sarah," Susanna told the staring little ones, and took hold of the rope about twenty feet from where it was tied to the door.

"Miss Alden, you stay inside," urged Dave.

"I can't." Susanna looked at the boys who were ready to brave that ferocious gale of pulverized ice. "Listen, boys. Hang on to the rope, and if you get so cold you can't grip anymore, start back along the line and get into the schoolhouse. We don't want to lose a one of you. Rosie, shut the door after us but wait here so you can hear if someone comes back and is too numbed to open the door. Sarah, whatever you do, don't let anyone come out."

"I'll head for the barn," Dave said, knit cap pulled down to his eyebrows, young face set in grim lines. "When I get as far as the ropes stretch, I'll start the sweep south—that'll put the wind to our backs. I don't think we can hear, so if you find Jenny, give the line three tugs. And like Miss Alden says, if your fingers start numbin', get back down the ropes to the school. Before we go out, be sure you've got a scarf or something fastened over your nose and lower face."

While those who didn't have mufflers borrowed them, Susanna had a sudden idea. "To make sure no one loses the rope," she said, "let's tie wrists to the line with knots that'll slide if anyone has to work their way back. Girls, can we have some apron strings?"

Taking these as Sarah snipped and Cobie fetched them, Susanna anchored the ties around mittened and gauntleted wrists while Dave and Ridge secured them to the line, fixing each other's and Susanna's last. It took precious minutes, but these lives were as valuable as Jenny's and Susanna abhorred risking them.

Even though she couldn't think of any way she could have handled Jenny much differently, she felt terrible guilt. If she hadn't said that about the convent . . . If she hadn't tried to force an apology . . . But who could have dreamed the child would set off in this storm?

At least, she hadn't been gone more than half an hour. Please let her be within the compass of the ropes. Let her be all right. Let—

Dave opened the door. As quickly as they could, the boys and Susanna ran out, checked by the blasting wind and stinging blinding particles that scourged exposed faces and drove down collars and up coat sleeves. The cold stopped Susanna's breath, even through the wool scarf, but then she bowed her head and inched forward. Dave had been right about her skirts. The wind flailed them wide above the knee-high drifts and if her mantle hadn't restrained them to some extent, she could scarcely have moved.

No use trying to keep her eyes slitted. She couldn't see anything but gray white ice dust. Why had that wretched child gone out in this? Why, when she felt the overpowering force, the numbing cold, hadn't she turned back at once? Why hadn't she followed the rope to the barn and got her pony? On him, she might have had a chance of reaching home.

"I'd rather die!" Tormented, Susanna again heard those words. Jenny loved her horse and might not have wanted to risk him. Or she may have, under threat of the convent, stolen out with that bitter childish cry in her heart, *They'll be sorry when I'm dead.*

And so they would be, all of them, especially Susanna. But Jenny would be the dead one. Cav had come out after Susanna and she felt him by her skirts. Could he smell anything in this storm? She prayed that he wouldn't stray off and be lost.

The line tautened, then began to tug at an angle away from the wind. Turning laboriously, Susanna followed. The horrible thing was that if Jenny had fallen so the rope would pass over instead of striking her, she could be missed in the twenty feet or so between each searcher.

What if they made the sweep and found nothing? Susanna was determined that none of these boys should freeze or lose hands and feet. If they completed the circle, she'd make them go in. But she herself couldn't. She simply couldn't take shelter while Jenny was out here.

Lashed by gusts that drove Susanna repeatedly to her knees so that it was harder to stumble up each time, she existed in a blind, eerie world of wailing shrieks. Except for the rope, the horsehair one the cowboys had made for her, she was isolated in a merciless eternity that had no bounds, no limits, nothing solid. Her feet were clumsy blocks with no feeling and she had to lift them from the ankle and knee, each step a labored push into the drifts. Good Dave. He was keeping them going.

The rope. She had to hold to it. Was Val still pushing his way to her right? If any of the boys fell, the apron string would drag down the line. Maybe they weren't going in a circular swing. . . . Maybe they were just floundering. . . . No, the rope was taut.

They must be rounding the school for Susanna's end of the rope grew tighter. As they circled the school, twining the rope around it, she'd have to move up the line. And when they reached the door— She'd give the rope three tugs and make the boys go in.

Where was Cav? Was that him barking, above the baying wind? She strained to hear but it was useless. That lost-soul shrieking of the wind sounded like a hundred things. Cav, though, was no longer plunging along beside her.

And then he was, gripping her mantle, trying to drag her backwards. Should she give three tugs? No. She hadn't found Jenny and whatever Cav wanted her to come to was probably beyond the stretch of the rope. She wouldn't risk the boys. And she dared not think what would happen if they reached the door and found she was gone. She had to trust that Cav could lead her back to the school, that he could lead her now, pray God, to Jenny.

She fumbled the apron string over her mitten, drew in a stabbing breath, and let go of the rope.

❊ *Eighteen* ❊

Now she was in that slashing, piercing void. Panic darkened her mind, who knew for how long, but when she was aware again, she was forcing through the frigid mounds, Cav hauling at her. What if he let go? What if he wasn't leading her to Jenny but to a dead cow or horse?

What if he couldn't find the way to the school? *Father, help me!* Suddenly, she felt his presence, his love, and then she knew he would be with her when she walked the valley of death, whether that was fated to be now or many years away. Fear left her. Beyond that valley was endless day. Beyond the storm . . .

Cav stopped. She tripped against something. Bending down, thrusting her deadened hands through several inches of ice particles, she found a bundle, heaved it up against her with wrists and arms rather than wooden fingers, and knew she held Jenny.

A Jenny who didn't stir or respond to Susanna's calling her name. Surely it couldn't be too late! Wresting the body from the drift, Susanna bent almost double, dragging the child more than carrying her, each breath an agonized gasp as Cav tugged them along.

It seemed forever. They would all freeze here. *Matt, I wish you knew I loved you.* Then she staggered against something—someone. Val, just reaching the door. Somehow, still dragging Jenny, she stumbled in and was caught and supported.

Sarah wavered before her as her frozen eyelashes unmeshed, and she gazed around to count the muffled blanched faces of the boys. All of them were safe. Dave scooped up Jenny while Sarah brushed powdery ice from her. Jenny was limp, her eyes were closed and her face was without color, the willful sweetly bowed mouth bluish.

Bending close, Susanna felt a faint breath. "We've got to get her warm." Susanna herself was too chilled to generate extra heat. "Sarah, you and Rosie and Charlotte take off your dresses and shoes and we'll tuck Jenny in amongst you."

"Take off my dress?" gasped Charlotte, flushing. "That ... that'd be wicked!"

"I'll do it," said Berenice, already unbuttoning.

"We'll be just like hot-water bottles," Sarah told the younger girls as she swept them into the bedroom where Dave was gently taking off Jenny's shoes.

Susanna's fingers were so numb that Sarah took over unbuttoning Jenny's coat. Together, they undressed her to her chemise as Dave went back to take charge of the other youngsters. Thank goodness, though Jenny's face was pale, when Susanna lay her palm against it, it wasn't frozen but was resilient. Jenny must have pillowed her face in her arms, covering even her ears. Susanna was glad of that. She'd once watched with horrified fascination as the frost-bitten ears of one of her father's patients had thawed to swollen discoloration that withered over a period of time, turned black, and fell off. Jenny had luckily escaped with more than her life.

Nesting the girl against Rosie and Berenice, Susanna held the covers while Sarah slipped in and gathered Jenny in her arms so that the child was completely surrounded by the bodies of her schoolmates.

From her father's and Matt's dictums, Susanna remembered that fluids shouldn't be forced down unconscious people but she made tea and gave several cups to each of the boys shivering by the fire. Having them take off their boots or shoes, she examined the feet, rejoiced at finding no chalky white toes, and asked the younger children to each take one of the older boy's feet and warm them between their arms and chests. She wouldn't let the boys rub their faces and hands till she'd made sure that these, too, had escaped frostbite. That done, Susanna gratefully sipped some tea herself, the fragrant steaming brew quickening blood that felt as if it had frozen in her veins.

Hovering over Jenny, who was completely covered, Susanna lifted the quilts enough to peer at her face. She was less pallid and the lips were pinker. "Jenny," Susanna said. "Jenny, can you hear me?"

Golden eyelashes fluttered. The girl whimpered, a sound that came strangely from imperious, scoffing Jenny. "Jenny!" Susanna insisted, calling her back from the place into which she had almost vanished. "You're with us, you're safe, dear."

The dark blue eyes opened slowly, staring at something the rest couldn't see. It was a moment before they focused on Susanna and widened. "It . . . it was you. You found me."

"Cav found you," Susanna said, smoothing the yellow hair.

"It was you."

"No. It was all of us." Without being asked, Dave brought a cup of tea. While Sarah sat up, cradling Jenny and keeping her wrapped to the chin, Susanna held the tea while Jenny took little, hesitant sips and Susanna explained how Ridge had thought of tying the ropes together and how the boys had spaced themselves to make the circle.

Jenny's gaze wandered around her schoolmates who

were all crowding at the foot and sides of the bed. Her glance slipped from Ridge as if in shame, wonderingly considered Val. "You . . . you cared about me," she whispered. Tears glistened in her eyes. "I was so nasty—especially to you, Val, and you, Ridge!"

Ridge said gravely, "You ought to know, Jenny, that Miss Alden let go of the rope to find you."

Color rushed into Jenny's face. For a minute, she ducked against Sarah, but then she lifted her chin and looked at Susanna straight and unflinching. "I've been hateful and jealous. When I sneaked out, I was so mad at you that I just wanted to make you sorry and cause a lot of trouble, but after I was in the storm a while I knew I didn't want to die. I yelled and tried to come back but I couldn't find the way. Then I couldn't make my feet go. I got warm and sleepy and it felt like someone I can't remember was holding me—" She gulped. Tears spilled over and ran down her cheeks. "I'm sorry—really sorry. If . . . if you don't want me in your school anymore, Miss Alden, I . . . I'll let Daddy send me to that convent."

Susanna sank down and took Jenny in her arms. "We want you, honey. We all want you here."

A few hours later, the storm slackened, but the drifts were too high for safe travel and Susanna and the children passed the night as they had the one before, staying up late with songs and stories and sleeping in the two improvised beds. Jenny had no frostbitten toes, fingers, nose, or ears. Cav, the hero, graciously accepted tidbits and caresses.

Seizing a moment when she caught Frank by the water bucket, Susanna said, "It was brave and good of you to help look for Jenny."

He shrugged. "Didn't want anyone to think I was scared to go out." His green eyes were flat. Before she could say anything else, he moved off and took up his usual solitary reading post by the fire.

The next day, the sun dawned in a burst of fiery brilliance, turning the prairie to a dazzling field of diamonds flashing myriad colors. The wind had scoured the higher slopes so that purple, dun, white, and black grasses thrust out of the ice dust, but what had been swirled from higher ground piled up in the hollows.

Dave went out with the shovel and cleared a path to the privies and well. Ridge and Val took over and shoveled their way to the barn where they cleaned out the accumulation of manure and fed the animals. Freck cleared the outside windows, and Sarah helped Susanna clear the sills inside.

No one, not even Magdalena and Helen, cried for their parents or complained. The sun was out, they were all alive, and that was wonderful.

Fortunately, the sun carried warmth as well as light. The sparkling carpet melted off the slopes well before noon and began to diminish elsewhere. The released horses and Flora mule lunged through the drifts to the thawed grass, frisked like colts, and grazed when they could stop racing each other.

At noon, operating from the shoveled paths, the children made a family of snow people, man, woman, boy, and girl. Jenny didn't go out, but stayed close to the fire, a most subdued little girl. Susanna let the others play an extra half-hour. When they trooped in, they stood on both sides of the fireplace to dry themselves while they had spelling.

At afternoon recess, Susanna kept the youngsters in. It was the concerted opinion of the mounted ones that they could get safely home and she didn't want them to be cold and wet from slush before they started.

"What about us?" Charlotte asked. "Mama will be so worried."

"I can't let you walk home while some drifts are still so high," Susanna explained. "Maybe your father will come for you in the wagon."

As it happened, all the fathers appeared except Cash

Hardy, beginning shortly after recess with Ase McCanless. "I knew you'd keep the kids corraled inside and that you had plenty fuel and food," he said, glancing up in some surprise from awkwardly returning Jenny's fervent hug. "Hold on, sweetheart, what's got into you?"

"Oh, Daddy! I . . . I've been so bad and I'd be froze to death out there if Susanna hadn't let go the rope—"

Ase set her back and glanced from her to Susanna. "What's this?"

Jenny blurted out her story, drooping her head when she whispered what she'd said to Ridge, and how she'd been searched for by homestead boys as well as ranch ones. Ase knelt to let her sob against his shoulder, patting her hair and making soothing rumbles. When she quieted, snuffling, he rose and looked at Dave whose gangling height almost equaled that of the rancher though he was just starting to fill in flesh around muscle and bone.

"Thank you, son," said Ase. "And you, Frank, and you, Val. Freck, Ridge, I'm most mightily obliged." He shook hands with them all, though they shuffled in embarrassed protest and insisted that Jenny was beyond the line, that she'd be dead if Cav hadn't found her and Susanna hadn't left the rope to search in the blinding, killing storm.

Shaking his head, Ase muttered, "Can't think how I'll ever settle with you, Miss Alden. But you must know how I feel."

"I know." Her own eyes were misty. "I'm just so thankful the storm's over and everyone's all right."

Will Taylor and Saul Prade drove up almost at the same time, just as Luke Tarrant rode along the slope. Kermit Brown brought his horse through mounded snow that was now only hock deep and Jacob rode up on a plow horse.

Amid joyous greetings, it was agreed that there'd be no school tomorrow. Girls hugged Susanna and each other, homestead and ranch, before clambering into wagons or onto saddles, Cobie behind Jacob. The boys all said good-bye to Dave with special respect, for during that blizzard he had used his quiet strength for them all and emerged the leader.

Ase insisted on telling of Jenny's rescue, praising the boys and the girls who'd warmed her back to consciousness, and lauded Susanna till, blushing, she covered her ears. "It was Cav!" she declared. "Besides, I'm the teacher. It was my place to hunt for Jenny."

Only Prade regarded her with a cold half-smile and spoke no word. Would he be pleased or angry that Frank had joined the hunt? Fearing that commending the boy might get him into trouble with his father, Susanna thanked Sarah warmly for all her help and said she'd see them day after tomorrow.

Following Val on Schatzie, Rosie and Georgie had ridden off on Zuleika and would be left at their home. Dave and Ethan walked. The footlog was clear of ice and the Krause horses had trampled a path for them. "We live so close that Dad didn't bother to come," was Dave's offhand comment on Cash's conspicuous absence.

On Thursday morning, the Hardy children didn't come to school but Jem Howe rode into the yard as Susanna was ringing the bell. Dismounting, his gray eyes full of trouble, he said that Cash had left for town the day of the blizzard, mounted on the horse Matt had traded for Margaret's sewing and baking. He hadn't come home. Riding to the Hardys' to check on the family on the morning of the thaw, Jem assured the frantic Margaret that the children were bound to be safe at the school and had gone to search for Cash.

He'd found him late last evening on the prairie, hand protruding from a drift in silent pleading while the horse lipped grass where it was free of the snow. After all, the storm had found its victim.

Earth was frozen a few inches beneath the slushy surface but the men of the Mason-Dixon community used pickaxes and shovels to make Cash Hardy's grave on a knoll situated between the Hardys' and Jem Howe's which Jem said he'd give for a local cemetery. To keep the body from deteriorating, Cash was buried the day after he was discovered.

Susanna had joined Laura Prade and Mavis McGuinn in sitting up with Margaret and the body the night before. Cash looked peaceful and nearly as young as Dave who comforted his mother, brothers, and sister, in spite of his own grief. The Krauses brought a simple coffin made of lumber left over from their roofs, and it seemed to relieve Margaret beyond measure that Cash wouldn't have to be lowered into the prairie sod wrapped in a blanket.

There was no minister. Jem Howe read the Lord's Prayer and said a few words about Cash and his service in the war. Naturally, no one said what most must have been thinking, that Margaret and her children would do a lot better without Cash than when he was drinking up their painfully earned savings. There'd been no harm in him and perhaps his back had given him miseries that only a frolic could make him ignore. When there was a dance or singing, they'd all remember him, Margaret especially; there was no mistaking her grief for her husband but a dancing man usually doesn't fit well behind a plow.

After the burial, the neighbors accompanied the bereaved family back to their home and the women put out the food they'd brought, the best of what they had. There was enough left to last the Hardys for a week. Outside, Ase and Luke had rigged a pole hanger, out of the reach of coyotes and wolves, for the half beef Ase had hauled over.

"Would you like me to stay all night?" Susanna asked when the other guests were gone, except for Jem Howe, who seemed more than eager to assume any responsibility Dave would allow him.

Margaret shook her head, arms around Rosie and

Georgie while Dave and Ethan stood nearby. "Thank you, dear, but I've got my children. We'll manage together."

Susanna knew they would.

The burial was on Friday, and school, of course, was impossible. A death in such a small group of people affected all of them. On Saturday, Susanna stopped to see Margaret for a short time before riding on to the Krauses'. On the track near the knoll with its fresh grave, she met Jem in his wagon, hauling a keg of molasses, a bushel of potatoes, and several bags full of something or other. He squirmed as if caught in some nefarious act but Susanna greeted him approvingly, happy to know that in time there'd be another man in the Hardy house. So long as his scapegrace father had been around, Dave had had to do the work and take care of the family, but with Jem to take over, Dave would be free to go on with his schooling and teach or do whatever he chose.

Susanna glanced quickly away from the grave. Not only was she sad for Cash and his family, but his fate made her worry about Matt. More than likely he was still in Texas, perfectly safe, but she would feel a lot better when he was back. Her heart ached as she passed his forlorn-looking house but she was glad to see that all his horses had survived the storm. That made her think what an ingrate she was. Instead of moping over a man, she could be in a grave beside Cash, and Jenny, too. Life was good, life was sweet, and whatever else happened, she'd fill her days with all of old Marcus's "work of a human being" that she could find to do!

Morning and evening of the lengthening days as January yielded to February, Susanna heard the low fluting notes of prairie cocks from the booming ground Ridge had shown her about a mile south. The birds had separated now into male and female flocks and Susanna had several times walked over early to watch the hens feed unconcernedly around the bare circle which was large enough for a hundred cocks to display. One would dash in, pat the ground with his feet, lift comic orange eyebrows while erecting the feathers on his neck and inflating the brilliant orange air sacs at the sides of his throat, open his tail with a snap like that of flirting open a fan, and begin to boom. Sometimes the males flew at each other with much flailing of wings but these conflicts were more show than action.

As the ground thawed, farmers started breaking sod with their ox teams, tilling perhaps an acre in a long hard day. The great horned owls began their nest, and still Matt Rawdon had not returned.

It was on the last Saturday of February, and the last day the Krauses felt they could spare for study, that Susanna saw smoke lifting from his chimney and approached with mingled joy and trepidation. Had he come alone? What had happened in Texas? She was wrestling with whether she should stop when the door opened and he came toward her, black head atilt, eyes that shining gray, the sharp angles of that beloved face even gaunter than she remembered.

"Well, Miss Alden," he said, after bending to play-tussle Cav who had streaked, belly to ground, to meet him, and now flopped over on his back, waving his paws in worshipful submission. "I hear you've tamed the terrible-tempered Jenny and become quite the heroine."

Hurt by his mocking tone, Susanna said stiffly, "I keep telling everyone it was Cav that found Jenny."

"All the same, I reckon she'd welcome you now as her stepmother."

"As to that, Dr. Rawdon, I cannot say."

"You swallow a poker this morning?"

"I'm supposed to smile when you're so . . . so damned vile?"

"Truce!" His smile flashed as he lifted a hand but it didn't reach his eyes. "Am I to take it, then, that Ase McCanless hasn't taken advantage of his daughter's tractability to press his suit?"

"Perhaps you've forgotten, sir, but women in mourning do not entertain proposals."

"I stand rebuked, but unless memory fails me, next month, March, will make it a year since your father's death."

"That's true, but I trust that Mr. McCanless has more kindness and sense of propriety than to mark the date of my father's death on the calendar and come tearing over next morning with a ring. Even, that is, if he intends to—"

Matt made a rude sound. "You know damned well what he intends. I'm only amazed you've bluffed him into waiting."

"He's a gentleman—which you are not!"

"That was never my ambition," he retorted with an infuriating smile. "Well, then, Miss Susanna, since it seems I don't immediately have to find you a wedding gift, I'll let you get on to your Saturday pupils."

"Wait!" she called as he started to turn away. Her cheeks burned and the words scalded her throat, but if he could ask so many prying questions, why couldn't she? "Why are you so concerned about whether Mr. McCanless has proposed to me or not?"

He took a long stride back to her before he checked. A mask settled over the pleading eagerness she'd glimpsed, just for a second, in his eyes. "I wondered if you might be more amenable to that suggestion I made last winter."

How dare he? Swallowing wrathful tears, she hurled at him, "I . . . I'll never be your fancy woman! Not if I'm an old maid all the rest of my life!"

He raised an eyebrow. "Oh, I'd reckon in about ten years you'll be safe from me, ma'am."

Speechless, she brought her heel against Schatzie's flank, something she had never done before, and had to grab for the front of the saddle as Schatzie soared into a lope.

Matt's laughter floated after her; and she was no wiser than before about what had happened down in Texas. Her lungs expanded and vexed as she was at his arrogance, she was filled with a dizzying flood of guilty thanksgiving. He hadn't returned with a woman.

Though the Krauses had seemed genuinely sorry to give up their "school," they had made such progress that Susanna was certain they would continue to study on their own and practice English with their children. In any case, school ended the last of March and in addition to attending the summer institute for teachers, she intended to yield to her aunt's importunings and make a visit to Ohio.

That might give her a better perspective on Matt. The board, with Prade voting against it, had already offered her a contract for the next school year with a five-dollar-a-month increase in salary. She wanted to teach here, work with these children she had come to care about so deeply, but in a way that was folly for she couldn't imagine ever getting interested in another man so long as she was where she'd even occasionally have a glimpse of Matt.

Considered in that light, when school ended, she should pack all her things and look for a school a long way from the Mason-Dixon district, perhaps in Nebraska or Colorado. She didn't expect to love another man as she did Matt, but there were many kinds of love. Perhaps with him firmly put behind her and no chance of encountering that wild sweet lightning that flowed between them, she could come to care enough for a man who was able to let himself love, a man who didn't wall himself away from human involvements.

And yet ... not to know if Dave went on to higher schooling; if Sarah found an outlet for that calm, wonderful temperament of hers; if Jenny resigned herself to being a girl instead of her father's son; if Charlotte grew out of her silliness as she now and then showed signs of doing; if Val found a way to be an artist. Oh, she wondered about each one, most of all about Frank, longed to see him act as if moved by his own will, not in that curious dead fashion that followed the exorcism of his possession by his father. If she left now, she would feel she was abandoning him.

Another year would see Berenice firmly ensconced in the pleasures of learning that made her, beside Charlotte, less of an ugly duckling. It would give the Krause children enough proficiency in English to manage with whoever came to teach. Dave, at the rate he was going, might even finish eighth grade, and Ridge would be that much further along in learning to mesh his Cheyenne heritage with his father's.

A year. She could surely manage one more year. This stretch of prairie, these people, had become hers in a way that Pleasant Grove and claimed places could never be. If only she hadn't had to love a man so bitter about the past that he wouldn't reach for the present . . .

March was waking before dawn to meadowlarks fluting, red-winged blackbirds shrilling *kong-ka-reee,* and a medley of other songs. Through the day, geese and cranes called overhead, joyful on their return to their northern breeding grounds. The sun leaned closer with each lengthening day, caressing the prairie, which took on a soft green hue as new grasses and plants pushed through dead stalks. Leafless spires of white pussytoes appeared, along with yellow Johnny-jump-ups, daisies, delicate pink anemones, the four-pointed stars of pink, purplish, and white bluets, lily-like wild onions, blue-eyed grass, and splashes of yellow paintbrush. The moisture-holding buffalo wallows bloomed gold with buttercups and purple-disked black-eyed Susans.

Pronghorns feasted daintily on tender green shoots, relished, too, by rabbits, prairie dogs, and many other creatures. Willows and cottonwoods budded along the creek and the red-tailed hawks were nesting in the tallest cottonwood south of the one claimed by the owls.

The Turkey Red winter wheat sown the autumn before by the Krauses had sprouted and grown enough before frosts to be used for pasture during the winter but now the cattle and horses were put to graze on the prairie while the wheat shot up like magic—this at the time other homesteaders were planting potatoes, corn, and sorghum cane before they could sow their wheat. Frank was kept home to help most of that month. Dave could only come a few days—no putting off plowing and planting till school was out—but he kept his brother Ethan out only when absolutely necessary. It was the highest mark of the Krauses' esteem for education that Val didn't have to miss a day.

Charles Alden had died in his sleep on March 10, 1874. As the anniversary approached, Susanna thought of him almost constantly, but now it was the good times that came back, and a sense of sharing the present. When she woke to birdsong, she thought he heard it, too, and when, last thing at night, she looked out to see the Pleiades setting, she could hear him telling her their story. Her real mourning had ended when she sang for him at the Christmas ball. She didn't feel nearly as separated from him now as during those painful years when the drink that eased his hurting also destroyed the father she'd adored. Best of all, she felt that he was pleased with her, proud of the life she'd made on this broad prairie he had never seen, at least not in his mortal body.

It seemed almost wrong to keep the children inside the dim soddie while the door stood open, spilling light and an enticing blend of the odors of soil, grasses, and flowers. Nature study lengthened to an hour and the recitation bench, on mornings when it wasn't too windy, was moved outside and Susanna heard classes there. Even conscientious Berenice found it hard to concentrate, and for the last few weeks, Susanna held her pupils' attention by integrating study around preparation for the school year's grand finale, the closing day program.

Sarah and Berenice wrote a play, a simplified *Midsummer Night's Dream* with parts for all the children. With the older girls' help, Susanna assembled costumes of cheesecloth—airy tunics for the girls, for the boys, cloaks dyed an indeterminate greenish tan by boiling the material with a variety of leaves steeped in water. Betty contributed gilt paper for fairy diadems and wands. Ridge created a hollow donkey's head, maned with real horsehair, from rawhide stretched over a willow frame and padded with grass.

The play was the main feature, but Dave had long ago memorized Mark Antony's stirring address over the body of Julius Caesar. The Krause children were going to sing some folk songs in Plattdeutsch. Charlotte had been ridiculed by her fellow students out of simpering as she intoned Elizabeth Barrett Browning's "How Do I Love Thee"; Ridge wanted to give the story of Hiawatha's hunting from Longfellow's poem; and Ethan could declaim Edgar Allan Poe's "Telltale Heart" in a way to chill the blood. Jenny, Rosie, Cobie, Dottie, and Berenice had worked up an amusing little skit where they discussed the drawbacks to marrying either a cowboy or a farmer, decided to stay single, and then battled each other to greet a man coming up the road though they couldn't tell what line of work he followed.

For that single day, farmers would leave their plows, cowmen would stop hunting for bogged-down cattle and cows having trouble calving, and the whole community would arrive midmorning for the program. The noon feast would be followed with games for the children and a play party for the grown-ups.

On the great day, as horses and wagons arrived, benches were carried outside for the spectators and the play was presented with the soddie used as backstage. Matt Rawdon came late, and it was only when she saw him trotting up on his tall gray horse that Susanna let herself admit how much it mattered that he be here on this festive day—and not because, in that first hour they'd met, he'd scoffed that she'd never survive the Mason-Dixon district.

Freck, in the donkey's head, brought roars of laughter as Charlotte-Titania made over him, and Sarah and Ridge, Jenny and Val burlesqued the mixed-up lovers while Athenians and fairies played their roles. Shakespeare wouldn't have recognized the paraphrased dialogue but the production was ringingly applauded as were the dramatic readings, the Krause children's singing, and the girls' skit.

In conclusion, Susanna handed written reports to each child along with the family histories the older ones had done that year, and with the children gathered around her, she thanked the parents for their cooperation and understanding. Freck got out his guitar and they finished with the Kansas rivers song.

Planks spread across wagons sagged with food and when everyone had eaten, the play party began. The Krauses departed, but no one raised eyebrows, smirked, or made belittling remarks. The Mennonites might not dance with their neighbors, but they had made a coffin for Cash Hardy, the dancing man, and their growing wheat, which had also supplied winter pasture, impressed everyone and led Will Taylor to remark that if they'd sell him some seed, he'd plant Turkey Red next fall. Matt Rawdon, mounted on Saladin, reined in by Susanna as she waved good-bye to the Krauses. Val was riding Schatzie home though he insisted that next fall, he'd again share her with Susanna.

"Well done, Miss Alden." Attuned to sarcasm in his tone, she was surprised to detect none. "A most satisfactory last day of school. Is it true that you're departing soon for Ohio?"

"As soon as I catch up my records, Dr. Rawdon."

"Since, when I brought you here last September, I predicted that you wouldn't last long, don't you think it would be enjoyable to make me eat my words all the way to Dodge City?" When she looked confused, he chuckled. "In other words, may I take you to catch your train?"

"It's not your responsibility, sir. I'm sure one of the trustees will offer."

"No doubt. I'm amazed that Ase McCanless hasn't already. The point is, I am offering. Will you let me? Cav can ride along and see you off. I presume you planned to leave him with me."

"I was going to ask."

"Fine. When shall I call for you? Four days? A week?"

"A week, if you're sure—"

"I'm sure." He touched his hat and cantered toward the creek.

Susanna turned to find Prade coming toward her. Again, she wondered how such a comely man could give off such an aura of malevolence. Even in daylight, with the whole community near, he caused the back of her neck to prickle and sent a chill through her. Was he still beating Frank? And if he wasn't, what was he doing instead to render the boy so lifeless?

"If you're smart, Miss Alden, you'll stay in Ohio."

Startled at this direct attack, she lifted a shoulder. "I've signed the contract, Mr. Prade." She tried to walk past him but he blocked her way.

"I know what you want to do. Carry on with the doctor, commit whoredom. I'll be watching and when there's proof—well, then we'll see what everybody says—"

"You . . . you must be out of your mind to talk to me like this!"

His green eyes smoldered. "Want to run to Ase McCanless? I've got my bullwhip in the wagon."

"You know I don't want a fight." She started past him but he blocked her way.

"I'll be watching. If you come back, I'll see you broken. And when you're shown up for a harlot, what'll all these fools who're eating out of your hand now think about you?"

"What's the matter with you?" she cried.

"You've ruined my son."

She gasped. *"I've* ruined him?"

"You filled him full of your soft notions. For a woman, that may work, but not for a man."

Susanna shook her head. "That can't be all of it. You've hated me ever since I wouldn't take those switches, since I said I wouldn't whip."

His face contorted, then froze in a hard mask in which only those eyes showed feeling. "That's what my mother used to whine, the bitch, and beg with my father— But he did what he had to. Many a time he bloodied my back, taught me to stand up to it like a man. He beat me but he was the one who clothed and fed and kept me years after she ran off with some pretty music master who was spineless as she was."

"Maybe she couldn't stand to see you beaten."

Prade's lip curled back from his white teeth. "She had a salve that used to help when she spread it on. When she went away, she left me four tins of it. I threw them out."

"Yet you don't seem to blame your father when he caused it all."

"My father did what a father should." He held out a mocking hand as they neared the circle just forming, but, evading him, she slipped in between Tom Chadron and Bert Mulroy.

Jem Howe, instead of Cash, was calling the measures. That must have made the whole company remember the feckless, good-natured man with the pleasing voice, and it must have been especially poignant for Margaret in her old calico dyed black, but only Delia looked down her nose when Nate Steele urged her into the singing game. Shaken by Prade's cold hatred and the glimpse of what had formed him, Susanna mechanically followed Jem's sing-song. Prade had guessed how she felt about Matt; had anybody else?

Writhing at the thought of being pitied as an old maid schoolmarm pining after an unobtainable man, Susanna desperately wished for a moment that she hadn't signed the contract. But then she lifted her chin and smiled so brightly at young Tom that his brown eyes glowed and his Adam's apple pumped up and down.

There was no shame in loving. God knew, it was better than hate. All the same, she thought one more year at Mason-Dixon was all that she dare risk.

❋ *Nineteen* ❋

Johnny had driven Betty home in the buckboard while Jenny raced with Freck and Dottie, so Ase was the last person at the school. His broad, square, weathered face had a determined set as he listened patiently to Susanna's increasingly nervous remarks about the program and the children.

"Reckon there couldn't be a better closing-day fandango," he said. "But as of now, school's out, Miss Alden, ma'am. You're not the teacher. I'm not the head of the board." He surveyed her dark green tarlatan which she had graced with white lace collar and cuffs. "And you're not in mourning."

Her hand went involuntarily to her throat. "Mr. McCanless——"

The blue eyes searched her in a questing male way that made her blush but didn't find what they looked for. He gave a shrug. "No need to get skittery. I'm plumb growed up and if I can wait for rain, I can wait on a woman. I hope, though, you'll let me take you to town when you leave for Ohio."

Her blush deepened. "That's kind of you, very kind, but Dr. Rawdon's taking me." The rancher's eyes narrowed and she found herself almost stammering. "There's Cav, you see. Dr. Rawdon's going to keep him while I'm away."

Ase's gaze probed deep till she could endure it no longer and looked away. He shook his head and she couldn't tell if it was pity, anger, or both that roughened his voice.

"Doc's a fine man, but from piecin' things together, folks reckon he came up here because the woman he was engaged to took a horror of his hand. Seein' that, he naturally wouldn't hold her to her word, but it sure has soured his notions of females. He might love you, Miss Alden. Might even marry you. But he'll never trust you."

Now two men knew. How long before everyone did? Burning with humiliation, she sucked in her breath and bent all her will to keep from crying. "I know he's unlikely to marry, sir."

"Not in your guts you don't—pardon the plain speakin', ma'am, but it's a fact. Lord knows I got a lot of respect for your mind—but you're a woman, too, and what can your heart know except that there he is, by himself?"

It would help if she could claim insult and overflow with righteous outrage, but Ase's tone, while frustrated, was also understanding and genuinely concerned. Her tears spilled over but as she blindly spun away, Ase took her in his arms, buried her face on his shoulder, and patted her head as he might have soothed Jenny.

"It's rotten damned luck, honey. You sure deserve the man you want. But, look, it's not the end of the world. Hearts are tough things. When my wife died, I thought I'd never care about another woman—not in the marryin' way. But here you are!"

She sobbed harder at that, regretting for both their sakes that she didn't love him. He held her till she began to sniff and pull away in embarrassment. Producing a clean handkerchief, he mopped at her face and made her blow her nose. Then, grasping her shoulders, he held her at arm's length and, though those deep blue eyes were serious, they also held merriment.

"If you'll give me a chance, Susanna, I reckon I can make you love me. I hope for both of us—and Jenny, too, who sure would love to have you for a mother—that up the road a little, you'll let me court you. But if you won't—when I see it's no use for good and all, then you know what?"

"What?"

"Well, honey, I'll shine up my boots, slick down my hair, and find me somebody who can love me back."

Now, why did that make her feel more than a trifle piqued? She didn't want him to yearn after her—well, not for very long—but his gay resolve struck her as, yes, indecent. Removing herself from his hands, she straightened her ruffled hair.

"A laudably practical decision, Mr. McCanless. Instead of wasting time on me, you'd better start your courting immediately or who knows how many prospects you'll lose? Margaret Hardy, for instance."

His grin broadened. "I sure admire Mrs. Hardy, but even if Jem wasn't set to propose soon as it's respectable—and let me tell you, ma'am, that out here no one blames a woman who needs a man to work for her and her kids if she marries sooner'n she might back east—anyhow, with all respect, I'll be lookin' elsewhere." He fumbled in an inner vest pocket and produced an envelope. "The trustees figgered you have a bonus comin'."

She eyed him skeptically. "I think you mean *you* did."

He colored like a boy caught in mischief. "There's no price I can put on Jenny's life."

"I don't want a reward for doing my duty."

"You are sure one hard-headed woman." Grimacing, he opened the envelope and produced what looked like a railway ticket. "Take this, anyhow. If we've got to import a teacher, least we can do is pay her fare back and forth."

That seemed equitable. After considering, Susanna

thanked him and took it with a smile. A round-trip ticket would have taken half her savings and there were a lot of things on her shopping list. Encouraged, Ase ventured, "What would you think about movin' to a good school buildin' next fall?"

"Not unless you've deeded it to the district," she said with implacable sweetness.

He shook his head. "Boy, are you stubborn!" They stared at each other and burst into laughter. He threw up his hands. Striding toward Rusty, he called over his shoulder, "If you want me to collect you in Dodge when you come back, just drop me a line. And have a good visit!"

At the crest of the slope, he turned to wave, then sent Rusty into his deceptively smooth swinging pace. Staring after him, Susanna didn't know whether to be glad or sorry that he knew her secret; on the whole, she decided to be relieved that he didn't now believe she was fancy-free. On the whole, too, she appreciated his jaunty declaration and even smiled ruefully as a line of a play-party song ran through her head: "I'll find another one prettier'n you!"

If only she could say the same. Absently stroking Cav, she moved into the soddie and for the first time noticed a ruffled calico-covered box on her desk. The calico matched one of Sarah's dresses. A neat card was fastened to a bow—a ribbon she'd given one of the girls at Christmas? "To our Dearest Miss Susanna Alden. From all of us."

As she took off the lid, folded papers spilled out. Opening the first one, she recognized Magdalena's laborious printing. "I love you and Cav and school, but I love you best!" On a piece of cardboard, Val had done a drawing of Susanna standing by the globe, one hand on it, the other stretched out in smiling invitation. What a remembrance of her first year! There were notes or letters from all the children, some several pages long, some with drawings, some, like Frank's, very brief. "You are a good teacher. I hope you come back." Ridge wrote, "You are like White

Buffalo Woman who showed people how to do things right."

Some brought a lump to her throat, Charlotte's gush, a quizzical smile, but the last one was Rosie's. "I love Mama and Dave and Ethan and Georgie when he's nice, and I love God and Miss Alden."

Susanna laughed till, overwhelmed, she cried and gathered the letters to her as if they had been the children. Six months till school began again. It seemed too long a time.

Spring cleaning in a soddie was work without much obvious effect, but Susanna scrubbed sooty curtains on the washboard, gently washed the quilt she'd used for a coverlet, and soaked the rug overnight before rubbing at the spots, rinsing and wringing it, and hanging it to dry on the plum bushes. The cheesecloth sagging from the rafters was so disreputable and clogged with litter that she decided to buy a new bolt.

Except for the money she'd sent Aunt Mollie to buy Christmas presents, she had saved almost all her wages, and that was fortunate because she was sick of the drab garments she'd worn this past year. She had already given the brown calico to Margaret Hardy, and would refurbish the gray grenadine and green tarlatan for they had plenty of wear left in them, but she hungered for something airy and bright.

As she toiled at the washboard, she dreamed of daffodil gauze, flowered dimity, dotted Swiss, or perhaps muslin or lawn though she knew she couldn't indulge in more than one such garment. The others would have to be dark enough to hide the results of sweeping an earthen floor, sometimes a muddy one, with her skirts. But, oh, she could have a plaid, and a floral of some kind, or stripes and checks! She thirsted for color. And ruffles? Why not? *She* would enjoy them and if Delia Taylor thought a schoolteacher had no business looking as feminine as she could, that was too bad, the devil with Delia! Of course, Susanna wondered what colors and styles Matt would think most becoming, but she wouldn't allow herself to dwell on this. She suspected that he couldn't remember later what a woman wore, only whether or not she looked nice.

Before she bought material and had the dress made up, though, she was buying Christmas presents for all the children, and some little thing to welcome them back to school. She also had to find sketch pads for Val, some good pencils, and pastels. There was a comprehensive list of items she'd learned were not available in Dodge. She intended to take as few things as possible with her to Ohio for she'd be traveling back with a very full new trunk. The one she already had would have to hold her clothing and bedding to protect them from mice and pack rats.

Remembering the rattlesnake and tarantula that had greeted her last fall, she sighed to think of the cobwebs and debris that would inevitably accumulate before her return. She would arrive in Dodge in August and attend the two-day summer institute before going home.

Home? Straightening and flexing her aching shoulders, she gazed toward the creek where yellow-headed blackbirds had again joined their hardier red-winged brethren, followed the hawk circling above the prairie, watched the spring grass, mostly bluestem, shimmer light green since she saw it from the wind's direction. Facing the other way, it would resemble dark green velvet. And the sky, the boundless azure sky, meeting the earth without woods or mountains to hide that union.

Yes, it was home, the one she'd chosen, and even though she would have to leave next year, and even though she could happily do without so much wind, she wouldn't leave the prairies and the open sky. Her soul had come to need them.

*　　*　　*

Matt, arriving shortly after sunrise a week after closing day, frowned at her satchel and one large bundle. "You must be forgetting a trunk or valise, Miss Susanna."

"No." She took a final look around both rooms. Yesterday she'd taken her leftover food stores to Margaret. The hearth was swept; the lids were on all the three-legged iron pots; shuck mattress and rug hung on a line stretched from one wall to another in a hopeful attempt to keep them free of scorpions, centipedes, and rodents; the lamp was emptied and cleaned; her books were packed in the trunk beneath clothes and bedding. In the schoolroom, she touched her desk, glanced at the washed blackboard, the tarp-covered globe.

How empty and silent it was without the children. Turning to Matt, she found him watching her in a way that sent her pulse racing and began to melt her knees. Tearing her eyes away, she hurried outside and said a little breathlessly, "I have a lot of things to shop for. Besides, I hate my clothes and I'm going to get some new ones."

He whistled Cav into the buckboard and lifted her up. For a moment, their faces were perilously close and she went faint, remembering that one harshly sweet kiss, the one she would choose, if such wishes were granted, to remember in the grave. His eyes touched her mouth. He quickly moved away, going around to climb up beside her.

"Will you do something for me?"

How she wished she could answer yes to anything he asked. But she had to say with forced lightness, "That depends on what it is."

"Get yourself a dress the color of the sky on a clear, fine day like this." He grimaced. "Something that doesn't button right up to the chin and down to the wrists—something with a little flow and grace."

"Flow and grace aren't what I need in the schoolroom."

"Don't see they could hurt. Just as easy to wear pretty clothes as dowdy ones."

"So I'm dowdy?"

"Aren't you?"

That was exactly how she'd been feeling but she choked at this matter-of-fact indictment. Before she could think of a withering retort, he scowled at her brown bonnet. "And for Pete's sake, take that thing off, at least till the sun gets high enough to pink up your face! It makes you look like a missionary or a preacher's wife."

"I don't see anything wrong with looking like either, Dr. Rawdon, and if you're going to criticize me all the way to Dodge, kindly drop me off at the Tarrants and I'll ask Mr. Tarrant if he'll drive me in."

"You took off your bonnet the day I fetched you from Dodge," he said so softly that she could scarcely hear him above the creak and rattle of the buckboard. "That was when I really looked at you. That was when I decided there was more to you than a prim, proper Yankee school-marm who was careful of her—"

"Clothes, money, and reputation," Susanna finished.

"Just so." He chuckled, casting her a mirthful glance, and she was undone.

After all, why not let the wind finger her hair this last day she'd feel it for a while? She was with Matt. Why not be happy as they could, this one time? She untied the ribbons, and though it wasn't hot the way it had been that September afternoon and her head didn't ache from wearing pins in her hair for three days, she reached up and loosed the coiled hair, threw back her head and laughed, reveling in the freedom.

He laughed, too, and Cav, eager to share this pleasure, thrust a companionable nose between them. As they followed the track worn by Freck and Dottie to the main road, Susanna's heart soared with each meadowlark and the pungent smell of earth and old growth mixed with the fresh scent of new grass and flowers. Just to be alive on such a morning was glorious. To be with Matt, too, wheeling across the prairie, filled her with such joyous exhilaration that she felt light enough to float right off the seat and wing with the birds. That thought was so comic that she laughed again, and Matt gave an approving nod.

"You have a sweet laugh, Susanna." It seemed right, natural, for him to drop her title. "I haven't heard it much."

"That," she shot back, still in good humor, "is because you're forever telling me what to do, fussing at me for being a Yankee, or tricking me into keeping Cav or using Schatzie. I've learned, Dr. Rawdon, that I have to be on guard around you."

It was meant playfully but she bit her tongue the instant the words were out, for he stiffened and for a very long moment, stared straight ahead before he half shrugged. "Just for the trip, Susanna, let's drive a bargain. I won't transgress so you can safely relax. You won't bedevil me to practice medicine or chide me for my varied shortcomings. Agreed?"

"Agreed." She hesitated. "May I ask something?"

"So long as it's not why I'm not delivering babies or patching up my fellow man."

How to put the question that had been consuming her? She phrased and rephrased it several times and her mouth was dry when she finally got it out. "Did you have a good trip to Texas?"

His mouth jerked down. "The trip was fine," he said after a moment when Susanna held her breath. "What happened while I was there—" He broke off. "Listen, I'll tell you about it while we're having dinner, because we're having dinner at the Dodge House before I put you on your train. I plan to take a room and stay overnight so you're welcome to use it to freshen up and rest a bit while I attend to business." Before she could argue, he gave her a challenging smile. "May I ask *you* something?"

"You may ask. Maybe I won't answer, or perhaps you'll have to wait till dinner, too."

"Fair enough." He turned enough to watch her closely and Susanna's blood coursed through her with tingling shocks before it slowed, grew warm and thick as honey wine, and she had to look away. "Has Ase proposed to you?"

Her blush answered so she nodded. His hands tightened on the lines. In an elaborately casual tone, he asked, "What did you tell him?"

Susanna's heart pounded and she felt as if she were suffocating. "I . . . I told him no."

The hands gripping the reins loosened and color flowed back into his fingernails. "Knowing Ase, I don't reckon that's the last time you'll get asked."

Susanna tried to turn it into a joke. "He let me know if I don't wake up to my good fortune in whatever he considers a reasonable time, he's going to find somebody else, and I'm sure he can and will."

"Wonder is that some enterprising lady didn't rope him long ago. He's by way of being the biggest cattleman north of the XIT down in Texas, he's still got all his teeth, and from what Betty says, he's not a fussy eater as long as it's beef."

"Mr. McCanless is a handsome man." Illogically, Susanna felt bound to defend him, partly in justice but more because she wanted Matt to know that she, an old-maid Yankee teacher, had turned down what Aunt Mollie and her friends would have termed "a catch." "Furthermore, according to Betty, he was devoted to his wife."

"And his new one wouldn't have to keep house in a soddie," added Matt. "Well, at least you'll have the satisfaction of telling the homefolk that you've got a rich, good-looking rancher at your feet."

"That will be nice," Susanna admitted sunnily, gratified at what could only be jealousy on Matt's part. It wouldn't hurt him to get a taste of the way she felt when she thought of that woman in Texas he must love, or how tormented she had been all the time he was away. Honesty, however, compelled her to chuckle. "Mr. McCanless isn't at my feet. He towers over me. And I don't really think it's me so much as just that he's suddenly got tired of being single."

"It's you."

Matt gave her such a glance that her heart skipped. Time, more than time, to talk of something else. "Is Val too busy with farm work to help now with the horses?"

"He's breaking sod. All the men are except for old Anselm. These folks don't farm by a season or even two or three. They farm by the decade, even by the century. That's why they'll last."

"They brought enough money to make a good start," Susanna pointed out and voiced the misgivings that had grown as she came to understand the homesteaders' unending struggles with drought, grasshoppers, searing winds, and blizzards. "It seems there are bound to be several bad years for every one of good crops. The land may be free but traveling here isn't, and a family needs oxen and implements, seed, enough to live on till they get a crop, and enough to tide them over if the crops fail. It seems really almost cruel to have a Homestead Act when it lures people to try farming when they don't know how or have money for what they need."

Matt nodded. "Lots of people spent all they had or could borrow, went broke, and headed back east a lot poorer than they'd been. That's why a few legislators who understand the problem have tried to get Congress to pass a law authorizing loans to help homesteaders get started. They've got nowhere and probably won't, though one big reason the Homestead Act was passed was to ease conditions in the East and give unemployed people a chance to be independent. I feel sorry for them even if they are Yankees."

"Well, maybe after the election this fall, Congress will do something."

"Fat chance." He eyed her quizzically. "I'm surprised you're not out preaching woman suffrage like Susan B. Anthony, who's made some swings through the state. Or maybe, since women can vote at school board elections, you think that's sufficient."

"You know perfectly well I don't. Of course I think women should have the vote. I just haven't felt called to campaign for it."

"So you'll wait till men get ready to bestow the franchise on you or till women like Susan B. Anthony and Lucy Stone galvanize them into action?"

"I suppose I will." He made her feel as if she should be out making speeches and importuning legislators, but she simply did not have the passion to wage that war.

"Voting's a strange thing," he mused. "In order to rejoin the Union and get rid of military Reconstruction, the Southern states had to ratify the Fourteenth Amendment which gives Negro men the vote though it disenfranchises Confederate soldiers and bars them from holding office."

"But Reconstruction's over!"

"I hope you didn't teach your students that. Florida, Louisiana, and South Carolina are still garrisoned by Federal troops and ruled by carpetbaggers. Texas didn't get rid of carpetbaggers till 1874. And it was only in 1872 that Congress passed a General Amnesty Act which lets former Confederates hold office—except the most important five hundred or so. Being defeated on the battlefield was one thing. Reconstruction—having our state governments destroyed and being placed under military law two years after the war ended—that's what it'll take generations for the South to forget."

"I'm sorry for that. But how long will it take Negroes to forget slavery?"

"I told you before, teacher. The war wasn't fought over slavery. But let's not start a war of our own, not today. Do you think your aunt will believe you when you tell her about the soddie?"

"She can't quite believe that we burn prairie coal instead of wood." Susanna laughed, and the rest of the way to town they talked about neighbors, Matt's horses, the children, and other safe topics, holding the dangerous ones at bay.

It was only when they fell silent that tension mounted between them, charged with unspoken questions. What was he going to tell her? Susanna wondered. That his old love had gotten over her revulsion for his hand? That he was going back to Texas to live with her? There was no possible way he could have good tidings, so Susanna, resolving to enjoy these hours, perhaps the last they'd have together, would ask some question or tell him some amusing school story.

Six months ago, Dodge City had looked raw and make-shift with its false-front buildings and soddies, but Susanna hadn't set foot in any kind of settlement since then and now it seemed a hub of commerce and activity. Freight wagons creaked along Front Street, the broad thorough-fare through which the railroad passed, and wagons and horses were hitched in front of stores and other establishments.

"None of the men are wearing guns," Susanna exclaimed. "Last fall, they all did."

"You've got to remember Dodge is only five years old even if you date it from the trading post Charlie Myers set up close to H. L. Sittler's soddie in 1871. For quite a while, the only law here was what vigilantes doled out. Then a couple of gunmen were brought in to try to keep some sort of order but that didn't work. I hear a bunch of the steadier citizens got together last Christmas Eve, made up a set of ordinances, and elected a law-and-order mayor. They sent for Wyatt Earp. South of the railroad track, any-thing goes, but north of the line, guns aren't allowed."

Stopping in front of the Dodge House, he hitched the team and helped her down. "Dodge is still wild enough but you'll be fine as long as you keep north of the railroad. It'll still be a couple of weeks before the cowboys start hitting town with the trail herds. I'll get a room and you can tidy up while I take the horses to the livery stable."

He grinned as they stepped up on the boardwalk which, in anticipation of fires, had large water barrels placed at intervals. "From the way you crammed your hair under your bonnet, it'll need brushing before you can come down to dinner. Take your time. I have to stop at the mercantile and the barber's."

He got the room and carried her satchel and bundle up the stairs. "You don't have to get ready to ward me off," he told Susanna, a touch of exasperation in his voice, for she was lagging, feeling very ill at ease. Ladies most certainly didn't enter a gentleman's hotel room, but just as certainly she needed privacy to repair the effects of the five-hour journey. "I'm not coming in, Susanna. I'll be waiting for you in the lobby."

Unlocking the first door on their right, he set her things inside without stepping into the room himself. "Disappointed?" he teased. Before, cheeks burning, she could answer, he went quickly down the stairs.

The big brass bed looked as if it had a real mattress. Doing her best to ignore it, Susanna took off her bonnet, and groaned at the tangle of long, waving hair revealed in the dresser's large plate-glass mirror. As she bent to wash her face and hands at the flowered porcelain bowl, her corset dug at a body unaccustomed to its constricting rigidity.

Wear the thing throughout the train trip? She'd be on a sleeper out of Kansas City but she'd have to sit up this first night and standing in a corset was bad enough, but to sit was a form of torture augmented with each hour. Susanna felt she couldn't endure it. Once in Pleasant Grove, she would don the accursed thing when not doing so might disgrace her aunt, but for now it was coming off even if it was a nuisance to have to undress.

Undressing might be an exciting pleasure, helped by the hands of the man you loved ... Rebuking the futile thought, Susanna hurriedly escaped her garments and undid the hated contrivance, wishing she could throw it away forever. Resuming her three petticoats, she wished they, too, could be consigned to a missionary barrel and reflected that if she were to take up a crusade it would be against garments that impeded women's movements and torturing styles that compressed inner organs. She buttoned her cuffs and bodice and attacked her hair, again reflecting that wind felt glorious in loosened tresses, but the delight had to be paid for.

Soon, now, soon, she'd learn what had happened in Texas. Dreading it yet consumed with the desire to know, she almost welcomed the painful tugs as she worked tangles out of her hair for they diverted her a little from what she was to hear. At least, she had this day to remember. This day and a kiss.

After months in a soddie, the hotel dining room seemed opulent with its chandelier, white tablecloths, and gleaming silver plate. The diners appeared to be mostly prosperous businessmen or ranchers with a scattering of officers from the fort five miles away. There were only two other women, matronly ranchers' wives. In her whole life, Susanna had dined out only a few times. This was a rare treat and delicious odors floated from the kitchen, but bracing for what Matt had to tell her had robbed her of appetite. She looked helplessly at the bill of fare and murmured that she'd have tomato soup.

"The lady will have the soup," Matt told the white-aproned waitress. "Welsh rarebit, Saratoga chips, Russian salad, and—" He raised an eyebrow at Susanna. "My dear, would you prefer Bavarian cream or lemon tart? Sauterne or champagne wine? Coffee, tea, or chocolate?"

My dear, as if they were married. It would be ungracious to argue in front of the waitress so Susanna contented herself by saying, "Oh, please, *dear*, do go ahead and finish making up my mind for me."

Not in the least chastened, he said, "The lady will have

Bavarian cream and lemon tart, sauterne, and French coffee to end. I'll have the same except for roast beef in place of the rarebit. And we'd like Parker House rolls if they're fresh."

"Just out of the oven, sir," the middle-aged woman promised before she whisked away.

Matt leaned forward. "Susanna, can you do something for me?"

"If you mean to eat all that food, I have serious doubts."

"Have what you fancy, but I didn't bring you here to have a bowl of soup. Can't we just enjoy our meal and each other's company before I tell you what I need to?"

"No!" She started to tremble.

"Oh, Susanna! Oh, my sweet—"

He looked so stricken and remorseful that she wove her fingers together beneath the starched tablecloth and swallowed hard. "Tell me this." She was past pretending. "Are you going back to Texas? Is your . . . your fiancée coming here?"

"Neither."

The pressure on her lungs and heart slackened, though she was puzzled. If it wasn't either of those unthinkable happenings, what could he have in mind? With a sigh of reprieve, she said, "All right. Let's eat, drink, and be merry."

The waitress brought the sauterne, and he raised his glass to Susanna.

❋ *Twenty* ❋

Assured that neither of the things she most dreaded was going to happen, Susanna found that she was indeed hungry. The tangy rarebit whetted her appetite for the egg salad and rather thickly sliced potatoes fried to a crisp golden brown. Matt exerted himself to beguile her with amusing stories from his childhood and student days and she so treasured these intimate glimpses that delighting in his company drove all foreboding from her.

This was the nearest to a honeymoon she would probably ever have, the sauterne made everything sparkle, and, slightly dizzy, she allowed herself, just this once, to imagine that when night fell, they'd walk up those stairs, enter that room, and Matt would take her in his arms again. He would free her from the dress, the petticoats, applaud her for discarding the corset so they could more swiftly be together with nothing in between. . . .

She glanced up to find his eyes dwelling on her, blushed from head to toe, and thought distractedly that she shouldn't have had that second glass of sauterne. But oh, she felt so deliciously happy, so light and floating. That light in his eyes entered her and glowed within her depths, in her most hidden parts.

"Susanna," he said again, in a queer, muffled voice, as if he hurt inside. "Oh, my love, Susanna!"

She closed her eyes. If this were their honeymoon, they wouldn't wait till dark. He'd take her arm and support her up the stairs, for her legs felt as if they hadn't a bone in them, or her spine, either. Out of people's sight, he'd sweep her up and carry her to that big bed. At the very thought, a quivering began in her.

Matt said something beneath his breath, reached across the table and took her hand in both of his, warming it. "Susanna, what I have to tell is quickly said. My sister's been imploring me to come for a visit. She thinks I'm at the ends of the earth and should come back and start a practice among 'our own kind,' whatever that is. I tried to set her mind at rest, unsuccessfully, I fear, but my real mission was to ask my former sweetheart to explain to me frankly how she felt about my hand."

Susanna started to speak but he motioned her to silence. "Melanie wept. She said she still loved me though she's married to a wealthy banker and has two children. She'd been ashamed of her shrinking and tried to conceal it when I first returned, but when I touched her, she flinched. She could close her eyes, she said, try not to ever look at my ruined fingers. But when she felt them on her, it was ... her very descriptive phrase was 'like being gripped by a corpse hand.'"

Susanna blenched. "How ... how could she say such a dreadful thing?"

"Because it was true."

Susanna tried to take his hand but he hid it beneath the table. "Matt, I don't feel that way!"

"How do you know how you'd feel when I touched your naked body?" Shock made her catch in her breath. Roughly, before she could speak, he said, "I'd rather die,

Susanna, than have you shrink from my touch, or even worse, endure it with gritted teeth."

It took her a long moment to realize the enormity of what he was saying. "You mean," she demanded, "that because one woman was squeamish, you won't make love to another—won't even try?"

"I didn't say that." His tone held its old brittle cynicism. "Women paid for companionship can put up with worse than my hand. But you—" That proud head lowered. "I couldn't stand it, Susanna."

The myriad small sharp blades razoring at her unified in a slashing thrust that pierced her through. "I love you," she said on a swift breath. Except to her father, she hadn't spoken those words to a man since Richard left to join his regiment twelve years ago. It was like breaking tight bonds and this time she spoke softly and slowly, for it was surely the last time that they could speak like this. "I love you, Matt."

Reaching beneath the table, she dared to take his hand in both of hers. It was a corpse hand, cold, the ridged tissue hard and uneven. For an instant, it rested between her palms. Then, with a stifled sound, he snatched it away, shaking his head. "You can nerve yourself to touch my scars, but that's a far cry, my darling, from feeling them on your body."

"I don't understand," she pleaded desperately. "You— once you asked me to—"

"That was when I was trying to convince myself that I couldn't be falling in love with a Yankee teacher who kept trying to drag me back into the human race."

"What if I'd said yes?"

"I knew you wouldn't."

"But if I had?"

"I was sure you'd recoil, just as Melanie did, and that would effectively cauterize the feelings I didn't want to have for you." His voice dropped. "But it was too late. I think it's been too late since the minute you took down your hair, gave it to the wind, and laughed."

"It's wicked, Matt Rawdon! To not even give me a chance—"

He stiffened as if she'd slapped him. After a silence during which it was all she could do not to cry, he said harshly, "I'm giving you the best chance I can. To marry someone like Ase McCanless, someone who can touch you without wondering when you're going to wince away."

"I'm not going to marry Ase."

"You might. If I went away."

"Don't talk like that!"

His mouth twisted. "In spite of my resolves, Susanna, how long do you think I can live three miles from you without someday doing what I'm convinced would be disastrous for us both?"

That made her hope. If he did make love to her and find that she'd cherish his hand because it was his, then he'd have to give up this ingrained certainty that his caress was bound to be distasteful to her.

"Please don't leave," she urged. "You've got your homestead and horses. People need you." She swallowed hard. "I'm leaving after this coming year. Till then—oh, Matt, I want to see you sometimes—the way we have this year—even if it hurts."

A tremor swept her body, a yearning so intense it was physical pain. The lights in his eyes were now twin fires and magnetic shocks radiated between them. "My love, my innocent, I'll do my best, but I'm not sure that I can last the year even if you can."

He got abruptly to his feet and drew back her chair. "It's three hours till train time. Would you like to rest or have a tour of the town's respectable establishments?"

Impossible to sleep. Lying down now on that large, comfortable bed would be utter torment. "I'd like to look in the mercantile," she said, to her surprise managing a steady voice. "I need a new comb and some shoelaces."

328

They promenaded down Front Street, Matt's hand beneath her elbow to keep her from tripping on the uneven planks. When they entered the store, redolent of everything from cloth to saddles, the way he joked with Bob Wright, the dark-browed, thick-mustached owner, who had been both buffalo hunter and bull-whacker, made her wonder if men were that different from women, able to shut away feelings and behave as if nothing at all had happened.

She found her shoelaces and studied the array of material and trims, but didn't find a comb of the sort she preferred till they had canvassed the other general stores. "Could I get a bone for Cav?" she asked.

This was easily done at the butcher's and Cav, moping in the livery yard where Matt had ordered him to stay, accepted the bone and her caresses with euphoric wags of his tail which slackened as they turned to go. He dropped the bone and looked piteous.

"I'll be back, you rascal, and we'll have a walk soon as this lady's on the train," Matt promised.

"It's a shame we can't tell them why we do the things we do," Susanna said, bending to cup the dog's face between her hands. "Good-bye, Cavalier. I'm going to find a good, stiff brush for you so that I can keep you nicely groomed when I come back."

"Now don't you reckon that'll tickle him to death?" Matt drawled. "Come along and have some tea or chocolate before we head for the depot."

Their day was ending, this sweet, terrible day she would never forget, when she had known for certain she was loved, when she had confessed that she loved this man, and then faced the bitterness of his determination that nothing must come of it. It made her wish she could catch him off guard, prove to him that his dread was groundless—yet did she really know that herself? She was sure that loving him as she did, she could get used to his maiming, but with him watchful for the slightest sign, he might take modesty, the inevitable awkwardness of a virgin, for repugnance. She wouldn't get a second chance. That made her afraid to try to take the first one.

Back at the hotel, they had tea and collected her bag before going to the station. There weren't many passengers on the train because the line only extended west to Pueblo, Colorado. Several men got off with their baggage and an air of staying for a while. Matt helped Susanna locate a seat as far as possible from some drummers and a black-clad dandyish man she took for a gambler. Stowing her baggage beneath a seat across from two respectable looking middle-aged ladies, behind a young mother and father with a baby, and in front of an elderly gentleman who was absorbed in his paper, Matt straightened.

Susanna felt as if her heart filled her body and had turned into the heaviest of stones. Much as she loathed sniffling in public, tears blurred her eyes, and as she blinked, one ran down her cheek. Matt caught in his breath. Then suddenly, devilishly, his smile flashed.

Embracing her soundly, he kissed her astonished mouth, drew back and patted her cheek. "Have a good visit with your aunt, my love," he said, loudly enough to be heard by the men at the back of the car. "Don't worry about a thing. I'll take good care of the children." He dropped another kiss on her forehead and went down the aisle before she could think of words to chastise him without betraying to the interested onlookers that there were no children and he was not her husband.

In spite of the desolation she felt at leaving him, she had to smile at his roguishness which had let him kiss her good-bye while warning off the raffish single men. As she settled into her seat, the woman across from her said in a cheering way, "Never mind, dear, he'll be just that much gladder to see you when your visit's up."

Susanna murmured something and turned to look out the window for Matt. He wasn't there. She felt irrationally disappointed, but then he came in sight, Cav at his heels.

He'd brought him to see her off. The train groaned into motion. Between tears and laughter, Susanna waved back at man and dog as long as she could see them and wished that instead of chugging toward Ohio, she could go back with them to a prairie home where they could be together.

In Topeka, she changed lines and had a sleeper car for the rest of her journey, though she got little enough sleep in her upper berth. It was suspended from the ceiling above the lower berth made up from two seats that faced each other across a small table which was removed at night. The skimpy curtains defied her struggles to get them to meet and it was difficult to ascend or descend or put on or take off her robe so that she could decently repair to the ladies' boudoir at the end of the car. It was worth it all, though, to be hugged and petted by her aunt and uncle who were waiting at the station.

"Well, child, you've thinned a bit and your complexion's got a touch of sun, but it becomes you." Aunt Mollie's quick hazel eyes appraised Susanna and she smiled. "I like that color in your cheeks. Come along now. Dinner'll be ready, all your favorite things, by the time you've had a bath and changed."

After months of living in a dirt-floored soddie and being responsible for nineteen children, it was as delicious as Aunt Mollie's cooking to be cosseted and live in a real house with waxed oak floors, a sound roof, and plenty of windows.

Susanna spoke to all the classes at the academy, telling them about life on the Kansas frontier. They shuddered or giggled incredulously as she described her school and, comparing these girls with Sarah, she thought most of them would never manage as pioneers, though their attitudes were really not too different from Charlotte's. It was nothing against them; not everyone should move west, but though she envied the well-lit schoolrooms, excellent library, and uniform texts, she realized that after dealing with the mixture of pupils that had gathered in that one dim room in the soddie, she'd find teaching these biddable young ladies a boring occupation.

Even in her hopeless yearning for Matt, she missed her children, all of them, and frequently wondered how these days passed with them, especially with Frank. Now that he was older, perhaps Saul wouldn't beat him, for boys of that age often ran away when maltreated, and he could do a man's work in the fields.

Susanna's own days passed quickly. While her aunt was busy with the academy, she took over the housekeeping and most of the cooking. Her gifts to her aunt and uncle were a bag of jerky and another of Turkey Red flour, which she now made into nutty-tasting bread. Shopping took up considerable time as did delving into stored books and belongings for things she wanted to take back to Kansas.

The trunk in her room filled by the day: scented bath soap for Betty and Margaret; a plaid tie for Ase; fitted pencil boxes for each child, and for each, at Christmas, a carefully chosen book. For Catherine and Jacob's wedding gift, Susanna found a beautiful ruby cut-glass creamer-and-sugar in a trunk of her stored things. She hesitated long over a handsome silver-gray brocade waistcoat for Matt till acknowledging with a sigh that it was too intimate a gift. She bought him instead a volume on equine diseases and their treatment. When Val's sketch pads and pastels were tucked away, she spent pleasant hours deliberating with her aunt over styles pictures in *Harper's Bazaar,* and more time choosing material and trim for two new dresses, olive sateen with a floral print of bronze and golden brown and the one she had promised Matt, sky-blue bengaline, a corded cotton and wool fabric that would be trimmed with velvet ribbon of a deeper blue. Seeing this inspired Aunt Mollie to surprise her niece with a flounced petticoat of midnight blue taffeta, which made such an intriguing rustle when she wore it that Susanna felt quite dashing even in her old tarlatan. One of her stored trunks yielded some materials she'd folded away when her father died—a summery sprigged muslin and a daffodil poplin. Since a sod schoolhouse was no place for looped-up polonaises and elaborate poufs, her new dresses could be simple. Susanna decided to conserve her dwindling funds by making the gowns herself, using Aunt Mollie's sewing machine and some help from her aunt on the trickier aspects.

Benjamin Harris had called on her first Sunday back in Pleasant Grove, bearing French chocolates and flowers. When she'd glimpsed him coming up the walk, Susanna hurriedly asked her aunt and uncle not to leave her alone with him. The lawyer's hair had receded to start a tonsure and after the tanned faces of prairie men, his skin looked pallid and unhealthy. He boasted of his practice which had just been moved into sumptuous new offices, but Susanna could not forgive that he'd built that practice while Richard, his classmate at Harvard, had been fighting at the front where he died.

With her aunt and uncle joining in, they passed an hour in amiable but innocuous chat, and Susanna, after a second remember-your-manners glance from her aunt, suggested tea and served it. Vastly relieved when he rose to go, she declined an invitation to a church social without murmuring a softening excuse.

As they looked after his well-tailored, retreating shoulders, Aunt Mollie sighed. "Susanna dearest, that was close to rude. You might have pled another engagement or sounded a bit regretful."

"So he'd ask me to something else? No, thank you, darling. If I wouldn't let him come courting before, I certainly won't now."

Aunt Mollie leaned forward. "Really, Susanna? Have you—is there a gentleman?"

No use letting this aunt and uncle who'd been almost

like parents build up dreams of never-to-be grandnieces and nephews. "There's a man I care for but because of an injury he got in the war, he refuses to consider marriage. That's why I plan to look for a new school next spring." At their distressed expressions, she added quickly, "Cheer up, dears, it's not that I haven't had other opportunities. There are cowboys and homesteaders who'd besiege me at the flutter of even an eyelash as rusty as mine, and I've been proposed to by Ase McCanless, the rancher I've often written you about."

"You have?" Aunt Mollie beamed. "Oh, Susanna, now that you've won over that wild little girl of his, he sounds a wonderful match!" The sparkle in her eyes faded as she studied her niece. "You've refused him."

Collecting tea things, Susanna brushed a kiss on the plump pink cheek. "Yes, darling, I did." She laughed with a brightness she was far from feeling. "You should have heard him tell me he wasn't giving me long to change my mind. It was a little like that song, 'I can and I will get married for the fit's come on me now.'"

"It's too bad you don't get taken by the same kind of fit." Aunt Mollie sniffed, and caught Susanna's hand. "You've lost all those years looking after your father, child. It's time you started a nice family. That'd put the other man—I suppose he has to be that Confederate doctor—out of your mind."

Meeting the anxious, motherly hazel eyes, Susanna replied in all truth and soberness. "Mr. McCanless deserves better than that. Anyway, I just can't do it. You'd better get used to admitting to an old-maid niece."

Aunt Mollie brooded but Susanna's gaze stopped several entreaties on her lips. Turning up her hands, she said philosophically, "At least I can tell everyone that you've been proposed to by one of the country's most important cattlemen."

"Yes." Susanna chuckled as she picked up the loaded tray. "What's more, you can tell them he's not spavined and he's got all his teeth."

Uncle Frank chortled at that and though Susanna often saw her aunt's concern in her eyes, by tacit agreement, there was no more discussion of possible husbands. In this place full of old memories and so far removed from things that would remind her of Matt, Susanna sometimes succeeded in going for an hour or more without explicitly thinking of him, though his presence, the image of his lean face and piercing gray eyes, was always at the back of her mind. In moments before she sank into sleep at night, though, or awakened in the mornings, he was there.

Would he haunt her, she wondered, all the rest of her life? And yet, could she have banished him with a wish, she would not have done it; remembering him was painful but it was her deepest pleasure.

The luxuriant green of early April grass had paled to the soft yellows and browns of late summer, but as Susanna watched from the train with the eagerness of homecoming, she saw tall spikes of pink and lilac gayfeather, splashes of large-petaled white prickly poppies, and all the swaying golden family of various kinds of sunflowers. Less than a year ago, she'd compared them unfavorably with roses and peonies but now she found them beautiful, a welcome to the plains.

She had written Henry Morton that she'd be arriving the day before the institute began, and he was at the train to meet her, wispy brown sideburns ruffling in the wind and mournful brown eyes alight, to make up for his absence of last September and convey her with her baggage to the Dodge House.

"Mr. McCanless will be in to take you out to Mason-Dixon after the institute." Morton gave her a benevolent side glance. "Downright set on it, he was."

Now, against all reason, since she'd written to no one but the superintendent, why had she hoped Matt would be the one to find out when the institute was over and be there to drive her home?

Ironically, Morton had reserved the same room for her that Matt had taken in the spring, over four months ago. She thought she could not stay there, that as soon as Henry Morton vanished, she'd ask to be changed, simple enough since the heavy trunk was residing in a downstairs closet.

She halted, though, hand on the doorknob. She was committed to living till April amid not only reminders of Matt, but with at least occasional meetings and the constant awareness that he lived and worked and slept only three miles away. She couldn't avoid memories of him and the sooner she steeled herself to that, the better.

True. But, she derided her conscience, aren't you staying because this will be the only time you can lie where he has, fit your body to the mattress and imagine you feel the imprint left by him?

Yes! Yes, and I'll have that, and I'm not ashamed. She wasn't ashamed, but she was weary and heavy-eyed next morning. In spite of fatigue from traveling, she had scarcely slept and her thoughts of Matt were tormented.

Fortunately, the institute was absorbing, the sessions taught by professors from the state normal school and the state university. In algebra, she got a review of parallelograms; in civil government, a study of constitutional amendments and the Kansas Constitution; history and geography dealt with Kansas, and for botany, they walked out of town to classify grasses and flowers.

Perhaps the main benefit was talking with other teachers about their problems and solutions. Last year, Susanna had felt very much a lone guerrilla fighter, and her school was still the most distant from town, but now she knew she had allies in the battle to educate children under adverse conditions. Several of the young women and one young man enrolled in the institute were just out of eighth grade themselves, sixteen and seventeen years old, but if they passed the examination, they would get a third-class certificate to teach in a rural school. They could continue their education in the summers until they qualified for first-class certificates. This was what Dave might do.

Retha Cunningham, a vibrant blond, blue-eyed widow who would probably not long remain so, taught eight miles south of Susanna and they agreed, if the parents consented, to take their pupils to visit each other's schools with programs prepared to show what they'd been learning.

Pleasantly tired from the crammed hours of the two-day session, Susanna slept soundly the next night, and came down to the dining room the morning after the institute ended to find Ase McCanless drinking coffee and watching the door.

"Here you are." Rising, he reached her in two long strides, taking both her hands and squeezing them in his. She wore her daffodil dress, ruffled at hem, wrists, and yoke, and he gave a soft whistle. "Doggoned if you haven't gone and got purtier'n ever." His dark blue eyes were glowing. "How were your folks? How was Ohio?"

"First, how are Jenny and Betty and Johnny? And Ridge? Is Margaret Hardy managing? How——"

"Light and have your breakfast." He escorted her to the table and pulled out her chair. "Tell the waitress what you want and then I'll give you the news, such as it is."

Everyone was fine, he said. A dry summer, but that was nothing new. The Krauses' Turkey Red wheat had been cut early in July. They'd given a bushel of seed wheat to anyone who wanted it and that had proved to be all the homesteaders except Saul Prade. The regular wheat and corn and cane had grown well but were now beginning to wither from drought.

"That Turkey Red probably means the end of western Kansas as cattle country," Ase said with a wry grin. "Long as farmers use spring wheat, they're goin' to lose a lot of crops to drought and 'hoppers, but with winter wheat they can harvest before it starts dryin' up——" He shrugged.

"Guess I better be thankful no Mennonites have taken it into their heads to settle in the Neutral Strip or the Texas panhandle."

Though he must have known she was burning to hear about Matt, Ase spoke of everyone else, and there was something in his manner that made Susanna sure he was concealing something. "I've got a favor to ask," he said as Susanna finished her toothsome apple fritters. "Will you help pick out material for some dresses for Jenny? Betty says she's plumb outgrown her old things. I've fixed it with Mrs. Prade to make up the duds. She is sure a nice lady—a sight too good for Saul."

Sipping her coffee, Susanna stared at Ase. "Of course I'll help choose Jenny's material. But Ase, you've been fidgeting. What is it you haven't told me?"

He looked sheepish. "I . . . well . . . Oh hell, Miss Susanna! Beg your pardon but though I reckon I should be tickled, I'm not. Doc Rawdon's sister, Miss Amanda, she's come to keep house for him. What she's really after is to close herd him back to Texas. She's more mother than sister to him. Looked after him when their folks died though she was just a kid herself and worked hard to send him to medical school." Ase sighed. "She's a nice lady, but she sure is—determined."

The cup had almost dropped from Susanna's fingers. She set it down with extreme care, unable to breathe for a moment. It struck her as grimly amusing that as if they were warders of a condemned person, first Matt and now Ase had urged her to have a hearty meal before they gave their bad news. Susanna realized that in spite of Matt's dogged resolve not to make love to her, she had been unconsciously hoping that he'd change his mind, that something would happen to give her a chance to prove to him that his infirmity didn't matter. Having her adored brother marry a Yankee schoolteacher was surely no more part of Amanda's plans for him than his staying on the homestead.

Commanding her hand not to shake as she took several

bracing swallows of coffee, Susanna said, "Having a woman to look after him must be a welcome change for the doctor. But I should think she won't like the soddie."

Ase grinned. "That's not half of it. She hired carpenters, had lumber freighted in, and the house ought to be about finished. Jem Howe says when she turned up with her maid, cook, and housekeeper, Doc moved out to the barn and let her have the soddie."

The thought of a Southern lady crowding into a soddie with three servants struck Susanna as so ludicrous that she laughed. It was ludicrous, too, for her to be jealous of this sister, but she was.

Rising, she defied the embarrassed commiseration in Ase McCanless's eyes. "Let's look for Jenny's material," she said. "Her best color's blue, of course."

That stabbed her with the thought of her own blue dress, the one Matt had asked for. She could almost hear Amanda saying, after she'd cajoled Matt back to Dallas: *"My dears, can you believe Matthew conceived this passion for a droll old-maid Yankee schoolteacher? Of course, it was only because he was out on those awful prairies far from his own kind."* With the taste of copper in her mouth, Susanna stepped out into the scorching wind.

❋ *Twenty-one* ❋

As she had before in times of grief or distress, Susanna found relief in the dailyness of life and was rescued by its being organized around routines of eating, sleeping, and occupations. The Ace High had been her first home here and it was good, during the three weeks she visited, to share tasks and chat with Betty, listen to Johnny's yarns, and ride with Jenny. Ase was busy with roundup so she didn't see him often.

Jenny had practiced her penmanship that summer and with a shy pride unlike her usual confidence, showed Susanna several filled tablets that demonstrated hard-won progress. Jenny's twelve-year-old figure was just beginning to bud and her face was losing its childish roundness. With sun-browned skin, deep blue eyes, and that yellow, yellow hair, she gave promise of real beauty. When Susanna complimented her penmanship, Jenny flushed with pleasure.

"Miss Alden?"

"Yes, dear?"

"Thank you for talking Daddy into letting me have a divided skirt—and such a pretty blue one! If I can't wear Levi's, it's the next best thing." Hesitating for a moment,

Jenny touched Susanna's arm. "If . . . if you ever want to marry Daddy, I'll still like you."

"Thank you, Jenny," said Susanna gravely. "Your father's bound to find a nice woman he'd like to bring home. Give her a chance, sweetheart."

The blue eyes, so like Ase's, widened and the sweet, willful mouth dropped open. "You . . . you don't want to marry Daddy?"

"I like and admire him tremendously, Jenny, but you see, I don't love him."

Jenny pondered. "You mean the way I like Dave and Val and Freck, but it's Ridge I love?"

If that love ripened with Jenny, Susanna wondered what it would bring, but she wasn't going to warn the girl or argue. "Yes, honey." Susanna gathered the child to her. "That's exactly how it is."

Ase, too, had his question, the evening that she said she must get to the soddie next day and start preparing for school. Searching her face across the table, he said, "You haven't changed your mind about the school? Or—anything else?"

Why couldn't she love him when she liked him so much? It was fitting and proper and Jenny would welcome her. Ase was potently male. In this house where she felt so comfortably at home, couldn't she grow into loving him enough to make a happier life for all of them than she was likely to find if she left the district next spring? It was no use haranguing herself, though. Longing for a home and family would certainly have induced her to accept Ase if she hadn't met and loved Matt.

But she had. Meeting Ase's wistful eyes, she said regretfully but firmly, "No, Mr. McCanless. I haven't changed my mind."

No sunflowers or grass swayed on top of the soddie, and

it took her a stunned moment to believe her eyes. "The soddie! It's got a shingled roof! A real roof!"

Ase had seemed pensive but he chuckled at her delight as he helped her out of the buckboard. "Didn't want you and the kids gettin' rained on again and I was purty sure you hadn't decided to move. Makes it lighter inside, too."

It did, though after her months away and the drive in the blazing sunlight, the soddie seemed murkily dark as she stepped inside. This was compensated for by the comparative coolness. No rattlesnake slithered across the floor and no tarantula swung down in her face. In fact, as her eyes grew accustomed to the dimness, she saw that the floors were freshly swept, everything was neat, and the fuel basket was full.

When she turned to thank Ase, he shook his head. "Dave helped with the shingling as much as he could. I told him about when you'd be coming. Guess all you need's a bucket of water."

He got that while Susanna lightened the trunk of books, handing them to Jenny who had ridden along on her pony. With help from the two of them, Ase got the trunk inside and brought in the provisions Betty had amassed for the first month.

"I smell chocolate cream pie," Ase said, sniffing like the giant in "Jack and the Beanstalk."

"Let's all have a piece," Susanna said, and that was her homecoming.

She missed Cav as she made her bed, put away books, and hung up her dresses, wincing at the blue one. Would Matt think it became her? It wouldn't matter if he did, now that a vigilant sister-chaperon was added to his own stubborn conviction that a woman could only endure his caresses, never enjoy them. Amanda didn't sound like the sort to attend the Friday visitors' afternoons so it was quite possible that they'd meet only at affairs like the Christmas ball.

As for Matt, the joy of seeing him could only be matched by chagrined disappointment that now she'd have no chance at all to make him change his mind.

Would he bring Cav to her? Susanna supposed she should refuse to take back her companion but knew she wouldn't if he was offered. Though far from being as timorous as she'd been a year ago, she would still feel much safer with Cav and, besides, how lonely the winter evenings would be without him stretched on the rug beside her, chin between his paws.

There was a sound and then, as if the thought had conjured him, Cav thrust his head under her hand and pressed against her with such rapturous tail-waggings that Susanna staggered.

"Oh, Cav!" Bending, she hugged him while he slathered her cheek. "Cavalier!"

"His name's Hank." Matt stood just outside the door, washed in bitter yellow sunlight that leached his face, carved shadows beneath his cheekbones. "How are you, Susanna?"

Feeling as if her bones had dissolved and she might crumple like a rag doll, Susanna straightened slowly. "I'm well." She couldn't bear to look into those eyes, dreamed of so often. Turning to the trunk, she almost babbled. "I . . . I have a book for you."

She handed him the heavy volume, drawing back her hand so swiftly that the book nearly dropped. "Why, this is Mayhew's *The Illustrated Horse Doctor: Being an accurate and detailed account of the various diseases to which the equine race are subjected, together with the latest modes of treatment, and all the requisite prescriptions. Written in Plain English.'*" Laughing, he caught his breath. "Thank you, Susanna. It's a famous tome and should be useful though I hope I won't often have cause to refer to it." He cleared his throat. "I suppose you've heard my sister's come. Allegedly, she's seeing that I don't live in male squalor. What she really wants, of course, is to plague me into setting up shop in Dallas and prescribing nerve tonics and sleeping potions to her high-strung, idle friends."

"If that's so, it's strange that she'd build such a fine house."

"After a starving youth when she worked at anything decent to keep us together, Amanda married a very wealthy, very old man. The spread of his investments and holdings and her own shrewdness enabled her to recoup a comfortable part of his fortune after the war. Amanda's generous with her money and contributes to many worthy causes, but she hasn't the slightest nostalgia for hardship." He made a rueful grimace. "She can't believe that I was a lot more comfortable in my soddie. But after she's gone to all this trouble, I can't refuse to live in her home."

"Can you refuse to become a Dallas society doctor?"

"Can and will." He shrugged philosophically. "Amanda can't stick this out too long. When she finally sees that I won't move, she will. The winter should do it."

By then I'll be leaving. Anything that might have happened without your being in her house and under her eye, won't have. "Matt," began Susanna. "Please, can't we—"

He raised his hand, the scarred one, held it between them, almost imploring her. "Susanna, my love, my darling, I know I must seem a coward to you, a poor-spirited thin-skinned whimperer, but I don't dare risk marrying you. I simply don't dare."

"You . . . you don't have to."

His eyes went almost black and his nostrils paled white at the creases. "Do you think I'd take from you what some men deem the most important thing about a bride and then not give you the protection of my name, even if you loathed my fondling?"

"Don't worry about that." She would beg this one time, then never again. "I love you. I'm asking you. You'll owe me nothing."

He turned away. "You're so much braver than I am, my

sweetheart, that you make me ashamed. But it's all the more reason that I can't wrong you. Let's not talk about it again. This is the last time I'll call you my love. I dare not even kiss you."

He moved away like an old man, as if he couldn't see. She huddled down by Cavalier, held him tight, and wept.

The next day, she visited Margaret Hardy. Rosie and Georgie, gathering chips and stalks, saw her and came running, and after Rosie got her hug and kiss, they curvetted around her like frisky colts, quieting only when she gave them a bag of cinnamon drops.

"We'll save some for Dave and Ethan," Rosie promised. Like Jenny, she had grown though there'd still be no difference in the measurement of chest, waist, and hips. Georgie was taller and his yellow hair was turning brown. They dashed ahead of her, shouting, "Mama! Mama! Miss Alden's here!"

Thinner, but looking well, Margaret's golden eyes danced at the large bar of lilac-scented soap. "Dave and Ethan are planting that Turkey Red wheat the Krauses gave us," she said. "They've worked like men, and of course Dave almost is—he turned sixteen in July. The wheat'll be ready for cutting soon—if the Lord wills," she added hastily, for as much as on their own efforts, whether a farm family prospered or failed depended on enough moisture at the right time, not to mention a host of other uncontrollable plagues like grasshoppers, drought, blight, and unseasonable hail that in a few minutes could beat a proud field of ripe grain into the mud. "The corn's making good ears and I hope it and the sorghum cane can be cut before school starts." Her cheeks pinkened. "Jem will help. He doesn't want the boys to miss school."

To a woman with a farm and children, that was the kind of wooing that counted. Susanna was glad for her friend though she thought with a stifled sigh that Margaret would marry soon, and Ase, once he embarked on a search, would quickly find any number of beautiful ladies to thrill at the notion of wedding a cattleman. In three or four years, her older pupils might start marrying and the others would be growing up. In ten years, she thought lugubriously, should she stay here, she could be teaching a second generation, even, God help her, children of those she was teaching now.

Well, she wouldn't, interesting as it would be. She had won a place here and it was her home as Ohio had never been, but closing day next March would be for her the closing of this part of her life. Among her qualifications for her next school, she could write, "Certified old maid." But in the midst of what verged dangerously near to self-pity, she knew she was loved, believed she would always be; and she knew that, however staid and proper she appeared, she would keep a green place in her heart to bloom with hidden flowers.

That bittersweet solace eroded as Margaret proffered her vinegar and water "beverage" and said, "Have you met Doc Rawdon's sister?"

"No," said Susanna dourly.

"Doc rode by here with her one day. She wore the fanciest riding habit, lilac trimmed with purple velvet and curlicues of braid, and wore a matching hat. Pretty but—" Margaret chuckled. "Know what Jem said? That he'd bet, compared to her, an icicle was plumb feverish. I invited them in, but my lady was having none of dugouts, or me, either, I guess. Looked down her long, straight nose like I was some kind of peculiar critter she couldn't quite place. Even with that new house she's building, I can't feature she'll like it here." Encircling Rosie with her arm, Margaret smoothed back her daughter's sun-streaked tawny hair. "It's a pity Doc doesn't have a wife to look after him instead of a bossy sister. But there, it's none of my business. Have some more beverage, dear. Did you have a nice time in Ohio? How were your aunt and uncle?"

* * *

Farmers were as busy in their fields as ranchers were with roundup, but Susanna, on different days, walked to visit the Taylors and Prades. Like Jenny, Berenice was just starting the change from girl to woman. She would never be beautiful, especially alongside Charlotte's willowy Dresden-doll prettiness, but her dark, deep-set eyes were lovely and her rare, tentative smile transformed her angular face.

"I read through the Fifth Reader this summer," she told Susanna when Laura paused in a recital of her latest symptoms and grudges against homesteading. "And I helped Helen through First Reader and we worked on her sums."

"The way she goes at it, you'd think she was already an old-maid teacher," Laura complained, then realized what she'd said and colored to the roots of her pale blond hair. "Forgive me, dear Miss Alden. Teaching the young is a necessary and estimable pursuit. But"—and here she gazed fondly at Charlotte, who sat on the footstool beside the chaise—"being a wife and mother is of course a woman's natural calling."

Susanna did not stay overlong. Next day, at the Prades', she found Laura's silvery blond head bent over her sewing machine and Jenny's blue riding habit while Sarah mended. The twins were gathering wild plums and Frank, of course, was in the fields with his father.

Fourteen now, Sarah was as tall as Susanna and her green calico dress strained across the tender curving of her breasts. With her golden hair caught back by a ribbon and her dark-lashed green eyes, she was startling to behold. Laura greeted Susanna warmly, but there was a shadow in the violet eyes. She spoke of the promising wheat crop with mingled hope and fear.

"Now that Mr. Prade's heard the Krauses are building frame houses this fall, he's bound we must have one. I've told him the soddie's fine. I'd rather get a milk cow, fence the garden, and save for a few years before putting everything into a new house, but he's absolutely set on it. This crop means so much to him that it ... well ..." The minister's daughter smiled uneasily. "It seems like tempting fate. Won't you stay for dinner, Miss Alden?"

Susanna glanced involuntarily at the coiled whip on the wall. She would like to have seen Frank, for she worried about him, but she was far from eager to encounter Saul Prade, particularly if his resentment of the Krauses had deepened. She declined the invitation but visited over a cup of warmed-over coffee. When she took her leave, Sarah asked if she might walk a little way with her, and both older women consented.

"I got through Seventh Reader this summer," Sarah told Susanna, as they walked along with Cav patrolling in front of them. "And I've been studying algebra with Frank—he likes it, you know."

The girl paused. Puzzled as to where this was leading, Susanna said, "That's wonderful, Sarah. If you want to, you may be able to do eighth-grade work and finish school next spring."

"Oh, do you think I can?"

"I'm sure of it, dear, if that's what you'd like." Susanna laughed. "I'll quit asking you to help the younger ones so much and then you can concentrate on your own studies."

"I loved helping. That's what I want to do—get a certificate next summer and find a school."

She would be neither the first nor the last fifteen-year-old to teach a frontier school but Susanna was disturbed by the desperation in the voice of this remarkably even-natured child. "You may not have to look far for a school," Susanna said. "I'm leaving next spring."

"You are?" Sarah looked amazed. "Oh, I hoped you'd be here for the twins but they'll be all right. It's Frank I have to get away, Miss Alden. I ... I'm scared for him."

"Why, dear?"

Drooping her head, Sarah whispered, "You know Father beats Frank. Mother knows Frank gets punished but she doesn't know how—and we don't want her to ever know!

Frank used to worry me because he was mean to animals and—you remember how he was at school till you wouldn't whip him when Father took him to you."

"He doesn't bully anymore," Susanna pointed out. "And I don't think he's—doing those other things."

"He's not. But in a way, it's worse than when he was!" Tears formed in Sarah's eyes as she caught Susanna's hands. "I have to get him away! He acts like he's dead inside. And that drives Father wild because he loves Frank better than any of us, maybe even more than Mother. He keeps trying to snap Frank out of it. I'm afraid something awful's going to happen."

Tears ran down her face and her breast heaved as she tried to choke back her sobs. Susanna took her in her arms and let her weep. What an unspeakable burden for a four-teen-year-old! "Maybe you should tell your mother," Susanna said haltingly.

"No!" Drawing away, Sarah wiped her eyes on her apron. "It would break her heart. And if she knew, she'd try to stop Father and then—I don't know what would happen. Sometimes I think if she finds out, something'll break loose in him and he won't care what he does."

There was such twisted perversion in Saul Prade that Susanna hesitated to ask the next question. "Have you tried to talk to your father?"

"Yes." The girl's face went so still that it was more frightening than her passion. "He says I don't understand how a father should raise a son. And when I've begged . . ." She shook her head, slender body trembling. "His eyes get so strange, Miss Alden, and his hands—when he touches me, it's not as if he's my father. I'm scared of him. I can't try again, not even for Frank."

"But will your father let you leave?"

"Frank's old enough to run off and get work. I'll try to get him to study hard so he can finish eighth this year, too." She drew herself up, considerably more grown-up than Delia Taylor would ever be. "I think Father'll let us go if I threaten to tell Mother about him and Frank. I won't do that, of course. We'll just run away. I'll put it to Frank that he's my brother and he has to look after me."

This was no childish scheming but a well-thought-out plan. "We'll get you through school," Susanna said, clasping Sarah's hand. "But remember this, dear. If anything happens so that you or Frank have to get away from your father quickly, come to me. Will you promise?"

"Father might—" Sarah's voice splintered. "I think he's hated you right from the start. We can't bring him down on you."

"Don't you worry about that. Promise, Sarah."

Some of the tension eased out of Sarah's body. Again, she was a child, trusting an elder. She gave her word and turned back with a lighter step.

Susanna went away the heavier. If anything irreparable happened to either child, she'd never forgive herself. She was more alarmed about what Prade might do to Sarah now than to Frank, though she told herself that surely no father would molest his own daughter. But what could she do?

Even if she appealed to Ase, he'd be reluctant to interfere in another man's family affairs. He hadn't seen Frank's mutilated back. If he spoke to Prade, it could lead to killing or compel Laura to know things about her husband that would make it impossible for her to live with him.

Chilled in spite of the warm autumn day, Susanna thought that Sarah had struck on the best answer and prayed that the evil she had sensed in Prade from their first meeting would somehow contain itself till Frank and Sarah could safely get away.

With the exception of martially erect old Anselm, the Krauses, from Magdalena to Peter, had been practicing English and spoke it at the huge noon meal they insisted Susanna share with them. To keep from seeming partial to Val with her gift of sketch pads and pastels, which delighted him to incoherence, Susanna brought candy for the younger children and a scarf for Cobie.

"Our Turkey Red thinks it at home is," laughed Jacob. "Sixty bushels to the acre we harvested and we had fifteen acres." He smiled at blue-eyed Catherine who blushed happily. "When the fall work is done, our houses we will build."

Catherine's mother, Anna, spoke slowly, smiling as she searched for the correct words. "The wedding, we will hold it a small time before Christmas." In a matter-of-fact way that would have scandalized Delia Taylor, she added, "The land, we begin to feel it ours when grain sprouts from seeds we plant. But when we bury our dead or a child is born, we belong truly."

Smiling at the young couple, so tenderly and honestly in love, Susanna thought they would doubtless be as fruit-ful as their fields and suspected that these quiet folk, come halfway around the world to keep their faith, might well endure on these prairies where others failed.

When she started to leave, Val offered to lend her Schatzie, but she said, "Thank you, Val, but she's your horse, and I won't need her since we won't be having Saturday classes." Freda had said, with Anna nodding agreement, that they would continue to study with their children and Jacob, but they wouldn't dream of taking up more of Susanna's free time.

Laden with a basket of good things, Susanna, Cav trot-ting ahead, cut through the fields of grasses browning for lack of rain, avoiding the Rawdons' as she had in coming. Matt had already cut his hay in the field across the creek from the school. She was glad of that. Most of the time, by staying occupied and fiercely wresting her thoughts away from him, she managed better than she'd expected to, but now and then, like this, she was seized with such longing that she wondered if she could possibly endure the situation through the term of her contract. It would help when school started and she was immersed in teaching nineteen young and different minds.

The creek was so low that by kilting up her skirts, she could jump across. The level of the well had sunk, she had noticed, till she had to uncoil almost all the windlass rope to bring up water. Cav pricked up his ears and began to sniff the tracks of a shod horse that had forded the creek and gone along the track, which was overgrown from six months' disuse.

Matt? Susanna's heart leaped into her throat. She should ask him not to come. It just made things harder. But it wasn't gray Saladin waiting in front of the soddie but a clean-limbed chestnut mare with a white-blazed face and three white stockings. Nor was that a regular saddle. It had the side hook that Jenny so detested. Cav loped toward the house to welcome the guest who'd arrived while he was away, and ran through the open door as if he smelled someone familiar.

"Get away, you disgusting beast!" Cav emerged, head and tail down, crushed at the rebuke. He was followed by a woman in lilac trimmed with purple, so tall she had to duck her head to keep from dislodging a plumed hat held on by chiffon ties. The ties formed a graceful bow that softened a pointed chin, just as the high, narrowing forehead was disguised with golden ringlets. She had the long, straight nose Margaret had described, similar to Matt's, and was looking down it.

"No wonder the dog runs in," she said in a soft Southern voice. Her eyes were a deep jade green and only a few faint, fine lines at the corners of her eyes betrayed that she was older than Matt. "I must say, my dear, that I admire you for being able to endure such conditions." Smiling graciously, she offered a gloved hand. "I'm Dr. Rawdon's sister, Mrs. Farwell. And you have to be Miss Alden."

There was nothing for it but to shake hands. "Will you have some tea or coffee?" Susanna offered.

"Thank you very much, but I won't make myself a nuisance." Again that charming smile. "From the way Matthew speaks of you, it's clear that you have his highest esteem." Golden eyebrows arched. "Am I correct to assume that you return his regard?"

"I love him." Susanna's voice was so fierce that it astonished her.

Amanda Farwell gave a silvery laugh. "You speak to the point, my dear. I admire that. If you love Matthew, you must want what's best for him."

"What, Mrs. Farwell, do you consider best?"

The dark green eyes widened. "Why, to leave this dismal place! Move to a city where he can practice his profession, be in contact with our own kind, and eventually find a suitable wife."

Flushing angrily in spite of herself, Susanna said, "Your brother doesn't seem inclined to do any of those things."

"He's always been stubborn," said Amanda airily. "But in time, I've always led him around to reason. Why, if you can credit it, instead of going to medical school, he almost went off mustanging in the brush of South Texas."

"He's no longer a boy, Mrs. Farwell."

"But you must see that he's wasted here."

"The community wouldn't agree with you. Even though he won't begin regular practice, he helps when he's needed. If he could just get over the idea that taking care of ordinary ills isn't as important as surgery—"

"You'd really have him waste himself in this wretched place? Be paid in scrawny chickens and vegetables if he's paid at all?"

"Oh, there's so much more pay than that! Being part of a community, doing useful work—"

Pityingly, Amanda shook her head till the plume danced. "You are a Yankee, aren't you, dear? All that rock-ribbed duty! But from what I hear, you have good sense. Soon or late, Matthew will come back where he belongs and will need a wife who belongs. With all respect, Miss Alden, a person of your—um—background would never be truly accepted in Dallas."

Or by you, thought Susanna. Not that it matters. "Let me allay your fear on one score, Mrs. Farwell. Dr. Rawdon has not proposed to me. I don't think he ever will."

Relief glowed in Amanda's eyes. Obviously, Matt hadn't explained their relationship. "It's commendably honest of you to tell me that, Miss Alden. Still, you have great influence with Matthew. If you'll consider deeply, I believe you'll come to my opinion of where his happiness lies and convey that in any conversations you have with him."

The woman was so assured and condescending that Susanna longed to do something rude and shocking, but that would only confirm Amanda's view of her as a Northern savage. "I doubt we'll have many conversations, Mrs. Farwell." The words stuck in Susanna's throat and she clamped her jaw to restrain a rising temper. "Thank you for calling."

Amanda slanted her a glance that showed the beginnings of respect. "I see I've worn out my welcome," she said with a small, self-deprecating laugh. Moving gracefully to her mare, she mounted with an ease Susanna was sure she'd never attain. "Again, my dear, thank you for your candor. I believe that however our views differ, we both want what's best for Matthew."

She nodded, turned the mare, and was off at a smooth canter.

"I wish you'd bitten her," Susanna said to Cav, patting him to restore his happiness. "Or at least jumped up and got mud all over her clothes."

Too angry and upset to work on her lesson plans, Susanna got soap and water and attacked the windows, saying with each scrub, "Damn her, the patronizing witch! Damn her!"

❀ *Twenty-two* ❀

As she reviewed her notes on each pupil and worked on her lesson plans, Susanna thought of all kinds of crushingly polite things she should have said to Amanda and grew more outraged each time she remembered the woman's audacity. Sarah's frightened face kept rising before her, too, and she wondered anxiously if she were imperiling the girl and her brother by keeping quiet. The alternatives were so dreadful that she always came back to hoping the two could finish school this year and go away together. Her father used to say that doctors knew a lot more about people than was comfortable. That, Susanna concluded, was even truer of teachers.

She was working at her desk, trying to concentrate on reading groups, when Cav ran in, whining, and tugged at her skirt. He'd never done that except when he was trying to lead her through the storm to Jenny.

"What is it, boy?" The wind carried a scorched odor. Hurrying outside, Susanna froze. The whole southeastern sky swelled with a roiling cloud of coppery brown, boiling thicker at one place and then at another, rolling across the plains. From miles away, the gusting wind brought the acrid smell of burning grass.

Prairie fire. Terror drenched Susanna with cold sweat but her mind recalled with sharp clarity all she'd ever heard about this scourge of the grasslands. People in soddies or dugouts should be fairly safe. Since the men were in the fields, they'd see the conflagration in time to take shelter with their animals, possibly even plow fireguards around their homes, sets of furrows with a space in between that was burned to leave a wide belt where the fire would have nothing to devour.

The unharvested crops would be consumed. There was no time to plow fireguards around acres of grain. Matt's horses—could he get them into the barns and soddie? A good thing the Krauses hadn't built their frame houses yet.

Would the fire leap the creek? As low and sluggishly as the water flowed and thick as rushes and willows were along the banks, it wouldn't be much of a barrier. It was out of the question to run. She and Cav would be as safe in the soddie or barn as anywhere the fire reached.

Every man was expected to help fight a fire once he'd secured his family and stock. Ase and the other ranchers were probably already battling the fire, or heading toward it with some unfortunate cattle that would be killed, split in half, and used as drags, hind and front legs tied with ropes to saddle horns of two riders who dragged the half-carcasses, bloody side down, along the line of fire to smother it while other men followed on foot to beat out smoldering flames with wet blankets, slickers, or whatever they had.

Susanna's gaze fixed on the shingled roof. That would burn! On the realization, she ran inside, seized the water bucket and dashed water upon the low, slanted roof. Bucket after bucket she drew up from the well, trying to soothe Cav who whined and pleaded with her to flee. Smoke now rolled above what looked like a sunset blazing across the entire horizon.

In spite of all warnings and common sense, Susanna had to battle panic that impelled her to run like the antelope that skimmed past, heedless of Cav. Prairie dogs, rabbits, and other burrowing creatures should find safety in the deepest parts of their burrows, but coyotes loped by, blending with the sere grass, and she thought she glimpsed the larger, grayer shadows of a pair of wolves, followed by several half-grown ones.

The writhing ocean of tossing flame with its towering pall of billowing smoke surged hungrily across the small eminence of the cemetery and poured toward the Hardys'. Dear God, let them all be safe inside that dugout. Almost as impervious to fire as the earth of the slope it was cut into, the cave-like dwelling that had been Margaret's bane should now be her salvation.

All this time, Susanna kept tossing water on the shingles, running from back to front and making sure the log roof leading to the fuel shed was well-soaked. Since everyone was busy with autumn work, no new fuel had been hauled over and the dwindled heap left from last spring was in the far corner and didn't seem too likely to catch fire.

In order to have water ready for dousing flames, Susanna filled the washtubs as the fire licked greedily toward Matt's and the Taylors' and swept toward the creek. Her eyes stinging from smoke and cinders, Susanna brought up a final bucket of water and dashed for the house. The smoke hid sky and sun, everything but waves of fire that crested and ebbed and swelled again.

Panting, Cav at her heels, she barred the door—as if that would keep out this invader! Thank heaven, six months' pounding of feet, horses, and wagons around the school had trampled out the roots of the grass surrounding the building, reaching pretty much to the privies and barn.

If the flame did crack the windows and dart inside, she'd slosh water on the bedding and roll herself and Cav up in it. But oh, her books! Grandmother Alden's china! And the wonderful globe the children loved so much . . .

Keeping up a flow of encouragement to the frightened dog which helped calm her as well, Susanna put the china and her favorite books in the trunk. The smoke was thick and strangling bitter. She wet a handkerchief and held it over her eyes and nose.

That hissing roar, like a multitude of whirring rattlers! It was almost dark as night. In spite of the thick sod walls, the room began to heat. Even if they didn't burn, would she and Cav be baked to death or suffocated? The air next to the ground was better. Bucket at hand, Susanna knelt on the rug beside Cav, embracing him as she lowered her head, breathed through the cloth, and waited.

If only no one died, and no creatures! Amanda Farwell may have finally found some virtue in a soddie. Had her frame house burned? The yard of the Ace High dwelling was clear of grass and Johnny kept it scythed for a wide radius around the headquarters buildings and corrals. Since the monster had vaulted the creek, there was no guessing how far it would rage.

Sweat matted Susanna's hair to her scalp, trickled down her face and neck. Even through the cloth, which she kept wet, the air burned her nose and throat. Were things desperate enough to soak the bedding? Were her ears playing tricks or had the fury hurtled past?

Waiting till she was sure the voracious snarling had dulled, Susanna started to rise, found the smoke stifling, and went down on her knees, creeping into the other room where she reached the window, held her breath, and tried to peer out.

The glass she'd polished to exorcise her indignation at Amanda hadn't cracked but was so blackened it was almost opaque. Squinting through a thinner haze at one corner, she could faintly make out the barn, and she could *see* the wind, for it was charged with blackened ash of every size from fine dust to swirling particles. This followed behind the fire, so thick that she could scarcely see the flames.

Choking, she sank down on the earth again, blessing the sod that had been her refuge. Just as sleet had sifted through cracks and windows and the door, black powder was still settling everywhere, but Susanna was too grateful to feel anything but rejoicing that they were alive. Her own danger past, she thought with fresh concern about her neighbors, but that she had escaped harm in spite of a shingled roof made her assure herself that they, too, must be safe, at least in their lives. Losing crops and belongings was serious. After the other adversities, the new failure might force some homesteaders to sell out, just as grasshoppers and drought had. But as long as a person had health and life, losses could be gained back.

If only no one had been caught out on the prairie, far from any refuge! Fear weakened her. She wouldn't breathe freely, even in clean air, till she knew Matt was safe—and Dave and Jem, the Wrights, McGuinns and Harrises—everyone. She thought of Saul Prade with a chill of dread.

This crop was to have financed the building of a frame house. If he lost it when the Krauses had already made a bountiful harvest of the Turkey Red he'd despised . . . Shuddering at the thought, Susanna crouched beside Cav and kept her head down till the air was somewhat better, though dust that looked like pulverized coal continued to thicken the layers that covered the bed and other furniture, drifted in at the windows and door, and coated the bucket of water.

The daffodil dress, the sprigged muslin, the sky-blue gown she'd bought for Matt, all her hanging clothes were black as her best silk. Why, why, hadn't she covered them with something? She was wearing the green tarlatan but it too was smudged black. Cav rose and gave himself a prodigious shake that added to the cindery haze. At her shriek, he licked her sooty hands, beseeching forgiveness for whatever he had done.

"It didn't matter, boy," Susanna told him with a sigh. She thought of hurrying across the creek to see if the Hardys were all right but the black wind was blinding. Besides, if anyone came looking for her and she was gone, it might set off a frenzied search, the last thing the community needed.

Skimming charred dust and chaff off the water in the bucket, Susanna filled Cav's water bowl and drank herself before she began to clean off the food supplies and pots and pans. She hoped cinders were healthy. They'd be eating and drinking them, sleeping and sitting and walking in them, for a long time to come. But what did that matter, if only no lives were lost?

Anxiety grew in her as she worked but she knew she'd have to endure it for the men would be fighting the fire and till it died or was defeated, she wasn't likely to hear anything. Increasingly haunted by the possibility that Matt had been caught riding out on the plains, she built a fire—what an irony that was—and put on water to brew tea which always heartened her, especially from one of Grandmother Alden's cups which could now add a prairie fire to disasters they'd lasted through.

She'd seen the fire shortly before noon and it was now four o'clock though it seemed as if an eternity had passed and another was starting that would end only when she heard everyone was safe. Black powder had filtered under the lid of the pan that held mush she'd made for breakfast that morning. She scraped it off, thanked goodness the canned foods would be clean, and opened some Borden's milk. Cav deserved a treat so she splashed milk over his mush, poured the rest on her own, and after forcing a few bites, ate with more appetite than she'd dreamed she could summon and sipped at tea which had never been more revivifying.

Was the wind slackening? Staring out through the darkened glass, she thought it looked like late twilight, but gusts no longer beat at the house. As she watched, she saw the faint outline of the sun in the west. She simply couldn't go through the night without learning how at least the Hardys were. She found a relatively clean washcloth in the dresser and was washing her begrimed face when a rap sounded on the door.

Hurrying to unbar it, she pushed it open. She knew Matt by his eyes, not his blackened face, and went limp. Saladin, also black, snorted and fidgeted. "Oh, Matt!"

They were in each other's arms, clinging as if to make sure they were really there, really alive. They held each other a long time in blessed relief and thanksgiving that asked for nothing more. At last, he kissed her gently and stepped back.

"The Hardys are fine—Jem's with them now we've stopped the fire, which we couldn't have done without the cattlemen and their drags. Stopped it at the bend of the creek beyond Prades' though it burned Ase's school to the ground."

"Is everyone all right?"

"Seem to be. Will Taylor had gone over to Jem's to borrow his mowing machine and didn't have time to get to shelter so he tied his shirt over his horse's eyes and just stayed in the middle of five acres Jem broke from sod a few weeks ago."

"Your horses?"

"I got them all in the barn or soddie, and besides, it was so dry I'd already made a fireguard, so mostly the flames went around us, same as they did at Krauses'. They'd plowed and burned a fireguard so wide it stopped the fire on that side." Answering her unspoken question, he said wryly, "Amanda had a fit because I left her to fight the fire, but besides the fireguard around the buildings and main corral, I'd made another one around her wooden house. She's fine, except for her temper."

"The crops?"

"Burned. Except at the Krauses'. Their Turkey Red was already harvested, of course, but they saved their corn and sorghum, too, because of the fireguards they made around all their planted fields."

"Was Saul Prade fighting the fire?"

"In a way. He and Frank tried to plow some furrows and start a backfire around the crops, but the backfire jumped the furrows and burned the fields before the main fire got there. Frank joined in to help us but Saul had burned his hands too bad."

Susanna shook her head. "I wish he'd saved his crops."

"He's lucky to be alive and have his family and stock safe."

"I'm afraid he won't see it that way. He's already jealous of the Krauses. Since they saved their grain, he'll really hate them."

Matt shrugged. "The Krauses plowed the furrows that helped check the fire, and they were in there helping though their own places were safe. They've said they'll share their grain with whoever needs it and give seed wheat to anyone who wants to plant this fall. Ase is giving half a beef to every family that lost its crops. He's not forgotten how Dave and the others circled with the rope to look for Jenny in that blizzard. No one's going to starve or have to give up." He grinned slightly. "Unless they think they've had enough of Kansas. The only disaster we haven't had around yet is a tornado."

"Don't even mention it," Susanna said. "Are you hungry?"

He looked at her comically. "I guess I am. Didn't think about it, I was so anxious to make sure you were all right."

"Come in. Wash your face and hands—don't worry, you can't make anything dirtier than it is." She stoked the fire and while the water reheated for tea she fried up the remainder of the mush, unwrapped the last of the cheese the Krauses had given her, and opened a can of peaches. While he started on that, she mixed corn fritters and dropped them in the frying pan.

Plain fare, when she longed to prepare a feast for her love, but how wonderful it was, after her fears, to watch him eat and drink and know that he was safe. As long as he was well and sharing sun and earth with her, she'd thank heaven for that.

He was ravenous and that pleased her. It made her amazingly happy to set food before him. She was spooning more fritters on his plate when someone knocked.

"Come in," she called, setting down the pan and going to the door.

It was Ase, blackened and red-eyed as Matt had been. "Wanted to be sure you're all right." His gaze went past her to Matt who raised a hand.

"Come in and wash up," Susanna said. "Have some fritters and peaches. I'll put on coffee." Ase disdained tea.

"Obliged, but I better get home."

"Sit down, Ase," Matt urged. "Your hands'll tell Betty and Jenny the fire's out, and you must be as starved as I was."

Susanna put her hand on his begrimed shirt. "Please, Mr. McCanless."

His cindery face widened in a smile. "Well, how can I do anything but what you want when you talk nice like that, Miss Susanna? Sounds like you don't even aim to rub it in that my school burned down—damned glad you weren't in it! I'll wash outside, scoop the ash off one of those tubs you were smart enough to have ready."

While he finished a can of peaches and the remaining fritters, Susanna made more. He had three cups of coffee while they talked about the fire, but when Matt rose to go, Ase jumped up, too. They departed at the same time, riding off in opposite directions into the haze that stung eyes and throats and thickened what was now really twilight.

Putting on several kettles of water to heat for a bath and hair-washing, Susanna did the dishes, carried the bedding out to shake it, and began wiping off the furniture with dampened cloths. Black dust would be settling in the house for days, but she had to make a start.

Thanks to the frequently cursed sodhouses, their inhabitants had survived the fire. Because of the Krauses' and

Ase's generosity, no one would go hungry or be forced to sell out. But Prade ... Susanna's spine chilled. He must have been a little mad to start with. What would he be like now?

A few days later, she visited the Hardys, wearing the tarlatan, for walking across the charred prairie blackened hems and stockings. In this wood-hungry land, dead limbs and fallen trees weren't allowed to accumulate along the creek, so after consuming reeds, grass, and smaller willows, the fire surged on without doing much harm to the cottonwoods beyond scorching their trunks. The crows and blackbirds were thick as ever, so even in this singed world they must be finding something to eat. The young of ground nesters like the meadowlark were long fledged so perhaps most small creatures had escaped.

Susanna arrived at the dugout as Jem, Dave, and Ethan were hitching up after dinner to finish planting more Turkey Red. As they started for the fields, Jem called over his shoulder, "Margaret, better give Miss Alden our news."

"What news?" asked Susanna, turning to Margaret who was blushing like a girl.

"Well, dear, we've been planning to marry a year after poor Cash died, but the fire scared Jem so that he swears it's plain crazy to worry about customs that don't make sense out here. I've talked with the children. They loved their daddy but they like Jem. Just so's they don't have to call him Father, they'll be tickled to have him live with us. Not in the dugout," she added with pride. "Soon as the wheat's planted, Jack Harris and Ben Wright will come over and help build a good soddie—four rooms. They owe Jem work because he's helped them a lot."

Margaret's golden eyes shone as she led the way inside and poured them glasses of the familiar much-diluted vinegar. "We lost our crops, but Jem has enough money put by to pay the Krauses for the grain we need—he says he's not taking advantage of their good hearts though he says we can take half a beef from Ase and repay him next year with molasses and flour. We won't have money for a wood roof, but listen! Jem knows where there's lots of cedar a little over a hundred miles south of Dodge down in Indian Territory. He'll haul enough to make shakes for the roof! Isn't that wonderful?"

Susanna nodded. "All the same, you'd better build near the dugout in case there's another fire."

"Or tornado," Margaret said with a rueful but still exuberant laugh. Sobering, she leaned forward. "But you know what's the best thing of all about Jem?"

Smiling, Susanna said, "It sounds as if it'd be hard to decide that."

"No, it's easy. He says of course Dave can be a teacher, and if things go well enough, we'll help him attend the university. What's sure is Dave won't have to stay here and support us."

Susanna was glad for her friend. After hard years with a feckless man, she deserved someone who'd try to give her a good life. Ignoble as it was, though, Susanna couldn't suppress an envious heart cry. Still, it was her own fault if she refused a good man like Ase for one who was afraid to claim her. Vinegar was an appropriate drink for anyone so noodle-headed. When Margaret offered to refill her glass, Susanna nodded and drank it as chastisement.

Apart from crops, the blaze had consumed the cow chips and stalks used for fuel. Settlers would have to range beyond the seared region to fill their wagons. The ranchers welcomed them to the unburned range, and Ase, Kermit Brown, and Luke Tarrant each brought a load and filled the shed when they attended the trustees' meeting the day before school started.

"Appreciate it, friends," Will Taylor said. "I've got to cut and haul a mountain of hay for that dadburned cylinder stove, and I just finished planting wheat. I'll deliver my share of fuel sure as you're born, but it's a big help not to have to do it right now." His usual harried look relaxed in a smile. "Nothin' beats good neighbors. And it was a lucky day for us when the Krauses settled here. Lendin' us wheat and corn and there'll be molasses, too, for anyone who'll help strip the cane, feed it through the crusher, and keep the pans of juice simmerin'. They're settin' up a mill and Pete and Fred say when we get another sorghum crop, we'll all be welcome to use it in return for a share of the molasses. They—"

"Pete and Fred!" Prade mimicked. His burned hands and arms were still bandaged and his gold hair and eyebrows were singed. "Those damn Dutchies! They'll get rich off our sweat!"

"How's that?" demanded Will.

"They're lending you grain to get through the winter and the mealymouthed hypocrites say you can pay them back just what you borrowed—no extra bushels."

"That's right. And how can you figger anythin' but good out of that, Saul?"

Again, Prade cut the gangling Missourian short. "You're obligated, though, aren't you, Will? Grateful to the Dutchies? So likely you'll help them build those new houses they're stickin' up while the rest of us are glad to have a roof over our heads. And you'll bust your guts breaking sod for them—they'll get their wheat back, and get a lot of work out of you just like they will from the others."

Will's brow furrowed. "Fellow ought to show he's grateful, seems to me," he said slowly.

"Maybe there's not all that much to be grateful for."

Ase had been scowling at the exchange. Now he said, "What're you drivin' at, Prade?"

The man swung to face him. "Doesn't it strike anyone else as damn peculiar that the fire stopped at their fancy fireguard? How come they were the only ones who'd plowed around their fields?"

Ase stared. When he spoke at last, it was in a hard, dry voice. "If you think folks like that would start a fire, Prade, you're plumb crazy. Best not go around spoutin' such flap-doodle. Come on now, let's get to school business."

Greetings and laughter filled the air as the children met again after months when most of them had been too busy to visit each other and play. Since there was no grass, the ranchers had already filled the haymow and dumped several stacks near the barn. The smaller boys were leaping into the stacks with boisterous shouts when Susanna stepped to the door to ring the bell. She smiled to see that Sarah was already chiding the exuberant children, telling them they mustn't trample the horses' food.

As the youngsters trooped in and spied the pencil boxes at each place, there was fresh delight, and seeing that most were too excited to settle down at once, Susanna let them stand and sing the Kansas rivers song and several more before she read from Walt Whitman. "The spelling assignment for each class is on the board," she said. "The rest of you study those while I hear seventh-grade reading."

As she had suspected, all the class—Sarah, Dave, and Frank—could read the last part of the Seventh Reader without a mistake. With no misgivings, she advanced them to the Eighth Reader. "The three of you want to finish school next spring," she told them, glancing from Dave's steady light brown eyes to Sarah's intent green ones. Frank didn't evade her gaze but there was no answering flicker of expression. "You'll have to work extra hard in algebra and geometry since you have two years to cover. I've appreciated your help with the younger children, but now you need to concentrate on your own studies. Berenice and Ethan are in fifth grade—Berenice is reading sixth—and they'll be able to work with the others. I'll have more time, too, since the Krause children are speaking English so well that they won't need special tutoring."

From the determination in Sarah's and Dave's faces, she knew they'd conquer the eighth-grade work along with seventh. As for Frank, who could tell? At least he didn't move with stiffness as if he'd been beaten.

As she heard each child read, Susanna was pleased to find that most of them had gone through their old or next readers during the summer, so she did some regrouping. Ridge had advanced to Third Reader to join Jenny, Rosie, Dottie, and his former protégé, Val. Freck and Charlotte were weak fourth readers and would need a lot of drill, but Susanna didn't expect any unusual difficulties. That was good since it would give her more time to teach her two-years-in-one class.

Giving them their diplomas would be a gratifying close to her service in the district, and, if possible, she'd slip in some Latin roots and other high school material. Comparing the ease of beginning studies this year with last October's confusion, Susanna wondered with a pang who would ring the bell for her children next year, who would guide them into the next books and watch them growing up. It was going to be so hard to leave! But not as hard, she thought, steeling herself, as living near Matt when he refused, refused absolutely, to give their love a chance.

Jem built the new soddie, hauled up the cedar, and by mid-November had shingled the roof. He and Margaret went to Dodge to be married quietly and have a few days' honeymoon. Fond as Jem was of the Hardy youngsters, and they of him, it would have been intimidating for newly-weds to spend their bridal night with the bride's children in adjoining rooms.

Since they were no young couple and Cash was not long dead, there was no raucously ebullient charivari, a raid on the couple with cowbells ringing, guns firing, whoops and shouts, and perhaps a dunking of the groom in the creek, but Betty organized a festive dinner where the countryside, laden with choice victuals and useful gifts, descended on the new home. Only the Prades were absent, though Matt Rawdon came by himself, wished the couple happy, left his gift, a brass Rochester hanging lamp, and departed, speaking to Susanna only in passing.

Had he even noticed the blue dress? He certainly hadn't heard the rustle of her taffeta petticoat. Braced to put up with Amanda's condescension, Susanna had worn her pretty new dress to bolster her spirits. Now the man who above all she wanted to admire it had scarcely glanced at her.

Susanna hoped Margaret didn't feel snubbed by Amanda's reputed headache. It seemed that Amanda was trying to isolate Matt from his neighbors. If she succeeded, he might eventually give up and return with her to Dallas.

Forcing these glum thoughts aside, Susanna joined in the feast and the following play party. Ase, in a manner, was her escort, for he'd brought Betty and Johnny in the buckboard and stopped for Susanna. Jenny had ridden beside them in her new divided skirt.

It was ample chaperonage, certainly, but they were dancing outside by the light from windows and lanterns, and at the end of a reel, Ase swept her out of the flickering illumination to stand in the darkness by the old dugout. She tried to pull away but his arms and hands were relentless.

Short of creating an embarrassing furor, there was nothing she could do except retreat from him and, back against the door, say reproachfully, "Mr. McCanless!"

"Miss Susanna!" Surely he hadn't been drinking.

"This . . . isn't proper, sir." She started around him. He blocked her way.

"Have you changed your mind?"

"I haven't." Pushed to plain speaking by this high-handed abduction, she didn't try to gentle the answer. "And I won't."

A long breath went out of him. "All right, Miss Alden, ma'am, reckon I got nothin' to lose." He brought her against him, found her lips with his, bruisingly male, and kissed her hard and thoroughly.

After the first seconds when she found it was useless, Susanna didn't resist, but she didn't yield, either, didn't allow her body to soften as it tried to do. Stepping back, Ase said, "I did it, and I'm glad. I won't pester you again, Miss Susanna. In fact, I'm going to St. Louis and start huntin'."

"Good luck," she said.

He waited in the darkness for her to return to the party. As young Tom Chadron beseeched her to be his partner, she hoped Ase would find his bride—but not till she'd left the district. She had no wish at all to dance at his wedding.

❀ *Twenty-three* ❀

Fall rains washed away some of the charred stubble and encouraged fresh green growth like a second spring, though this didn't have time to grow high before frosts came that purpled the bluestem and bleached the dropseed and sideoats grama on unburned grassland. Chevrons of cranes and geese no longer glinted high against the sun, and prairie chickens flocked in numbers that testified most had escaped the fire. The nighthawk was gone, and the yellow-headed blackbird, but the big, iridescent green blackbird and flocks of white-crowned sparrows took up winter residence, the red-tailed hawks hunted, crows gossiped with red-winged blackbirds along the creek, and the meadowlark winged up from the prairie like its very spirit.

With a sound roof over her head, Susanna enjoyed the rain that rinsed away the lingering odor of burned grass, and she greeted the rising Pleiades like old friends, but with a tinge of sadness. By the time they disappeared next spring, she'd be gone, too.

Fortunately, teaching left her little time to brood over Matt. The election of 1876 gave her an excellent chance to illustrate how the political system worked. Though the

Prohibition party and the National Greenback party had nominated candidates, the real contest was between Republican Rutherford B. Hayes and Democrat Samuel Tilden. On the day of the election, officials from Dodge City opened the polls in Susanna's room and she thought the slight disruptions when someone passed through the school on the way to vote were more than compensated for by the children seeing their fathers exercise their franchise—and noting that their mothers could not.

There were further lessons in actual politics because the election was disputed. Tilden had a heavy popular vote margin but the electoral vote in four states was contested and in three Southern states Republican election boards threw out Democratic votes for alleged irregularities and certified Hayes, which gave him enough electoral votes to win. The Democrats were protesting this, of course, and how the issue would be decided remained to be seen.

Berenice and Ethan took up Sarah's and Dave's tutoring of younger children. There was no primer class this year; under the tutelage of Cobie and Val, Magdalena and Freddie had studied hard enough to be in first grade on equal terms with Helen and Georgie. Susanna was able to spend a considerable part of the time with Dave, Sarah, and Frank, and it was a joy to encourage such good students, especially when they were as eager as Sarah and Dave were. Frank absorbed her teaching and he must have studied, for his compositions and test papers were near perfect, but he never exhibited interest except in biology and physiology.

Would he make a scientist or doctor? Susanna wondered. With a hastily suppressed memory of the crushed turtle, she thought that might have been the perverted side of a curiosity and analytical ability that would make him outstanding in some profession—if only he'd rouse from his strange torpor.

Susanna's pleasure in her students was marred by only

one thing. Saul Prade. When he stopped by the first time, she wasn't much concerned. She'd invited parents to visit if they wished outside the regular Friday afternoons. Besides, as a trustee, he had a right, if not a duty, to stop by unannounced to see how she was carrying out her charge. When he came the second time within a week, she grew nervous and her anxiety mounted with each visit as he began to drop in as often as three times a week.

What was his intention? If it had been any other home-steader, she'd have thought he was simply passing time idled by the loss of the crops. There was no corn to shuck this winter, no sorghum to take to the mill, no hay to cut. He was the only settler who hadn't planted Turkey Red in the burned fields, so except for ranging on unburned land for cow chips, he had little in the way of occupation. Will Taylor, Jack Harris, and Ben Wright had all turned to freighting to offset their crop losses, hauling supplies from Dodge to Camp Supply in Indiana Territory and Tascosa and Fort Elliott down in Texas.

Since Prade had been a bull-whacker, it was odd that he didn't do the same. Instead, a frequent and increasingly unwelcome onlooker, he would come in noiselessly except for the opening of the door, stand by the water bench, and silently observe.

At first Susanna greeted him, but soon gave him only a nod and went on with her class. Blessedly, he never stayed long. Fifteen or twenty minutes and he was gone as noiselessly as he'd come, but not before Susanna's stomach had twisted into a tight, cold knot.

She could complain to Ase, but, after all, what could she say? Prade didn't interrupt classes or heckle her. He was just *there.* It was like being stalked by a giant cat. Watching him as much as she could without seeming to, Susanna found the lack of expression on his handsome face more worrying than ridicule or malice. He looked at his son with chill eyes that made Frank, in recitation, stumble over things he knew by heart. Toward the twins, Prade

Jeanne Williams

seemed totally indifferent. Only when Sarah, slim, womanly, and golden-haired, rose to speak, did his tight lips
soften a trifle and his gaze hold pride and tenderness.

Early in December, he came one morning a little before
recess, watched quietly till Susanna dismissed the children, and when she started to follow them out, he stepped
in front of her, filling the door.

Fear shot through her. It took all her will not to fall back,
but when he spoke, his tone was civil enough. "Seems to
me you're spending a lot of time on the older kids, miss.
I don't recall studying half what you're teaching them."

Susanna's heart skipped before she assured herself that
he couldn't possibly guess what she and Sarah had
planned. "I'm trying to make up for last year," she
explained truthfully enough. "Because some of the pupils
had never been in school before and so many were just
starting to read, I tended to let Sarah and Dave help a lot
with them, and because they and Frank are such good students, I left them to study on their own more than I would
have if I'd had more time."

He gave her a wintry smile. "Sounds like you're admitting what I told the other trustees. Taking on those
Dutchies robbed our kids of the schooling we were paying for."

"The Krauses have given their share, and more," Susanna
reminded him. "It's true I had to give them extra time, but
I think that was made up for by the way they got the
others interested in foreign countries and why people
come to America."

"That's your opinion."

"Every child passed last year. None failed in any subject,
and most did extremely well. If you have any complaints,
Mr. Prade, please take them to the trustees."

"Now wouldn't that do a lot of good? Ase McCanless was
sweet on you before but after you found his girl in that
storm he thinks you hung the moon."

"As to my duties, sir, I should be out on the playground supervising. If you'll excuse me."

He stepped aside. "I'll be watching. And someday you'll make a mistake even McCanless can't shrug off."

"I'll have to do it before April," she said. "It should delight you, Mr. Prade, to know that I won't sign a contract for next fall."

He stared at her. She met those hard green eyes, but with difficulty. After a moment, he gave a bark of laughter. "Can't stand having Doc Rawdon's sister so close, can you? She put a stop to your whoring little games!"

Susanna drew herself up. "You're a trustee, Mr. Prade, but that gives you no right to insult me. In future, kindly visit only on Friday afternoons."

"I'll come when I please."

She took a deep breath. "It's my agreement with the board that I'm responsible for and thus have control of the school so long as my work is satisfactory. I find your . . . your surveillance annoying and distracting."

"Going to run to McCanless?"

"I will if necessary."

Casting her a glance so full of hatred that Susanna felt lanced by white-hot steel, he turned and strode off. Shaken, Susanna steadied herself against the door. All her strength had been spent in that conflict, brief as it was. If he knew what she purposed with Sarah . . .

Susanna thought him capable of murder. Certainly she wouldn't dare precipitate a fight between him and Ase. She just hoped Prade, though she was sure he wasn't afraid of Ase or anyone, would choose not to have a confrontation. Picking up the bell, she rang the children in.

Snow fell, cloaking the ravaged plain. Prade brought Laura on two Friday afternoons, but ceased his unnerving visits. Cobie and Val reported excitedly on the progress of their new homes. Peter and Freda's house was finished, Frederick and Anna's lacked only some indoor carpentry that was being left for stormy days, and the house where Jacob and Catherine would live was nearing completion.

"Jacob, so eager he is, works even at night." Cobie laughed. "Soon we'll have the wedding." She held out her hands to the other pupils. "All of you must come. Dancing we will not have, but there will be such food. And so much——" Pausing, green eyes alight, she groped for the word. "Joy! To our joy you must come."

Susanna had not seen Matt since the wedding party for Margaret and Jem. That was best, she told herself, though she hungered for sight of him and was disappointed and rather hurt when he hadn't come to the Thanksgiving program and dinner at the school. That was doubtless how it would be till she left. She'd meet him only at other people's weddings or at the Christmas ball. Perhaps, since it was held by a wealthy rancher, Amanda would deign to attend. If she did, thought Susanna, firmly tilting her chin, she'd see Susanna dancing gaily in her sky-blue gown—no need for that infuriatingly superior woman to know that later the despised Yankee schoolmarm would weep into her pillow!

Susanna had dismissed school Monday afternoon the week before Christmas when she heard the rumble of a wagon. All the children were gone except the Prade youngsters who were waiting while Sarah asked about a complicated geometry problem.

"Just a minute, Sarah." Susanna went to the door and found Jacob pulling up with a load of hay on a jaunty green wagon. Beaming, he pulled his cloth cap off the yellow hair that made him look even younger than he was.

"The hay in the barn I will put," he said. "But I am come to invite you to our wedding, mine and Catherine's. One day before Christmas, we will married be, and our friends must come and be glad with us."

"That's wonderful, Jacob." Susanna reached up her hand to shake his. "Tell Catherine how happy I am for her, for both of you. I'll surely be there if it doesn't storm."

"A storm comes, we marry a little later," Jacob said philosophically. There was something Biblical, reminiscent of his patriarchal namesake, in his toiling for the family of his betrothed. Except here was no sore-eyed Leah to be foisted off on a suitor who'd have to work seven more years to gain his Rachel. "To Ase McCanless I have already been. He will stop for you with his buckboard. All arranged it is."

"Thank you, Jacob." Susanna smiled. "I'll look forward to it—though not as much as you!"

He clucked to the horses and Susanna returned to help Sarah. After solving several examples, Sarah nodded. "I understand now, Miss Alden. Thanks for being patient."

"You learn much faster than I did." Susanna laughed. "You'd best be getting home now before your mother worries."

As she walked to the door with the children, she heard voices from the direction of the barn. Stepping out, she was in time to see Saul Prade lash Jacob with the doubled horsehair rope that was kept in the barn.

"Stop!" Susanna shouted. Sarah cried out, too, and they both ran forward.

Jacob was as big as Prade and much younger, but he didn't try to take the rope away or attack Prade. He didn't even shield his face with his arms as the end of the plaited horsehair raised a bloody weal from cheek to brow. Advancing, Prade redoubled the rope, slashed again and again at Jacob till the young man reeled.

"Dirty damn Dutchie!" shouted Prade. "You set that fire! Wanted to burn the rest of us out—turn us into your hired men! Didn't you? Didn't you?"

"No! We do not do bad things, Mr. Prade!"

The rope bloodied Jacob's mouth. Sarah caught her father's arm. "Daddy! Stop it, Daddy!"

Jeanne Williams

He wrested loose and began to scourge the unresisting man. Sarah vainly pleaded and tugged at Prade. Susanna frantically glanced around for a weapon, found none, and did the only thing she could think of—moved in front of Jacob, protecting him with her body.

Prade checked a moment, arm raised, then with a laughing snarl, drew his arm back further and swung the rope. The looped ends wrapped stingingly around Susanna's throat and upper body. With a cry, Jacob dragged her away. In the same instant, Frank seized his father's wrist and grappled for the rope. Prade knocked him aside with a doubled fist.

Frank went down, staggered up, rushed blindly at Prade, got the full force of a mighty swing of the quadrupled rope. "Raise your hand to me, you whelp?" panted Saul. He kicked the boy in the groin and while Frank doubled up on the ground, gasping, his father swung back the rope.

Susanna knelt over Frank, shielded him, braced for the lashing. It never came. Slowly, still cradling Frank, she looked over her shoulder. Sarah stood between her and Prade, arms outstretched, slender body straight and defiant as a sword.

The glazed look faded from the man's eyes. Breathing heavily, he twisted the rope, flung it away. "You're no son of mine," he said to Frank in a choking voice. "I won't have you under my roof! Stay with the Dutchies or this damn meddling woman! Come in, Sarah, you and the twins."

Sarah hesitated. Frank had managed to sit up though his face was ashen. "Go on, Sarah. I . . . I'll be all right."

Susanna nodded. Even in her dazed state, she knew it would be impossible for Frank to live with his father now. It could lead to the killing of one or the other. If Prade wasn't insane, he was dangerously near it.

The man stalked off with Sarah. Paul and Pauline trailed behind, casting tearful glances back at their brother. "Are you all right?" Susanna asked Frank as she and Jacob

380

helped him to his feet. Sweat broke out on his face and he couldn't straighten up.

"I . . . hurt pretty bad."

"A kick like that—" Jacob, blood still seeping from his mouth, shook his head. "Very painful it is. Perhaps to the doctor I should take you, Frank. With us, of course, you are welcome to live."

"That might make matters worse," Susanna said. "But, Frank, it probably is a good idea for you to see Dr. Rawdon. I'm sure the Howes have room for you. Jacob, you'd better let the doctor examine that slash across the mouth."

"You, too, should go, Miss Alden."

Turn up at Amanda's house and ask Matt to examine her wealed breasts and throat? The very notion provoked a wry smile from Susanna. "I feel as if I'd been strangled," she said. "But I'm not bleeding and nothing's broken. Please, both of you, don't tell anyone that Mr. Prade hit me. It could start a lot more grief than we've already got, and Laura and the children don't deserve it." When they both nodded assent, she said, "Jacob, let's put some hay back in the wagon for a cushion and I'll get some quilts so Frank can lie down. I'll ride along with you as far as the Hardys'. More than likely Jem or Dave will hitch up a wagon and bring Frank back to their place after the doctor sees him."

Margaret responded as Susanna was sure she would. "Of course the lad can stay with us. Dave, take the wagon and fetch him here if Doc Rawdon thinks it's all right." She shook her head. "Poor Laura! What's she going to do? Her man's plain daft, it seems, but she's got the other kiddies to think about."

Susanna was in fact more worried about Laura and Sarah than about Frank. He was out of Prade's way. But how could Laura live with what her husband had done, not only to Frank, but to Jacob and a woman? Susanna hadn't told Margaret that Prade had lashed her; the fewer people who knew that the better. If Ase or Matt found out—well, it could yet be deadly.

She had the collar of her mantle draped around her throat but as she turned to go, the collar slipped. She immediately covered her throat again but Margaret's eyes widened and she pulled the cloth down, gasping.

"He hit you, too, the devil!"

"Just once. It hurt, but I'm all right."

"I'll make sure of that, my dear. Come in the bedroom." At her insistence, Susanna unbuttoned her bodice and slipped it off her shoulders. She winced even at Margaret's gently exploring touch and winced again when Margaret, with fierce mutterings, smoothed ointment on the welted bruises. "Your throat's the worst, bare as it was. Flailin' a man who can't fight back because it's against his religion, that's bad enough, but hittin' you! Stark mad, he is!"

They returned to the main room to find Jem slipping into his coat. "I'm going to get Will Taylor, maybe McCanless, and we'll have a talk with Saul Prade."

"Don't!" Susanna implored. "We've got to think about his family. I'm sure when he calms down he'll know he went too far and won't do anything like this again."

Jem knotted his brawny fists. "I'll see him by myself, then—find out if he's as brave with a man as he is with a woman and a kid!"

"Please don't." Susanna feared for Jem who was older than Prade and considerably smaller. "It'll be best for everybody if this stops right here."

Margaret put her hand on her husband's arm. "Leave it alone, Jem dear. The teacher's right. Prade ought to be whipped and run out of the country, but then what happens to Laura and the other children?" She caught Susanna's hands and gripped them strongly. "You're probably right, that he'll pull in his horns. But if he doesn't—if he causes you the least bit of trouble, you've got to promise to let us know."

"You sure do," nodded Jem, who still had on his coat.

"I'll tell you," Susanna promised. "Thank you for taking Frank in."

Margaret shook her head. "Poor boy, and poor mother. But many's the boy younger than Frank that's run off from his pa's thrashings."

"I was one myself," grunted Jem. "Pa was beatin' me with his belt. I took it away from him, gave him a lick or two, and went down the road. It's gettin' dusk, Miss Alden. Want I should walk you home?"

"Thanks, but Cav's outside."

"Where was he durin' all that fracas?" Jem asked drily.

"He must have walked part way home with Rosie and Georgie the way he sometimes does," Susanna said. "I met him on your side of the creek." She added defensively, "I'm glad he wasn't there. Prade might have killed him."

"Poor Jacob." Margaret sighed. "For this to happen right before his wedding. Will his face be scarred?"

"I hope not, but he certainly will look awful for a while."

Jem shook his grizzled head. "I sure can't understand lettin' someone whale you, but it took nerve. I reckon he'll look good to that pretty Catherine of his, and who else matters?"

Susanna laughed a little shakily and stepped out into the twilight. Tomorrow was Friday. She'd have to keep a scarf looped high around her throat, and wear one at the wedding, too, which was Sunday. Jacob's injuries, some of them, couldn't be hid. She hoped he knew no one else shared Prade's wild notion that the Mennonites had started the disastrous prairie fire.

Did Prade believe it himself? Was he truly insane? If he were, what would he do next? Was she endangering other people by trying to keep his behavior at least partly secret?

They had crossed the creek and were halfway to the soddie when Cav stopped and sniffed, gave an eager whine, and trotted back. Susanna heard a horse coming, the splashing as it forded the creek, and in a moment, a rider loomed against the lighter, lower rim of the sky that met the dark horizon.

"Susanna?"

It was Matt. A rush of warm gladness filled her, followed by dismay. "Is Frank all right?"

"He will be. Dave's taking him home. I stopped to tell Margaret to keep cold packs on the swelling till it starts going down. She's leaving water out to freeze at night and using that inside a towel."

"Jacob? His mouth?"

"One tooth knocked out, a couple loosened. His face'll be bruised and puffed up a while, and he's got rope marks all over his chest and shoulders. Nothing serious." They had reached the school. He swung down and trailed Saladin's reins. "Come on, Susanna. I'm having a look at you."

"They said they wouldn't tell!" She tried to resist as he gripped her beneath the elbow, but he hustled her inside, fed the fire which was burning low, and lit the lamp.

"They didn't tell. But Jacob, don't forget, can't tell a lie. When I asked point blank if Prade had hurt you, he could only mumble that he couldn't answer that—and that answered. Come here."

"There's no need. Margaret put on some ointment."

"So she told me. Are you coming or shall I drag you?"

She moved reluctantly forward and obeyed his motion to sit down near the lamp. He tilted her head back, hands firm but gentle. The tautness hurt her bruised neck and she flinched. The black pupils swelled over the gray of his eyes as he peered and touched, but his tone was professionally detached. "Can you swallow?"

"I haven't tried."

He filled a glass with water from the dipper and handed it to her. "Try it."

Her throat knotted and ached throbbingly, but the water went down. "Now your chest and shoulders." At her anguished look, he said sharply, "I'm a doctor—and I'm too sick and furious at this moment, Susanna, to be roused to lust if you were naked."

As she had for Margaret, she slipped down the bodice. Could he see how her heart pounded beneath the chemise? Like his voice, his examining hands were cool and disciplined. She responded to his commands to raise her arms, rotate her shoulders and wrists, and flex her fingers.

"Nothing but bruising and contusions where the rope hit hardest," he said, helping her slip her arms back down the sleeves. "He could have killed you, though, with that blow across your trachea."

The cold rage in his voice terrified her. "Matt, you . . . you won't do anything?"

"What I would do, were it not for Laura Prade and four nice youngsters, is put a bullet in his head."

"Matt!"

"Oh, I won't. Not unless he compels me." Matt strode to the door and turned. "What I am doing is riding over and asking him to talk with me outside. Just the two of us. I'll tell that murderous lunatic that if I hear he's troubled you again in the slightest way, I'll kill him as if he were a rabid dog."

"You might be hanged for that!"

"Sheriff Earp has enough to keep him busy in Dodge. Prade's lucky to get another chance. If the men around here knew what he's done, how long do you think it'd take Kermit Brown, who was a Texas Ranger, and Ase and Luke to find a rope and a limb?"

"But Laura—"

"I have compassion for her, Susanna, but if that man were dead, she'd surely find a better one. She couldn't find worse."

His hand was on the door. Filled with dread, Susanna cried, "Oh, Matt, be careful! Please!"

"I will. But I'll be clear." Seeing her fright, his gaunt face softened. "So you won't worry, I'll ride past on my way home. I won't come in—just call a good night."

She caught in a relieved breath. "Thank you."

He nodded and stepped out. Susanna barred the door.

She raised her hand to the throat he had touched, and though there was pain, there was sweetness. But, oh God, dear God, let nothing terrible happen!

Matt not only called a good night several hours later, but shouted through the door, "Prade knows he's earned a hanging. I think he'll be damned careful from now on."

Grateful that Matt was safe and somewhat cheered at his report, she banked the fire and went to bed, Cav on the rug beside her. It was a long time since she'd had night terrors, but now she did, wave after wave of images, Prade beating Jacob, kicking Frank, swinging the rope at her. . . . She tried to run in her dream and could not; would wake, touch Cav for comfort, and, when she drowsed, be trapped again.

The only thing that eased her was to remember Matt's touch, warm and deft on her throat, her back and shoulders, but such thoughts were useless. At last, she got up, stoked the fire, lit the lamp, and, as she had done at other hard times in her life, found refuge in a book and read until morning.

Before class the next day, Sarah, who didn't look as if she'd slept either, hurried to her and whispered, "How are you, Miss Alden?"

"Fine. I suppose Dr. Rawdon told you that Frank should be back in school next week."

"Yes." Sarah kept her beautiful eyes lowered as if in shame. "Daddy told Mother Jacob caused a fight and Frank came in on Jacob's side. Of course, ever since the fire, he's been saying the Mennonites set it. When Mother wanted to go to Frank, he told her if she did not to come back, and that he'd keep the rest of us. She might have gone anyway, but I got her to one side and . . . and . . ." How cruel for a child to have to tell her mother such things! "I told her Frank and I are going away next spring, that we'll both be through school and able to get work. She . . . she cried and held me, but finally she said maybe that was best." Sarah was holding a tissue-wrapped parcel and now she handed it to Susanna. "We can't go to the wedding but mother asked you to give this to Mr. Reighard and his bride with all her wishes for their happiness. It's a pair of silver candlesticks that's been in her family since they were made by Paul Revere."

"Oh, she should save them for you."

Sarah gave a positive shake of her head. "No. I want the Reighards to have them." Her voice broke. "I'm so ashamed of what happened! And I'm so worried for Mother—"

"She has you and that's a lot."

Green eyes somber, the girl said, "She won't have me long." For that, Susanna had no answer.

❋ *Twenty-four* ❋

Snow fell softly Saturday night but the day of the wedding dawned bright and radiant, and though it stayed too cold for the snow to melt very much, it wasn't deep enough to impede travel. The service would be at noon, conducted by Anselm, who was both the elder and minister of the small congregation, and the feast would follow.

"Seems kind of a shame to hold such a big celebration without dancin' or even a play party," said Ase after he had helped Susanna up beside Betty, tucked robes around her, and snugged a warm brick at her feet. He may have given up hopes of winning her, but he was as kind and gallant as ever. "But tomorrow night's the Christmas ball."

"We'll stow away so much of that larrupin' good Roosian grub that we won't feel like shakin' a leg," predicted Johnny from the mound of covers in the back which he shared with Jenny who had preferred to ride in the wagon rather than use the odious sidesaddle. Even she had understood that her beloved divided skirt wouldn't do at a Mennonite wedding.

Cowboys passed them, and the whole Brown family, who were on horseback, Dottie not having Jenny's same hatred of sidesaddles. The Tarrants similarly rode by. Millie rode astride but her cloak covered her except for her exquisitely patterned moccasins. To match them, she surely had on one of her beautiful buckskin dresses.

At the Hardy-Howes', Dave, on the gelding Matt had traded them for Margaret's baking and sewing, reined over to say that Frank was getting around and would be at school Monday. He rode on to catch up with Ridge as Jem brought the wagon to the door for his family.

"What's this about Frank?" demanded Ase as they clopped along. "Somethin' wrong with him?"

"He had a falling out with his father," Susanna said briefly. "He'll be staying at Howes' till school's out."

"Must have been some fallin' out!"

"It was."

"Prade beat the kid up?"

"Yes. I—I'd really rather not talk about it, Mr. McCanless."

He gave her a searching glance but let it drop. "What a shame for that nice Laura Prade," Betty said sympathetically. "It's mighty hard for a woman when her husband and son can't get along—and men critters bein' what they are, often they don't."

"Thanks." Ase chuckled. "I reckon that means women don't ever have a time with their daughters when the gals start sashayin' around with the boys?"

"That's different, Ase, and you know it very well," Betty chided. "Women have to watch their daughters or you pesky men—well! And at that, they're not a patch on most fathers. When Jenny starts courtin'—"

"Don't even mention it," Ase pleaded, but Jenny called from the back, "Don't you worry, Daddy. Ridge is the one I'm going to marry and you already know him."

"Does Ridge know about this?" quizzed Ase.

"Not yet," returned Jenny confidently. "But he'll know by the time we're old enough."

Ase shook his head. "Fellas don't have a chance when

you ladies make up your minds. Look at Jacob—had to follow his gal all the way from Russia and work over a year 'fore her folks'd let 'em tie the knot. He sure has earned this party." He squinted eastward, shielding his eyes. "Hey, that's some house Miss Amanda built. Two stories and a big veranda. Bet they don't sit on it much though when the wind's blowin'."

"It's not as big as your house," said Susanna. That sounded childish and she could have bitten her tongue. Ase just grinned!

"Look at that! Doc's pullin' up to the back porch in a fancy carriage—looks like a landau. Sure not the thing for our kind of roads. Had to be his sister's notion."

"I haven't even met the Doc's sister yet," said Betty with a sniff. "Wonder how he got her to go to the wedding. She's bound to think she's better than Russian emigrants since she seems to think she's way above the rest of us."

Susanna didn't remark that she'd had the dubious distinction of being called on by Amanda. Thank goodness there'd be so many people at the celebration that they could ignore each other without it being noticeable.

Jacob had a muffler bundled up to obscure his mouth. He and Val, Peter, and Frederick met guests as they arrived and showed them where to leave their vehicles. Any horses or oxen that were likely to stray were hobbled or stalled in one of the spacious barns, converted from the sod houses the families had lived in before the new ones were built. The barns had roofed storage shelters in between them and formed a solid block adjoining the steep-roofed frame buildings, with the old barns forming an angle at the end to make a sort of courtyard providing some relief from north winds. Within this protected area, several large stacks of hay had been heaped up so the guests' animals could feed and not stray off hunting for grass beneath the snow.

A broad way had been cleared from the barns to the middle one of the three neatly painted identical square white houses trimmed in green. This proved to be the home of Anna and Frederick, Catherine's parents. The Krause women, including Cobie, and a glowing Catherine in her simple white bride's dress, made their neighbors welcome to a house filled with delicious aromas, accepting with gracious thanks the gifts everyone had brought. Susanna handed Catherine the silver candlesticks and the wrapped ruby cut-glass creamer-and-sugar set and tendered Laura Prade's good wishes and apologies for being absent.

Catherine's blue eyes darkened for a moment but she recovered and spoke softly so no one else would hear. "Tell Mrs. Prade very much we thank her and for . . . for all, she must not feel bad, it is not her fault."

She invited the women to warm themselves by the huge brick stove that heated the kitchen, *die grosse Stube* or main room, and the large bedroom where babies and coats were being deposited. A stair led to the half-story above, a kind of attic where the children had their sleeping quarters, and where Catherine, after today, would sleep no more.

Benches, chairs, and tables had been carried in from the other houses. Spread with snowy cloths, the tables held platters of cheese, sausages, and ham, all manner of pickles and preserves, and mounds of bread, cakes, rice pudding, prune and raisin pudding, zwieback, cookies, and dozens of pies. Three large samovars steamed on the sideboard. Guests were offered tea or coffee and then stood visiting at one end of the room while the women congregated by the stove and exclaimed on how nice it was and how wonderful it would be to have one like it. The polished wood floors had colorful rugs, the glass windows were curtained, and though this home had none of the luxuries of Ase's, its neat comfort was a tremendous contrast to the soddies most of the guests lived in.

Delia Taylor, the most tightly corseted woman there, sucked in her breath either from necessity or envy. "It doesn't seem fair they've got ahead so fast," she said in a lowered voice to Margaret.

Margaret gave her an astonished look. "They had to sell their houses, livestock, and most of their things for give-away prices in Russia. If you'll remember, they broke sod and planted crops almost the minute they got here, and they've worked hard ever since. What they have, they've earned."

"Yes, but we all lost our crops and they didn't," muttered Delia.

"A good thing for us they didn't," Margaret returned. "Could you have held on if they hadn't loaned you grain to get through the winter? Most of us couldn't have."

"Hold on!" Delia's tone was bitter. "I'm tired of holding on, Mrs. Hardy—I mean, Mrs. Howe." Was that a deliberate slip to hint that Margaret had married rather quickly after her husband's death? "I wish my husband would get sense and go back East. Don't expect me to thank the Krauses for lending us that Russian wheat! I like soft, fine, white flour, not the kind that's milled from this."

"Seems last year you were saying how sick you were of cornbread," said Margaret. "We like Turkey Red. It's got a lot more flavor and body than spring wheat. We've got twenty acres planted to it. God willing, we can pay back the Krauses next year and have plenty for us and some to sell."

"As far as I'm concerned," said Delia, "this prairie's only fit for buffalo and Indians and I wish we'd give it back to them."

"So do my people, Mrs. Taylor." Millie's voice was quiet but her dark eyes flashed and she held her head even more proudly. Though her hair was dressed back smoothly with silver combs, she wore a lovely dress of fringed, beaded, velvety soft buckskin. "But the buffalo are slaughtered and my people are told they cannot wander the plains any-more but must stay on reservations. To us, you who break the sod and divide the land into little parts you claim for your own are worse than grasshoppers or prairie fires, for you will not pass with a season and never again will our world be healed."

Delia flushed. There was no telling what she might have said but at that moment Matt Rawdon came in with his sister. Few of the gathering had met her and though no one exactly stared, Amanda was instantly the focus of attention except for Susanna's which fixed on Matt. He was too thin and his face was craggier, giving Susanna a glimpse of how he would look in later years, when she could not see him, would not know how he was.

Desolation overwhelmed her at that severing, final, forever, that must come in a few short months. Life, without at least now and then beholding that beloved face, stretched like a desert. Besides, she had made this community her own. She wanted to give all her children their eighth-grade diplomas, attend their weddings, teach their children.

This was home as no other place could be. Why must she leave it? Maybe, after all, she should ask Matt to leave, as he had offered last spring. But if she did, he'd probably go with Amanda. Susanna still hoped that as he found himself appealed to by his neighbors, he'd go wholeheartedly into practice, find fulfillment at least in his work.

Amanda shrugged her hooded fur-trimmed and -lined green velvet cloak into Matt's hands and handed him her matching gloves. While, nodding and speaking, he carried her appurtenances to the bedroom, she accepted a cup of tea from Catherine, smiled on her, and wished her joy on her wedding day.

Catherine hurried off to greet Mavis and Shell McGuinn. Sipping her tea, Amanda studied the furnishings of the room, very much the fairy tale dowager queen in iridescent deep green taffeta with a looped-up black lace overskirt. A ruched collar fluted stiffly in back and dipped low in front to the rounding of still firm, high breasts. Golden hair was swept up and secured with a large lace and taffeta bow, and matching rosettes adorned green satin slippers.

The elegant gown whispered Paris or London; it didn't take Amanda's pleasant nod and smile to bring humiliated burning to Susanna's cheeks, make her painfully conscious that the blue dress she'd been so proud of had been stitched by her inexpert hands with the finer details sewn by a Pleasant Grove, Ohio, seamstress. To hide the bruises on her neck, Susanna had contrived a sort of draped scarf from scraps of leftover blue fabric and though she had thought the result rather fetching, it now felt makeshift. Her petticoat *did* rustle, but what was that compared to the swish of yards and yards of flounced skirts?

Matt presented his sister to the women. She acknowledged them all with perfect courtesy but she looked astonished when Hettie Brown seized her hand and gave it a vigorous pumping. "Good to meet Doc's sister," boomed Hettie, blissfully uncorseted in her maroon velvet, freckled face beaming. "We'll sure look forward to seeing you at the Christmas ball."

"How kind you are," murmured Amanda. "Kansas hospitality is so ... refreshing, isn't it, Matthew?"

Matt grinned at Hettie. "You can bet we'll be there, Mrs. Brown, if we're not snowed in."

"Don't talk about that!" cried Hettie, and, amid laughter, Matt turned to introduce the men who had drifted over, all of them in varying degrees of bemusement except Ase who bowed and moved over to talk with their hosts.

Everyone was there except the Prades. Anselm appeared for the first time, his white hair and beard making him seem an Old Testament prophet. As his family hushed, so did the visitors, and Jacob, the marred lower part of his face now exposed, stood at the door and addressed the crowd.

"Dear neighbors, glad we are you have come. Elder Krause, our minister, will perform the service in German but we will tell you in English when it is time to feast!"

The ripple of laughter quieted as Anselm delivered an eloquent discourse on how Boaz had loved Ruth when she gleaned his fields in a foreign land; on how Jacob had served twice seven years to win Rachel, and how Jesus had blessed the wedding at Cana. Susanna caught the gist of it but for those who understood no German, it must have become a bit wearisome though not even the children audibly shifted a foot.

The crystalline sopranos of Catherine, Anna, Cobie, and Freda soared above the tenors and basses of the men. When the solemnly sweet hymns were finished, Anselm, quoting scripture, spoke with loving seriousness to his granddaughter and her bridegroom, explaining their duties to one another and the sanctity of marriage. He then pronounced them man and wife and as he blessed them, there wasn't a dry eye among the women excepting Amanda's, for the venerable patriarch's resonant tone conveyed the meaning although the words were strange.

There was a long reverent moment. With all her heart, Susanna prayed for their health and happiness in this new land, and felt a pang that she would never see their children or teach them how to read. Jacob, his bride's hand in his, turned, and the weals and bruises on his face couldn't obscure his joy.

"Please!" He spread his hand toward the laden tables as Peter and Frederick puffed in with a wash boiler full of steaming golden noodle and butter-ball soup which they set on a bench by the tables. "You are welcome, good neighbors and friends."

As a close friend, Susanna was invited to sit with Jacob and Catherine, her parents, and Anselm. Evidently, Matt was also regarded with special esteem for he and Amanda made up the rest of the bride's table. Most of the conversation was between Matt and Jacob. Tempting as the food was, Susanna had no appetite but she talked with Anna and the beatific Catherine who made attempts, in their halting English, to include Amanda.

Amanda was friendly in her regal way but she was so clearly out of place that it was a relief, at least to Susanna, when Freda served final cups of coffee and the honored guests could blend into the crowd. Susanna was joining the ladies who were again clustering by the stove when Anselm addressed her in German.

"Professorin!" He always gave her that title. Gradually, he had melted enough to converse with her in the High German which he explained older Mennonites had learned as children though the everyday language was Plattdeutsch. "Will you please to come with me? I would show you something. Get your mantle for we must go to the barn."

Puzzled, Susanna excused herself and, wrapped in her mantle, went out with the elder who marched down the cleared way to the last barn, which was across the court-yard from the new houses. Stalls and a manger filled one side of the building and the larger part was a haymow. Motioning her around behind the manger, Anselm pointed at the back of it, boards that ran almost the length of the building and rose over four feet high.

"Look!" Anselm pointed a quivering finger and from his tone Susanna could not guess whether he was shocked, pleased, angry, or a bit of all three. "This is what the boy does when he should be working!"

The broad expanse was a mural done in pastels. Obviously, Val hadn't expected anyone else to go behind the mangers since it would be his task to fill them. Horses he had drawn, Saladin and Schatzie and a score of others, some caught in motion with tails and manes flying, mares nuzzling foals, colts at play. At the far end, benignly sur-veying the animals, was Michelangelo's Creator God, white beard and hair flowing, with his fingers outstretched with the gift of life, not to Adam as in the Sistine painting Susanna had shown Val, but blessing the horses.

"See?" Anselm tried to scowl but un-Mennonitish pride

shone through. "He has drawn me, Professorin! Is it not a likeness?"

"Indeed it is, Elder Krause." Susanna wasn't about to tell him about the model. "Valentine has a rare gift."

"But Mennonites—we farm the land." Anselm tugged at his beard. "Artists loaf and drink and sponge off relations. We'll have none of that among us."

"God has surely given Valentine this talent," Susanna reasoned in her most persuasive tone. She searched for words, hoping she didn't mangle them too much. "He also has a natural bent for training horses. Ase McCanless would hire him in a second."

Anselm recoiled. "Valentine shall not go to work among carousing, blasphemous cowboys, especially not those who come up from Texas." He paused and the nervous plucking at his beard turned to a soothing caress. "Dr. Rawdon, though, possible that might be—"

Susanna smiled. "I don't think you have to worry about Valentine turning into a wastrel. Some artists do make their livings by their work, and until then your grandson's ability with horses will easily support him."

Anselm heaved a sigh. "I will think on it. I have not yet shown this to my son and Anna. I discovered it this morning only and giving a daughter in marriage is ordeal enough for one day."

"I'm sure they'll be guided by your opinion, Elder Krause."

He snorted. "They have not always been, as look at their learning English! One talks and talks and it falls on deaf ears." He brightened. "Sometimes those who seem not to hear do take good advice later. We have just learned that ten families of our village are leaving Russia. They will buy abandoned lands adjoining ours and we will have a real congregation. They waited, hoping the czar would change his laws, but now they see he will not. Better late than never!" He laughed triumphantly. "Next fall, Professorin, you will have many new children in your school. You have taught our young ones so well that I agree now it is good for them to be educated with neighbors—so long," he added emphatically, "as they are taught our religion and language at home and do not fall into worldly behavior."

It seemed inevitable to Susanna that if Mennonite children attended public school, they would become worldly but, known to classmates who would later be their adult neighbors, the association would keep the Mennonites from being viewed as outsiders with suspicious habits.

"I'm glad you're pleased with my teaching," she said. She feared she was mutilating the language though Anselm apparently understood her. "I've enjoyed working with your grandchildren. But I'm leaving when school's out in the spring."

"Leaving?" he echoed in dismay. "If your salary is not enough . . ."

Susanna shook her head. "The trustees voted me a substantial increase without my even asking." Ase's doing, of course, with Prade predictably dissenting. "And the children—I wish I could see them all through eighth grade. They are dear to me. But—"

A tall figure rose from behind the manger and at the same instant clubbed the unsuspecting Anselm from in back with a shovel. Susanna's scream, as she turned to run, was stifled by Prade's hands clamping her throat in an iron grip. He smelled strongly of kerosene. *What had he been doing?*

She clawed for his eyes but he laughed and squeezed till the world spun black in a midnight splashed with blood that roared and pounded in her ears. He hurled her down, and she knew dimly that he was gagging her, knotting ropes cruelly tight around her wrists and ankles.

Through flashing explosions, his face wavered before her, green eyes and golden hair capturing what light there was. "I'll be back and set you afire with the hay," he said in a calm voice. "Think about burning, you devil bitch, you who set my son against me! You just stay there and think about it while I burn those new frame houses! I'll teach those Dutchies to fire my wheat." He laughed eerily. "I won't burn anyone but you, though, Susanna Alden. Not if people have the sense to get out of that middle house when the empty ones start blazing—and they're going to blaze, because I was dousing the floors with kerosene when I saw you heading down here with this old scarecrow."

He prodded Anselm with his foot. "I'll drag him out now. Then, after I torch the houses, all I'll have to do is drop a match into that hay." Again that wild, strange laughter. "I won't be long, teacher, but I bet it'll seem that way!"

Blood stained Anselm's white mane as Prade caught him under the arms, dragged him toward the door, kicked it open, and hauled the limp body outside.

Footsteps crunched. Prade was moving to the houses already prepared for burning. Whatever his half-mad intention, what would keep the flames from leaping to the middle house before an alarm was raised, before there was time for everyone to escape?

Still giddy from strangulation, Susanna struggled with the ropes but they gave not a fraction, so tightly was she lashed. She searched for some way to give a warning— some way to stop Prade. . . .

There must be something in the barn, something sharp that she could fray the ropes against. The manger's edge? Struggling to her knees, she advanced on them to the corner and worked her wrists back and forth, but the rope was thick hemp and she saw despairingly that to wear through the fibers would take far longer than she had.

She couldn't walk, she couldn't use her hands. . . . The knees supporting her gave the answer. She couldn't run but maybe she could crawl.

It was the only chance.

❊ *Twenty-five* ❊

Hands all but useless, cumbered by her mantle and skirts, Susanna struggled forward on elbows and knees, using her weight to thrust herself along. Prade hadn't thought it necessary to bar the door. It yielded at a push from her shoulder.

Blinded by light, though it had become slightly overcast since morning, Susanna lurched onto the cleared, frozen ground. If only she could shout! If only someone would step outside or glance through a window! It was all too likely, though, that it was Prade who'd see her as he ran from lighting one house across to the other. She couldn't see him. He must already be inside, might already be striking a match.

Anselm lay crumpled before her like a heap of discarded clothes, blood still trickling from his scalp and dyeing the snow scraped to one side of the path. She couldn't see his face but his breathing was quick and stertorous.

Trying to keep the mantle beneath her elbows, Susanna inched along. The houses seemed an infinite distance away though she could hear laughter and the hum of voices from the middle dwelling. Feeding at the several haystacks in the courtyard, horses and oxen regarded her with no particular interest.

In a grotesque race, she forced herself on, passed the second soddie barn, sobbing for breath. Where was Prade, in which building? The last barn— She smelled kerosene strongly now.

Trying to hurl herself forward by sheer will, she wrenched past the first new house as a drift of smoke stung eyes, throat, and nostrils.

"Bitch!" Prade sprang out of the door of the house at the end, flames leaping behind him, a torch in his hand.

With frenzied strength, Susanna heaved to her knees and slammed her bound hands into the lowest window-pane. Glass shattered. The laughter stopped. She glimpsed Matt's face. Then Prade seized her wrists, was dragging her toward the nearest haystack as the horses tossed up their heads, snorted, and fled the torch. Bound as she was, there was nothing Susanna could do to stop that headlong rush. But if he stopped—if he gave her the slightest chance to throw herself against him . . .

Out of deference to their hosts, no one had worn a gun today. She could hear people shouting, footsteps pounding the frigid earth, but Prade was in the hay.

He bent to grip Susanna and toss her into the center. With all her might, she threw her body sideways against him, knocking him backwards, the torch still in his hand. When the fire touched the dry hay, it fairly exploded. In the same breath that she knocked Prade over, Susanna rolled toward the snow surrounding the stack. For Prade the hay was a pyre.

The flames and Matt reached her at the same time. Her hair and clothing blazed but he buried her in the snow as the stack flared into a withering inferno, crackling, hissing, finding more solid fare only near its center. Men scooped up snow and threw it on the blaze but nothing could stop it till it consumed itself so they ran to battle the fire in the end house, filling buckets, tubs, anything they could find, with snow, and dumping it on the floor and walls. Smoke billowed out door and windows in stifling pillars, but the flames were nearly vanquished in the time it took Matt to determine Susanna's hurts, cut the ropes from her bleeding wrists and ankles, and carry her into the house where a bed was readied.

So dazed that she scarcely knew what was happening except that Anselm had been found and was being supported into the house by his sons, Susanna rested in the arms where she would gladly die and clung to Matt as he lowered her to the pillows. "It's all right," he told her, and then, very softly, "All right, my love." Gently disengaging her, he said in a normal voice, "If a few ladies will help you undress, I'll make sure your only real hurts are slight burns on the face and hands. Another second . . ." He bowed his head and she saw that he was trembling.

"I'm all right," she told him, and in her heart, she added, *my dear love.* "How is Anselm?"

"I'm going to see."

Matt stepped out. Betty and Margaret took off Susanna's mantle and worked off her dress, the cherished taffeta petticoat and the warm red flannel one. All her garments were the worse for crawling on the ground, being dragged through snow, and singed by fire. They had protected her, though her knees and elbows were abraded, her throat ached from the new strangling, her hands and face smarted, and she had cuts on her hands from breaking the window.

"Your hair looks like you ran wild with a curling iron," Betty said. "And your eyelashes aren't as long as they were, but you got off lucky. If you hadn't knocked that maniac over . . ."

"There'll be some bones for poor Laura to bury," said Margaret, shivering as she took off Susanna's shoes and stockings. "Saul must have been plumb crazy. It's awful for his family but really, I guess it's better this way than if he'd lived."

Betty nodded, shooing Susanna into bed and pulling up the covers. "The kids and Laura can get on with their lives and Frank can go back home. Ase said Prade blamed the Mennonites for setting that prairie fire in September—that shows how warped he was getting."

Thinking of Frank's scarred back, Susanna knew Saul Prade, for all his male beauty, had been a twisted soul from childhood, but it was best for his family to let all that be buried with him. The women went out and Matt returned.

She pulled the quilt to her chin, flushing at her earlier behavior. "You needn't bother, Dr. Rawdon, I'm just fine. How is Elder Krause?"

"He'll have a lump, but unless concussion manifests itself later, he'll just have a headache for a day or two." He studied her with an expert eye. "Do those burns hurt?"

"Of course they do!"

"Not 'of course,' madam," he said imperturbably. "If the burns were serious, you wouldn't feel anything except at the periphery for all the nerves would be dead. In my experience, the best treatment for minor burns is immersion in cold water, and I've asked Catherine and her mother to bring several basins."

Folding back the covers as Catherine approached with a basin of water, Matt arranged the pillows so that Susanna could lower her face to the one basin and rest her hands in the other as they were held on the bed by Catherine and Anna. "When I saw you were hurt the other night, I should have done more than just talk to Prade," Matt said.

Emerging for air, Susanna said, "You might have been killed. And it seemed so awful for Laura. . . ."

None too gently, he guided her head down, holding her hair clear of the water. "No way of hiding what went on today, but I reckon there wouldn't be any use in the rest of it coming out. A farmer who lost his crops went sort of insane. That's all Laura and the neighbors have to know."

Cobie ran in with the news that the fire in the house was out. Most of the main room's floor would have to be replaced, but that was nothing compared to what could have happened. The haystack blaze was flickering its last. Susanna went sick at the thought of vestiges of what had been a strong, comely man charred to blackened bones.

What a waste, a terrible waste, not only today, but of a life. Still, he had fathered Sarah and Frank who had exceptional potential. They might prove his justification for having lived. Certainly, they would do much to comfort and sustain their mother and help raise the twins, who could blossom now they were out from under the shadow of their formidable father.

Susanna raised her head at Ase McCanless's voice, demanding of Matt how she was. "I'm all right," she answered for herself.

"Is she, Doc?"

Matt nodded. "Hair grows back and I don't think the burns will leave scars, except maybe on her right hand. It got the worst of it."

"You think she can travel? I can take her to my place where we can look after her."

"I'd better see to her." As Ase hesitated, Matt added, "Don't worry. She won't be left alone as long as she needs me."

That would be forever, Susanna thought. In spite of her annoyance at being spoken about as if she were incompetent or a child, a warm glow filled her, alleviating her hurts, at the way Matt was taking charge of her. Could it be that— She didn't dare think it, but she'd enjoy this as long as it lasted.

A terrible question raised itself and she voiced it aloud. "Who'll tell Laura? I should go see her."

"It'd make her feel awful to look at your burns," Ase said and reflectively rubbed an ear. "I guess the best thing is I'll pick up Frank and break the news to him, then we'll take him home. Getting him back ought to help. I'll see to anything she needs."

"And I'll stay if it looks like she wants someone," Betty

said. She glanced from Margaret to Hettie and Millie and the other women. "We have to show her she's got friends."

"I will go to her, too, in a few days," said Catherine, blue eyes dark with compassion.

Ase nodded. "We'll all help. She's a fine lady and we'll let her know we want her and the kids to stay right here."

Susanna remembered that he'd always admired Laura. Who knew? When Laura was through her shock and grief, she would be a lovely and still youthful woman in a world where these were scarce. Ase might not have to go to Saint Louis or Dallas to look for a bride. It was a ray of promise in this day's tragedy.

Guests taking their leave poked their heads into the bedroom to inquire after Susanna and urge her to take care of herself. Then they wished Jacob and Catherine happiness with a fervor increased by narrowly escaped disaster. Amanda stepped in, shook her head and commiserated with Susanna before turning to Matt.

"Have you done all you can for Miss Alden?" A nice way of saying she wanted him to take her home.

"If you're in a hurry, ride with the Howes or McGuinns," he suggested. "I'd only drop you off in any case, because I'm taking Miss Alden home."

Her eyebrows raised toward golden curls clustering over her high, narrow forehead. "Are you, indeed?"

"I am. And I'll stay till I'm sure she'll be all right alone so you'd better not wait up for me."

Amanda didn't speak for a moment. When she did, her tone was all kindly concern. "Let's take Miss Alden to our house, Matthew, if you judge her condition serious enough to require your continued attention. I'll help nurse her."

Susanna started to protest but Matt said firmly, "Thank you, Amanda, but Miss Alden will do better in her own home."

"We'll be glad to drop you off, ma'am," offered Ase, who had lingered near the door.

Amanda gave Susanna a long, considering look. "You

were very brave, Miss Alden. But for you, some of us would surely have perished. Thank you for what you did."

Astounded at this handsome speech, Susanna said faintly, "Anyone would have done it."

"Fiddlesticks! I, for one, couldn't have crawled that far in the snow." Amanda turned to her brother. "Take good care of her, Matthew, and send if I can do anything." She took Ase's arm and swept out in an opulent rustle.

Matt and Susanna exchanged startled glances before he said, "Lower that face again. We don't want you scarring."

"But—"

"Doctor's orders." He guided her head downward and she was forced to close her mouth and hold her breath.

For the next fifteen minutes, he repeated this tactic every time she came up for air and began to chide him. At the end of that period, he studied her hands and face. "Do the burns still hurt?"

"Not much."

"I think we'll get along then and have you in your own bed before dark." He turned to Catherine. "Could I borrow a couple of featherbeds to wrap around Miss Alden?"

"To be sure, you must have those in the bride chest," she cried, and hurried away.

"I'll hitch your team and bring the landau," said Val.

Feeling ridiculous at causing such a fuss—she had been hurt worse by Prade's previous assault—Susanna was bundled into the spacious upholstered carriage and enveloped in soft featherbeds with warm bricks tucked at her feet. She laid a reddened hand on Catherine's arm and tears sprang to her eyes. "I'm sorry, Catherine—sorry this happened, and on your wedding day."

Catherine gazed up at Jacob. They exchanged a look of such love that Susanna understood that the bond between them could only be strengthened by trials, and while she rejoiced for them, she couldn't quell a stab of envy.

"We will pray for that poor madman and for his family," Jacob said. "In our prayers, Miss Alden, you will be ever remembered, for if you had not done today what you did, some of us would surely be badly hurt if not burned along with our houses."

Anselm, head bandaged, said in High German, "God protect you, gracious lady. With His help, you were the instrument of our salvation." He smiled crookedly at Val. "If I had not taken you to see the work of this artist of ours . . . Yes, the hand of our Lord is surely in it."

"What everyone forgets," she told him, "is that I was saving myself."

"And us and our homes," he returned. He closed the door while Matt got up on the driver's seat in front.

She waved from the window till houses and figures grew tiny. Reveling in the bliss of being looked after, she sighed and closed her eyes. Prade's contorted face rose before her but had no reality, nor did the blazing pyre. Later, she would feel it, later she would know it was true, but for now the lulling motion of the carriage and the knowledge that Matt would take care of her drained away everything but the peace of trusting him and her relief that only one hate-crazed man had died that day.

She woke to Cav's joyful barking, the cessation of the rocking motion and the sounds of the carriage—even an elegant Landau creaked on rutted Kansas roads. Dashing from the barn where he napped on the rare occasions when Susanna went somewhere without him, Cav stretched low in his salute to Matt and danced along as Matt lifted Susanna, featherbeds and all, and carried her into the house.

"Stay in those till the place warms up," he commanded, depositing her on the bed and building up the fire from the few remaining banked coals. "I'll take care of the team and be right back."

Cav was so excited at the return of both his humans that he tried to slather her face. When Susanna ducked, he settled for her hands and she was still talking to him and scratching his ears when Matt returned.

"Well, the horses are cozy in the barn with plenty of hay," he said, taking off a cape of Confederate gray and hanging it on a peg with an air of finality. He put more fuel on the fire and lit the lamp, then pulled the curtains on the twilight.

Susanna watched him, torn between dismay and pleasure. He behaved exactly as if he were at home. If only he were.

He asked prosaically, "Anything we can heat up for supper? Wish I'd asked for some of that noodle soup."

"How about potato and onion soup?" Susanna asked. "It's in the kettle just inside the schoolroom. And there are leftover biscuits in the Dutch oven."

"Another feast." He grinned, and set the cast iron pots on the fire before he came purposefully to her. "I recommend that you put on your nightgown and get comfortable while I step into the other room." He eyed her critically. "Do you have some scissors?"

"Of course." She frowned her perplexity. "They're on the dresser."

"Good. I'm going to trim off those frizzed ends. But first, my love, out of your shimmy and into your gown."

"Matt—"

He raised a silencing hand. "Yes, I have taken advantage of you, and, yes, I brought you home under false pretense that you needed a doctor. Shameless of me, but damned if I could see you drive off with Ase McCanless when you'd come within a breath of dying. The gown, now!"

He went into the schoolroom, followed by Cav. Susanna made haste to extract her gown from its place beneath her pillow, pile the featherbeds to one side, and climb under her own quilts.

"Ready?" called Matt.

She made a noncommittal sound and found that she was quivering with delicious fright. What was he going to do?

Avoiding the tender spots, he took Susanna's face in his

hands, bent and kissed her eyes, then drew back, wrinkling his nose.

"You not only look frizzled, my sweetheart, you smell it." He got the scissors and began to snip, measuring out the tresses as if he were performing some critical operation. When he had finished, he evaluated the results and gave a nod of satisfaction. "Those short ringlets become you, darling, though I reckon I won't cut the back to match." The clippings he collected on a magazine. He put them and the scissors on the dresser, sat on the edge of the bed, and took her hands, again careful of the burns. He kissed her chafed and purpling wrists. "Susanna, you deserve better—but will you have me?"

"You . . . you mean—"

"I mean, will you marry me? Will you live with me and love me, even if I'm scarred, even if I'm cantankerous?"

"Oh, Matt! Are you sure?"

"Before I knew how badly you were burned, while I thought your face might be permanently changed, I knew it wouldn't matter to me. I love you—what's under the skin. You're a lot better and kinder and wiser than I am, Susanna. If I felt that way, I had to believe you did."

At first they embraced like survivors after a disaster, but after a time, he shifted to cradle the back of her head and seek her mouth. Trembling as their need for each other mounted, Susanna slipped free of the quilts to mold closer to him. With a groan, he wrested his mouth from hers and held her against his shoulder, stroking her hair, caressing her shoulders.

"Now I have to be as careful of your reputation as I once accused Yankee schoolmarms of being," he murmured against her ear. "It'll be hard, but we can wait because, my love, my sweetheart, my beloved Yankee, we're going to have our whole life long together."

Punctuating each name with a swift kiss, he finished with one that was as satisfactory as prudence allowed. "That's our ration for the evening, except for a good-night

kiss," he said, rising. "We're going to eat and then I'm tucking you in." At the question in her eyes, he said, "As your
doctor, it's my opinion that you shouldn't be alone tonight.
I'll put benches together in the schoolroom and repair to
them with the featherbeds."

"But Amanda—"

"It may help convince her of what I've already told her.
My life is here, and you're the only woman I'll ever trust
and love. Besides, from the way Amanda spoke when she
said good-bye, I think she's beginning to see why I need
you—and whatever else one can say about her, Amanda
really does want me to be happy."

Susanna took that in. He might be right. There'd been
no hint of superiority in his sister's voice during those last
remarks. In time, the two women who loved Matt might
be friends—so long as they didn't have to live too close
together. "I think tomorrow you should call on Laura,"
Susanna said, with a sudden pang of remembrance and
concern. "What a miserable Christmas it will be for her,
for the whole family!"

"Frank will be there," Matt pointed out. "Laura had to
know something was very wrong with her husband even
if she didn't understand it. This will be hard on her and
the kids but in the long run, they'll be a sight better off."

He brought her food on a tray and carefully poured tea
into Grandmother Alden's cups. Lifting his to her, he said
in a voice that reached and warmed her heart, "Here's to
our life, Susanna. Here's to our love."

There were nightmares—flashes of Prade's gloating face,
of Anselm's bloody head, of the blazing haystack with that
darker thing amid the instant flame of stems and leaves.
Several times, as she dreamed she was crawling toward
the house and Prade was running toward her, Susanna
waked to her own screams.

Each time, Matt was quickly there, holding her close,

assuring her that it was over. When she calmed, he brought the covers around her snugly, kissed her, and reminded her that nothing could hurt her; he was close by.

Since he fed the fire each time he was up with her, the room was fairly warm the next morning. After a Christmas morning kiss, he went to see to his horses while she dressed, and together they made breakfast, biscuits and oatmeal full of raisins, with plenty of strong coffee.

She'd made no present for him but before they started their meal, he took something out of a compartment in his wallet and slipped it on her finger. It was a broad gold band etched with leaves and flowers.

"My mother's wedding ring," he explained. "I know you can't wear it on your finger yet, but maybe you'll wear it on a ribbon around your neck. I know you'll want your aunt and uncle to be at the wedding if they can, but let's make it as soon as possible."

Eager as he, she sparkled up at him. "I'll write to ask them to come, and when we collect them in Dodge City, we can ask the minister to ride out the next Sunday. That'll give time to get the word around." She could hardly wait for him to meet her aunt and uncle and she looked forward to, in time, flaunting her handsome, accomplished husband in Pleasant Grove, where she'd been chalked off as an old maid.

Susanna looked up from the golden band and smiled at Matt. "It's the most beautiful ring in the world. I've got a chain for it." She took his scarred hand, pressed it to her breast, and then to her lips.

The Christmas ball had been canceled, of course. On the last day of Christmas vacation, Matt came by with a pretty bay mare saddled for Susanna. Where horses or wagons had passed, snow had melted from the track though snow still glittered across the prairie. Cav trotted ahead, now and then questing after intriguing scents. It was such a beautiful day and so wonderful to be riding with Matt that in spite of dreading what lay ahead, Susanna's spirits rose and rose even more when he told her Amanda was preparing to move back to Dallas.

"She'll stay for our wedding, though," he said. "And if you like it, she wants to give us the house for a wedding present. It seems big and formal now but some children should take care of that."

Even the best of soddies had no appeal for Susanna. She shook her head in wonderment. "Is it true? We're going to have a house? We're going to have children?"

"We're going to have a home," he said, and rode close, kissing her thoroughly. "I was over at the Krauses' this morning. They've already replaced that floor and Anselm's cantankerous as ever. Jacob and Catherine fairly shine, they're so blissful."

"I'm glad. It'll be fun to teach their children."

Matt's eyebrow shot up and he closed his hand over hers. "My sweetheart, you're a splendid teacher. I wouldn't dream of keeping you out of your school till we have youngsters of our own, and perhaps when they're school age, you'll want to take up your profession again. But I do hope that by the time the Reighards have a child in primer, we'll have one or two requiring their mother at home. I don't want our children thinking I'm their grandfather."

They bantered and she told him that among other neighbors, Ase had stopped by to say that Frank was a changed boy, taking his place as man of the family and, with Sarah, arranging a quiet private funeral with the minister Ase fetched from Dodge. Now the cemetery on the knoll had two graves, Cash on one end of the slope, Saul Prade on the other. After an interval, Catherine and Jacob would visit Laura, but, except for Delia, the other neighbors had already called and in his or her own manner shown sympathy and a wish to help.

"I doubt if that would have happened if folks hadn't got-

ten to know each other on your visitors' Friday afternoons," Matt said. "Some communities would ostracize the
family of a man who behaved as Prade did—but then, this
wasn't a community till you came, Susanna. You made us
one."

Overcome at such praise, Susanna protested, "I've only
done my job."

"And got Northern and Southern kids to care about
each other," he teased gently. "Brought in the Krause
youngsters and taught their families; rescued Jenny; kept
Prade from likely burning up some people. Oh yes, my
sweetheart. You've done your job." Chuckling tenderly at
her confusion, he mercifully changed the subject. "Say,
isn't that Ase's Rusty horse out in front of Prades'?"

It was. Laura, in black, looked fragile and lovely though
her violet eyes were hollowed. She and Sarah had been
mending by the fire while Frank, in his father's big chair,
read *Gulliver's Travels* to the twins who perched on
either side. The coiled bullwhip was gone. Ase, who was
standing by the fire with a cup of coffee, seemed a bit flustered, but while Laura and Sarah brought coffee to their
guests, he smiled at Susanna in a warm fond way that told
her they would always and ever be friends.

"Good to see you out, Miss Alden, ma'am. Don't forget,
the board of trustees is meetin' at the school this afternoon." Was that a delicate hint for Matt not to be there?
Draining his cup, Ase picked up his hat and stood bending
the brim as he addressed Laura. "If you're sure you can get
to it, ma'am, I'll bring that sewing of Jenny's over in a few
days. And just remember, if you need anything . . ."

"You've been more than kind, Mr. McCanless." Her eyes
brimmed and she bent her head over the sock she was
darning. "Everyone has been." She glanced around at her
children and her gaze lingered on Frank who had a light
in his eyes and a vibrant, warm ring to his voice as he imitated Gulliver to the twins' rapture. "But we'll be fine, I
know we will."

Laura saw Ase to the door. Then, with a look at Susanna that asked her to follow, she went into a bedroom and closed the door. The two women looked at each other a moment. Then they were in each other's arms, and wept and clung and spoke their hearts.

At last, straightening, Laura said, "It sounds terrible, but it's a relief to have it over. I was so upset when Saul told me he'd ordered Frank not to come home that I would have left if it hadn't been for the twins. I've known Saul was changing after the wheat burned—well, he got the way his father was before he went insane and killed himself."

"I'm sorry."

"So am I. But don't feel to blame for a moment for—for what happened. I'm just grateful no one else was killed or badly hurt." She stared at the window and the sparkling plain beyond. "Do you think I ought to leave, Miss Alden? Take the children where no one will know?"

"I think you belong here. Now more than ever."

Laura gave her a slight, swift smile of thanks and they returned to the warm room and the others.

After a quick bowl of soup and some slower kisses, Matt had to go, but he left the bay mare, Star. "Call her an engagement horse." He grinned. "We'll be riding every weekend, I hope, and with the kids' horses around, she won't get lonely in between."

She watched him ride off, glowingly aware of the ring suspended on the chain between her breasts. Very soon now, she would wear it on her finger.

Closing the door, she dusted the desks and gave an especially loving polish to the globe stand. The trustees would meet at two, so she put on fresh coffee and mixed up some apple muffins. She didn't have to feed the men, but on cold days coffee and a warm, sweet morsel would be welcome. Matt had taken her letter to Aunt Mollie and Uncle Frank to Dodge. Even with the mail's vagaries, she hoped to have an answer back in time to marry late in January or early the next month. She'd always thought of summer as the time for weddings, but she dreamed now of how sweet it would be, after rapture, to fall asleep with their arms around each other.

The rumble of a wagon roused her from this delightful musing. She rescued the muffins from overbaking, set the Dutch oven on the side of the hearth, and went to greet the arriving guest.

Strange that any of the trustees should travel in a wagon. She looked out to find Ase assisting Betty from the buckboard while Johnny clambered down and Jenny, at the barn, was unsaddling Scout. Well, after all, they were special friends, and from the look of towel-wrapped pans and dishes that exuded tempting aromas, they planned to stay on for supper.

Susanna had scarcely exchanged hugs and a kiss with Betty when a wagon with Jem Howe driving, Margaret beside him and the children in back, rattled across the creek. "Jem's a new trustee," said Ase blandly, unhitching his team.

Bewildered, Susanna might have accepted this, but as Jem pulled up, the whole Brown clan came riding across the prairie as the Tarrants appeared from the south. Here came the Taylors from the north, and behold, three small green Mennonite wagons were splashing across the creek.

"Ase McCanless! What's going on?" Susanna demanded.

His eyes danced. "I guess you might say it's a christenin'."

"A *what*?"

He lifted a canvas-wrapped object from the back of the buckboard, leaned it against the fuel shed. "Hold your horses, Miss Alden, ma'am. Soon's everybody gets here, you'll know all about it." He peered toward the creek. "Wonder where Doc is?"

"He's not a trustee or—"

"No," Ase said dryly. "But I reckon he has a right to be in on things concernin' you—doesn't he?"

She blushed at that and hurried to greet the newcomers, all of whom carried food. As if by magic, desks were scooted together to make tables and these were spread with cloths and set with dishes and tableware brought by each family. The array of food was arranged on Susanna's desk and the kitchen table while the Krauses' huge kettle of golden noodle soup was set on the hearth beside Millie's stew.

Outside, the children made snow families, played Fox and Geese, or piled up snow forts and besieged each other. Matt drove up in the Landau with Amanda, helped her out, and grinned at Susanna with no apologies for not having warned her. While he drove toward the barn and unhitched the horses, Amanda came in, advanced on Susanna and took both her hands between elegantly gloved ones. "I'm glad to see you recovered from your ordeal, my dear." She lowered her voice so that no one else could hear. "I regret, of course, that Matthew won't be coming back to Dallas but I can see that he's made a place for himself here, just as you have. I do wish you happy."

"Thank you." Susanna looked into her future sister-in-law's eyes and thought that in time they might even become fond of each other. "You're very dear to Matt, you know. It's kind and generous to give us your lovely house. I hope that you'll often come to visit us."

"I will," Amanda promised, "but I won't wear out my welcome." As Matt entered, she moved over to chat with the Krauses. What a strange, wonderful feeling to have Matt beside her, to have their friends and neighbors accept that soon they would be married! Susanna didn't think she'd ever get used to that, ever take it for granted. Sorry that the Prades weren't there, she was glad she'd visited them that morning and felt sure that in time they'd become much more a part of the community than when Saul was alive.

An air of expectancy filled the room. Ase stepped to the door and bellowed, "Hey, you kids! We're ready!"

Stamping off snow, the youngsters hurried in, hung up their coats, and gathered around Freck, who had his guitar. They launched into the rivers song, followed with "Kansas Land," "Starvin' to Death on My Government Claim," and one new to Susanna that had a chorus of "Home, home on the range . . ."

And then to Susanna's surprise, for these songs had never been sung in the school, the children—Northerners, Southerners, and Mennonites—sang "Dixie" in a spirited fashion that set their parents clapping and singing as much as they knew, and then the clear, sweet youthful voices soared in "The Battle Hymn of the Republic."

Unable to believe her ears, and then believing, seeming to see her father's smile and hear him say, "Well done, my daughter," she was overcome and bowed her head. Tears ran down her cheeks. Matt gave her a handkerchief, and as the voices stilled, she saw that his eyes were suspiciously bright. So were Ase's, and all of the women were using handkerchiefs.

Looking at her students, knowing and loving each face, Susanna couldn't speak on her first effort, but she swallowed hard and managed to say, "Thank you. Thank you so very, very much. . . ."

"Just one more thing before we eat," Ase said. He nodded to Will and Luke who stepped out and returned in a moment with a large, varnished cedar sign.

They held it up. Flowers and birds were carved all around the border. In the middle, large, deeply incised letters read SUSANNA SCHOOL.

"Guess Mason-Dixon don't fit us anymore," Ase said. "Now, folks, soon as we hang that sign over the door, Elder Krause's goin' to bless us, and we'll settle down to dinner."

The children flocked around Susanna. "We practiced at

418

noon and recess," Freck explained proudly. "Did you like it, ma'am?"

She shook her head. "Oh, Freck, I can't tell you how much I liked it. This . . . this must be the happiest day of all my life." She kissed him and he colored over his freckles. Dave looked eager, so she kissed him, too, and by the time she'd hugged and kissed all her pupils, the sign was pronounced satisfactorily hung. The crowd hushed as Elder Krause gave a blessing in German—and then, incredibly, prayed in English.

As guest of honor, Susanna was compelled to go first to fill her plate, but as she was hustled forward, she glanced up at Matt. "I . . . I'm so happy I don't think I can stand it!"

"Wait," he promised. "You're going to be happier."

The light in his eyes and her own heart made her believe him.